EVIL UNSEEN

DAVE SIVERS

Copyright © Dave Sivers, 2016

Cover design by Jessica Bell

All rights reserved. No part of this publication may be reproduced, stored, or transmitted in any form, or by any means electronic, mechanical or photocopying, recording or otherwise, without the prior permission of the copyright owner.

Evil Unseen is a work of fiction. Names, characters, places and incidents are the product of the author's imagination or are used fictitiously. Any resemblance to actual events, locales or persons, living or dead, is purely coincidental.

ISBN: 978-1523324583

For my father

ACKNOWLEDGEMENTS

As always, I owe a huge debt of gratitude to so many people who have helped me to see this book through from the first spark of an idea to the finished article.

I am hugely grateful to Rebecca Bradley, Debbie Porteous and Chris Sivers, who read the manuscript and provided invaluable insights; and to Ian Robertson, Clare Heron and Rosie Claverton for their respective input and guidance on police procedure, CSI techniques and psychology.

Praise is due to my brilliant cover designer, Jessica Bell, who has produced another gorgeous wrapper for my product; to my eagle-eyed and insightful copy-editor, Jane Hammett; and to Chris 'the Guru' Longmuir, who so generously helped me out with the technical aspects of publication.

I'm indebted to the real Karen Smart, Lara Moseley, Tracey Walsh and Claire Taylor for lending me their names, and to my wonderful network of writing mates, including the members of Chiltern Writers and very many more online, for their support and encouragement.

As ever, all mistakes are my own. The world of Archer and Baines is a shadowy twin of the real Aylesbury Vale, but those who know the area well will glimpse real places, even where I have used fictitious names. The Northfields estate does not exist outside the pages of these novels.

Very special thanks to my family: to my dad, who always believed in me and who never misses an opportunity to plug my books; and to my wife Chris, for her patience, love and endless support. I couldn't do this stuff without her.

And finally, thanks to all the readers who are as enthusiastic about Lizzie Archer and Dan Baines as I am, and who keep asking when the next instalment will be out. There can be no greater compliment, or encouragement, to a writer.

Dave Sivers
www.davesivers.co.uk
Buckinghamshire, 2016

1

Detective Inspector Lizzie Archer sat in the passenger seat, rigid and bolt upright. "There's no need to go quite so fast, Dan," she protested. "In my experience, bodies don't mind waiting."

Detective Sergeant Dan Baines mumbled an apology and eased his foot off the accelerator, reducing the Mondeo's speed by all of three miles per hour. A smile tugged at the corners of his mouth. It must be two years, give or take, since his boss had arrived here from the Met, where he imagined constant traffic jams made it impossible to go faster than the average tortoise, even with lights and sirens going. Yet she still didn't like negotiating narrow country lanes, and was always on edge when Baines floored the pedal.

He supposed she was right. The bodies wouldn't be going anywhere. There were two of them, on the Northfields estate. The place had been a thorn in the side of the Aylesbury Vale division of Thames Valley police for years, but the serious gang problems they had briefly feared a couple of years ago had been short-lived and, even at the height of the trouble, rivals had stopped short of killing each other.

"I thought things were too quiet," Archer commented. "Tumbleweed blowing through the office, Friday afternoon, the weekend starts here. Not that I had any plans," she added wistfully.

Baines knew Archer lived alone – he had helped her move in to her small house in the village of Great Marston – and that she didn't seem to have much in the way of a social life. He knew she'd been self-conscious about the facial disfigurement she'd sustained in the line of duty before her transfer, but she had undergone something of a transformation over the past year, with the skilful use of make-up and an artfully layered haircut disguising the crescent-shaped scar on her left cheek.

Only the slight droop of her mouth on that side told tales about her horrific encounter with a broken bottle. A lunchtime altercation in a London pub, Archer intervening despite being off duty. She'd paid a heavy price for that arrest.

If a quiet weekend watching repeats on TV had stretched out in front of Archer, Baines had begun to entertain a more romantic hope for two uninterrupted days with his partner, Karen. He'd even dared to imagine that he might get away early and surprise her with dinner on the table when she got in from work. Only spag bol, mind – the peak of his culinary repertoire. Dan Baines, MasterChef.

And now they had a double murder on their hands, and any sort of a weekend for either of them was fading like a mirage.

As he approached the scene of the crime – a street corner – he could see blue lights flashing: the first response patrol cars already there. He hoped they had secured the scene. He spotted Phil Gordon's van and marvelled at how the crime scene manager and his CSIs had once again managed to beat him to it.

He pulled up at the side of the road in an approximation of parking. He and Archer got out and approached the blue and white crime scene tape that the patrol car guys had already got up with commendable efficiency. A tent had also already been erected to conceal the bodies. Just as well. Quite a crowd had gathered to rubberneck the proceedings. It was still normal working hours, but Baines knew that many on the estate didn't work 'normal' hours, and there were plenty who didn't work at all.

In fairness, Northfields had never exactly been a hotbed of murder and mayhem, and Archer had assured him it was Disneyland compared to some parts of London, but to his eyes it was a grim concrete jungle that should have been bulldozed long since, and replaced by decent homes. Maybe some of the inhabitants would be indolent or criminal wherever they lived, but he couldn't imagine this sort of environment helped.

Archer flashed her warrant card at a stony-faced young constable who stood, arms folded, in front of the tape. He must be one of the new ones; certainly, Baines didn't recognise him, and Aylesbury nick wasn't that big.

"DI Archer and DS Baines. What have we got?"

"Two bodies, ma'am. Males. One maybe mid-thirties. The other, I reckon, mid-teens. Gunshots, both. No sign of a weapon."

It was a good report, brief and to the point. Baines winced at the age of the younger victim.

"You were first on the scene?" Archer checked.

"Yes, ma'am. Well, strictly, a neighbour was. Heard the gunshots and peeped out her window. Called it in, but didn't come out in case the shooter was still around."

"Didn't see the shooter?"

"No. Heard a vehicle drive off at speed, but didn't see that, either."

"We'll need to talk to them," Archer said. "Get someone to find her for us. And get the crime scene manager over. We don't want to blunder in there without suiting up unless he's okay with it."

While the uniform spoke into his radio, Archer looked, grim-faced, at Baines. "A teenager. Shit."

Baines nodded. Death was never pleasant. Murder was even worse, and it was most depressing of all when a victim had all their life in front of them.

Mid-teens. About his son Jack's age. If he were still alive. This one was going to get to him if he wasn't careful.

"So," she persisted, "I wonder how this played out."

Baines could think of a couple of scenarios, but they both knew it was way too soon to be playing speculation games.

The uniform came off his radio. "Witness – if you can call her that – is indoors. There's an officer with her. She had quite a shock. Crime scene manager's walking over now."

The last statement was superfluous, as they could see the familiar figure of Phil Gordon coming their way, his loping gait distinctive even in the anonymising white crime scene suit he wore.

"Well, this is a grim end to the week," he said, his Geordie accent somehow adding to the solemnity of his words. "I knew it was too quiet."

"What's it look like, Phil?" Archer wanted to know.

"You'll see for yourselves, but you'll have to suit up – it's early days yet, so Christ knows what's evidence and what isn't, in a road like this. In a nutshell, though, both look like executions – one shot to the body that probably knocked them down, and one through the head to finish the job."

Baines finally found his voice. "Anything to suggest who was shot first?"

"I've not spoken to the lady who heard the shots, so I've no idea how spaced out they were. Both body shots are from the front – not in the back, so neither of them appears to have been running away. But someone who knew what they were doing could probably have dropped the second one before the first hit the ground, then – bang, bang – two kill shots."

Archer sighed. "So... they could have been talking, or one could have come round the corner and just happened on the first shooting, so the gunman had to silence him."

"Both things are possible. The way they've fallen, I reckon the older guy was just ahead of the lad – maybe trying to shield him, but who knows? We've got an ID on him, by the way. One Matthew Butcher. Nothing on the kid, although we've recovered phones from both bodies."

"All right, Phil, thanks," Archer told him. "If you can find us some suits, we'll take a look first, then have a chat with this witness lady. I take it the pathologist has been notified?"

"Dr Carlisle is on her way, yes."

That was the first piece of good news since the incident had been called in. Barbara Carlisle was a stickler who sometimes drove them mad with her insistence on the facts – anything that smacked of speculation was anathema to her. But she was thorough and rarely missed a trick.

As the two detectives were struggling into their suits, the pathologist's elderly black Mercedes estate drew up. They waved to her and waited whilst she also suited up. Then the three of them ducked under the tape and headed for the tents.

"I gather one of them's quite young?" Carlisle commented. "I hate those. Not quite as bad as little children, but..." She trailed off, leaving the rest unsaid.

Gordon was waiting by the tent. "Might as well start your tour here."

"You didn't waste any time getting this up, did you?" Archer commented.

"You can get these up in five seconds flat," said Gordon, "and fortunately we had an idea what size to bring."

There was only space for one of them to squeeze inside, so they waited whilst a CSI with a camera slipped out, then let Carlisle go in. As she hunkered by the youth's body first, they hovered by the flap, giving her space. Baines found himself avoiding looking at the young victim's face.

"Shots were heard around 4pm," Gordon told them. "Judging by stuff found in his bag, he was on his way home from school."

"Dan?" There was something in Archer's tone. "We know this kid, don't we? Rather well, unless I'm mistaken."

He forced himself to look then, first a glance, then a longer double take. A deep chill seemed to be spreading out from the centre of his being.

Even with the hole in his forehead, the blood, and the frozen look of death on his face, there could be no mistake. He remembered an extremely bright boy who'd gone wrong, got himself shot a couple of years ago, and started turning his life around. In his mind's eye, he saw keen eyes, owlish behind bottle-thick spectacles, and a smile that somehow conveyed both sensitivity and wicked humour at the same time.

Now history seemed to have repeated itself, with fatal results.

"Brandon Clark," he confirmed, his voice hoarse. "Fuck. Poor kid doesn't have much luck around guns, does he?" As he spoke the last few words, the cold he felt inside bubbled, turned to hot, molten anger.

She must have heard the catch in his voice, because she looked at him with concern.

"You're right there," she said. "Poor little bugger."

"I saw him just last week, you know," he said. "Would you believe it? He was thinking about the police as a possible career and wanted to pick my brains. Said he saw me as some sort of role model." He tried to laugh, but his heart wasn't in it. "Incredible, right?"

Ever since the original shooting and its aftermath, he'd kept in occasional touch with the Clark family. He wasn't wholly sure why, but he'd hoped he could perhaps make a little difference just by being there for them.

"I know you liked him," Archer said softly.

"The one thing he couldn't do was get himself off this shitty estate," he said. "Now look at him."

"No great mystery here," Carlisle remarked from beside the body. "I'd say Phil had it right. First shot was to the body. Might have been fatal, given time, but it was the head shot that killed him. Within the last hour, but we know that already. I'll be able to have a proper look when I get him to the mortuary." She started to move away from the boy's corpse. "Better have a look at the other one."

As she moved to the second body, Baines felt his hands clenching into fists.

"He didn't deserve this, Lizzie. It'll kill Julie, you know."

They both knew Brandon's mother, a decent woman doing her very best to raise two boys on her own with not much in the way of income.

"Still," he spat, "we know where to look first, don't we?"

Archer touched his arm lightly. "I know you're upset about this, Dan. So am I. But there's no point in jumping to conclusions. Let's take a look at the other body, and then we can talk to the woman who called it in. I think we should get Jason over, too, to get a door-to-door going."

Jason Bell was a youngish Scottish Detective Constable: good at process, not so great when he had to be a bit more creative. Coordinating door-to-door enquiries was right up his street, and he could be relied on to separate the real nuggets of information from the chit-chat and gossip that some folk loved to share, without discarding anything until he was certain it was irrelevant.

Baines knew she was right. Whatever his feelings and suspicions, he needed to keep them in check, at least for now, or his judgement would be coloured from the off and he'd be pursuing the case with a less than open mind.

It was tough sometimes, though. It was true that the boy had led a gang that had caused trouble on the estate for a time, but Baines suspected he had first started it out of boredom and then disbanded it because it couldn't hold his interest. Baines knew he'd knuckled down at school, and there had even been talk of him taking his A-Levels early.

How old would he be now? Sixteen?

"Dan?" Archer's voice was soft, but firm.

"Yeah," he said. "Yeah, okay."

Carlisle was examining the older man – Matthew Butcher, according to Phil Gordon. He lay twisted slightly to one side. As with Brandon, there was a lot of blood on the pavement around his head. Forcing himself to focus on the second victim, Baines could see that this man was a little older than the uniform guarding the tape had thought. Baines had recently turned forty, and this guy was a year or two older, he thought. Leather biker-style jacket. More grey hair than brown. Wrinkles starting around the eyes and mouth. A fairly nondescript face: smooth, regular features.

Same hole in the forehead that Brandon Clark had presented.

"Well, the wounds are looking pretty similar," Carlisle decided. "Time of death too. How exactly it happened is your job to find out, but I'll let you know if I find anything interesting when I get them back to the mortuary."

They came away from the tent, leaving her to it. Archer took a breath.

"How's this for a theory?" she said. "One of them's targeted by our killer. A botched mugging, a deliberate execution – who knows? No sooner he's down than the other one comes round the corner, stumbles on the scene, sees the killer's face. Has to be silenced too."

"Sounds plausible," Baines agreed. "I thought we were keeping an open mind, though?"

"We are. I can think out loud, can't I?"

"The question is," he mused, "assuming you're right – who was the target, and who was in the wrong place at the wrong time?"

"Or there's another possibility," she said, her face grim now. "Maybe they both were."

"Meaning?"

"Meaning let's at least hope there was a motive for this. Otherwise we've got a lunatic in the Vale, choosing his victims at random."

2

It would have been fair to say that the nearest thing they had to a witness was still in a state.

Her name was Lorna Rees, she was around sixty, and her hands shook so much when she tried to make them tea that the uniformed constable who'd been with her had to take over. She stared into space as if she kept seeing the scene over and again. Archer was grateful – for her – that she had only seen it from an upstairs window. Up close and personal with a bird's-eye view of the blood would have given her even worse nightmares.

"I knew they were gunshots," she said, sitting on the edge of a saggy old sofa with a floral pattern so bright that it should have been handing round sunglasses. "I don't know why. You get all sorts of noises around here, but this… I don't know. I thought, firecrackers, and then I thought, no, too loud, and not quite right. Then I thought, my God, those were shots."

"How many?" Archer asked.

"Four. I'm sure it was four."

"Spaced out, or close together?"

There was an overflowing ashtray on the coffee table that sat between them, but that didn't deter Lorna Rees from taking up the packet beside it, extracting a cigarette and placing it between her lips. Archer, whose father had died too young from lung cancer, detested smoking and cigarette smoke, but this was the witness's own home and now wasn't the time to protest. Still, she did nothing to assist when the woman's trembling hands proved unequal to the task of flaming her lighter. Baines, maybe out of solidarity, also watched her struggle until the uniformed policewoman, barely concealing an eye roll at them, went over and helped her light up.

Rees drew deeply on the fag as if it was her last, and blew the smoke out and upwards. Archer's gaze was momentarily drawn to the yellowed ceiling.

Their witness closed her eyes for several seconds, then said, "Spaced out. At least, I think so. You know? Maybe I'm remembering it wrong, but a bang, a couple of seconds, then a second bang. That was when I thought, gunshots. Then I think there was a longer gap. I don't know. Perhaps five seconds. That third shot – that was when I really knew it was a gun. I was going upstairs to look out when I heard the last one."

"How big a gap that time?" Baines checked.

"Like between the first and second shots. Couple of seconds at the most. I ran upstairs. I'm not sure what I was thinking. I mean, what if he'd seen me looking out? I don't want to be next." She took another draw on her cigarette. "Well, anyway. I was at the bedroom door when I heard this car – I think it was a car – absolutely roar off, tyres squealing, the lot.

"I remember I squeezed up against the wall and edged along until I was next to the window, and I sort of looked round the side. Just in case it really was a gunman, and he was still there. But he wasn't. There was just… just…" She stubbed out the cigarette, even though most of it still remained unsmoked.

"You're doing fine," said Archer.

"I don't feel fine. I should have turned the telly up and taken no notice. But I didn't. Too bloody nosey for my own good."

"So what did you see?"

"The bodies. One on the pavement, one in the road. I couldn't see much, but I just *knew*. Same as I knew that car must have been the driven by the person who shot them both. You know what the stupidest thing is, though?"

"No."

"Part of me thought maybe they were just making a film. You know, a thriller or some such. I half expected them to get up and walk away. Thought there might be cameras, just where I couldn't see them. But no. I knew they were dead. Straight away, really."

She picked up her tea and drank greedily. Then she grimaced at the uniform.

"Blimey, I know they say sweet tea's good for shock, but you must have emptied half the sugar bowl in here."

"Sorry." The uniform blushed and moved towards her. "I'll make another."

"No, you're all right."

"Did you hear anything else?" Baines drew her back to the questioning. "Maybe before the shots? Raised voices, maybe?"

Lorna Rees shook her head. "I don't think so. I had the telly on, so it would probably have drowned out anything like that. I somehow heard the bangs over what was on telly. Funny, that."

"Is there anyone who can stay with you?" Archer asked. "A husband or partner coming home soon? A son or daughter?"

"No. I'm widowed – last year – and the kids have left home. My daughter, though – Vicky – lives in the town. Maybe she'd come round."

"Get PC...?" Archer looked at the uniform.

"Downes," she supplied.

"...to contact her for you." She held out a card. "If you think of anything, however small, give me a ring."

Lorna Rees took the card, and Archer made to get up, but Baines held up a finger.

"One last thing, Mrs Rees. You were home in the day. You don't work?"

She smiled. "I do, but I do the early shift at Tesco. I'm home mid-afternoon. Then it's all about killing time." She shrugged. "We should have been looking forward to retirement together. Then he had a massive heart attack, and that was that."

Archer lived alone in a house that still didn't feel like a home. She had a fleeting image of herself in twenty or thirty years' time, no longer working, still friendless, and wondering what to do with the days and nights stretching out before her. She crushed the thought and moved on.

"We'll be in touch about a formal statement," she said.

Outside the house, they watched as the body bags were loaded into an ambulance. Phil Gordon came back over.

"We'll be a while processing the scene. Oh, there's a parked car nearby, which comes up registered to our Mr Butcher. Might as well take it away and go over it with a fine-tooth comb, but I'll be amazed if it tells us anything we don't know."

"I say we stop dancing around," Baines said. "We know what happened here."

"Do we?" Gordon blinked.

Whatever Archer thought about the conclusion she knew Baines was jumping to, the last thing she wanted was for it to start spreading across Thames Valley – not that Phil Gordon was a gossip, but he might say something to someone who was.

"Let's talk about that later, Dan," she said. "Someone's got to break the news to Julie Clark, and it might as well be us, but we'd better find a family liaison officer. And we need to track down a next of kin for Matthew Butcher, too."

She could see Baines straining with impatience.

"We build this case. Same as any other," she told him firmly. "That way we don't cock it up and no one walks on any technicalities. All right?"

He breathed in, deeply. The breath came out as a sigh. "You're right, of course. Sorry." He turned to Gordon. "You said you had ID on Matthew Butcher. If you don't need it for your science stuff, can we have it? We can get Joan to find out more about him."

Joanne 'Joan' Collins was the real backbone of the team. Young, black and committed, she was highly organised and seemed to have an inexhaustible supply of ways to dredge up information.

The crime scene manager went off to get them what they needed, leaving Archer and Baines alone.

"I'm really sorry, Lizzie," Baines said again. "You know why I think Ryan Sturridge is at the bottom of this."

"Of course I do. And I know that Brandon isn't the only one who might have been on his list of scores to settle."

* * *

There was little about the Northfields estate to inspire cheerfulness. Whatever time of the day or night it was, the air seemed to reek of burned cabbage and wet washing. In the depressing blocks of flats, there was always some bulky item of rubbish abandoned in one of the stairwells, and the graffiti artists had long since given up hope of finding any remaining surfaces large enough to contain their next masterpiece.

Every so often some politician or other would be in the local media hand-wringing and making 'something must be done' remarks. Fine words that added not a jot to the quality of life here.

Yet Brandon Clark had lived here with his mother, Julie, and kid brother Marcus, in a house quite out of keeping with its surroundings: immaculate exterior paintwork, well-maintained front garden, and no sign of the litter that blew in through many a local gateway and never got picked up. Julie was hard-working and house-proud. Baines admired her immensely. When kids went off the rails, it was too easy to blame the parents. Julie Clark hadn't been to blame for her elder son's past misdemeanours.

It was two years since Brandon Clark had disbanded his gang, the Barracudas. Around the same time, Ryan Sturridge's younger sibling, Michael, had been sent to a young offenders' institute, leaving their rivals, the Bloods, leaderless. For a time, crime levels on the estate had dipped noticeably, but the past six months – dating back to a few months before Ryan's release – had seen statistics starting to ramp up again. And the crime was looking better-organised than before.

As they rang Julie Clark's doorbell, Baines felt sick. Breaking bad news to anyone was bad enough. Breaking the news of a dead child to a parent was a whole new level. When you knew the family... well, that was something he'd never get used to.

Julie opened the door, smiled in surprise, then saw the uniform and the looks on all their faces. Baines didn't have to say anything.

She knew.

Every drop of blood fled her face, and Baines had to be quick to catch her as her legs went.

"Please," she moaned, clinging to him. "Please. No. Not my Brandon."

They got her indoors and onto her sofa. Archer told the family liaison officer to stay put and went off to make drinks, taking Marcus with her to 'help'. The boy was almost as distraught as his mother, but she and Baines had agreed this strategy in advance. It would give Baines some space to do his best to get any useful information out of Julie without her worrying about her remaining son.

She sat staring ahead, her face damp with tears and snot. Baines sat opposite her, giving her a moment before starting the questioning. The FLO sat beside her, holding her hand. Finally her gaze swivelled his way.

"How?" she wanted to know.

"There was a shooting," he said, knowing no fancy preamble would soften the blow. "Another man's dead at the scene, also shot. His name's Matthew Butcher. Does that mean anything to you?"

She shook her head, although whether that was in answer to his question or in denial of what he had told her, he wasn't sure.

"Shot?" She shook her head once more. "Again? No, that can't be right."

"I'm so sorry, Julie."

"Ryan Sturridge," she said flatly. "He said he'd make people pay when he got out, and that little shit of a brother of his said Brandon was on the list, more than once."

Baines knew all about those threats. Baines had been involved in Ryan's arrest and had been threatened himself as the then teenager had been dragged away from the dock after his conviction for aggravated assault. Now it looked as though he'd been biding his time since his release. Baines wondered how many more were marked for death. He wanted to bring him in now, grill him until his skin bubbled, get the proof he needed by fair means or foul, and then get him put away for good.

The fact that he knew Archer was right about playing it by the numbers didn't make him feel a whole lot better.

"But has Sturridge been in contact?" he asked her. "Since he came out of prison?"

"Not to my knowledge. Although Brandon's been quiet lately. I asked him if everything was okay, and he said he was just working hard at school. I don't know. I was a bit worried, but Brandon was sure it was all just big talk. He was wrong, wasn't he?"

Archer returned with Marcus, each carrying two cups. There were times when Baines welcomed a cuppa when he was in someone's house, but he'd not long had one at Lorna Rees's home. There was such a thing as too much of a good thing. He thought he might leave his.

Archer melted into the background, not breaking his thread.

"We don't know if Ryan Sturridge was involved, Julie," Baines continued. "Not yet. We've got this other victim, this Matthew Butcher. We don't know if he was the intended victim or just a passer-by who saw too much. Matthew Butcher. Do you know the name?" he asked for the second time.

"I told you. No."

At least the ambiguity of her head-shake had been cleared up.

"Marcus?"

"No, Mr Baines. Is Brandon really dead?"

"I'm very sorry, Marcus, but yes."

"Oh." The boy looked down, tears leaking from his eyes. "He was going to take me to Disneyland Paris one day. I wanted to go."

He started to cry in earnest, and his mother went to him, the two clinging to each other like shipwreck victims holding on to floating wreckage.

"We're going to get some people to search Brandon's room later, if that's okay," Archer said, "but maybe Dan and I could take a quick look now?"

Julie merely nodded.

"We know the way." They'd been here before.

Hating the whole thing, Baines followed Archer to Brandon's room, both snapping on latex gloves.

The room wasn't so different to how he remembered it. Posters of pop stars had been replaced by more political ones about human rights and the environment: not such a surprise once you'd spoken – really spoken – to the lad. There was a pile of books by the bed. Brandon had been a serious bookworm, had been reading Dickens and Orwell last time Baines had seen him here. Now it appeared he'd graduated to Chinua Achebe and Martin Amis. Graham Swift's *Waterland* sat atop the pile, a bookmark poking out, about three-quarters of the way in. A book Brandon Clark would never finish. It made Baines's heart hurt.

Young males with unfulfilled potential were too close to home for his liking.

Archer pointed to a laptop on a small table in the corner. An old kitchen chair pushed underneath indicated that it had been used as a desk.

"We need to get the experts working on that," she said. "Phil mentioned a phone."

She opened drawers in a low chest, whilst Baines checked out a bedside cabinet.

"Nothing jumps out," he said.

"Nor here. Maybe the CSIs will find something."

"Maybe. Are we done here?"

Archer crouched down, peering under the bed, then stood up. "I guess we are. Let's finish up here, then get back to the station, brief the boss, and take stock."

"Ryan Sturridge?"

"We'll talk to him afterwards, but low-key. Him and his best bros. Just where were they at the time of the shooting, that sort of thing. I still want to know how our Mr Butcher fits into the picture."

"Unlucky passer-by. Got to be."

"Still. We need to talk to his nearest and dearest. Break the news, apart from anything else. Hopefully, Joan will have something for us by now."

3

Detective Chief Inspector Paul Gillingham was eating a bacon sandwich at his desk when Archer looked in on him. It was his usual fare when a late night was sprung on him. He would bribe one of the more rotund uniforms at the station to go and get it for him, with the invitation to get something for himself as well.

Archer leaned against the door frame and rapped her knuckles on it. Gillingham, who was in the act of taking a bite, eyed the remains of his snack wistfully, shoved it back inside its paper bag, and pointed to a chair opposite him.

"So what have we got?" he asked with his mouth full, leaning back in his fancy executive chair.

She brought him up to date, adding that Bell was orchestrating door-to-door enquiries even as they spoke, whilst Baines was seeing what Collins had turned up on Matthew Butcher.

"And Dan and Mrs Clark both think Ryan Sturridge is at the bottom of it? Do you think we should bring him in?"

She hesitated. "A bit soon for that, in my opinion, sir. At the moment, all we have against him is threats he made at his sentencing. Okay, his brother may have repeated them afterwards, but he was more mouth than substance, as I recall. Without evidence tying Ryan to what happened today, we've no grounds for arresting him. I thought we'd call round and try to have an informal chat, for all the good it'll probably do."

He looked gloomy. "A double shooting. All sorts of people will be jumping up and down, and it's the sort of thing the media love too. I'd really like a quick result. Bad boy goes straight? Arch enemy not long out of jail? Now he's dead?" He smiled. "You're right, of course, Lizzie. We need to join the dots. Let's just join them fast."

"I'll do my best."

"Do better. Rattle his cage a bit. Nothing to lose."

She left him with more than a few misgivings. It was too easy to home in on one suspect with little or nothing to back up those suspicions. She'd done it once herself. If Sturridge had nothing to do with these two murders, they could miss clues to the real killer.

Wanting a few minutes to draw breath, she went back to her desk and extracted her unofficial kettle and jar of good instant from a drawer before heading for the small kitchenette. When she returned, juggling the items along with a mug of black coffee, Baines and Collins made a beeline for her.

"Got an address for our Mr Butcher," Baines reported.

"Good."

"He had a credit card in his wallet," Collins explained. "That's what the CSIs based their ID on. But the bank is being cagey about his personal details: they want to do it by the book. To save time, I checked out the registration of his car, and we've got his address."

Baines brandished a slip of paper.

"Good work, Joan," Archer said. "Any chance you've been able to dredge up a next of kin, partner, whatever?"

"I've done the usual searches. Looks like he might live alone."

"What about that phone Phil recovered? Stored numbers?"

"It's password-protected, so it'll take a little time to get in to it. Could take up to an hour once we've roused the right expert."

"Damn. We really need someone who can tell us something about him – and besides, I don't like to think of someone who cared about him going about their business, not knowing he's gone."

"We need to get to that address," Baines said. "Knock on the door. If no one's in, we'll talk to neighbours. Someone must know something about him."

"He had some keys on him, and they're being sent over," Collins told them.

"Great. He must have had an address book or something. If need be, we can let ourselves in and have a look. Where's the address?"

"Old town," Baines said. "We'll be there in under five minutes."

She took an experimental sip of her coffee. Hot. "Okay. Give me maybe ten minutes to drink this, then we'll go. Afterwards, we can nip back to Northfields and look up Ryan Sturridge."

He looked at her. "I thought we weren't—"

"The boss thinks otherwise. Ten minutes."

* * *

Archer's coffee interlude at least gave Baines time to call Karen and tell her he was likely to be late and then working over the weekend. Again.

As always, she understood. She never complained. One more thing he loved about her – just as he had loved the same thing about her sister.

Karen Smart was the identical twin sister of Baines's dead wife, Louise, who had been gone some thirteen years now, the victim of a serial killer. That shared loss had bonded Baines and Karen in a close friendship that had grown into love. It had taken Baines time to be sure that it really was Karen he loved, and that he wasn't simply trying to replace Louise with a carbon copy – someone who looked, talked and acted exactly the same as she had done.

Not that re-creating his old life was ever going to be possible without Jack.

The killer had preyed on mothers with children around the age of two. His routine had been to murder the mother and abduct the child. Exactly one week later – always on a Friday – he would kill that stolen child at the scene of his next murder and, like some sick variation of the old changeling fairy tales, take the child he found there.

Except that he had stopped after Louise's death. Baines had agonised for the week whilst he and his colleagues had made desperate, but fruitless, efforts to catch the killer and find Jack. But there had been no new crime scene, no body. The boy had simply never been seen or heard of again.

Apart from in Baines's dreams – and in strange waking visions, for which he had yet to find any explanation.

Now Brandon Clark's death had somehow brought those early feelings of loss flooding back. A kid similar in age to what Jack would now be, and whom Baines had come to care about. He had hoped Brandon would escape the estate and make something of his life.

"It was on the local news," Karen said. "Not much, and no names yet. But one of the victims was sixteen?"

"I knew him, Karen. His name's not being released yet…"

"You don't have to tell me, if you'd rather not."

"I trust you to keep it to yourself. It was Brandon Clark. Remember?"

"Oh, God. Brandon? Dan, I'm so sorry. His poor mother."

"So here we go again, I'm afraid. All hands to the pump, and little or no weekend."

"Don't worry about that. Just catch the bastard who did it."

"That's the plan."

He'd made the call from the car park, for some privacy from the open office and to enable him to hear her over the rattle of fingers on computer keys, the blare of telephones, and the loud voices of officers trying to make themselves heard above the racket. He went back inside, to find Archer waiting by his desk.

"I've got those keys," she said. "Your car?"

"For a change," he said with a smile. He usually drove. For all that she hung on with white knuckles when he was in a hurry, she preferred to be driven. Not that they'd encounter any of the narrow lanes she disliked here in Aylesbury. Traffic congestion in the market town was becoming, he imagined, increasingly similar to what she'd known in London during her days at the Met.

Indeed, his estimate of under five minutes to get to Matthew Butcher's Monument Street address had reckoned without the Friday evening snarl-up on the A41, but they still managed to draw up outside the terraced house in less than ten.

As the name suggested, Aylesbury's old town contained some of the town's oldest buildings, some of them late mediaeval and Tudor. Buckinghamshire County Museum was also here, and Castle Street had once been the main point of entry to Aylesbury from nearby Thame. Monument Street itself was close to the twelfth-century St Mary's Church and was, Baines thought, mostly Victorian. Matthew Butcher's home, number 11, looked as if it was possibly the smallest property in the road.

Collins had arranged for a couple of uniforms to meet them there, and they were waiting in their squad car. CSIs were also on their way. Whether anyone else was there or not, the property would need to be treated as a crime scene.

There was no bell push, but a very robust-looking knocker made a satisfying sound. The noise seemed to echo ominously. They waited a full minute and then tried again.

"Use the key?" he suggested when there was still no reply.

Archer pursed her lips, a move that emphasised the droop of the left corner of her mouth.

"Maybe try the neighbours on either side. Doesn't feel right to just barge in when we don't know the situation. There could be someone in there having a shower or sitting on the loo."

Baines thought the house fairly emanated emptiness, but he didn't argue. There was no one home to the left of the property, but they struck gold at number 13. A harassed-looking woman in an apron, patting at her hair, opened the door with a bogus-looking smile slapped on. Enticing cooking smells wafted down the hall.

"Hi," she said, all false bonhomie. "You must be Ian and Sandra."

They showed their warrant cards. "Sorry, no," Archer said. "We're Dan and Lizzie – I'm DI Archer and this is DS Baines."

"Oh," she said, face falling. "*Police?* Are you sure?"

Archer raised a bemused eyebrow in Baines's direction. "Well, I'm fairly sure, yes." She nodded towards the squad car.

"Oh. Only we're expecting Tom's stupid boss and his stupid wife to dinner. Sorry. I thought you were them."

"Sorry to disappoint, especially as something smells good. But we're here about your neighbour at number 11. Mr Butcher?"

"Is that his name?" The woman shrugged. "We don't really know him. Said hello a couple of times, putting the bins out and the like, but that's about it. Mr Chatty, Tom calls him. Been here a year, give or take. We still don't know his name – although, in fairness, we've not introduced ourselves to him either. He comes and goes at odd hours. No idea what he does. What little I've seen of him, he's always in a hurry."

She stopped prattling. Looked from one to the other. "What's all this about?"

Archer kept her tone casual. "Mr Butcher's been involved in an accident, and we're wondering who to inform. Does anyone else live here?"

"Not that I've ever seen. Never seen anyone else go in or come out, but then neither of us are curtain-flappers."

"You've been very helpful, Mrs...?"

"Mitchell – Linda Mitchell."

A Mercedes drew up behind Baines's Mondeo. Linda Mitchell fell silent as a middle-aged couple got out. He was carrying a bottle of red, and she held a small bouquet that looked as though it had been grabbed at a petrol station. They approached number 13.

"Ian and Sandra?" The pasted-on smile was back.

"I didn't know we were going to be six," the man said, sounding irked and looking pointedly at Archer and Baines.

"Are you ever going to let them in?" a male voice bellowed from inside the house.

"We'll leave you to your evening," Baines said, moving away. Archer thanked the reluctant hostess once more and followed him.

They waited until the door had closed.

"Christ on a bike," said Archer. "There's a dinner party I want no part of."

"Wouldn't mind a doggie bag, though. The cooking smelled good. Well, it doesn't sound as if we're going to disturb anyone."

Archer asked the uniforms to keep an eye on the front door and also look out for the CSIs, then drew a bunch of keys from her bag. The third one opened the door and they went inside, slipping on latex gloves. There was mail on the mat, mostly what looked like junk, plus something official: possibly a bank statement.

"Open it?" Baines proposed.

"Let's have a look round first."

Baines's first thought as they moved around the premises was that it was all very neat, arguably too neat for a man living alone. Everything was clean, cushions on the two sofas in the living room were properly plumped, and a mug and a cereal bowl lay on the drainer by the kitchen sink. He took a cursory look in a bin tucked out of sight in the cupboard under the sink. It was almost empty.

Upstairs told the same story. The bed had been made, and wardrobe and drawers revealed clothes immaculately organised. The whole house reminded him of a head without a hair out of place.

The second bedroom seemed to serve as an office-cum-gym. A small desk shared the space with an exercise bike, a mat, and some hand weights. A TV was strategically placed so that the screen could be seen whilst using the bike.

"What do you make of it?" he asked.

"Seriously?" She made a face. "Just a little bit off, if not creepy. Check the desk and see if you can find any clues to who might have known this guy. I'll be back in a tick."

The desk was locked. He went in search of Archer. Found her back in the bedroom, peering into a laundry basket.

"He's not a complete neat freak," she said. "There are some clothes in here waiting to be washed. I'm going to see if he irons every day."

"Why?"

"Because, if that Linda Mitchell woman hadn't said she saw him around, I'd be wondering if anyone really lived here." She shook her head. "Can't put my finger on why it bothers me. But I'd be interested in what he was even doing on the Northfields estate."

"Desk's locked. Any chance one of the keys on that ring will fit?"

It did. Archer left him opening drawers. The top one contained bank statements, utility bills, some stationery, and a few pens and pencils. He moved on to the second drawer down. Here he found a solid metal box: heavy, also locked. None of the keys on the ring fitted it. He shook it, but was none the wiser.

The bottom drawer contained a few framed photos: a woman smiling at the camera. A couple of kids, a boy and a girl. One with Matthew Butcher and the woman and kids.

Archer returned. "Yes, there's ironing in a basket in the under-stairs cupboard. So maybe he is just excessively tidy. Some sort of OCD?"

"Could be. Look at these pictures."

He set the frames up on the desk.

"A family? Divorced, perhaps."

"But why keep them in the bottom drawer? Why not keep them out, at least those of the kids?"

"You've got me. Just another mystery about this guy. We left Joan trawling the databases, and with luck someone will be working on his phone by now. I'm sure once we've found a parent, or a sibling, maybe this woman in the pictures, then we can find out something about him."

He showed her the metal box.

"Key must be hidden somewhere," she mused. "Bag it for now. Could be something or nothing. We'll get it opened up somehow. Seen enough?"

"Yeah." He took a last look round. "This," he swept the room with his arm, "this doesn't speak to me of a life. Makes me almost as sad about Matthew as I feel about Brandon."

"The CSIs can do the detailed stuff, show us what we missed."

"Meanwhile," he slipped off his gloves, "Let's get at Ryan bloody Sturridge."

4

Ryan Sturridge was back living with his mum in a block of flats that was more in keeping with the estate's image than Julie Clark's smart home. At least the half-dead furniture that used to sit scattered about in the communal area at the front of the building had been tidied up since Archer had last seen it.

The litter, weeds and dog mess, not so much.

They found mother and son at home, eating some sort of ready meal. It made the stuff Archer kept in both the fridge and freezer, to make a change from takeaways, look and smell positively appetising.

Ryan as good as ordered his mother to rustle up tea for 'our guests'. He would brook no refusal, but insisted on finishing his meal before he gave them his attention.

So they sat watching him eat surprisingly daintily, Archer trying not to gag at the greasy aromas wafting from his plate. Just as the tea arrived, he set down his cutlery, pushed the plate away, and patted his washboard stomach.

"That was great, Mum," he declared, sounding like a judge on a cooking programme. He turned his chair round to face Archer and Baines. "So what can I do for you?"

"Where were you at around 4pm today?" she asked.

"Why?"

"Just answer the question," Baines snarled.

"I was having a drink with friends. What's it to you?"

Archer ignored the question. "Who are your friends, and where did you go?"

"Anyone see you?" Baines added.

Sturridge smiled. "If I didn't know better, I'd think I was being fitted up for something again. Not those shootings, by any chance?"

"What do you know about those?" Baines asked sharply.

"Only what I heard on the news. One of them not much more than a kid, yeah?" He sighed. "Tragic. What's the world coming to, eh?"

"The kid was Brandon Clark. It's not been announced yet. Still tragic?"

"Brandon?" He made a big show of whistling. "Oh, dear, how sad. Second time he's been shot, wasn't it? You harassed my family last time, too."

"Not entirely without good reason," Archer said. His smugness was getting under her skin. Baines was keeping his own emotions on a tight leash, she knew. One of them had to remain objective. She silently counted to ten.

When she didn't say any more, Sturridge shrugged. "Just have to agree to disagree, won't we?" He picked up his mug of tea and blew on it.

"When you went inside," Baines said, "you made a lot of threats. You said a lot of people were going to pay."

"I said a lot of things. I was upset. I'd been fitted up."

"Happens to you a lot, doesn't it?"

"You should know, Mr Baines."

Archer had been toying with her none-too-clean mug, debating whether to drink from it or not. Now she put it down on the table with a bang. Tea slopped over the side.

"Oops," Sturridge remarked. "Fetch a cloth, Mum."

She had started loading the dishwasher but now hurried over with a damp cloth and started wiping at the spill, only succeeding in spreading it over the table.

"Ryan," Archer said evenly, "we can do this here, informally, with a bit of cooperation from you, or we can do it at the station."

"Only if I want to come," he replied, offering them another insolent shrug. His gaze lingered on the drooping corner of Archer's mouth in a way that made her want to punch him. "Unless you're going to arrest me. On what grounds? I know my rights – a bloody sight better than I did before I did my time. Five minutes out and you're trying to pin a double murder on me?"

"Three months out, actually," Baines said, "and it's already sounding like you're up to your old tricks, and worse. In fact, crime was ramping up on the estate, and beyond, even before you came out. Ben and the guys paving the way for you, were they?"

"If you had proof to back up what you say, you'd be slapping the cuffs on me. Now, are you going to arrest me with good reason to suspect me of anything? Or ask me some questions? Or piss off so Mum can get me my pudding?"

"All right." Archer tried to claw back control of the conversation, which was getting away from them. "Where was this drink you say you had? And who was with you?"

"That's more like it. I was with my mate, Ben Loftus, and my girlfriend, Laine Shaw. We were in the Falcon. The bar manager, Raphael, will tell you. Check it out."

"We will. We'll need contact details for both your friends. Convenient you having an alibi like that."

He laughed. "It's not an alibi. It's a drink."

"Do you own a gun?"

His hand moved towards his mouth, then upwards to remove an imaginary strand of hair from his forehead. "That would be illegal."

"You had one before."

"I was never charged for that."

"Your fingerprints were on it."

"Doesn't make it mine."

She sighed. "So you've been out of prison for three months. Have you done anything about looking for work? You seem to be spending your weekdays and your money in pubs. What are you living on?"

"Let's just say I'm pursuing some business opportunities. I won't be living in this shithole much longer. Sorry, Mum," he said casually.

"Before you went *away*," Baines said, "it was all kicking off. Gangs on the estate. The Bloods and the Barracudas. You against Brandon. Then you go down, making threats from the dock. Now Brandon's dead."

"Brandon was a stupid little kid."

"Not so stupid."

"Whatever. They were stupid little gangs. I was growing out of all that when I got put away. He's not worth my time now."

"No?" Baines scratched his head. "You sounded pretty passionate at the time. Said the police were pigs, we'd fitted you up, and we were going to pay."

"Compensation, yeah? Nothing else. I expected the conviction to be quashed."

"It was never going to happen. The case against you was cast-iron."

"So you say." Sturridge gave him a sly look. "I hear that DI Britton, him that arrested me, has kicked the bucket. Karma, see. Who needs to dish out revenge, when you've got karma?"

DI Britton had been Archer's predecessor and mentor. He still felt his loss keenly, she knew.

"You've something to say about DI Britton?" he demanded.

"Only that he was as bent as... as anything," he concluded lamely. "So what? He's gone. Now so is Brandon. If ever I had a list, it looks like the names are being ticked off without my help. Now, are we done?"

Before things got out of hand, Archer handed him a card. It was time to go. She practically stood over him whilst he jotted down addresses for Ben Loftus and Laine Shaw, then she and Baines left.

Outside, she stood with her arms folded, surveying the estate's relentless gloom. It was easy to say that bad guys were a product of their environment, but she knew that was grossly over-simplistic. Just as she knew that Sturridge being a little shit didn't necessarily make him a killer.

She'd found it hard to judge whether he was surprised by the news about Brandon Clark or not.

"He was lying about the gun, wasn't he?" Baines ventured. She'd expected an outburst from him, but he seemed a little subdued, if anything.

"He was lying about something, probably the gun. Question is, do we have enough to turn his gaffe over? Especially as that alibi will almost certainly hold up. Chances are, even if he has a weapon, he's not keeping it there. What did you make of that big talk about business interests? Onwards and upwards and getting out of the estate? Fantasy?"

"Probably. Or he's spreading his wings. We know drug supply in the area seems to be up lately, and no one can pin down where it's coming from. And have you spoken to the guys who keep an eye on the sex trade recently?"

She hadn't.

"They say people are jumpier than they've ever known," he said, "and more close-mouthed, too. Like they're scared of something."

"Scared of Ryan?" She was sceptical. "I don't get the impression that he's half as bright, or as tough, as he thinks he is."

He laughed without a trace of humour. "I don't think he'd be what's got them scared, no. But I'd say he's got cockier, if anything. Maybe some seriously heavy people are muscling in around here and Ryan's coat-tailing them." He shrugged. "That was the first time you've met him. What did you make of him?"

Archer thought about the question for a moment. "Well, we do know he's capable of brutality. That was what got him put away, wasn't it? And did you see the way he was ordering his mother about, and she just meekly did as she was told?"

"That's true. You'd never have seen her running around after him like that before. Most of the time she was off her face on drink or drugs, or both, and she always had some scumbag man or other warming her bed until he got bored with her. She didn't give a stuff what the kids did, so long as it didn't interfere with her."

"You think he's knocking her about?"

"Or maybe supplying her. Something's got her under his thumb, hasn't it?"

"Still." She shuddered. "His own mother."

"I know. But the question is whether he had anything to do with those shootings. I don't think we can rule it out. Maybe he met some hard cases in prison and is stupid enough to think he's one of them now."

"And stupid enough to start shooting people?"

"Maybe."

She started walking towards the car. "Let's get back to the station. We can get his alibis checked out in the morning. I've no doubt they'll confirm what he said and everyone will be word-perfect."

"As in a manufactured alibi for the murders?"

"Maybe." She frowned. "Or maybe he's got something else going on that he wants to cover up."

Baines pressed his key fob to unlock the car, and they got in.

"You know, all three of those names he gave us will say he was with them this afternoon. I can't imagine his girlfriend giving him up, and Ben's always been a loyal lieutenant. He backed up Michael Sturridge after his brother was jailed, then Michael went and blotted his own copybook."

Archer looked at him as he drove away. "What about the barman he mentioned?"

"I don't know any Raphael, but the word was that the Bloods traded drugs in the Falcon and gave the bar staff backhanders to turn a blind eye. Not that any evidence ever turned up."

"How come you know all that?"

"Steve Ashby's had quite a bit of involvement with that scene. If you believe him." Ashby was one of three DIs at Aylesbury, along with Archer and Lara Moseley.

Archer and Ashby had rubbed each other up the wrong way from the start.

"Well," she said, "plenty to get our teeth into there. I'd still love to find someone who knew our Mr Butcher. Let's hope we can find a quick way into that box – and that there's some useful information inside it."

"I think we can find a suitable key. A bloody big screwdriver should bust the lock a treat."

"Maybe we can find a more subtle method."

He pulled a face. "There are times when you're just no fun."

* * *

Ryan Sturridge watched from the window as the Mondeo's brake lights flashed at the end of the road before turning. Then he took out his mobile phone and speed-dialled a number. He tapped his foot impatiently until it was answered.

"Hiya, Benny boy, it's me. Change of plan. Get your arse over here now."

He listened to Ben start to complain about being in the middle of his dinner.

"Shut up," he snapped. He looked at his watch. "If you leave now, it'll take a couple of minutes to get your shoes on, three minutes max to get here. I'm all heart, so I'll give you ten, starting now. You'd better not be fucking late. We need to talk."

* * *

Archer gathered the team for a quick update when they returned to the station, starting off by updating them about their uninformative conversation with Ryan Sturridge and the unnaturally neat house on Monument Street that Matthew Butcher had occupied.

"Joan, how have you got on with tracking down family for Mr Butcher?"

The DC furrowed her brow. "It's weird. I've been through all the usual databases and, if you go back more than three years, it's as though he didn't exist before. Half the places you'd expect to find some information on him, he's just not there."

"You're sure?" Archer held up a hand to forestall Collins's answer. "Of course you're sure. You'll have checked and rechecked, right?"

"Yes, guv. Not a sniff of a family – nor a job, come to that."

"Any joy from that phone?"

"Haven't heard back yet. I'll chase it up when we're done."

But a shiver of disquiet was already running across the back of her neck. She had a queasy feeling about this, but decided that it would keep for a few minutes longer.

"So," she said, trying to sound calm, "we're no wiser, but we have got pictures, possibly of family." She held them up. "And we've got a mysterious locked box. Any ideas about getting it open before DS Baines applies brute force and ignorance?"

"Um, I might sort of be able to help you there, guv," piped up DC Jason Bell. He didn't blush quite as much as he used to when speaking in front of the team, but there were still a few red patches on his neck and face. "Does anyone have a paper clip?"

Collins was able to oblige. They watched as he straightened the clip, bent it in a few places, then inserted it into the lock. Everyone watched expectantly whilst he wiggled it about. Then he withdrew it.

"Better get that screwdriver," Baines remarked.

"Ye of little faith," the Scot replied, adjusting the bends and then trying again. This time they all heard a click. "Learned that in Glasgow," he said. "Just don't ever ask how."

He opened the box. Archer, Baines and Collins peered inside.

"Bloody hell," Baines said.

There were three passports, three driving licences, and several credit cards in Matthew Butcher's name and in two other names, but the picture in each piece of ID was of the man who'd died earlier today.

There was also cash. Wads of it.

Archer shoved her fingers through her hair, realising even as she did so that she was exposing her scar. She hastily pushed her hair back into place, flustered.

"Someone get the boss. Now."

Collins moved fastest. She returned a couple of minutes later with DCI Gillingham in tow.

"What's so urgent?" he wanted to know. "I've just had the Assistant Chief Constable on the phone. In person. Wanting quick results. Please tell me you have something."

Archer grimaced. "At the moment, sir, we have a dead man who probably doesn't exist."

"What are you on about?"

She told him about the overly pristine flat, showed him the photographs, and explained about Collins's failure to find any trace of him going back more than three years.

Then showed him the contents of Matthew Butcher's box.

He looked sharply at her.

"What do you think all these identities are about?"

"Search me. Several possibilities. Not many of them good."

"Such as?"

She'd given it some rapid thought. "Well, at one end of the spectrum, I suppose he could be one of the good guys. Security services, that kind of thing."

"What, MI5? Here in Aylesbury? I can't see that. What else?"

"There's terrorism, of course. Or some sort of international criminal – maybe a hit man – who might have to burn an identity and move at the drop of a hat. Or maybe he's just a con man who plays different parts to get rich widows to part with their savings." She shrugged. "Take your pick."

He looked at the documents and cards again. "Do we even know if these are real?"

Archer picked up a passport and studied it. "In the sense of properly issued versus forgeries? I suppose they could be good fakes, but they wouldn't get him very far these days. The passports and driving licences might be useful as bogus ID if you took them at face value. He might even manage to hire a car. But they wouldn't get him out of the country. Fake credit cards would be easy enough if you could get past the ID checks. I reckon they're genuine, with a pukka credit limit on each card."

"You know," Baines chipped in, "it might explain why that house was so well organised if the person living there wanted to be able to leave in a hurry. All it needed to complete the picture was a packed suitcase in the hall."

Gillingham pulled up a seat. "So what does that say to us? Are we buying Lizzie's international hit man idea?"

Archer bit her lip. "I'm not sure we should rule anything out. We just don't know. Something's not right, though."

"It could be enough to make *him*, not the young lad, the target of those shootings."

"We don't know, and we don't want to fixate on one scenario. There are still three possibilities. Brandon and the man we've been calling Butcher knew each other and were together when the gunman struck. Or Butcher was the target and

Brandon was collateral damage. Or vice versa." She shook her head, thoughts and questions swirling in her brain. "We've got those pictures. So why don't we circulate them to police forces across the country and also to news agencies? Someone must recognise him, the woman, the kids. Also, we need to contact the National Crime Agency – let them know we have a dead body here with these multiple IDs and see if it means anything to them."

"Sounds like a plan. What else?"

"We've got alleged witnesses who can put Ryan Sturridge elsewhere at the time of the shootings. Tomorrow, we'll talk to them and also to friends of Brandon." She looked Bell's way. "Anything come of the door-to-door, Jason?"

"Sorry, guv, no. A few people heard what turned out to be the shots, but only Ms Rees, the one you spoke to, bothered to investigate. So no one saw or heard anything. At least, that's what they say. I suppose it's just possible they don't want to get involved, but I've no reason to think anyone was lying."

"Did you check whether anyone knew Matthew Butcher?"

"Drew a blank there, too."

"All right," Gillingham said. "Let's get those photos out there, and then everyone go home and get some sleep. We've got someone on our patch who's got a gun and doesn't mind using it. We don't want any more bodies, so it looks like being a very long weekend."

5

When Baines and Karen finally got together, she had moved in with him almost immediately, and they were currently renting out her own home, waiting for a more buoyant housing market before attempting to sell it. He came home to find her on the sofa, nursing a glass of wine and watching a repeat of a cop show on ITV3.

"You're earlier than I expected," she commented as she put the glass down and rose for a kiss and a long hug.

"Early start tomorrow, though," he said. "This one's a bastard. And looking a bit of a puzzle."

"Well, I made lasagne. How do you fancy puzzling round that? And one of these?" She pointed to her glass.

"I could kill for one of those," he said.

He followed her into the kitchen. She'd done a day's work herself and then come in and cooked, but still had a bounce about her on a Friday night. Baines, by contrast, felt knackered, depressed and angry.

"How are Brandon's family?" she asked as she poured wine for him.

He took the glass. "Not good, as you'd imagine." He took a sip. Watched her put the remains of the lasagne in the microwave. She turned it on, then put a plate in the oven on a high temperature to warm it quickly.

"I'd have waited for you if I'd known it wasn't going to be an all-nighter."

"You make it sound like some sort of rave. No, we'd got as far as we reasonably could. There are things we need to bottom out. Motive would be a good start. It's possible that Brandon wasn't even the main target, although I'll take some convincing."

She spoke above the roar of the microwave's fan. "Is there a suspect?"

"Yeah, but we have to prove it."

"So who was the other victim?"

"That's the thing. We're not sure yet."

"Really?"

He hesitated. Something told him he needed to be cagey about this, even with Karen, but he also knew the photographs would be all over the media soon. He decided to give her an edited version

"We can't pin an ID on him. There are some things that don't add up. He might have been going by an assumed name – we found some ID that could be fake."

She raised an eyebrow. "Really? What does that mean?"

"We simply don't know right now. We did find pictures of what looked like family, and those will be with the media and other police forces by now, or at least on their way. We're hoping that, by tomorrow, someone will have laid claim to him."

She'd brought her own wine with her, and she took a sip. "I guess you can't make a proper plan for the investigation until you know exactly what you're looking at."

"Or *who* we're looking at, for that matter. I know who I think is responsible – or at least I thought I did. Now I'm not so sure, but at the moment it's like doing a jigsaw with no picture on the box and half the pieces blank."

"You'll figure it out. You always do."

"Not always," he said quietly.

She regarded him with a sudden sadness in her eyes. "No. Not always. Have you seen Jack lately?"

She knew that he no longer reported every dream or waking vision of his son – or the figure he imagined was his son – to her.

"Not so much," he said. "There was that case about six months ago – the piece of shit who imprisoned and tortured his ex-girlfriend for three days? Remember? I saw him a couple of times during that time. And maybe once since, but that was no more than a flash."

That was how it went sometimes. For reasons he couldn't fathom, the phantom – mirage, whatever it was – always appeared to him in the guise of a teenager, about the age Jack would be if he was still alive. He'd been abducted thirteen years ago, and for most of those years Baines had locked his emotional reaction to Louise's murder and his son's disappearance away in a mental box. Almost three years ago, the box had inexplicably burst open. First had come the dreams, then the sightings.

Sometimes, Jack would stand before him, as solid as any flesh-and-blood being. At other times, all Baines might see would be a flash in his peripheral vision of the blue and white Queens Park Rangers replica shirt the boy always appeared in.

Baines thought the shirt might represent a lost future in which he would have taken Jack to see the football team he, his father and his grandfather had all supported – a throwback to the family's West London roots. But, short of insanity, he could see no reason for these manifestations, nor why they had started when they had.

There was no point in asking Jack, either. Apart from a handful of words he had spoken to Baines in a dream, about a year ago, the apparition had never spoken to him.

The insanity angle he utterly rejected. Karen had tentatively suggested he see a shrink a couple of times, and it had simply annoyed him. He saw enough charlatans in his day job, without seeing another in his own time.

True, she had managed to cajole him along to a 'mediumship night' in Aylesbury. But it had left him none the wiser – had made matters worse, if anything – and the passage of time had enabled him to rationalise the things the so-called clairvoyant had seemed to know about him.

"Dan?"

He realised he'd allowed his mind to wander.

"Sorry?"

"I said, this new case... a boy about Jack's age, who you liked. Do you think it'll trigger more sightings?"

"No idea, since I don't know what 'triggers' them in the first place."

"They seem to be most intense when you're working a difficult case."

It immediately got under his skin, like the opening bars of a particularly annoying tune. He stared at her, the day's shocks and frustrations coming to the boil. "Not this again."

The microwave pinged, but she didn't immediately open the door. "Not what again?"

"You still think it might all be in my mind, don't you?"

"I didn't say that."

"You're determined to get some quack to look inside my head."

He knew his tone was hectoring, but he didn't give a damn – nor did the hurt look in her eye have any impression on him.

She opened the microwave without another word, took out the lasagne, removed the plate from the oven, and started to serve it.

"There's some parmesan cheese in the fridge," she said. "I grated some earlier for you."

From the living room, the low voices of onscreen characters could still be heard.

She put the plate of food in front of his usual chair at the kitchen table.

"I'll leave you to it and watch the rest of my programme," she said. "Join me when you're in a better mood."

"I just don't enjoy being called a nutter," he said to her retreating back.

"Whatever," she threw over her shoulder.

* * *

Whilst Baines was picking at his lasagne and seething over Karen's attempts to reopen a subject that, as far as he was concerned, was off-limits, Archer was seated at her own kitchen table, a takeaway in its foil trays in front of her, her laptop open by her right hand. Florence and the Machine were playing on her iPod.

The dating website stared back at her, enticing her, promising her that her soul mate, her perfect partner, was out there somewhere.

She kept coming back to these sites. She wasn't even sure she was looking for a partner, certainly not a long-term one. The last two relationships she'd had – one before, one after the incident that had disfigured her – had ended painfully, for very different reasons.

All she thought she really wanted was a bit of company now and then, with the bonus of some good sex. She was still very self-conscious about her looks, and she knew she would probably always have to endure the occasional stare, such as Ryan Sturridge had inflicted on her today, and the odd insensitive – or even cruel – remark. But her 'new look', as she thought of it, had given her confidence a boost. Part of her felt ready to take the plunge into dating again, and she thought this was as good a way as any.

Part of her was bloody terrified, for all sorts of reasons. For starters, she would advise any other woman to be wary about trundling off to meet a total stranger, with no idea as to whether they bore any resemblance to the online persona she thought she had warmed to.

Today's murders were a case in point. Who was Matthew Butcher really? A good guy with secrets to keep, or a dangerous criminal? And had either of those truths got him killed, or had he just been unlucky today?

Leaving aside the risks, there was her scar. What would the protocol be? Just see how the guy reacted when he saw it? Prepare him in advance? If she did that, how could she be sure he didn't just have some sort of freak show fetish thing going on?

She speared a piece of chicken and popped it in her mouth, the flavours barely registering.

Even if, by some miracle, she got lucky and found someone who seemed to like her and with whom she could have some fun, there was the job. Take the case that had kicked off today. The hours would probably be insane, starting tomorrow. This was why so many police officers had relationships with other members of the emergency services. They were the ones most likely to understand the pressures of the job, but it was a cliché she was keen to avoid. She'd tried that twice, and neither had turned out well.

She knew of a notorious pick-up bar in Aylesbury. Maybe it would be simpler to just go in there late one night, perch on a stool, and book into a cheap hotel with the first decent-looking stranger who showed an interest. Or maybe just have a quickie in his car. No complications. Just a bit of human contact for a little while.

Great plan. Either scenario could end with her being fished out of the canal, or dug out of a shallow grave by some inquisitive dog on an early morning walk.

She stared at the screen again. Should she register? She felt sure she'd have to send in a photo, and she didn't really have a good one. A selfie would be naff, but who else could she get to take one?

She'd lost touch with, or just plain lost, all her friends since what had happened to her. Both her parents were dead, and her brother hadn't spoken to her for a couple of years. She hadn't had so much as a Christmas card from him. He'd made it clear that she had no place in his life any more, resenting having – as he saw it – had to be the one who made sacrifices to support their mother when she was dying, while her own job pressures had constantly thwarted her attempts to play her part.

She often thought that Dan Baines was possibly the nearest thing she had to a friend, and their relationship was almost all work. They never discussed personal stuff. She was fairly sure he had a partner who'd moved in with him sometime in the past year, but he'd never actually said, and she'd never asked.

Asking him to take a photograph of her was out of the question. She'd feel duty-bound to explain what she wanted it for. Could she really expose herself to that humiliation with him? With anyone?

It hardly mattered at the moment. She had enough on her plate with these murders, and the idea that she could find a spare evening to meet a potential Mr Right was risible. At least until the case was closed, there wasn't much point in wasting time with this website.

She laughed at herself as she shut down the laptop. Maybe she should just get herself a cat, and take up knitting.

* * *

Baines walked into the living room with two mugs. Karen was in the centre of the sofa, her legs folded underneath her, and showed no sign of budging up so he could join her.

"I made some tea," he said.

"It'll take more than that to get round me." She didn't take her eyes off the TV screen.

"I know," he said, feeling absurd. "I'm sorry. I shouldn't have been like that."

"No."

"It's been a bad day."

She looked at him then. "I know it has. And I'm sorry. But you do need to ask yourself why this young man's death has affected you so much."

He examined the question. "I just liked him, and I admired the way he'd gone about changing his life. We had some sort of connection."

"You can't save everyone, Dan," she said softly, reaching out for his hand.

"I know I can't. It's just…" He couldn't explain, not even to himself. He just hated what had happened.

"And, by the way, I wasn't trying to get you to see a shrink, even though I still think it's worth a try. It's your mind, not mine, at the end of the day."

"I can handle it."

"You're seeing things that are not there. Or at least that nobody else can see. That's not normal, Dan. And it's not really going away, is it?"

"Maybe I don't want it to go away," he said softly.

"I get that. I do. It feels like some sort of link with Jack. But what if it turns into something else?"

"I'll handle it."

"What if you can't?"

"I will."

She rolled her eyes. "Don't expect me to come and see you when you're in a straitjacket." But she made room for him on the sofa. "You don't have to be tough with me, you know. Lou was my sister, and Jack was my nephew."

"*Is* your nephew," he corrected.

"Is. Look, you're all I've really got now, Dan. My family haven't been the same since I moved in with you. They think it's sick."

He remembered her anguish when they had accused her of trying to take Louise's place.

"I think mine only tolerate the situation." His parents and siblings were not hostile about it, but he could tell they felt awkward.

"All I'm saying," she said, "is that I couldn't bear it if anything happened to you, or to us. Don't close your mind to getting some help if you feel you need it. Can you at least promise that?"

"Of course," he said. And he would, if he really had to.

6

Archer stifled a yawn as she walked into the office. The case and her mixed feelings about online dating had kept her awake half the night. She had vague recollections of a bad dream: a restaurant, a date whose face she couldn't remember placing a bunch of red roses in front of her. The flowers had started to bleed, the blood pooling out from them, running over the edge of the table and dripping onto her lap. She'd awoken with a strangled cry of horror. After that, she'd been wide awake.

She'd expected to be first in the office, but Joan Collins had beaten her to it, and hurried over to her even before she got her coat off.

"Guv, Matthew Butcher's phone. Unregistered pay-as-you-go with no SIM card. One number stored in the phone's memory, also unregistered."

"You've tried ringing it?"

"Just rings and rings. No way we can trace it."

"Keep trying."

"We will. There's more, though."

Archer blinked. "There could hardly be less."

"No, but listen to this. His leather jacket had pockets all over the place and the CSIs found one they'd overlooked, right up by his shoulder. They reckon it's meant to be a secret pocket, and it almost worked. Anyhow, you'll never guess what they found?"

"You're doing it again, Joan."

Collins had an occasional tendency to play guessing games about what she'd found out rather than come to the point. It was one of her – very few – faults.

"Sorry, guv. There was a small wallet thing inside with about a dozen unused SIM cards. They reckon he was using them once and then disposing of them."

"But why?"

"So the phone couldn't be traced, and there's no information on it even if someone got their hands on it."

"Again – why?" Then she answered her own question. "He had something to hide. And maybe he was scared, too. What of, I wonder?" She pulled off her raincoat. It was one of those days when it might rain, or might be warm enough for the coat to be a nuisance.

"That's all very well," she said, hanging it on a hook, "but how does anyone call him, if the number keeps changing?"

"Ah," Collins grinned. "They reckon he must have had another phone – sort of an everyday phone – and the killer took it."

"The killer rummaged in his jacket after killing him and Brandon? Risky."

"Maybe he already had it out."

"Maybe. Why take it, though?" She thought some more. "Maybe for safety's sake. The killer thought there might be something incriminating or useful on it. So does that make Brandon the unlucky victim? I'm just not seeing the whole picture here. Where are they with Brandon's phone?"

"Checking that out now. They wanted to give Mr Butcher, or whatever his name is, priority."

"Put a rocket up them. And find out when someone will have gone through the two victims' computers. For all we know, Brandon and Butcher did know each other." A thought flashed through her mind. "We don't know too much about Brandon's family – or at least, I don't. I seem to recall Dan saying his father had been a gambler and general waste of space who committed suicide. I wonder if there's anyone who's ever been a father figure to the boys."

"Someone a bit dodgy?"

"A stretch, I know. I don't think the father had a criminal record – he just got way over his head in debt. Can you get on to Julie Clark, just in case, and see if she's seen the pictures of Matthew Butcher we released – ask if she recognises him?"

"On it, guv."

Archer made herself a coffee and sat, deep in thought. What had the man she would call Butcher, until she knew differently, been into? Was that what had got him and Brandon killed?

It was relatively quiet in the office. She normally welcomed the opportunity to work without noise or interruption, but she couldn't settle today. She was tired, and she was grumpy from lack of sleep, so she didn't appreciate it when DI Stephen Ashby came waltzing in – unbelievably early for him, especially on a Saturday – and came to perch insolently on her desk.

"Insomnia, Steve?" she asked without a trace of humour.

"Oh," he said, "I've got a busy day ahead. We can't all have big murder cases that drag us in at the weekend. I'm seeing some mates for a pie and a pint later, then we're watching footie on the big screen."

"Well, don't let me keep you." She made a big show of studying her computer screen.

"Christ," he muttered. "You really have a problem, don't you? I've come in here at sparrow's fart, just to do you a favour. Perhaps I'll just fuck off home."

Now she was really suspicious. "What favour?"

"No, no. I can still get an hour's kip before I have to head for the pub." He stood up as if he was leaving.

"Suit yourself."

Bluff called, he sighed heavily.

"Look. I saw those pictures you put out yesterday."

She regarded him curiously. "And? Don't tell me you recognised our victim?"

He shook his head. "Nothing as good as that. But may I?" He gestured to her computer. Saw the suspicion in her eyes. "You can be such hard work. What, you think I'll upload porn, something like that?"

"Nothing would surprise me." She shrugged and stood up. "All right. But this had better be good."

"It is." He settled himself in her chair and started tapping keys, real hunt-and-peck stuff, but pretty quick for all that. She watched him do a search, choose a link, type in the search box on the site it took him to, then click through further sets of results.

Numerous family group photographs filled the screen. Ashby scrolled down, then hovered the cursor over an image of a smiling woman with two children.

"Recognise that?"

She studied it until she was sure there was no mistake.

"It's the woman – looks like the kids, too – from our photo."

"Not just the same mum and kids – the same picture. These aren't your man's family – they're stock pictures, probably all models. The single pictures are on here too."

"But... he was in one of the pictures."

"Photoshop, most likely. Someone who understands all this techno crap better than I do will be able to confirm it. These are not his family," he said again. "They're props. Now don't say I don't do you any favours."

She didn't like him any better, but she had the grace to thank him.

"How did you find them?"

"Stroke of luck, really. I've got a mate who designs and prints brochures and all that for local businesses. I watched him work on one, looking through the stock image sites for pictures to include – it's much cheaper than doing a photoshoot."

"Okay. But *these* pictures?"

"That? Oh, yeah." He looked at his shoes. "Thing is, I remember this woman because she reminded me of my ex-wife. Matter of fact, my mate was thinking of using her, but I talked him out of it. So when I saw the pictures you released, they jogged my memory."

"Well, thanks. Funny thing is, he didn't have these out anywhere – just tucked in a drawer. And why have them at all?"

He vacated her chair. "Buggered if I know. This is your mystery. I'm off to enjoy my weekend."

He strolled off, whistling. She watched him go. People never failed to surprise her. In her experience, Ashby was a lazy law unto himself, yet he'd put himself out to help her. She supposed a copper was a copper, when all was said and done.

She called Collins over and showed her the site Ashby had pulled up.

"Can you talk to Jason when he gets in, Joan? Ask him to get hold of the people who run the site and see if there's any way they can get us a list of who've accessed these pictures. You never know what information we might get hold of. Also," she added, "find out when Dr Carlisle is doing the post-mortems. I want to be there."

She finished her coffee and dealt with emails until Baines showed up, ten minutes or so later. They decided to question Ryan Sturridge's so-called alibi together and then visit the Falcon pub and speak to the barman he had claimed would vouch for him.

Ben Loftus was outside his block of flats when they called round, washing an old car that looked as though the dirt might be all that held it together.

Baines recognised him from previous run-ins, and the alarm in his eyes was as unmistakable as the dark bruise he sported round his left eye.

"What happened to the other fellow?"

Loftus gawped at him. "Eh?" Light dawned and he pointed to the shiner. "Oh, this. Nah, walked into a door, didn't I? Silly sod."

Baines showed his warrant card and did the introductions. The young man just shrugged.

"I know who you are, don't I?" He glanced dismissively at Archer, then stared at Baines. "You want something?"

Baines ignored the question. "You'd be surprised how many people I come across who walk into doors, slip in the shower, fall down the stairs."

"Yeah? Maybe you're some sort of jinx." He shoved his cloth in a bucket of murky water, brought it out dripping, and attacked the fading paintwork again.

"Stop doing that," Baines said.

Ben Loftus carried on scrubbing at a patch of bird shit.

Archer's patience began to run out. "Ben, put the cloth in the bucket right now and look at us. We want to ask you some questions. Now, we can have a nice chat, or DS Baines here can start admiring that heap of crap you're washing. Me, I know bugger all about cars – just where the petrol goes – but I reckon

DS Baines can find a number of breaches of the Motor Vehicle Roadworthiness Act 2008, each carrying a fine of £1,000. Five breaches is a cool five grand. Ouch."

His eyes widened. "You can't do that."

"No? Sergeant, best inspect the vehicle."

Baines took a step towards Loftus's pride and joy.

"Whoa." The cloth disappeared into the bucket. "No need for all that. How can I help?" His smile was insincere but wide.

"Where were you around 4pm yesterday?" Baines asked.

"Me? I was at the Falcon with Ryan Sturridge and his girlfriend, Laine. That's Laine Shaw. Raphael the barman—"

"—can vouch for you. I bet he can. You seem keen to get your witnesses out there. You haven't even asked why we want to know."

"So why?"

"Oh," Baines's tone was casual, "you may have heard about the shootings on the estate around that time. One of the victims was Brandon Clark. I'm sure you knew him."

He didn't look shocked. "Yeah, course I did. Poor Brandon, what a shame. Nothing to do with me, though. As I said—"

"—you were at the Falcon. When did you last see Brandon?"

Loftus made a show of scratching his head. "Don't rightly know. Months, maybe. He used to be a bit of a bad lad, but lately…"

"Is that what you are, Ben?" Archer wanted to know. "A bad lad?"

"Me? Law-abiding citizen, me."

"Do you know anyone who might want to harm Brandon?"

"Nah."

Baines produced the photo of Matthew Butcher and his bogus family and indicated the man. "Recognise him?"

"No." Too quickly.

"Take your time."

He studied it. "No."

"All right. That's all for now. I hope we don't have to come back and repeat any of these questions." Baines made as if to go, then turned back to him. "I'd stay away from doors if I were you."

They returned to the car. Baines put the key in the ignition, then looked at Archer.

"Motor Vehicle Roadworthiness Act? 2008?"

She looked at him as if butter wouldn't melt. "Is there no such thing? Oops. Thing is, you know that. I know that…"

"You deliberately misled him." He started the engine, grinning. "Shocking."

7

Ryan Sturridge's girlfriend, Laine Shaw, was similarly certain that both Sturridge and Loftus had been at the Falcon pub at the time when Brandon Clark and Matthew Butcher were being gunned down in the street.

Baines remembered her from her boyfriend's trial: she had been girlishly distraught when his sentence had been handed down. Whilst Sturridge himself had hollered curses and threats before and as he was led away, she had tearfully declared her love and sworn she would wait for him. She could have been no more than sixteen then – not much more than a child. Baines wasn't convinced that the intervening years had matured her much.

Sturridge's final alibi was the barman at the Falcon, Raphael. It had been refurbished five or six years ago with lots of chrome and padded seats in orange. Pictures of palm trees and American cars adorned the walls. There was a small dance floor.

Beyond the décor, the place seemed to have something of an identity issue. Food was Tex-Mex, music was Latino, and the whole ambience screamed that it saw itself as a young person's pub, at least by night. So there was something incongruous about its offering all-day breakfasts from 9am. When Baines and Archer walked in at around ten, there were a few middle-aged guys at tables, with sausages, bacon, eggs and all the trimmings piled in front of them, studying the form in the racing pages.

The guy polishing glasses behind the bar was muscled to grotesque proportions, his black tee-shirt straining across his pecs. His skin was the shade of burnished teak, either fake tan or the real thing, and his long black hair was tied back in a ponytail. As they approached the bar, the corners of his mouth turned up, but there was no warmth about his eyes.

"Hi, guys. What can I get you?"

"Looking for a guy called Raphael," Baines said.

The eyes became a little shiftier. "Who's looking for him?" Warrant cards were shown and Baines did the introductions.

"Well," the barman shrugged. "Guilty as charged. How can I help our heroes of law enforcement make Aylesbury a safer city?"

"It's a town," Baines said bluntly, before asking him if he knew Ryan Sturridge.

"Ryan? Sure. He was in here yesterday afternoon, with his mate and his girlfriend." He proceeded to give times that tallied a little too well with the others' stories, and then over-embellished it with a detailed account of what they'd had to drink and eat.

"Quiet in here, was it?" Baines said casually.

"Not bad, really. We usually do a decent trade on a Friday afternoon. Weekend starts here, that sort of stuff."

"And yet you remember what every one of your punters ordered?"

The smile faltered. "Well, no, I..." He swallowed. "You see, the thing is, those three are sort of regulars. Predictable. Always order the same thing. Boring, really."

"So who else might have been in that would remember seeing them?"

His hand covered his mouth. "I can't remember now."

"Just those three."

"Like I say, they're—"

"—regulars, right. Tell me, Raphael, how's the sideline been doing?"

"Sideline?"

"Oh, come on. We know small-time drug dealing's been going down in the loos for years and that the staff are probably in on it."

Raphael's dark eyes flashed. "You'd better watch what you say. Sure, we get raided maybe once a year, but half the time with no results. And none of the staff have been charged with anything. We can't be looking over the punters' shoulders all the time."

Baines shrugged. "And yet the suspicions persist. Ah, well." He showed Raphael a photograph of Brandon Clark. "Know this boy?"

The barman looked at it. "No."

"What about him?" He showed him the picture of Matthew Butcher.

This time there was a slight pause before he said, "No," again.

"You're sure? Both these pictures have been on the news."

"I don't watch the news. Too busy. Now, is there anything else? Because I've got work to do." His eyes scanned the tables briefly. "And you're bad for business. The customers can smell you. The feds."

Archer spoke for the first time. "That's a bit rude, don't you think, sergeant?"

"Very rude. Maybe we'll stick around. Have breakfast?"

"No," she said. "I don't care for the smell."

They walked back to the car.

"He was either lying, or jumpy, or both," Archer said. "Did you think he recognised the picture of Butcher?"

"Maybe, maybe not. The jumpiness could just be because he's worried the drugs thing will finally come home to roost."

A white van pulled into the car park. Two scruffily dressed men got out and headed for the pub. They looked as if they might have been out all night. Maybe they had.

"Could be the drugs," Archer said. "Or at least they might be part of it. My gut tells me there's a much bigger picture here, and we're not seeing it. Let's hope Joan and Jason have something for us."

* * *

But the two DCs had only a little to show for their morning's endeavours. Julie Clark hadn't recognised the photograph of the man called Butcher, nor any of his aliases. She'd insisted there had been no one in her life since her husband had killed himself, less than a year after young Marcus's birth. She'd believed that Brandon didn't really remember his father, but occasionally suspected that losing him had nevertheless had an impact on him; had been one of the reasons he'd gone off the rails for a time.

So, there was no apparent connection between Brandon and Butcher on a family level.

"No go with those stock images, either, guv," Bell said. "I had a good trawl and found the same pictures on two more sites. They could be on more. I spoke to a couple of the sites, and they don't hold ready information on who had what pictures. They'd have to go through each and every order received, and they really don't have the resources."

"Did you think to ask whether they hold customer accounts in any of the names?" Archer wanted to know.

"I did, guv. They were able to check Butcher's name and known aliases on that database. Drew a blank. There could be more aliases, of course. All you really need is a name, a credit card and an email address."

They were in the briefing room. Photographs and notes were pinned to a large paper-covered cork board. Archer cast her eyes over them, her frustration mounting.

"So we've nothing?"

"I wouldn't quite say that, guv," Collins told her. "They broke into Brandon's phone. Found nothing untoward, so far as we can tell."

"Any numbers he started calling or being called by recently? A change of pattern? A particular friend?"

"Brandon didn't really do friends, not after the gang broke up. He became a loner. I got hold of his class teacher, though. He sat next to a Becky Parks and seemed to talk to her a lot. I spoke to her. They weren't friends out of school, and if there was anything worrying him he didn't confide in her."

"Great. Brandon's almost as much a man of bloody mystery as Butcher or whatever his real name was." She sighed. "And no one's come forward about the pictures of Butcher?"

"Not so far, no."

"No missing persons reports?"

Collins and Bell shook their heads.

"You spoke to the National Crime Agency?"

"They said they'd make enquiries."

She returned to her seat, sat down, and put her head in her hands for a few moments.

"For Christ's sake," she said, "someone must know the man." She stood up and paced. "We've got sod all worth having. We can't connect the victims, don't know if they were connected, don't even have a scooby who one of them was."

"I checked out his other IDs, guv," Bell said. "They go back about as far as Butcher's."

"Good initiative, Jason, thanks. At least we know"

"Post-mortems are at 1pm, guv," Collins offered.

She gave a weary shrug. "I might as well go – watch two perfectly good human bodies being hacked about, gag at the stink of their last meal, and then get told that the cause of death was gunshot wound to the head."

"Okay," Baines said, "so how about this? We know Ryan Sturridge has dabbled with guns before; we know he threatened Brandon before he went to jail. We doubt he'd have the murder weapon in his possession, but we know the most likely candidates for having it in safekeeping."

"That's true. We should get warrants to search his home, Ben Loftus's and Laine Shaw's. Do all three simultaneously, so they can't tip each other off – otherwise, if there's evidence to find, it'll be at the bottom of the canal."

"We could have it dragged if needs be," Baines pointed out.

"Agreed, but one step at a time. Dan, can you set all that in motion? I'll update the boss, and then I'd better head off to the mortuary."

* * *

Archer never ceased to wonder at how far removed the modern mortuary at Stoke Mandeville was from some of the dispiriting, ancient morgues she had encountered in her time at the Met. It was ironic that one of the few tangible improvements to her life following the move was that she had a slightly less depressing environment in which to witness an ugly, but essential, procedure.

"Before we start," Carlisle began, "there's something you should see."

Archer followed her over to where Butcher's body lay.

"Note the head of dark hair," the pathologist said. "Now observe the pubic hair."

Much as Archer always wanted to be detached, professional and dispassionate about post-mortems, there was something about examining a corpse's private parts, especially when the deceased was male, that made her slightly uncomfortable. Nonetheless, it took little more than a cursory glance to see what the issue was.

"So he wasn't a natural brunette?"

Carlisle moved back to the head and combed the corpse's hair. "Not only that, but his roots need doing."

Archer puffed out her cheeks. "Unusual for a man to dye his hair like that."

"Especially from blond to dark, yes. Not unheard of, I'd imagine. But Joan said you were having trouble establishing an identity for him? Put the two together, and it makes sense."

"Trying to change his look?"

"Ever so subtly, perhaps. I mean, as I always say, you're the detective, but…" She left the thought hanging and reached up to the light above the table, adjusting it so it illuminated the man's face. Then she carefully pulled up one of the eyelids.

"Just as I thought," she remarked. "Contact lenses."

"Can we remove them?"

Carlisle certainly could and, in short order, the brown eyes had transformed to blue.

"I'll bet they're also corrective," Archer said, "and that he normally wore glasses."

"So might I," Carlisle commented. "At least, I would if I were a betting woman."

"Glasses, hair colour, eye colour. Not exactly a master of disguise. But maybe enough of a change for him not to be recognised at a casual glance. We'd better keep an eye out for distinguishing marks."

Carlisle proceeded with the examination, but found no great surprises. She strongly doubted that the first bullet, the one that had entered Butcher's torso, would have proved fatal.

"Well, I suppose it might if he'd been left to bleed indefinitely, but really, it was the shot to the head that finished it."

With the help of her assistant, Bruce Davenport, she turned the body over. The ruin of the back of the skull, where the bullet had exited, was shocking. As Carlisle worked, Davenport took photographs.

"Nothing I can see, apart from a couple of small moles on his back. I suppose if someone really knew him well..."

"Maybe." They didn't look the sort of marks that would ring any bells in a description. "I hate this." Archer looked across the room to where Brandon Clark's body waited its turn. "We've reason to suspect Brandon might have been the main target, yet everything's telling me this guy had way too much to hide to have been an innocent bystander."

She frowned as some semblance of a theory came to her. "All right. Say our man here was on the run. For some reason, Brandon's seen him before. He recognises him, says a word out of place, or perhaps Butcher realises he's been rumbled. But someone else has reason to want Butcher's identity to remain a secret too? Maybe that was who he was running from."

The pathologist smiled. "That's a lot of if, buts and maybes, Lizzie. Are you expecting an answer from me?"

"Thinking out loud, really. The only thing I can think of that might tie Brandon in with Butcher is that Brandon knew him for some reason, and it somehow got them both killed. But it's pretty meaningless without more detail. I'll see if one of my Photoshop wizards can produce some pictures that look more like the undisguised Butcher, and see if they jog any more memories than the ones we stumbled on yesterday."

"Perhaps he was some sort of con man?" Carlisle suggested.

"Perhaps. Shall we press on?"

The rest of the procedure went smoothly, with nothing else to remark upon. Cause of death was identical in each case.

Archer was given the bullets in an evidence bag for ballistics to examine.

"Thanks," she said. "Let's hope we have some luck with these. God knows, we need it."

8

Baines had got the go-ahead from DCI Gillingham for the three searches Archer had asked for, and warrants had been quickly obtained. Whilst he and two uniforms were turning over Ryan Sturridge's place, two other teams were at the Loftus and Shaw abodes doing the same.

Sturridge's mother stood by, wringing her hands, but her son's were curled into fists. Baines noted that the knuckles on his right hand had been recently skinned.

"How'd you do that?" he asked whilst the uniforms went through kitchen units. "Not on Ben Loftus's eye, by any chance?"

"Nah. Slipped and put my hand out to steady myself. Scraped it on a wall."

"Really? Only Ben's sporting quite a bruise this morning. Walked into a door, he says."

"Yeah? A lot of clumsiness going around. Must be the weather. I hope you're going to put everything back when you're done."

"Oh, don't worry," Baines said. "We've got aprons and feather dusters in the car."

Sturridge's mother looked hopeful. "Really?"

Her son looked at her, disgust plain on his face. "Don't be stupid, Ma." To Baines: "What do you think you're going to find, anyway?"

"Evidence," Baines said with a smile.

"This is just harassment. I've paid my debt to society. Now I'm trying to get back on my feet."

"Yes? Been going for job interviews?"

It was Sturridge's turn to smile. "Nah. Working for someone else? Mug's game. I'm looking at investing in a business."

"Really? What, a burger van?"

"Very good. Something more in the entertainment line."

"Don't tell me you're opening a lap dancing club?"

"You'll find out, Mr Baines. Wouldn't do to show my hand and let other people muscle in, would it?"

The search moved on. They found no gun. No pay-as-you-go phone.

"I hope you're satisfied," Sturridge said as they stood on his doorstep. "I might complain to my MP about this."

"Oh, no," Baines said, "not your MP. I'm wetting my boxers. Yours isn't the only gaffe we're turning over, Ryan, so you're nowhere near out of the woods yet."

Still, he was disappointed as he got back in his car. The uniforms drove off in their patrol car, but he sat sifting the few crumbs he'd gathered from this visit.

The damage to Sturridge's knuckles, on the same day that Ben Loftus looked as if he'd walked into a fist. What was that all about? Ryan had ruled the Bloods as much by brawn as by brain before he'd gone to prison, and it was his liking for violence that had earned him his sentence – aggravated assault on an Asian youth who he claimed had 'looked at him funny'.

Now maybe Loftus had done something to enrage him. Something small? Or something that Sturridge took seriously? Something that jeopardised his 'business plans'?

Baines found those plans hard to take seriously. Something 'in the entertainment line'? Whatever it was, assuming it was more than just fantasy, surely someone would have to bankroll him. A twenty-one-year-old who'd spent most of his adult life behind bars and still lived in a grotty social housing flat with his mother would have to be shifting a lot of drugs to finance plans for any sort of serious investment.

It was true that, according to Steve Ashby, drug crime was enjoying a slow but steady increase in the town. But was it credible that Sturridge owned a piece of that action? Was he, against all probabilities, a serious player?

If so, what of Matthew Butcher? Had he been a player too, someone who'd got in Sturridge's way? If so, it seemed unlikely that someone organised enough to have multiple identities would be working alone.

Suddenly, Baines found himself fervently hoping that Ryan Sturridge would prove to be nothing more than a delusional braggart. Otherwise, there was just a chance that a turf war was brewing that would make the old juvenile Bloods vs Barracudas feud look like flies fighting over a cowpat.

His phone rang. Jason Bell, calling from Laine Shaw's home. They had found a gun.

* * *

Laine Shaw looked younger and more vulnerable than the sullen young woman Archer and Baines had interviewed that morning. Maybe her lack of make-up had given her looks a hard edge that cosmetics had now softened, but somehow Archer doubted it. The kid was in trouble, and she knew it. She was scared.

The duty solicitor was Andy Knight, one of the good guys as far as Archer was concerned – at least compared to some – but still the enemy in situations like this.

The Colt .45, found wrapped in a tea towel and stashed at the back of a shelf in her wardrobe, was already on its way to ballistics for comparison with the bullets that had killed Brandon Clark and Matthew Butcher. The calibre was right, which was a good start. Disappointingly, it seemed clean of prints, but if it proved to be the murder weapon and could be traced back to Ryan Sturridge or one of his mates, then they could really start to sweat out of them what had happened yesterday afternoon. Maybe they'd even crack the case by Sunday evening.

"Now, Laine," Archer began, "you know why you're here. You're under arrest for possession of a firearm. So what I want to know is how you came by it."

The girl's gaze flickered towards her solicitor, then returned to its previous focus on a speck on the table. "No comment."

"Oh, don't start with that," Baines said. "This isn't a TV show. Going no comment isn't going to get you out of trouble. You've been caught with a deadly weapon in your room. It must have got there somehow, Laine."

"You remember what we talked about this morning?" Archer threw in. "Brandon Clark and the other man who was shot yesterday? Same sort of gun as the one we found in your room. We have experts checking whether it was the actual gun. And, if it is, then it's a murder weapon, and the only person in the frame right now is you."

"Come on," said Baines. "We're sure you were looking after it for someone. Probably Ryan. They're sitting there, fat, dumb and happy, while you're the one in this nasty little room on a warm day. You could already be looking at six months in prison or, if you're lucky, a fine of up to £1,000 – much more if it's the gun that killed those people. Of course, if you were holding it for someone else, maybe under duress…"

"No comment."

"I don't get it," said Archer. "You don't seem such a bad girl. What is it? Love's young dream? You see Ryan as some sort of swashbuckling rogue?" She looked at the girl's arm, bare in a sleeveless dress. No track marks there, at least, but maybe if she was shooting up she injected somewhere less visible. "Is it drugs? Does he supply you?"

That at least got a different answer. "I don't do drugs."

"See, now we're making progress. It wasn't so hard, was it? We ask a simple question, you give us a simple answer. How about we start again? How did you come by the gun?"

"No comment."

Baines brought his fist crashing down on the table, making the plastic cups of water jump and slop. Laine and her brief winced.

"For Christ's sake, girl, what's the matter with you? You're in the shit. Ryan's probably laughing at you. You could be up for accessory to murder, even if you didn't pull the trigger. Now start answering the bloody questions."

"All right," said Andy Knight. "That's enough. You're entitled to question my client, but she has a right to silence, without being bullied."

"She has a right to silence," Archer agreed. "She's also under caution and has been advised of the possible consequences of not mentioning anything she might later rely on in her defence. Maybe you should have talked a little more sense into her before we started this interview."

The look in Knight's eyes suggested that he may have tried to do just that. "With respect, Inspector, we each have our jobs to do. So I'll do mine, you can do yours, and we'll try not to tell each other how to do them. How does that work for you?"

Whatever response Archer might have thought of was forestalled by a tap on the door. Joan Collins slipped in and placed a piece of paper in front of her. Archer read it, then glanced at Baines and then the suspect.

"Interview suspended." She added the time and switched off the recorder.

"Sorry. DS Baines and I have been called away for a few moments. We'll resume as soon as possible." She looked the solicitor in the eye. "Andy, I know we both have our jobs, but your client really isn't helping herself. You need to get her to see that."

Outside the interview room, Baines looked at Archer. "What's going on?"

"Search me. We have to see the boss immediately. Beyond that, your guess is as good as mine."

"We can't have the ballistics results already."

"No way. Let's go and find out."

But Baines didn't move immediately. "Do you think she's going no comment to protect that little shit out of love or loyalty? Or is she scared of him?"

"Something else I don't know. Damn," she added, "today would have been a good day to bring my crystal ball into work."

They made their way to Gillingham's office. He was seated at his little meeting table, along with an attractive black woman in a dark tailored trouser suit and a white cotton blouse. With her high cheekbones and almond-shaped eyes, she bore a passing resemblance to the model Naomi Campbell. Gillingham gestured to the remaining seats at the table.

"DI Archer, DS Baines, this is DCI Catherine Sheppard from the Organised Crime Command at the National Crime Agency."

Archer blinked. "NCA? What brings you to this part of the world on a Saturday afternoon?"

Sheppard smiled, showing very white teeth. "You guys did, actually. You're investigating a double shooting in Aylesbury yesterday afternoon?"

"That's right." The penny dropped. "The guy with the multiple IDs? We circulated his picture?"

Sheppard nodded. "It's raised a flag. I'm afraid you've inadvertently stumbled onto our turf."

"Organised crime? Of NCA proportions?" Archer stared at her. "Really?"

"It looks like your case is connected to a major investigation of ours."

Archer absorbed this. "So what's your case about?"

Sheppard examined her flawlessly manicured fingernails. "I'm really sorry, and don't take this the wrong way, but it's an operation that's been compromised before. I can't say any more than that." She looked Archer in the eye. "You're not going to like this, but I'll be taking charge of the investigation from now on."

Archer shot a glance at Gillingham, who sat tight-lipped. The look in his eyes suggested that he was barely containing apoplexy, but he said nothing.

"Since when?" Archer was thrown.

"Since my director and your Chief Constable agreed on it."

Archer glanced at Gillingham, who merely nodded his confirmation. She took a breath, assimilating the information.

"So... what? I'll be reporting direct to you? Or through DCI Gillingham?"

"Sorry," Sheppard said again, "I don't seem to be making myself clear. This is what's going to happen." She held Archer's gaze. "I'm going to have to pull a team of NCA officers together quickly to work out of the local Serious and Organised Crime unit in Oxford. I'm going to need the file on the case so far and, until we're properly up and running, you'll need to report to me and check before you open new avenues of investigation. I'll leave you all my contact details." She handed out cards.

"That's going to cramp our style. It'll slow us down on the first day of a murder enquiry, and you know what a crucial time that is. And then if my team is going to have to liaise with your team—"

"I'm sorry," Sheppard said yet again. "You still don't get it." She sought inspiration from the ceiling. "I would hope to have my team in place and up to speed by Monday morning latest. After that, you bow out. There is no liaison. I know it sucks, but there are some big things at stake here, believe me—"

Baines had been keeping quiet up to now. "Yeah, well, two lives are a pretty big thing, actually. One of the victims wasn't much more than a child. A good kid. What the fuck does he have to do with organised crime? Because the only enemy he had in the world couldn't organise a game of Scrabble without someone's hand up his back."

Ever since this case had started, Baines had reminded Archer of a pressure cooker with the lid screwed down too tight. Now he looked in danger of exploding.

Sheppard's dark eyes flashed. "I sympathise, DS Baines. But there's nothing more to say. As I said, my director has cleared it all with your Chief Constable. That trumps whatever you or I might think about it."

"I don't fucking believe it."

"Get a grip, DS Baines," snapped Gillingham. "I don't like it any more than you do, but this is way above our pay grades."

"Really?" Archer interjected, pretty irate herself. "Organised crime here in Aylesbury Vale? And we're not even allowed to know what's going on?"

"Someone knows what's going on," Sheppard said. "Someone who gives you your orders. It's a question of the big picture."

Archer drew a long breath, calming herself. "All right, then. What do you want us to do about our suspect? Did DCI Gillingham mention we have someone in custody?"

The NCA officer shrugged. "Something about a gun? I doubt very much whether it's anything to do with my investigation. Hold her, bail her, whatever. Have your lab turn their ballistics reports and the gun over to us on Monday for completeness. We'll haul her back in if we need to. We do value your cooperation."

"Of course you do." Archer's mind was racing. "This is about the other victim, right? Matthew Butcher, aka Philip Bowler, aka Martin Cleaver." As she recited Butcher's aliases, tumblers fell into place. "Was he one of yours?" Sheppard's face was unreadable. "Under cover, yes?"

Sheppard sighed. "I don't know how many times I can put this in a nice way. I can't tell you anything, except that the NCA is taking over this case. Oh, and you three are the most junior people at this station who know any of this. Keep it that way."

"But we know the patch." Archer spread her palms, frustrated. "We can work with you. Help you. Why wouldn't you want that? Why wouldn't you trust us?"

"Let me have those files soonest. I'll get my team in place, and their priority will be to look at your case in the context of our own operation and see how it connects."

"And meanwhile?"

"Carry on investigating, obviously, but keep me informed of developments, and check with me before you open any new cans of worms. I should be in a position to transition the case to Oxford first thing on Monday."

"Oxford!" spat Baines. "Might as well be Timbuctoo."

"It's a difficult situation all round, Dan," Archer said, hating it but determined to avoid a full-scale row. "We'll just have to make the best of it."

"Thank you," Sheppard said, looking relieved. "Look, I hate to come in throwing my weight about…"

"We get it," Archer told her.

"I don't," muttered Baines.

Sheppard rose and held her hand out for Gillingham to shake. "Well, I'll see myself out, and I'll be in touch."

She strode across the room, all high heels and majesty. The three of them watched as she closed the door behind her.

"For fuck's sake," snarled Baines.

"It was an ambush," Gillingham confided. "I'd barely been told she was in reception than I had the Assistant Chief Constable on the phone, in person, making it clear we should give Sheppard whatever she wanted – hand the case over to her and leave her to get on with it."

Baines opened his mouth again, jaw jutting, but Archer got in first. "And did she tell you anything at all about what her interest is?"

"You know what I know."

"Bloody hotshots," Baines said. "Waltzing on to people's turf…"

"It's her job, Dan," Archer said. "I've been there myself, at the Met. Parachuted into other parts of London for one reason or another. I never really understood before why the locals resented it so much. Now I do."

"Sure. We've had people from Headquarters coming in before, and we often work with other forces and agencies. But the key words are 'work' and 'with'."

"I'm sure the NCA has its reasons," Gillingham said.

"Well, I'm not having it," Baines said.

"We're stuck with it."

"But… you can see she's just interested in Butcher Boy. She doesn't give a shit about Brandon. For all we know about this 'investigation' of hers, she's going to sweep this whole thing under the carpet."

Archer had to admit she feared the same. "Did you see how dismissive she was of the gun we found? How can she say it'll be nothing to do with the case?"

"And what about those pictures?" Baines seemed at least a little less het up now. "The NCA won't be the only people who recognise him."

"Yes, but they'll manage that in their own way. Damn it," she added. "I asked for pictures of Butcher with blond hair and glasses to be mocked up. I suppose that's a waste of time now."

Gillingham stroked his chin. "Actually, no. Let's do that. If someone comes forward in response to the original photos, we can show them to them. At least we might find out who this guy really was."

"I suppose we might as well," Archer agreed. "Although it's precious little."

"Yeah," Baines said, "but if we have a name, we can do a little digging around."

Gillingham shook his head. "That would be career-limiting for us all. It's not as if we don't have any other work to do, and we're all supposed to be on the same side at the end of the day."

"Right. Serious and organised crime happening on our doorstep, if we're to believe a word she says, and we're being kept in the dark."

"What shall we do with Laine Shaw?" Archer wanted to know.

The DCI shrugged. "What Sheppard said. Bail her for now. But I want those ballistics results coming through us. Oh, pass them straight on, but I want to know if that gun killed our two victims. That way, at least they won't get away with ignoring Brandon Clark."

"You say that now." Baines's tone was cynical. "What if they say it's for the greater good?"

"Then I'll complain up the chain of command." He saw the looks on both their faces. "What more can I do?"

9

Ryan Sturridge pulled into the pub car park next to Aylesbury police station. Since his release, he'd given Ben plenty of stick about his piece-of-shit car being embarrassing to be seen in. It was a bashed-up old Rover, the sort of thing his grandad might drive. But Sturridge knew his own clapped-out VW Passat wasn't that much better. When he started it up, it made a noise like a machine gun before the engine caught, and the exhaust made a farting noise if he tried to get away from the lights too quickly. More than once it had stalled on him. He hoped the cash started rolling in before the bastard thing fell apart underneath him.

Laine was waiting beside a soft-top Audi. Now that was a car more in keeping, he thought. She walked over and got in beside him.

"All right, babe?" he asked lightly. "Didn't think you'd get out this quick. I couldn't believe it when you called."

"I don't know why," she said, her lip trembling. "They'd been talking jail and all sorts. I was so scared. But I told them nothing."

"So why did they let you go?" He turned out onto the Wendover Road.

"Don't know. They said I was on police bail, whatever that is. They say I could still be charged with possession of a firearm."

He shook his head. "You must have said something. About me. You're not wearing a wire, are you?"

"What? No!"

"I'm going to have to check. Let's not talk for a while."

He drove on for a bit, then made a couple of turns before taking a left into an alleyway. It bent left at the end, and he parked out of sight of anyone passing the entrance.

"Now," he said, "about that wire."

He slid the dress off her shoulders, reached around behind her and unfastened her bra.

"Not here," she protested.

His hands cupped her breasts.

"Nope," he said with a teasing smile. "No wire." His mouth closed over hers, and he forced his tongue between her teeth as one hand began to slide up the inside of her thigh.

It didn't take long. Sturridge was in a hurry.

"There," he said as she cleaned herself up and sorted out her clothing, "that wasn't so bad, was it?"

"You hurt me."

"You like it rough." He looked at her, and the softness faded from his eyes. "Now, then. What did you really tell them about me?"

"I told you. Nothing. I went no comment."

"No comment?" He barked a laugh. "She went no comment. All right." He drummed his fingers on the steering wheel. "All right, then. Next question. How did they find the gun so easily?"

He saw the fear in her eyes. Enjoyed seeing it.

"Well," she gabbled, almost stammering, "you know they took the place apart."

"And?"

"And, well, they found it in the end."

"Where, babe? Where did they find it?"

"It... it was in my wardrobe. On the shelf. Right at the back, though."

"Oh." He smiled at her. "Right at the back. Well, that's all right, then. Right at the back of the sodding shelf of your fucking wardrobe."

"I had to put it somewhere."

"No, Laine. You needed to use your imagination."

Her lower lip trembled. "I'm sorry."

He backhanded her, his hand a blur, the impact resounding in the confines of the car. "You stupid cow." Blood leaked from her nose. "You stupid little cow."

* * *

There was still plenty to do until the NCA formally hijacked the case – checking statements and following them up, liaising with forensics, and casting around for new leads. Archer knew she had to say something to the team about where the case was going and had given them a half-truth, cooked up with Gillingham, about it turning out that another force had a prior interest in the case and would be running with it from Monday. She hated doing it.

Damn Sheppard and her bloody National Crime Agency. Dubbed 'the UK's FBI', it had replaced the Serious and Organised Crime Agency, and had only become fully operational in October 2013 as the UK's lead agency for fighting organised crime, cybercrime, economic crime, and the trafficking of people, weapons and drugs across regional and international borders.

Its role included taking a UK-wide overview of how criminals operated and how their business could be disrupted; as such, it worked closely with regional organised crime units, the Serious Fraud Office, and individual police forces, as well as acting as a UK point of contact for international law enforcement agencies, including Interpol and Europol.

At least, that was the theory. The last time Archer had looked, 'working closely' involved a degree of sharing and cooperation. But Catherine Sheppard was playing her cards close to her chest. She knew a lot more than she was saying, but what exactly did she know?

Collins had looked puzzled. "Why not a joint investigation, guv? Or will we be back on the case at some point?"

"Let's just see how it pans out, Joan." She had asked Collins to organise a copy of the case file so far and have it couriered to Oxford for Sheppard's attention.

Meanwhile she was waiting for the ballistic results that she also needed to pass on to Oxford. DCI Sheppard had already applied pressure for quick results and was keen to see what story they told. Baines was hanging around too.

She had just about concluded that they weren't going to come when her mobile rang.

She'd met Ed Fielding on one occasion and liked him. He was enthusiastic about his job and had a wicked sense of humour.

"I knew you'd be waiting for these," he said, "so I took the liberty of calling you direct."

"Good of you to turn it around for me."

"Now, I'm emailing you a written report, but I thought you'd want the headlines. Are you ready for this?"

"Go ahead, please."

"Okay. Well, the first thing is that the gun you sent us is not the one that fired those shots yesterday. In fact, it hasn't been fired recently, I'd say."

She digested this. "Any history?"

"Not that I can find. It's not a match for any bullets recovered from crime scenes – although it might have been used in robberies without being fired. So you've still got someone in possession of an illegal weapon, but they're not your killer."

She cursed mentally. She'd wanted it to be the murder weapon. They could have been well on the way to closing the case, and she would have loved to make DCI Bloody Sheppard eat her words.

"All right," she said, pushing her disappointment away. "Anything on those bullets?"

"Aha!" he exclaimed dramatically. "The bullets! Now, they're a different matter entirely. They *are* on the system. Or, at least, they're a match for a gun on the system."

She sat up straight. "Really? The actual gun?"

"The actual gun. But it's strange."

"In what way?" She saw Baines earwigging from his desk. There was no one else about, so she beckoned him over. "Hang on, Ed, just putting you on speaker." She did so. "You were saying the gun we found isn't our murder weapon, but you've got something on those bullets. And you say it's strange?"

Baines raised an eyebrow at her.

"The thing is," Fielding said, "they're a match for a gun used in a robbery nine years ago. A post office in Reading."

"Reading?"

"They fired a shot into the ceiling to scare the postmaster, and the bullet was recovered. It got a conviction."

"But…" She shot a puzzled frown at Baines. "I don't get it. If it got a conviction, surely the gun was found in one of the robbers' possession. Match the slugs, bang to rights."

"Give the girl a coconut."

"But that would mean we have the gun, surely."

"And if we have the gun – somewhere in Reading…" Baines chimed in.

"… then what's it doing being used in a murder here in Aylesbury?" Archer completed.

"Excellent questions, Lizzie. I wondered that myself. So I pulled in a few favours to get you an answer. Turns out the gun's disappeared from the evidence store in Reading. No one knows how or why. Or when."

"What?" She processed the information. "Shit. It's not going to disappear by itself, is it?"

"No. Which almost certainly means that someone on the inside has removed it at some point. And they've either passed it on to a third party, and it finally got used in your killings…"

"Or a cop pulled the trigger."

"Not necessarily a cop. But yes, maybe someone at Reading who would have had access to the evidence store."

"But that's Thames Valley. Our own force." A headache was coming. "Ed, I need you to do me a whopping favour."

"I can try."

"Send me that report, but keep it under your hat for the time being."

She heard his intake of breath. "Not sure I can do that. There'll need to be an enquiry at Reading. This is a bloody serious matter, Lizzie."

"Which is why I need you to help me out here."

"Ed," Baines cut in, "we need you to trust us, mate. How about we pretend this conversation hasn't taken place? You couldn't get hold of us. Hang on to the report and say nothing until late Monday morning. It's nothing dodgy, but we need to be careful how we handle this with certain people."

"I don't know." He sounded extremely uncomfortable.

"Monday morning," Baines pressed. "Come on, Ed. Remember that favour I did you that time. The shit never did hit the fan, did it?" He winked at Archer. "Monday morning. What harm can it do? No one's going to investigate it over the weekend now."

There was a long silence on the line, then a sigh.

"All right. I know I'm going to regret it, but yeah. Only up to half ten on Monday, mind. I'm not sticking my neck out on this. It's not exactly the same as that other little favour, is it?"

They hung up soon afterwards.

"What favour?" Archer arched an eyebrow.

"You don't want to know." Baines gave a heartfelt sigh. "This is becoming more and more of a mess. Mystery men in disguise. NCA muscling in. Now a murder weapon stolen from police custody."

"Butcher, or whoever he was, has to be the key. Sheppard didn't deny he was an undercover cop, did she?"

"She didn't really confirm it, either. But he has to be something to do with something big. Something that got him killed. And a dirty cop is involved somewhere."

"Let's not get ahead of ourselves." Archer rummaged in her desk drawer and fished out some paracetamol. "We're only seeing half the picture. Still, it looks like poor Brandon Clark was just an innocent bystander after all, doesn't it?"

"Beginning to look that way." Baines shook his head. "Poor bloody kid. His poor family, too. But you're right. I reckon all this work we've done, trying to tie Ryan Sturridge in, has been a waste of time."

* * *

Ryan Sturridge pulled his Passat into the nearest available parking slot to his flats. He glanced dolefully at the plum-coloured stain on the passenger seat. The car might not be in great shape, but he tried to keep it reasonably clean. Now that stupid bitch Laine had bled on it. He should have given her a slap or two more for that, but he hadn't wanted to make any more mess.

It still worried him that the police had simply let her go like that. He knew the law. They could have held her a lot longer, questioned her until they broke her. He very much doubted she could have kept saying 'no comment' indefinitely. Toughness wasn't her strong suit – which was normally something he liked about her.

He remembered the day he'd walked out of Feltham Young Offenders Institution, leaner than he'd gone in, the suit he'd worn for his trial hanging off him. Ben had been waiting for him with his joke of a car, and Laine had been waiting with him. He'd shagged her senseless that night. There wasn't much she wouldn't let him do to her, or that she couldn't be persuaded to do to him.

He thought maybe the silly cow imagined he was in love with her.

In lust, that was for sure, but now he'd seen her with blood and snot running down her face, he wasn't sure he could look at her in the same way again.

Still, he had to keep her sweet until this business with the gun blew over. If it did. He'd been a bit of an idiot, he saw now, asking her to keep it for him in the first place. It was just that he'd known, if the police had decided to try and pin something on him, they'd have searched his flat, and probably Ben's, too.

Thing was, he'd *wanted* a gun. For backup, if anyone needed persuading as he started to make a serious name for himself. But he couldn't afford to be caught with it. It would be straight back to prison, and he wasn't about to let that happen.

He should have realised they'd check out his girlfriend as well. It was going to come back to him anyway now. Unless he could think of something.

He knew they wouldn't be able to prove that his gun had killed Brandon Clark, for the simple reason that it hadn't. He'd wondered about Ben, though – had slapped him around until he was fairly sure his mate hadn't been using his own initiative.

Why had Laine been let go?

They needed to get together tomorrow, the three of them, to get their story straight. If Laine kept saying no comment – and he thought he could scare her enough that she'd be able to tough it out after all – then maybe if he and Ben just denied everything, it would be all right.

He got out of the car and walked towards the flats, wondering what was for dinner. He'd rather not be still living at home, but there were compensations. His mum might be a waste of space in most respects, but she wasn't a bad cook when she put her mind to it. Not a great one, either, but at least her meals didn't taste like shit.

He was almost at the front door of the block when he heard a click from his left, followed by a voice from the same direction speaking his name.

He turned. Saw the gun.

10

Lara Moseley had drawn the short straw as duty DI for the weekend and had been the first detective to be summoned to the Northfields estate when news of the shooting came in. A single head shot from close quarters had made a mess of Ryan Sturridge, but not so much that she didn't recognise him. She knew he had been a person of interest in Friday night's killings and, unaware of the NCA's interest in – and usurping of – the case, she had summoned Lizzie Archer from her home.

Archer had decided to spread the pain around and had turfed Baines out of his bed. He hadn't been delighted at the time, but he forgot his irritation within seconds of arriving at the scene.

Archer had beaten him by minutes, and stood by the body with Moseley. They all wore crime scene suits.

"Looks like a clean kill this time," Archer commented as he joined them. "Single shot to the head – but as clinical as the other two. I think maybe we were wrong to think Sturridge or any other local gang members were responsible. This is someone who really knows what they're doing."

"Doesn't mean the hits weren't ordered."

"True. Although I reckon a good pro must cost pretty big money. I'll bet heavily on this being the same gun that killed Brandon Clark and Matthew Butcher." She looked at Moseley. "Does the mother know what's happened yet?"

The other woman gestured to an ambulance parked across the road. "She's in there. I think she came out to see what the fuss was about. She was half off her face. Collapsed on the spot, by all accounts."

"I'll talk to her in a moment. We need to organise another door-to-door."

"I've got some uniforms on it already."

A van came round the corner and halted.

"Here's the CSIs," Moseley said. "Shall I brief them, or do you want to do it, Lizzie?"

"You were here first," Archer said with a smile. "Be my guest."

As soon as the other DI was out of earshot, Archer took a step closer to Baines and spoke softly to him.

"By rights, we should probably get on to DCI Sheppard. It's clearly part of the case she thinks she's nicked from us."

He felt the corners of his mouth twitch. "Only thinks?"

"We'll see. It's pretty obvious she's really focused on Butcher's death. Which leaves us with two young men who were both local gang leaders up to a couple of years ago. I think we're entitled to look into that a bit deeper – at least until someone orders us to stop."

He wondered if Gillingham would see it that way.

"I'll have to brief him, obviously, but I'll try and persuade him not to bother the NCA with this until we next hear from her."

"She'll see it on the news."

"Maybe. All the more reason to poke around while we still can."

He was sceptical and showed it.

"I'm not just handing everything over to her tied up with a pink ribbon."

He didn't disagree with the sentiment. He very badly wanted it to be his team that got its hands on Brandon's killer. He was taking Sturridge's death less personally, but the implications were worrying. He wasn't even sure he bought Archer's apparent assumption that Sturridge's death meant he was out of the frame for Friday night's killings.

"You know, maybe there are two killers after all. Who knows? Ryan gets out of jail and takes revenge on Brandon. Perhaps the gun Laine was holding wasn't the only one he had access to. Then one of Brandon's old buddies takes it into his head to avenge him."

"What buddies? According to Brandon's mum, he's had no contact with the old gang for ages. We questioned them and got the same story."

"Doesn't mean one of them didn't have a warped sense of honour." He could see that Moseley and Phil Gordon were headed their way. "What is it? Two years since the Bloods and the Barracudas were acting tough around the estate? Go back a bit further, and Ryan and Brandon were the two founders. Now they've both been gunned down. If we didn't have a spare, mystery body and the NCA barging in with their size nines, I'd say it was all kicking off again."

"Lara thought it looked professional."

He shrugged. "Maybe, maybe not. We've both done firearms training. Shooting someone in the head at close range doesn't involve that much skill, if you can handle the recoil."

Moseley, with Phil Gordon in tow, joined Archer and Baines. The CSIs started to get down to their work, photographing and measuring. One of them erected a tent over the body. One of them started examining a VW Passat, which Moseley said had been Sturridge's

"And there was I, hoping for a quiet night in with *Match of the Day*," the crime scene manager moaned. "Newcastle got a decent result today, as well."

"Get used to it," Archer told him. "If the bodies are going to start piling up on this estate, this could become a habit."

"You think it's the Bloods and Barracudas thing starting up again?"

"Dan thinks so."

"Dan thinks maybe," Baines corrected her. "I guess another possibility is a new kid on the block making a pre-emptive strike on potential opposition."

Gordon puffed out his cheeks. "I don't know. All that gang crap before, it was just kids being a bloody nuisance. Okay, there was the odd stabbing. But this is something else. Have you worked out where that other poor bugger fits in yet? Butcher?"

Baines opened his mouth, but Archer got in first.

"I'm still waiting for someone to lay claim to him," she said, "but for now we have to assume that he might have been an innocent bystander. Look," she turned to Moseley, "you might as well get home, Lara. Dan and I have got this."

She hesitated. "You're sure?"

"It's our case. No point in everyone's Saturday night being ruined."

Moseley made a show of reluctance, then headed for her car, wishing them luck.

"Aye," Gordon commented, "we could all do with a bit of luck." He went to talk to a couple of CSIs.

"Dan," said Archer, "I'm going to see what Mrs Sturridge has to say for herself. Who was Brandon Clark's main sidekick when he had the gang?"

He searched his memory for a moment.

"Aaron Briggs. Aggressive little sod. Only Brandon held him back. Remember after the Barracudas started falling apart, after Brandon walked away from them? It was Aaron who wanted to keep it going. He tried to keep the other guys involved by tough talk and a bit of violence, but he had the organisational skills of a drunken sheepdog."

"Doesn't sound like he'd have any reason to avenge Brandon's death."

He frowned. "Not really. But how's this for a scenario? He wants to start building up a new gang. He's older, thinks he's tougher, wants something a bit more big-time. But before he gets it off the ground, Ryan Sturridge comes out of jail. So Aaron's already decided to remove Ryan from the scene, but then he thinks he might as well take out Brandon as well."

"But why? Brandon had left all that behind, right?"

"You know that. I know that. But if Aaron still harboured ambitions to be a big-shot gang-banger, maybe the last thing he wanted was Brandon deciding he wanted to come back and take over again."

"Still not convinced."

"You have to imagine yourself into the head of a halfwit. If it was what Aaron wanted, he might have assumed everyone else would want it too."

"And Butcher? It's obvious he's the NCA's real interest, despite what I just told Phil. He must be significant in some way."

"Undercover cop who blundered into something? Rival hit man?" Even as the words left his lips, they sounded utterly implausible to him. He said as much. "I just don't get it. Surely Ryan's and Brandon's deaths are linked? Yet someone on NCA's radar gets whacked along with Brandon. That can't be a coincidence either."

"We can write scenarios all night." He knew when she was getting impatient and scratchy. "Find this Aaron Briggs and see what you think. Ben Loftus, too. Maybe his nose was out of joint with Ryan coming back to reclaim his kingdom. Your notion of someone knocking off both the old gang leaders works equally well with him."

"And you?"

"I'll talk to Ryan's mother and then stick around to see if the CSIs come up with anything useful."

A familiar black Mercedes rounded the corner and parked.

"I'll have a word with Dr Carlisle, too."

* * *

Grief and drugs were rarely a great combination, and that was certainly the case with Ryan Sturridge's mother, Keeley. She was a washed-out, bleary-eyed puddle of misery.

"I know he wasn't much," she snivelled, "but he was still my boy. And you love them, don't you?" She thumped her stomach. "In here."

"Of course you do."

"He was a little bastard. He was, you know. Any one of half a dozen blokes could have been his dad. Not much different with Michael. You know it was Ryan's fault Michael went away?"

That wasn't exactly the case, but now wasn't the time for that argument.

"Have you any idea who'd want to kill him?"

"How the fuck do I know? All I know is, he came out of jail all cocky and said things was changing at home. He was going to tell me when he was coming in, and I was to have his bloody meal on the table. Like he was the lord of the fucking manor and I was the, what's it, domestic staff."

"So…?"

"So I asked him who he thought he was, and he told me he wouldn't want to get rough with his own mother."

"And did he ever?"

"No. I think he would, though, given half an excuse. There were times I could have killed him, but I was scared of him. I know he slapped Ben about, and his girlfriend was afraid of him. You want to know who'd want to kill him? All I know is, he was out there, doing Christ knows what. New friends, he said he had, friends who'd give him a leg up." She sobbed. "Where's his big mates now? Eh?"

"These friends. He ever mention a Matthew Butcher? Philip Bowler? Martin Cleaver?"

She shook her head at each name.

"Any names?"

"No. But he said dinner on the table wasn't all that'd be changing around here. There'd be no more shitty cars or scrabbling around buying and selling drugs." Her face crumpled again. "I reckon these new mates of his either killed him, or they got him killed."

* * *

Baines had taken a uniformed PC with him in search of Aaron Briggs and Ben Loftus, just in case either of them gave any trouble. Neither was at home, and their parents claimed not to have a clue where they were. This effectively meant they could be anywhere, but Baines decided to make a quick tour of the estate. It wasn't a bad evening for April, and there were a few hangouts he thought were worth trying.

They found Briggs with a dark-haired girl, sitting on a piece of litter-strewn waste ground that went by the name of the Common, along with several other young people. They were smoking cigarettes that didn't look as if they'd come out of a packet, and were initially oblivious to the officers' approach.

"Evening, Aaron," Baines said when they were within three yards of the pair. He could already smell the cannabis.

The young couple looked their way, open-mouthed. So did everyone else on the Common. The next moment, the entire gathering sprang up and scattered like a startled flock of birds, Briggs and his lady friend bolting in opposite directions.

"Oh, for Christ's sake," Baines said. "Quick – after him."

The uniform took off, but Baines could see immediately that Briggs was easily outstripping a PC who really needed to work on his fitness. Spitting curses, he joined the chase, taking off after the young man.

If the PC was no sprinter, he was certainly no middle-distance runner either. As Baines overtook him, he could hear his breath sawing, and he caught a glimpse of a red face under the helmet. But Aaron Briggs was no athlete either. Baines didn't consider himself super-fit but, having left his colleague for dead, he found himself gaining fast on his quarry.

Beyond the scrubby grass was a road, and Briggs was headed directly for it. Out of the corner of his eye, Baines saw a car approaching and judged that the kid would be forced to stop to let it pass, and then he would have him. He was closing the gap rapidly now. But Briggs suddenly found an extra burst of speed from somewhere and shot across the road, forcing the driver to brake violently and hoot his horn. Baines changed direction to go around the back of the car, almost lost his footing, swore, righted himself, and charged on.

Baines realised now where Briggs was headed – the main road called The Northfields, and a maze-like block of flats that many a villain had disappeared in over the years. There had been plenty of talk about making it harder for suspects to hide there, but meanwhile the block remained stubbornly the same, its staircases and walkways creating a labyrinth in which you could easily get lost.

The lad was never going to make it, though. He was some way from his goal when his wind gave out. He stood, bent over, hands on knees, puffing, as Baines jogged up to him.

"Well, that was fun," Baines said. "Fancy a spot of exercise, did we?"

With a visible effort, Aaron Briggs straightened up. He gave a few rasping coughs. "Mr Baines." His feigned surprise suggested he would never make a living as an actor. "Yeah." Another cough. He sucked in ragged breaths. "Fancied a jog."

"Sure." Baines gave his head a weary shake. "So why did you really run?"

There had been a time when Aaron Briggs would have been all brashness and cockiness. Not now. "It was only a bit," he protested. "My own use, yeah?"

Baines raised an eyebrow. "You seriously think this is about what you've been smoking?"

"Innit?"

"How long have you been on the Common?"

"I dunno. Couple of hours. Izzy'll tell you."

"The young lady you were smoking with?"

"Isabel Moss, her name is. I'll give you her number and everything. But so what?"

"You used to fancy yourself as a bit of a gangster, right? Back when Brandon Clark was running the Barracudas. You were the brawn to his brain, yes?"

Briggs looked a tad insulted. "What you saying?"

"You even tried to keep it going when Brandon, shall we say, retired. But you can't run something on brawn alone."

"You saying I got no brains? What's this about?"

"Oh, come on. You know Brandon was killed yesterday?"

The corners of the young man's mouth turned down. "Yeah. Yeah, course I heard. He was my bro, for a while."

"But not any more?"

"I dunno. I don't hardly see him since he dumped us. Not since he walked away. But yeah. I suppose he's still my bro, even though…"

He trailed off, as if whatever concept he wanted to convey to Baines was too big for him to get his head around.

"And how do you feel about the person who killed your bro, Aaron? They shot him down in the street like a dog. Does that make you angry?"

"I suppose. Yeah. That's not right."

There was something about his eyes and his manner that Baines just couldn't read. It was an emotion of sorts, he was sure of it, but he couldn't decide what it was.

He studied the young man's face. "And now Ryan Sturridge is dead too."

Confusion. Or, at least, that was what he wanted to convey. "Ryan? Really? When?" His eyes widened, and then he was looking anywhere but at Baines. "You don't think...? Nah, you're joking me."

"There's a bullet hole in his head – that doesn't seem so funny. Do you know anything about it?"

"No. No!" It was the most animated he'd been in the whole exchange. "You don't want to go looking at me. I never done guns – no one in the Barracudas did. Someone done Brandon and Ryan, both the same way? Look a bit closer to Ryan... you know what I'm saying?"

"Suppose you spell it out?"

"I ain't saying no more."

"Maybe I'm interested in that spliff of yours after all."

Aaron Briggs stood shifting his weight from one foot to the other, his eyes fixed on the tarmac at his feet. "All right. All I'm saying is this. The couple of months before Ryan got out, Ben Loftus was, what'd he call it, recruiting, yeah?"

"What does that mean?"

"He came to me. He said that Ryan would be setting up something big. Not the sort of kids' shit we used to do. Some serious action that would make us some serious cash, you know? He said he had some new friends."

"And you said no?"

"I'm out of all that, Mr Baines. I got a girlfriend, a job and all that. I don't need to be getting in big trouble, you know? And it sounded like big trouble. Ben said these people didn't mess about."

"So, when you say look closer to Ryan...?"

"Maybe Ben had been making these new friends, but then Ryan comes back and thinks he can just take over. He was always a bully. That guy he got banged up for, he beat him up just cos he didn't like the way he looked at him, and I heard he slapped Ben around more than once."

Baines remembered the bruising around Loftus's eye. If Ryan Sturridge had caused that, maybe his sidekick had cause to be angry. Maybe the second gun was in his possession. And maybe Briggs was right. Maybe Ryan Sturridge waltzing back and taking over hadn't been acceptable.

"All right – that's it for now, Aaron," Baines said. "If you hear anything else, I want to know. I might want to talk to you again."

"Right." Briggs chewed his lip. "You know, I dunno about these new guys Ben was on about."

"In what way?"

"I couldn't work out who was going to be the boss. And, you know, I reckon Ben wasn't so sure either."

11

Whilst Baines tried to track down Aaron Briggs and Ben Loftus, Archer finished up what was a largely unhelpful interview with Ryan Sturridge's mother and went back to talk to Barbara Carlisle, who had arrived on the scene, wearing a light coat over a nice dress and moaning about being dragged away from a rare evening out.

For Archer, who knew next to nothing about the pathologist's private life, after some two years' association with her, it had been an opportunity to be nosy.

"Theatre? Ballet?"

"Just dinner with friends, but we don't get out much."

The 'we' was another open invitation. "So did you leave your husband – or is it partner – there?"

The green eyes had danced behind silver-rimmed spectacles. "Fiancé, actually. We're tying the knot in a few weeks' time. Just a small wedding – a few friends and family."

"I had no idea." She really must pay more attention to colleagues,.

"We've been together about two years. I was a friend of his wife, but she died. We kept in touch and, well, here we are. And I'd been thinking I was a confirmed spinster."

"Congratulations. I hope the sun shines."

"Thanks." Carlisle looked down at her attire. "This isn't exactly practical for getting suited up in front of a crowd. I'll have to get changed in the CSIs' van."

Now Archer asked her for her take on how this evening's shooting compared to yesterday. Carlisle's face said it all.

"Yeah, yeah," Archer said. "Wait for the post-mortem. Thing is, this might not be my case much longer if you can't give me something quicker than that."

"Why—" Carlisle stopped. "Best I don't ask? Well, I'll think about it."

Phil Gordon came and joined them.

"Blood in Sturridge's car. Passenger seat."

She looked at him. "His? Could he have been killed elsewhere, driven here and dumped?"

"No, no, this is definitely the primary scene. Blood pooled around the head says he died right where he's lying. There's bone fragments, too."

"The bullet?"

"Still looking."

"You need to find it, Phil. I want a comparison with the bullets that killed our other two victims, soon as you can. Mind you," she added, "a verbal report will do for starters. I'm sure you're much too busy to produce a written one any time soon."

"We'll do what we can..."

"*Much* too busy."

A slow smile creased his face. "What are you up to?"

She smiled back. "To quote a certain pathologist, best not ask." Then she nodded towards the tent that covered the body. "How are you reading the scene?"

"Interesting," he said. "Looking at the position of the body, and how it looks to have fallen, my guess is that Ryan was turning to his left when he was shot through the forehead at close range. So how do I read it? The killer was hiding, waiting for him. As Ryan comes up to the door, he hears a sound, or maybe the killer even calls his name. He turns and presents the perfect target."

"Hiding, you say?" Archer was intrigued.

Gordon led her to a waist-height coping wall with a tall, scrubby bush behind it.

"He could easily have hidden behind this," the crime scene manager told her. "Crouched down, no one would have spotted him. He would have seen Ryan Sturridge coming, though. All he'd have needed to do was stand up."

Archer leaned over for a closer look. The ground was litter-free, and she guessed that any litter or debris, however unpromising, would have been taken away to be sifted through at the lab for forensic gold dust.

"Anything interesting?"

"A few fag ends. I'd doubt if he'd have drawn attention to himself by smoking – the glow of the lit end, the smell of smoke – but it depends how much of a pro this guy is. I know Lara thinks it's a proper hit, but to my eyes any clown with a gun could have done it." He grinned. "I prefer clowns. They make my job easier."

"You'll be testing the dog ends for DNA, though, to see if any of them match anyone with form?"

"Of course. Although," he gestured vaguely, "who doesn't have form around here?"

It was a sweeping generalisation, but a fair point.

"You know the budget as well as I do, Phil, but any strings you can pull to get us early answers on this…"

He grimaced. "I don't know, Lizzie. I'm not exactly in credit at the favour bank, but I'll try."

"Look out, Phil," said Barbara Carlisle. "Now she's trying to pressure you into hasty conclusions too."

"Aye, Barbara," Gordon confirmed. "But we don't do hasty, do we? We do it all ploddy and scientific-like."

"Ploddy works for me."

"Good grief," laughed Archer, "you're like some comedy double act. Only without the comedy."

By the time Baines returned, the body was already being loaded up to take away. The CSIs were still working, but the crowd of gawkers had long since grown bored and gone home. Carlisle had finished her initial appraisal, adding nothing to what Archer had already known or Phil Gordon surmised. The immediate difference between this killing and the two last night was the absence of a body shot. As Lara Moseley had observed, it had been a no-nonsense, straight-through-the-head shot. But that, of itself, didn't necessarily say too much about the killer.

"I'm getting back to my dinner," Carlisle said. "Maybe they saved me some pudding. I just hope I don't stink too much of death. I'll do the PM early tomorrow, if you want to be there, Lizzie. About 8am?"

"I'll be there."

Archer stifled a yawn as the pathologist headed for the CSIs' van to retrieve her dress and coat.

"I don't think we can do much more here, Dan. Why don't we sit in your car and you can tell me how you've got on, and I can bring you up to date on what I've learned here – which isn't a lot. Then I think we'll call it a night, but have a proper team meeting in the morning."

They sat in Baines's Mondeo and Archer relayed her conversation with Ryan Sturridge's mother. Baines told her what he'd learned from Aaron Briggs.

"There's a common thread here, isn't there?" she commented. "The big 'new friends' who were going to get Ryan into the big-time."

"Yeah. But who was the tail and who was the dog?" He pursed his lips. "I was thinking on the way back here. It sounds like he came out of prison with a bit of extra swagger. You reckon he met someone in there who was connected?"

"Or at least claimed to be. There's always the possibility of two fantasists bullshitting each other. Although it's interesting that all his big talk ends here, with a bullet through his head. It can't be a coincidence, surely? But his mate, Ben, must know more. Did you get anything out of him?"

"Couldn't find him. Not in his usual haunts, not at home – no one knows where he is. We can't track his phone either."

"He's gone off the radar? Right after his best mate's been murdered?"

"A best mate who apparently slapped him around a bit and humiliated him. What if Aaron was right, and he decided to cut Ryan out of the new action we've been hearing about?"

"What, and then go to ground?" Archer shook her head. "Not sure I'm buying that. He must know it'll look suspicious, and he can't exactly get a piece of that action if he's in hiding. More likely he thinks he might be next, and he's running scared."

"I've got an all vehicles alert out for him."

"All right." She fought another yawn. "Not much more we can do for now. Can you make sure the team are in the office for

9am tomorrow? We'll get together straight after the post-mortem."

"Will do. And should I talk to Ashby? He's the big network man with all his contacts. Maybe he's heard about these characters Ryan was allegedly getting into bed with."

"Good idea, if you believe in the networks. Although…" She thought again. "No, leave that for now. I want to keep as much of this in my own team as possible for the moment, or DCI Sheppard will be in like a flash, shutting us down again. I don't trust Ashby to keep his mouth shut."

"What about the boss? He'll have heard about this shooting by now. I'm amazed he's not been on the phone to you. You think he'll go head-to-head with the NCA and the top brass over this?"

"He did talk about complaining."

"For form's sake, yes. But he's never been one to risk harming his career."

She sighed. "You're probably right. But I want at least to know what's happening on my own patch before I'm told to wind my neck in. If Sheppard won't tell me, I'll find out some other way."

He nodded. "You won't hear me arguing."

"That's how I'm hoping the boss will think too, if I put it to him the right way. I think you're right. He won't push his luck, but he seemed as pissed off about the situation as we are, and just as keen to know what the hell's going on."

Baines looked troubled, but he said, "Fair enough, then. See you in the morning."

* * *

Baines drove home thinking about two young men, neither of whom had had the best start in life. Just a few years ago, both had seemed to have very similar futures mapped out for them: getting deeper into trouble and criminal activity. Probably plenty of prison time.

For Ryan, that had remained the outlook, but Brandon seemed to have taken the other fork at the crossroads.

Now neither of them would fulfil their potential. By rights, Baines should be mourning one of them more than the other, but he found that his feelings were more complicated than that. Brandon's mother had always tried to do her best for her boys and had made as decent a home for them as she could. His lack of a father figure may have contributed to Brandon's wayward patch: boredom may have played a bigger part, and he'd had the wit to see a better way.

Ryan, by contrast, hadn't stood a chance. Baines wouldn't have minded betting that life inside, rubbing shoulders with some serious bad guys and hard men, had been an education of sorts, in the worst possible way.

He hadn't had much time for Ryan Sturridge. But he pitied him. And he wanted his killer caught as much as Archer did. Maybe more. He had been enraged by the waste of Brandon's life, and now Ryan's death had fanned the flames. He also felt indignation that someone could come on to his patch with a firearm and start using it. It wasn't the first time it had happened, and he doubted it would be the last, but he doubted if Archer realised how close he was to exploding. Even Karen probably had no idea.

As he made to turn into his drive, he stood on the brakes. Just for a moment, a figure seemed to stand in his path: a teenager in a blue and white replica football shirt. There was something sad, and at the same time fearful, about his expression.

This figure had disappeared so many times before, and had never uttered a word. His heart pounding, Baines gently eased open the door. As he got out, a shadow seemed to fall upon the boy – maybe the shadow of a man, or perhaps something infinitely more terrible. Jack seemed to flinch, to diminish in size, before the shadow engulfed him, darkness swallowing him, and he was gone.

Baines was shaking. There was a constriction in his throat. He sat in the driver's seat and held his trembling hands out in front of him. What did this latest vision mean? Did it mean anything at all, beyond the probability that he really was going mad? Had the deaths of two young men pushed him closer to the edge?

He laughed weakly at himself, a sound more like a sob, and clambered out of the Mondeo on jelly legs. Karen had been right all along. He was deluding himself if he thought this could continue. He needed help. And he would find it.

* * *

Archer arrived at her own home in Great Marston an hour or so after Baines's latest encounter with the figure that continued to haunt him.

As she walked to her front door, she noticed that the side gate into her garden was ajar.

She stared at it. She always kept it closed. Ever since she had moved in, she had been meaning to get a couple of bolts fitted to the inside. But then, she had been meaning to do all manner of things since arriving here.

She supposed it was just possible that an enterprising courier had left a package of some description by the back door. It had happened a couple of times in the past. The trouble was, she was pretty sure she hadn't ordered anything.

Feeling tension growing in the pit of her stomach, she walked along the little brick path between the house and the unkempt front lawn – getting a gardener was yet another thing she had meant to do. Glad she wore flat shoes that made little or no sound, she arrived by the gate and walked quietly down the side of the house.

The light of the waxing gibbous moon illuminated a male figure standing on her patio. He was talking to someone in a stage whisper she couldn't quite hear. Had they broken in? Was a second person inside the house, rummaging through her stuff, whilst this guy kept watch?

Maybe the sensible course was to summon assistance, but she was tired and outraged at the thought that she might be being robbed. She located her warrant card and stepped into the garden.

"Police," she said. "Identify yourself."

The figure turned her way. Tall, hair close-cropped, dressed in a tee-shirt and jeans. Archer had always been in the top three in her class at self-defence at the Met, but she'd allowed herself to get rusty in the Vale and was by no means certain she could take this man. Perhaps she had made a mistake.

His gaze slid from her warrant card to her face and then he smiled, an awkward but not unpleasant smile.

"Hello," he said. "I think you're my neighbour."

"Really?" She vaguely knew her neighbours on both sides, mostly by sight. There was an older couple – Brian and Jean, wasn't it? And Jake and Nicky, who she thought were a few years younger than herself. The last glimpse she'd caught of Nicky, she'd looked decidedly pregnant.

"I don't think so," she said. "Which side?"

He indicated Jake and Nicky's house. "We've not met. I'm Dominic – Dominic Newman." He held out a hand for her to shake. She ignored it.

"You think I don't know my own neighbours?"

"Well," he said cagily, "I've been there almost two months and we've never properly met, though I've seen you a couple of times. Jake and Nicky, who were there before me, said they hardly ever saw you. Long hours in the police, right?"

She felt the first stirrings of confusion. "You're saying Jake and Nicky moved out? When?"

"Like I said, two months, give or take."

"Nice try. There would have been a for sale board, there'd have been vans."

Irritation flashed across his face. If he was going to give up on the bluff and turn ugly, it would be any time now. "Look, what is this? You weren't in and I've lost my cat. He's wandered off before. He doesn't know the area well enough yet…"

"You're having a laugh, yes? A lost moggie? Maybe we should continue this discussion down at the station."

"You're arresting me? For what? For trespass?" He shook his head. "Cat's not here, anyway. I'm going home."

Her ire was up now. "Not so fast. What are you really doing here?"

"Oh, for Christ's sake." He took a deep breath. "Look. Jake and Nicky wanted to move before their first child was born. It was a close-run thing in the end. There was no for sale board because the estate agent knew their house was exactly what I wanted. And you wouldn't have seen the removal van because, from what I've seen, you're always out early and home late. It's not exactly a mansion. You can't get that much in. Moving in didn't take so long."

The moon lit up his face well enough that she could see him clearly. She detected not a hint of a lie. Could it really be that the house next door had changed hands two months ago and she hadn't noticed?

Even as she relaxed, mortification started to set in. Her gaze shifted to the back door, which was plainly still secure. What had she been doing two months ago? There had been a nasty assault case: a couple hospitalised by a jealous ex-boyfriend and his brother. She had worked long hours, divided between hospital and station, until the victims were able to tell their tale, then she'd had to run the attackers to ground. She'd missed her neighbours moving out, and since then she had lived next door to this easy-on-the-eye man and never even noticed him.

"Sorry," she said. "You must think I'm mad."

"I suppose your job makes you suspicious. The things you must see." He smiled again. "So am I off the hook, then? Not a potential axe murderer?"

"Well…" She waggled her hand from side to side. "I don't see an axe. So is it just you and your wife?"

"Me and Monty. Monty's the cat," he added. "Just me now, I suppose, unless he shows up."

"And your name was… Dominic?"

He nodded, and she held out her hand. "I'm Lizzie."

"I know. Jake and Nicky again." His grip was firm, but not crushing. "Pleased to meet you."

"Maybe I could help you look for...?"

"Monty? No, a bit needle in haystack, I reckon, especially now it's dark. But look, why don't you come in for a drink? I don't know too many people in the village."

She hesitated. It was tempting. He was good-looking and, now they'd got over their dodgy start, he seemed nice. But she was knackered, she hadn't eaten, and she had the joys of an early morning post-mortem to look forward to.

"Best not," she said. "Work tomorrow."

"Really? On a Sunday?"

"Blame it on the bad guys. A drink some time would be good, though." She fished out a card and offered it to him. "Maybe you could give me a call?"

"It's a date."

They walked to the front of the house and she wished him luck with finding his cat. She watched him make his way to his own front door. She was about to put her key in her lock when she heard a purr.

"Monty!" she heard him say. "Where have you been this time, old chap?"

She went indoors, smiling to herself. She really needed to get a life. She called herself a detective, and she'd had a fanciable next door neighbour for eight weeks or so and hadn't even noticed! She'd been thinking about getting a cat, and this guy already had one. Maybe it was a sign.

Mind you, he'd probably turn out to be gay, or in a relationship.

The thought reminded her again of her conversation with Barbara Carlisle and her revelation this evening. She'd always liked the pathologist, but had had no idea that she was about to get married. She didn't know much about the personal lives of Joan Collins or Jason Bell, either. At the Met, she'd been genuinely close to her team and had known a fair bit about them and their lives outside work. Was it different here because people were more reserved? Or had she put up the barriers herself?

As she foraged in the fridge for something she could eat with minimal fuss, she decided something had to change in her life. She should try letting down the drawbridge a bit and let people in.

Easily said. She just didn't have a clue how to do it.

12

Baines sat in the incident room with the rest of the team, most of his mind on the briefing that was about to begin, but part of it on his decision to seek professional help with what appeared to be a worsening problem. He still wasn't convinced that his sightings of Jack indicated a mental health problem. But there were times when he felt so close to some invisible edge that the slightest nudge would send him over, spinning into mental oblivion.

Part of him continued to cling to the hope that his son was still alive and trying in some inexplicable way to communicate with him. But these sightings took a toll on his emotions. He needed answers of some kind, even if he didn't like what he heard. Seeing a shrink would at least eliminate a possibility. Or, if he really was going mad, he could start to deal with it.

He'd talked it over with Karen, who'd said she would have a discreet word with one of the HR people at work and see if she could get a recommendation for someone to see.

"Once this case is out of the way, though," he'd said, earning himself a sharp look.

"All right," she'd said. "It can't be something we keep putting off, though. There'll always be another case, and another."

He'd had to hold in his temper, biting back the retort that sprang too readily to his lips, even though he knew she didn't deserve it. "I'm finishing this case first."

"I know you are. Do it when you're ready. I love you."

"Are you with us, Dan?" Archer's voice cut through his musings. "You've got that faraway look."

"Sorry," he said, caught out. "Yes, I'm with it."

"Okay, then." Archer was standing in front of the cork board. "Three murders we think are connected." She tapped photographs. "Brandon Clark. Ryan Sturridge. And a man we're calling Matthew Butcher, but who has multiple identities, and we can't be sure any of them is real. So what do we know?"

The lines and handwritten notes on the board had grown since the start of the investigation. As Archer spoke, she indicated any that she thought were significant, recapping the links between Brandon and Ryan, the threats Ryan Sturridge had made to Brandon, and Sturridge's recent release from prison. And the enigma that was Matthew Butcher.

"We don't know the circumstances. Did they know each other? Or were they in the same place at the same time by coincidence?"

Her gaze swept the room. "What we do know about Butcher is that our attempts to find out who he was have raised flags at the National Crime Agency. They want to make his murder their case, and they're not telling us anything. Which means they'll probably want us to back off on the other two killings as well, but I'm pressing ahead with those investigations for the time being."

Joan Collins's hand went up. "Guv, do we know for certain that Ryan's death is connected? I know it would be an almighty coincidence for it to be two unrelated shootings, but…"

"I'm still waiting on ballistics," Archer replied. "Phil Gordon was going to see what he could do to fast-track the bullet that killed Ryan."

"They found it in the end?" Baines checked.

"Embedded in a wall, yes. Phil phoned to tell me. Same sort of bullet as Friday, a .45, but they'll need to do tests to see if it was fired by the same gun. We do know it wasn't fired by the gun Laine was probably holding for Ryan. Fair point though, Joan – we need to keep an open mind. My instinct is still that all three murders must be linked, but I suppose you never know. Meanwhile, I've just come from Ryan's post-mortem. No surprises there. Dan, I don't suppose Ben Loftus has turned up?"

For the benefit of the others, Baines recapped the possibility that Ben's relationship with Ryan wasn't all friendship. Also the talk of powerful new allies.

"The answer is, though, guv, that he hasn't been seen since last night. I checked with his home and usual haunts. No one's seen him. No one seems that worried, either. It seems he comes and goes as he pleases. But I can't believe that his disappearing act just as Ryan gets whacked is another coincidence. Either he's the killer and he's decided to lie low for a while, or he's scared that he'll be next."

"Or he's already dead," Jason Bell suggested. "Maybe we just haven't found his body yet."

Before anyone could respond to this cheery thought, the door was flung open and DCI Gillingham stalked in with a face that could have curdled milk. He looked around the room, stared at the board, and then finally fixed his gaze on Archer.

"A word in my office, Detective Inspector," he said. "If you'd be so kind."

* * *

"Right," Gillingham snarled from behind his desk. "So suppose you tell me what the fucking fuck's going on, and how come I've got another fucking murder on my patch that I only heard about when the Super phoned me an hour ago? Maybe you could explain why the fuck the first the Super heard of it was on the fucking news?"

Archer hadn't been offered a seat, but she slid into one anyway. She was damned if she'd stand there and be dressed down like a naughty schoolgirl in the headmaster's office. And she wasn't going to stay on the back foot, either.

"If you've quite finished swearing at me, Paul," she said, "I can explain everything."

"Really?" He said it in a way that somehow accused her of barefaced lying. "Let's hear it, then. And, by Christ, it had better be good, or you'll be making tea for the traffic boys before the day is out."

She took a deep breath. "I was just obeying your instructions."

"Eh?" It clearly wasn't what he'd expected to hear.

She gave him her sweetest smile. "Remember? You said, and we all agreed what a good idea of yours it was, that we should get some pictures of Matthew Butcher with blond hair and glasses mocked up to show to anyone who contacted us about the original ones. So we could talk to them before Sheppard got her hands on them. Same with the ballistics reports – which, by the by, I've asked to have ASAP verbally, but encouraged Phil to soft-pedal on the written version."

"What's that got to do with—"

"We were obviously singing from the same hymn sheet yesterday: try to stay a step ahead of the NCA. So when we got another murder that looked connected – another local lad whom DCI Sheppard will probably see as an irrelevance compared to mystery man Butcher – I used my initiative and decided it was better all round not to rush into briefing you until we had our ducks in a row."

"But…" His jaw worked silently. "But that's insane. It was on the fucking news. The Super heard it. I looked an absolute bloody fool. Jesus, *Sheppard* will have heard it."

"Sheppard probably won't give a flying fart. For all she knows, people are popping each other in Aylesbury every other day. Come on, Paul," she wheedled. "This is our turf, not hers."

"You should have told me," he said, looking only marginally less apoplectic. "You'd better tell me now."

So she told him. When she'd finished, she'd have sworn that 'sly' was the best word to describe the expression that flitted across his face. She wasn't sure she liked it.

"Well," he said, "my take on it is that some serious players are making moves on the Vale and knocking off potential opposition. The boy Loftus is, as you say, either part of that or running for his life. But one thing's for sure, Lizzie. Butcher – or whoever he is – is at the heart of it, so the NCA really ought to be running this. Really ought to be informed." She opened her mouth to protest, but he raised an index finger. "And yet," he went on, "why should they come swaggering into our area, running the show, while we sit in the dark eating their shit?" He stood up. "I might as well come to your briefing. Phone on silent, I think. You know, if anyone calls, I might just miss them."

* * *

In the event, there hadn't been too much more to the briefing. Gillingham had sat at the back, as was his wont, and listened whilst Archer asked Bell to analyse the information that had come from last night's door-to-door enquiries and make sure any doors that hadn't been answered got knocked again. Collins's job would be to get hold of CCTV footage from around the Northfields estate around the time of each of the murders. The owners of any cars that had been on the move on both occasions were to be visited and questioned.

Meanwhile, Laine Shaw was to be dragged back in and asked more questions. It would be interesting to see how she was taking her boyfriend's death. It was also another chance, now she had no reason to fear Ryan, to find out what she really knew about these murders.

To this plan, Gillingham added that Steve Ashby should be asked to put some feelers out among his contacts. He would listen to no protests.

"We're a team, Lizzie," he said sternly. "We've all got a part to play. There's been enough maverick goings-on for one day. Speak to Steve, and for God's sake keep me in the loop."

Baines could see her feelings about that written plainly on her face. He thought the others would too. But this was no time for her to be having a major bust-up with the boss, and she seemed to know it.

He followed her out of the room after the meeting broke up. "Would you like me to speak to Steve? I know how he gets under your skin."

"I don't get it," she said. "I really don't. He opts for getting one over Sheppard and her team, even though he could drop himself in the shit for it. Then he decides to bring his mate Ashby in on it. The most indiscreet man I've ever met." She sighed. "You know, I'm still amazed Ashby came in so early yesterday, just to help us out with those photographs."

"There must have been an angle," Baines opined. "My experience is that Steve Ashby doesn't go out of his way to do anything that doesn't benefit Steve Ashby. As for Gillingham... well, you know they go back a long way."

"Yeah, but..." She paused, her eyes closed in concentration. Then she looked at him. "Remind me just how far they go back."

"Christ, Lizzie, I don't know. Let's see..." He racked his brains. "Gillingham came here maybe six, seven years ago. Steve followed him a year later. There was a vacancy, and—"

She made an impatient twirling gesture. "Yes, yes. And they came from...?"

"Reading."

They were standing in a corridor, keeping their voices down. Archer tried the door of the nearest office. It was empty, so she dragged him inside.

"Lizzie, what are we doing?"

"Look, this is probably nothing, but the gun used to kill Brandon and Butcher – Ryan Sturridge too, I'll bet – was used in a robbery in Reading, right?"

He saw where this was going. Sat down in the nearest chair. "Yeah, but come on, Lizzie. What are you saying?"

She stood fidgeting. "I don't know. But it's an interesting coincidence, don't you think?"

He felt the short leash on his patience straining once more. "No, not really. It's a hell of a reach, that's what it is."

"You think it's bollocks."

"I *know* it's bollocks. I mean, neither of us thinks much of Ashby, and we've often joked that he has some sort of hold over the boss. But liberating a gun from the evidence store in Reading nick, and years later starting to blow people away in our neighbourhood? They're not Butch Cassidy and the Sundance Kid."

"Someone took that gun." She shook her head. "But I suppose I'm being stupid. It's just that I thought I saw something in Gillingham's face when I was in his office just now. Something crafty. I thought at the time it was just because he'd decided to go along with leaving the NCA out of the loop as long as we could get away with it. But it somehow didn't quite feel that way." She sighed. "I'm not getting enough sleep, that's my trouble."

"Besides," he added, "you said yourself, Ashby helped you with those pictures."

"And, as you said, there must be an angle to that. But it's probably nothing to do with any of..." She shrugged "Any of this."

He felt a sharp pang of discomfort. Their working relationship had never run entirely smoothly, but he'd felt it had improved over the past year. Now she was going all weird on him.

"Tell you what, though," he said. "Ashby's always reckoning he's the networking king around here. It'll be funny to ask him to put his money where his mouth is." A new thought came to him. "You know, he's not the only one with contacts, Lizzie."

"No?"

"No. I bet you've got a few of your own from your Met days. Maybe you should stir a few of them up. See if anyone's heard any whispers about our neck of the woods."

She wouldn't meet his eye. "I don't know, Dan. I might have burned those bridges."

"You don't keep in touch?"

"Well, I... It's complicated."

"Just a thought."

She looked indecisive for a moment or two, then shrugged. "Maybe I could make a couple of calls. It's worth a try. Thanks..."

"For what?"

She smiled her lopsided smile. "Oh, for listening. For not having me certified."

"Yes, well. I might do that yet."

They returned to their desks, Baines to spoil Steve Ashby's weekend, Archer to get Laine Shaw picked up.

As he dialled Ashby's number, the conversation he'd just had with his DI played back in his mind.

Ashby and Gillingham mixed up with serious organised crime. It was ridiculous.

Wasn't it?

The conversation he and Archer had had with Ryan Sturridge at his home popped into his head. The thug had been baiting him about DI Britton.

He was as bent as... as anything.

Baines had thought Sturridge was just blowing smoke about Britton, to wind him up. But there had been that little pause. Had he been about to say a name – another copper he really did think was corrupt – and then thought better of it? If so, whose name had he been about to say?

Suddenly Archer's theory didn't seem quite so absurd.

13

Laine Shaw was back in the same interview room where, only yesterday, she'd been quizzed over the gun found at her home. She was ghost-pale and had a sticking plaster over the bridge of her nose. Andy Knight had dropped his Sunday plans to be here advising her, making sure she at least had some continuity of legal representation.

For a girl whose boyfriend – the one she'd apparently waited for while he'd been inside – had been gunned down last evening, she seemed less broken up than might have been expected. Archer wondered if that was significant.

"Laine," she began, "I'd like to start by reminding you you're under caution. And that you're still in trouble over that gun we found in your possession. We know you were holding it for Ryan, and we also suspect that Ben Loftus… shall we say… procured it for him. Now Ryan's dead. We know the gun you had wasn't involved in his shooting, or the two last night. Because we have that under lock and key here, and we now know a different gun was used in all three murders."

Preliminary ballistics results had just confirmed this.

"What we don't know, Laine, is who'd want to hurt Ryan. To kill him. Do you know? Oh," she added, "and before you go no comment on us again, you should know that we've no idea who's next on the hit list. Ben Loftus has disappeared. Do you think he's the killer? Do you think he's scared he'll be next? Or do you think he's already dead in a ditch?"

"And, more to the point," Baines added from beside her, "how can you be sure *you're* not on that list?"

Her lower lip trembled. For the first time, Archer noticed that her hands were shaking.

"Laine," Baines said, more gently, "we can't help you if you won't talk to us. What happened to your nose?"

She didn't answer, but her hand strayed to her face, touching the sticking plaster.

"What I mean is," Baines continued, "if you were only keeping that gun for Ryan because you were scared of him, because he had a habit of hurting you – well, that might help with the trouble you're in. We know he had a temper. People around him have a habit of turning up with bruises. With plasters on. We know he hit Ben."

"Ben walked into a door," she said.

"Of course. I guess you slipped in the shower. We've heard it all before. And we weren't born yesterday. You remember that DNA swab we took when we found Ryan's gun in your possession? Well, our forensics people found blood in his car, and it matches yours. Now why don't you tell us the truth? Ryan's beyond your protection now, but we're very worried about Ben."

She started to weep, very quietly, tears leaking from the corners of her eyes and trickling down her face.

Andy Knight whispered something to his client. Laine stared in front of her for a moment or so, and then nodded.

"Ryan did hit me," she said, so softly that Archer had to strain to hear her.

"Can you speak up a little? For the recording?"

"Ryan hit me." At little louder. "Last night. He was angry that you'd found the gun. I'd never wanted it, didn't want it in the house. I was scared of it, like it was going to go off on its own. He made me keep it. Said I had to look after it for him – he couldn't risk being caught with it. Got angry when I tried to say no."

She took a breath. "He changed in prison. Before he went in, he was, I don't know, like this lost little boy, playing the tough guy. He came out *hard*. Always wanting to lash out. Any excuse. He never used to hit me before. Now it was like hitting was his answer to everything.

"It was Ben who got him the gun. Me and Ben collected him when he came out, and Ben gave it to him on the way home.

He'd been talking big, even when he was inside. He'd met someone in prison, someone who had contacts. He'd said Ryan could join up with them, make some serious money. Ryan had got Ben talking to people around the town. What he called recruiting. Ryan came out full of talk, saying stupid stuff – like how in five years he'd be driving some big fuck-off car, and we'd be drinking champagne around his swimming pool."

"You didn't take him seriously?" Archer asked.

"You didn't *not* take him seriously, or he'd get angry. He was always off to meetings – sometimes with Ben, sometimes by himself. A lot were in the back room at the Falcon, but I don't know what the deal was there."

"Do you know who he met?"

She shook her head.

"You're sure?"

"Ryan said it was better I didn't know."

"What about the man who was shot on Friday night? You said you'd never seen him. Was that true?"

"It is true. Honest."

"What about Brandon Clark? Did Ryan ever mention him?"

"Well, yeah, but I never took it seriously. When he'd had a few beers and a joint, he'd say how everyone who'd ever done the dirty on him was going to pay. Sometimes he mentioned Brandon. Sometimes he mentioned you, Mr Baines." She inspected the table top again. "I knew he had the gun – yeah, all right, I was looking after it for him. But I thought it was just something to make himself feel tough. I never thought he'd really shoot anyone, and he didn't, did he?"

Archer ignored the question. "What about Ben? He obviously knew how to get hold of a gun? Could he have got one for himself too?"

"You searched his place, didn't you?"

"Doesn't mean he didn't have it stashed somewhere else."

"You think he might have shot Ryan? I mean, I know you said before, but..." Her eyes widened. "Oh my God. You're serious. But he wouldn't."

A thought flitted across Archer's mind. "So you and Ben picked up Ryan together from the prison?"

"Yes. So?"

"I'd imagine the two of you got close while he was away."

Her eyes flashed. "Not in that way."

"No? But maybe Ben wished it was in that way?"

"If he did, he didn't let on."

"We know Ben did a lot of work setting up this mysterious new operation. And then Ryan swans back in, taking over and knocking you both about. Maybe Ben decided he'd done the donkey work, and now he ought to be the one in charge. Brandon and that other guy – Ben shoots them both, he has his reasons. Ryan gets angry and hits him. And when he hits you – well, that's the last straw for Ben."

"No. I mean, I did tell Ben what Ryan did to me. I was pretty upset."

"Where is he, Laine? We really need to know, because he's either dangerous or in danger."

"I'd tell you if I knew." She swallowed. "Am I in any danger?"

"Until we can unravel what the hell's going on, Laine, your guess is as good as mine. If you know anything, someone might want to shut you up. If they only *think* you know anything, maybe they'll do it anyway."

Archer knew it was harsh, but she didn't think a softer approach would do Laine any favours.

"Okay," the girl said, "maybe I haven't told the whole truth."

Andy Knight interrupted. "Laine, before you say any more, we need to talk alone."

"No," she said. "Honest, I don't know who these people were that Ryan was working with. But I wasn't at the Falcon with them on Friday, like I said I was. I was home in my room. Mum and Dad were out at work, so they wouldn't know. Ryan told me to say it."

"You lied to us," Archer said flatly.

"Yes." Barely audible.

"You don't know for sure Ben and Ryan were there either."

"I'm sorry. Look, I don't know if Ben or Ryan had anything to do with shooting anyone. All I did was look after a gun." She was looking seriously panicked now. "Maybe you should lock me up. Keep me on remand, yeah?"

Archer couldn't be sure that Laine wasn't a target. She wasn't sure about anything right now. She might be able to make a case for holding her, but she feared for a kid like this, who really didn't belong in the system. On the other hand, if the killer saw her as a danger, the police couldn't protect her outside. Not without mounting a twenty-four-hour guard on her home, which wasn't going to happen, not with the budget the way it was.

"No," she said finally. "A girl like you in a women's prison? They'd eat you for breakfast. I can't make any promises, but possession of an illegal firearm under duress? If you're very lucky, you might just get away with a fine or a suspended sentence. Meanwhile, you want to stay away from that sort of environment."

"Maybe I'm better off in there than dead."

"No," Archer said again. "I'm going to bail you. Someone will take you home, and you need to stay there. You might be in no danger, but until we understand what the threat is…"

"All right." Laine looked unhappy. Scared.

"One other thing," said Baines. "You said some of Ryan's business meetings went down in the back room at the Falcon. They've got that barman there, calls himself Raphael, if that's even his real name. Do you know if he was in on Ryan's business? Or just providing a room, probably for a fee?"

"You'd have to ask him. I don't know."

"We will," said Archer.

* * *

"Right," Archer said, after Laine had left with a uniform, "what's next?"

They were back in the briefing room with the team.

"I've got that CCTV footage, guv," Collins said. "There's five cameras altogether – none of them covering our crime scenes, of course. But we're looking at small time windows, I guess – two lots of half an hour?"

"Sounds about right."

"Five hours' viewing, then. Maybe up to eight, if I keep going back over stuff to note numbers."

Archer thought of Sheppard, and how long it might be before she picked up on last night's murder. So far it had missed the national news headlines, thanks in part to events in Syria and pro-Russian unrest in Ukraine, but there were other sources. If Sheppard got wind of it, she was bound to wonder if it was connected to the case she had commandeered. If so, she might ring Gillingham, who might or might not stall her.

Or she might turn up on their doorstep at any moment.

"No," she said, "that's way too long. Rope in anyone you trust to do a good job, whether they're here or off duty. Jason, for a start, if he's finished looking through the door-to-door feedback."

"I have," Bell confirmed. "He's a lucky bugger, as well as a ruthless one. Perfectly happy to shoot people in broad daylight, but either no one saw or heard anything last night or people are keeping their mouths shut."

"Okay, so you're on that footage with Joan. See if you can get Ibrahim Iqbal on it too. I'm sure I saw him earlier." Iqbal was a civilian IT wizard who seemed to live at the station. "If you can pressgang two or three more, that's great, but don't waste hours of potential viewing time trying to rustle up support."

"Understood," Collins said.

"Okay, good. Dan, I've got a call to make, then you're with me. I think it's time we paid the Falcon a visit. I want to really lean on that Raphael character."

She made herself a coffee and brought it back to the briefing room. She had the room to herself now, which suited her fine for the call she had to make.

She'd spoken to DCI Nick Gibson, her old boss and mentor from the Met, less than half a dozen times since she'd transferred to Aylesbury in search of a new start. Most of the calls had been made by him, and the communication had dried up a year or so ago. But she knew Baines was right. Her erstwhile colleagues were too rich a source of potential information on organised crime to ignore.

He answered his mobile on the third ring. His delight when she announced herself was unconcealed.

"Lizzie! How the devil are you? How's life in the sticks?"

"Oh, you know." She tried to keep it light. "We have our moments."

"A couple of shootings the other night, for example. Are you working on those?"

"Yes, and another last night that you might not have picked up on. Same gun, so they're connected."

"Something tells me this isn't a social call."

She felt a twinge of guilt. "Sorry. Look, we must fix up lunch before we hang up. Get Sam along, too."

"You know it's *DI* Strong now?"

"That's great!" Her pleasure at her former DS's promotion was tinged with dismay that she hadn't heard it from him. "About time too. Recent?"

"Oh, I don't know. Six months? I thought he might have been in touch."

"No," she said quietly. "No, I didn't know. Is he still in your team?"

"No, he's on Serious and Organised Crime these days."

"That's a coincidence."

"Why?" He barely missed a beat before he answered his own question. "You're thinking the big boys might be involved in your case?"

She'd already decided not to mention the NCA connection to him, not wanting to mix him up in any repercussions from her continuing to investigate a case that was supposed to be off-limits. Instead, she made much of the gang links, Ben Loftus's recruitment activity, and his and Ryan Sturridge's boasting about some major league connections.

"As Loftus has gone off the radar, we can't rule him out as the killer," she said, "but my sense is that these killings have a professional feel about them."

"So you're thinking maybe a big – or maybe a medium-sized – player from London could be looking to expand onto your turf, using some of the existing infrastructure as a platform?"

It wasn't quite how she would have phrased it, but he was exactly right, and she said so.

"Could also be a mob from Birmingham, or a smaller Midlands town, like Nottingham," Gibson mused. "We can be as guilty of being London-centric as politicians and the media sometimes. You might speak to someone in the National Crime Agency."

Feeling herself blushing, she muttered that maybe she'd do that.

"Meanwhile, Sam's your man here, I reckon. You've still got his number?"

"Of course."

His voice took on a more serious tone. "How's it really going there, Lizzie? Are you finding whatever it was you were looking for?"

She hesitated, feeling ineffably sad. She wasn't about to moan about the crushing loneliness she felt when she retreated to a house she still couldn't call home, but she couldn't lie to this man either. Apart from anything else, he would see right through her.

"Too early to say," she compromised. "I've got a good team here, although we have our share of arseholes too. And I bought a house. In a village."

"Wow. You'll be joining the maypole dancers next."

"Ooh arr," she said in a Mummerset accent. "Real yokel, me."

"For what it's worth, I hope your career's back on track. You know how highly I rated you. I'd have backed you if you stayed; done all I could to help you through… you know."

"I do know," she said, "but we are where we are."

"We should do that lunch some time. Got to go, but give me a call when you've broken this case."

"Sure," she said, knowing it was never going to happen. The background noises from his end of the line told her that he too was in the office on a Sunday morning.

"Speak to Sam."

They hung up. She tried Sam Strong's number, but it went to voicemail. Feeling a little awkward about leaving a message after such a long time out of touch, she congratulated him on his promotion and asked him to call her.

"I need to pick your brains," she added, before breaking the connection. Then she went in search of Baines, feeling sad and more than a little irritable.

"Come on," she said. "Let's descend on the Falcon. Raphael backed up Ryan's lies about Laine being there with the boys, and I feel like giving someone a hard time."

14

The Falcon was in full Sunday lunchtime swing, with a number of drinkers inside. The day had turned overcast and chilly, so the outside tables weren't much in use. The weather made little difference to the overworked young woman behind the bar, though. She wore only a thin tee-shirt and an alarmingly short skirt.

"Raphael?" she spat. "If you catch up with him, tell him Wendy is utterly pissed off with him, and so's the landlord."

"He's not here?" Baines asked.

"Not here, not answering his phone, not answering his bloody door. He should have been here opening up. He should be here helping me. Instead, I had to try and rouse him, then go looking for the boss to get the spare keys. Then I had to deal with a lot of verbal from customers waiting outside."

He exchanged a glance with Archer. "Does he do this a lot?"

"What? Fail to roll up?" Wendy frowned. "Well, no. He's a lot of things – not all of them good – but unreliable isn't one of them. Jesus, I hope nothing's happened to him."

"I'm sure it's fine," Archer said with a confidence she didn't altogether feel, "but we do need to talk to him. Do you happen to have an address for him?"

She supplied it. A flat on the Fairford Leys estate.

"Do you happen to know a Ben Loftus?" Baines asked. "Comes in a lot?"

"Ben? Yeah, of course. Here, I heard his mate, Ryan, got himself shot last night. Is this what this is about? Only Raphael wouldn't have nothing to do with guns. I don't think, anyway," she added with a little less conviction.

"When did you last see Ben or Ryan?"

"Let me think. They were both in, it must have been Wednesday lunchtime."

"Not Friday afternoon?"

"I wouldn't know. I do the evening shift on a Friday, and it's bloody bedlam, so I try and get a bit of kip in the afternoon."

A bullet-headed man with designer stubble came and stood at the bar, an empty glass in one hand and a banknote in the other.

"With you in a tick, Peter," Wendy told him.

Baines dropped his voice, "Ryan and Ben," he prompted. "Raphael told us they were both there on Friday, with Ryan's girlfriend."

"Then they must have been."

"The girlfriend says she wasn't."

"I wouldn't know. I'd tell you if I did."

"I believe you. But – assuming they were here in the first place – could either Ryan or Ben have slipped out for a while and not been noticed?"

"Friday? I'd say so, yeah. It's mad in here on a Friday night, but not exactly quiet in the afternoon, either. I can't see how anyone could be sure who was there all the time."

"That's helpful," Archer said, turning to go.

"By the way," Baines said, "Do you happen to know his real name? Raphael – that's not his real name, is it now?"

She looked doubtful. "He really doesn't like people knowing it. I'm sworn to secrecy."

"Well, we're the police. He still owes us a written statement, and then we'll have it anyway."

She sighed heavily. "All right then. I dunno what his parents were on, but it's Ebenezer. Ebenezer Larkin."

Baines avoided eye contact with Archer. If they looked at one another now, they would laugh. Which would be unprofessional.

"The poor bastard," he said.

* * *

Fairford Leys was a fairly modern estate to the west of Aylesbury. Baines had once told Archer that the planners had wanted to create an environment similar to that of a village, and that the architecture had been inspired by traditional Aylesbury housing styles. It had Victorian-style lamp-posts and railings, and the centre of the 'village' was even encircled by a so-called 'city wall' modelled on the mediaeval, complete with gate towers.

When Archer had first seen it, she'd thought it a bit pretentious, but it had grown on her. And an effort had been made to provide some facilities for the people living in the 1,900 high-density homes. The estate had its own 'village centre' with shops, a small supermarket, restaurants, nursery, church, community centre, and a health club with a swimming pool. There were also play areas, open spaces, playing fields and a golf course.

The housing ranged from single-bedroom starter homes to five-bedroom detached properties, and the population was a mix of young singles, growing families, and the retired and elderly.

Ebenezer 'Raphael' Larkin had a ground-floor flat in Knightsbridge Place, not too far from the A41 Oxford Road. The building opened directly onto the pavement and had, to Archer's eye, a Victorian industrial feel, but quite well presented.

She looked at Baines. "Nice. Do you suppose he owns this or rents it?"

He pursed his lips. "Either way, it's hard to see how he can afford it on a bar manager's income."

"Even with a few kickbacks on petty drug deals. I think he must be into more shady stuff than we thought."

Entry was by intercom. When they got no response from Raphael's flat, Baines started pushing buttons until a female voice answered one of them.

"Police," he said. "Can you let us in, please?"

A pause. "Show me your badge," the voice said warily.

Archer spotted the small camera over the door and pointed to it. She and Baines dutifully held up their warrant cards. There was a click from the door, and Baines was able to open it.

"Thanks," he said. "We're looking for a Raphael Larkin."

But the intercom was already dead.

They located the flat easily enough, to the rear of the building, but hammering on the door elicited no more response than had the intercom system.

"Maybe he's had to leave town suddenly," Baines said. "A sick relative, something of that sort."

"Maybe." But Archer had an increasingly bad feeling about this. "If you go round the back, do you think you can have a look in through the windows? I'll stay here, in case he makes a run for it, and to let you back in."

"I'll give it a go."

Five minutes later, he was back, his face grim. "He's in the living room, on the floor. He's not moving, and there's a lot of blood. "

"Oh, fuck," she groaned. "Well, if there's any chance he's alive, we can't hang around waiting for someone to bring the Big Key." She was referring to a battering ram whose official name was the Enforcer. She eyeballed Baines. "What do you reckon?"

"I reckon we're too late, but we've got to try." He shrugged and walked back to Raphael's front door. It had fancy moulded panels, which he tapped. "These don't seem that sturdy."

He raised his foot and kicked out, striking the panel below the handle with the sole of his shoe. The third kick splintered the wood. The fifth punched a hole through. He reached inside, fumbled about until he found the latch, and opened the door.

"We probably ought to be suited up," Archer said, "but that all takes time, if there's any chance of saving him. Let's try not to touch too much."

Archer entered first, and Baines followed her through the little hallway. They located the living room, which was nicely furnished and decorated in an understated style. If she'd had time to think about it, Archer would have said the décor was not what she had expected, but the man lying in a pool of blood that soaked the pale oatmeal carpet had all her attention.

One glance at the hole in the centre of his forehead told her that checking for a pulse would be futile. A ruined cushion, colour-coordinated with a tan sofa, had been tossed aside.

"Looks as if he used that to muffle the shots," Baines said, pointing.

"Look at his knees," she said. Both of Raphael's kneecaps had been blasted, and the legs of his trousers were saturated with blood.

Baines moved towards the body.

"Careful," she warned, afraid he'd step in blood and start messing up the scene.

"I am being," he said without rancour. Stepping to the side of the body, he leaned over and touched the pale left arm below a black tee-shirt sleeve. "Cold," he remarked. "I'll leave it to the experts to do the science, but I reckon he's been dead several hours. Could be his killer was waiting for him when he got home from work."

"We'd best get CSIs and the pathologist here ASAP," she said. "Jesus, what a mess. The doc's just going to love having her weekend buggered up again."

She called Collins at the office and asked her to get hold of Phil Gordon and Barbara Carlisle. Collins pointed out that there was a duty roster, but Archer wanted consistency.

"Tell them I'm sorry," she said.

"I'll try."

She hung up. "Why do you think he shot his knees? That's a departure from the clinical hit."

Baines stared again at the corpse.

"Only one reason I can imagine. The killer wanted something, and he needed to encourage Raphael to give it up. I'd imagine a shattered kneecap, and the threat of more pain, is pretty good for loosening tongues."

She nodded. It made sense. "But what did he want? And did he get it?"

"Search me. Mind you, he must have made one hell of a noise, muffled shots or no."

"We'll knock on some doors while we wait. Surely neighbours will have heard something." She dragged her eyes back to the body. "Actually, maybe not. We need the scientists to check his mouth for traces of adhesive."

"You're thinking maybe his mouth was duct-taped?"

She nodded. "It's what I'd do. Probably make him apply it himself. You know, 'Nod when you're ready to talk'. But take it away with him in case of prints or DNA."

He shook his head. "You scare me sometimes."

"Sometimes I scare myself."

Her phone rang, and she checked the display.

"I need to take this," she said, moving towards the hall. She answered as she opened the front door.

"Sam!" she said as she reached the landing. "You got my call?"

"Nah," he replied, deadpan. "It just occurred to me to call you. Out of the blue, you know?"

She felt a surge of relief. She might have allowed their friendship to drift, but it didn't sound as if he'd changed. Same ironical sense of humour She imagined him on the other end of the line, either relaxing at home or, just as likely, up to his neck in work, an easy-going black guy from a hard-working London family who worked hard himself – and also played hard.

His full name was Samson Strong, which ought to have conjured up the image of a seven-foot muscle man. Instead, Sam Strong was five foot two and as weedy-looking a specimen of a policeman as she had encountered.

Back in the days before such discrimination had been abolished, the five-foot-eight minimum height requirement would have ensured that he didn't get a look-in, but Archer knew looks could deceive. He'd boxed for the police at light flyweight and had made some difficult arrests in his time. He wouldn't back down from a physical challenge, but he wasn't chippy, either. She had enjoyed working with him.

He was also a committed family man so, after congratulating him again on his promotion, she asked after his wife and children.

"They're all good, thanks," he said. "Two small kids are a handful, obviously, but I love it, you know?"

"Give them my love."

"But you didn't ring me up on a Sunday just to see how I was, did you, guv? I mean, Lizzie." Old habits died hard.

"It's a fair cop," she admitted. "I hear you're dabbling in organised crime these days."

"Not quite how I'd put it, but yeah."

"Do you pick up a lot of intel about who's doing what and where?"

"Maybe." His tone was suddenly wary. "But I'm not supposed to talk about—"

"Of course not."

"Only, a lot of our operations are pretty sensitive."

"I get it. It's just that we've got a case here that might be of interest to you."

It was a trick she'd learned from Nick Gibson. When you want something, make out you're giving them something instead. Of course, Sam probably knew this too, but it was worth a try.

"I'm listening," he said, still sounding cautious.

She outlined the sudden rash of shootings in the town, and the suggestion that some serious players might be gaining a foothold in her neck of the woods.

"I just thought it was worth seeing if someone with an ear to the ground might have heard anything about some of the big boys in London looking to expand out this way."

He let out something between a laugh and a cough. "Right. And this is a favour to me, because...?"

"Because if there is something of that kind going on here, somebody's making quite a mess on my doorstep. If we knew where to start looking, we might be able to kill two birds with one stone: catch our shooter and get a lead on one of your bad guys at the same time."

"NCA are a better bet if someone's crossing jurisdictions." He paused for a beat. "But then you knew that. So there's a reason why you're not approaching them." Another beat. "Because they're already involving themselves, right?"

She groaned. "I trained you too well."

"I'm not stupid, either. I listen to the news. Read the memos. One of your bodies on Friday night, you were trying to ID. Put out a photo. I tried to take another look at it before I called you back, and the link had been taken down. My guess? Your mystery man's of interest to the NCA and they've told you to back off."

"I definitely trained you too well."

"Shit." He didn't sound pleased. "And now you're mixing me up in something you've been told to leave alone. What happens to me if it all goes out of shape? And it will."

"Christ, Sam, no one's mixing you up in anything. I'm not asking you to tell me anything you don't want to. Just a hint is all I'm asking for. If you're comfortable."

He didn't reply immediately, and she let the silence stretch out. He knew that game too, and the buzz of the connection between them remained the only sound.

"This isn't like you, Lizzie," he said finally. "Going all maverick."

"I know. But I don't like this, Sam. You've heard about three deaths here, and I'm a few yards away from body number four. Yet I get the distinct feeling that the mystery guy is all anyone's interested in. And I think it's more to do with protecting his identity than finding out who's responsible for this bloodbath."

"That's their call."

"I don't like it," she said again. "One of the victims was just a kid. We're not even sure whether he was a target or just in the way. Another one wasn't that much older."

"Just as a matter of interest," he said, "who in the NCA is calling the shots?"

She told him.

"Marvellous."

"You've come across her?"

"Come across, yes. Crossed her, never. By all accounts, DCI Sheppard can be one scary lady." It was his turn to groan. "You're going to get me in trouble. I can feel it."

"Where's your sense of adventure?"

"If I ever had one, I lost it the day I got a mortgage." He sighed. "Look, I'll think about it. If I can think of something I'm – what was it? – comfortable with…"

"You'll let me know?"

"I'll let you know."

They hung up after agreeing to get together for a drink to celebrate Sam's promotion. Archer returned to where the body lay. Baines stood fiddling with his phone.

"CSIs and a grumpy doc on their way," he informed her. "Who was on the phone?"

"Best you don't know."

He looked at her sharply. "Best I do know, actually."

"You think?"

"I *know*. Think about it. We're sneaking around behind the NCA's back, and the clock is ticking. Soon they'll be coming in here demanding to know why we're keeping two new killings from them. Why we're even investigating them. Then you've got this idea that Gillingham and Ashby might be involved." He made a face.

"What?"

"Well, I know I said it was bollocks, but I'm not so sure now. It could explain why the boss was so keen for Ashby to be in the loop."

"Explain."

"What if they really are worried that this case could dig up some skeletons from the past? Having Ashby inside our tent might give them early warning, mightn't it?"

She absorbed what he had said. "It might. What's your point?"

His eyes bored into hers. "My point is, either way, we're in this together, Lizzie. I know we don't always see eye to eye, but I think we trust each other. Am I right?"

She found herself nodding without hesitation. "You are. Even if you're a pain sometimes."

He didn't crack a smile. "We might just be running out of people we know we can trust. So I don't think we can afford to keep secrets from each other. Now, who was the call from?"

She turned his words over in her mind and saw the truth in them. So she told him.

15

Baines and Archer finally returned to the station, to find that Collins and Bell had made some progress with the CCTV cameras. Between them, they'd captured no fewer than five vehicles that had definitely been on the move on the Northfields estate around the times of both shootings there. One of them was Ben Loftus's.

"We already knew he was lying about being at the Falcon at the time Brandon Clark and the so-called Mr Butcher were gunned down," Archer said. "And he could easily have been at the scene of Ryan Sturridge's murder. Now we need to see if he was anywhere near Fairford Leys in the early hours of this morning. Raphael's time of death was around three, according to Dr Carlisle. Might as well see if any of those other vehicles match as well."

"It'd be a big reach for Ben to be near the Leys by mere coincidence when Raphael was killed, guv," Bell remarked. "Almost a clincher."

"Not quite that," she told him. "But I agree that you, Joan and Ibrahim all need to apply your backsides to those chairs for a bit longer. He wasn't where he said he was Friday night. Now he's missing. If we can place him near all three shooting incidents, it at least makes him a strong suspect."

"On it, guv," Collins said.

"And can you get someone to track down Raphael's family? They'll need to be notified."

Collins made a note.

"One thing seems likely," Archer continued. "Raphael may well have known his killer. Three in the morning – he's getting home, or he's there already. Does he let the killer in because he knows him? Does the killer put him at his ease and then pull a gun?"

"So say it is Ben Loftus," Baines added. "Seems to me either he's got as far from here as possible – maybe even trying to get out of the country – or his work here's not done yet and he's hiding out somewhere local."

"That works if he's a potential victim, too," Collins pointed out.

"I spoke to the boss on the way back here," said Archer. "Do you know if he's sent Ben's picture out to ports and airports yet?"

"I took care of that myself," Bell said.

"Good. At least he can't flee abroad." She looked at Baines. "We need to check again with his parents – he still lives with them, yes?"

"Seems to be the pattern with Northfields tough nuts. Don't rush to fly the nest."

"So go and see them. See if his passport's still there."

"Will do." A thought struck him. "Unless he's like Butcher. Multiple IDs."

"Yeah, right," she scoffed. "From what I've seen of him, I doubt he could juggle an apple and an orange, let alone multiple identities, but maybe he's got hidden talents. While you're talking to them, push them on whether they can think of anywhere he might be."

"What'll you be doing?"

"I want to get a uniform outside Laine Shaw's home. We don't know what the motivation is for these killings yet, but silencing people might be a possibility. Maybe she knows more than she's letting on. Or, just maybe, more than she realises. Once I've done that, I need to brief the boss." She threw a glance at Collins. "Any idea what's been on the news about us this morning?"

"They've got hold of Ryan Sturridge's name from somewhere, guv, so they're naming him as a third victim."

Baines couldn't resist a laugh. "Probably his mum, falling over herself to sell her story to the papers. I wouldn't put it past her to want to cash in once the initial shock's worn off." He met her eyes. "But that's not the point, is it?"

She shook her head. They both knew it was a miracle that the NCA hadn't already closed their latest investigation down. From what Baines had seen of DCI Sheppard, she was no fool. She would surely have had some minion scanning the news for anything happening in or near Aylesbury and, with no contact from the Vale, would have been on the phone herself for information. Come to that, the top brass had ordered Gillingham to hand the Butcher case over to Sheppard and ought by now to have been checking that there had been some liaison over the latest developments.

So why had none of that happened?

"Go see the Loftus family," Archer told him. "If we're going to get hassle, it'll come in its own good time."

* * *

After Baines had departed, Archer returned to her desk and sat musing. It was almost as if there were two separate cases: the death of the man with many names, whose photograph had raised flags at the National Crime Agency, and the deaths of two young men who had fairly recent form on the local gang scene, plus the murder of a man who'd helped facilitate some of their dodgier deals.

Maybe Sheppard didn't care how many local scumbags died, and placed Brandon Clark in the same category. Perhaps she really was only interested in Butcher, and already knew what lines of enquiry needed pursuing there.

Archer thought she might as well bring Gillingham up to date, but her phone trilled when she was halfway out of her chair.

"All right," Sam Strong's voice said when she answered. "Just to be clear. You never got this from me."

"This is an anonymous call, right?" She smiled. "And I can be so clumsy. You never know when I might accidentally delete a record of an incoming call from my phone."

"Well, then. There are two London outfits that seem in expansionist mood at the moment. Of those, one seems to be extending its reach southwards, so Bucks would be a bit of a departure."

"The other?"

He paused before speaking. "The other's approach seems a bit more scattergun. Building a typical pyramid organisation, bringing in more and more small gangs, mainly for distribution."

"Of what?"

"You name it – drugs, guns. Some human trafficking – girls smuggled in from Eastern Europe and then made to work in the sex trade. They're buying into dodgy massage parlours and a few taxi firms too. It's quite corporate, and a family business."

"Pretty serious and organised then. So who's the kingpin?"

"Yes, well... If we had evidence, he'd be behind bars by now. We know who we think he is, but him and his family are like Teflon. Nothing sticks to them. Well, his youngest son did a bit of time for a spot of drug dealing recently, but even then we couldn't connect it back to the family firm."

"A name?"

Sam dropped his voice. "Before I answer that, you need to know what you could be getting into if you stick your nose into this. People who get in this firm's way end up dead, and the rumour is that they're not above killing coppers."

"What do you mean, 'rumour'?" She thought he was taking caginess to ridiculous extremes. She didn't recall him being so cautious when they had worked together. Maybe his new responsibilities had changed him.

"Just that," he replied. "A rumour. More of a Chinese whisper, really. The word is that an undercover cop infiltrated the organisation. Got quite close to the top. Then something went wrong. He was never seen or heard of again."

"When was this?"

"About four, five years ago. If you believe it, he was in the Serious and Organised Crime Agency." The NCA's forerunner.

Archer asked Sam to hold on, got out of her chair, and moved into the corridor. The tiny office Steve Ashby usually occupied was empty. Baines had phoned him and asked what intelligence he had on new players moving into the area, and he'd agreed to do some thinking and make some calls. He hadn't shown any inclination to disrupt his Sunday by coming in to work.

Archer closed the door behind her and almost gagged at the reek of stale cigarette smoke. Ashby had contempt for the anti-smoking laws and made only cursory attempts to conceal his use of tobacco in the workplace. It was one more thing Gillingham turned a blind eye to, and one of the many reasons Archer had refused to go on sharing this broom cupboard with him.

"Sorry," she said into her phone. "You say this copper who was killed was SOCA?"

"That's the story. But no one knows for sure. Those in the know reckon he'd have been disowned, rather than anyone confirming they had someone working under cover. Risk of jeopardising an operation, see?"

"Do we even know a name? An alias?"

"Nothing. It could be a load of old bollocks. But it's interesting you've got this mysterious corpse on your patch at the same time as the NCA are nosing around. I mean, what if they got another officer on the inside?"

"You think our dead guy could have been a cop?"

"Think about it, Lizzie. If he was, then the NCA could be trying to find out who killed him."

"Or hush it up all over again." She stroked her scar. "I don't suppose the rumour mill has a name for the first guy's handler?"

"Three guesses."

She stifled a gasp. "Sheppard?"

"It's only whispers, only rumours. But the fish we're talking about is big and getting bigger. Get something on the main man, cut off the head, and you could be talking about stopping an awful lot of lives being ruined – or worse – by these bastards. Undercover cops would know the risks."

Archer had never worked undercover, but she knew about those who went really deep, assuming a new identity, living double or even multiple lives: immersing themselves in their aliases, forging relationships, falling in love under those IDs. Some had been known to set up home with criminals or their contacts, even have children with them, all without their real families' knowledge. There were also tales of officers getting in so deep that the lines between their police role and their criminal persona became blurred.

There were well-documented cases of lines being crossed and the force in question being criticised. But how many other examples were there where the truth lay hidden, perhaps even buried?

She remembered Baines saying he thought they were running out of people to trust. Suddenly those words rang even truer.

"You said you had a name for me," she said softly.

"I don't know if I ought to give it you. Why not just let the NCA handle it, Lizzie? It's probably their case, maybe their mess. Let them clean it up."

"And in the meantime, this part of the world I'm supposed to be helping keep safe is getting more like the gunfight at the OK Corral. I'm not standing aside while that goes on, Sam, not for anyone." She knew she was thinking of crossing some lines herself. The thought made her stomach churn. But the thought of simply letting it go made her feel sick.

"All right," he said finally. "It's Connolly. Murray Connolly."

"Never heard of him."

"Originally from Glasgow, but came down south as a teenager in the 80s. Google him and you'll see a lot about his legitimate and charitable interests. There's a few images of him posing with celebs, too. Mr Teflon, the upstanding citizen. You'll find not a sniff of where most of his real income comes from."

"So how do you know he's into anything crooked?"

"It's well enough known. It's equally well known that he's got top lawyers and anyone suggesting he's even slightly bent will receive a hefty libel or slander writ."

"Where does he live?"

"What?" There was real panic in her erstwhile colleague's voice. "You're not thinking of paying him a visit? Jesus Christ, it's not your jurisdiction, and you'd be trampling over God knows what the Met and the NCA are doing."

"Whoa!" she said, amused. "Calm down, Sam. I was only asking. I'm not about to go knocking on his door, stirring it up."

"Google him," he said. "I'm not saying any more. And be careful. Remember – you never got this from me."

* * *

Baines returned to the station, no wiser after his visit to Ben Loftus's family. Their demeanour had changed somewhat since last night, when they'd been fairly laid-back about their son's apparent disappearance. They were used to, even resigned to, him being out all night, but that had been before Ryan Sturridge's death.

Since then, they'd been torturing themselves by imagining what might have happened to Ben, but had felt unable to go back to the police, in case Ben was alive and well and they said something that would get him into trouble.

Both the young man's parents were on benefits – his father apparently with a genuine back problem. They seemed decent enough people who couldn't understand how their son had managed to wander so far off-track. They'd known he'd been in with a bad crowd, and that his so-called best mate had done time, but they had much less of an idea what to do to bring him back into the light.

Nor did they have any idea where he might be now. They had already visited some of his haunts, and they mentioned others to Baines – all of which had already been checked out and checked out again.

"I don't know," Archer said when he'd finished filling her in. "Impressionable kid. Maybe someone's impressed him into doing some dirty work for them."

She related the phone call she'd had from Sam.

"He told me what he did on the basis that it didn't come from him."

"From who?" Baines smiled and shrugged. All he cared about was learning more about Murray Connolly.

"I looked him up," Archer said. "Like Sam said, there's nothing to ring alarm bells, until you start checking out his known associates. Several of them look shady or have shady connections. A handful of people separated from him by three or four points of contact have been charged with various offences, and one or two have gone down. None of them has given him up though, if he's involved."

"You said a son had done time?"

She smiled: a smile he recognised. It meant she thought she was on to something.

"Desmond Connolly. He was sent to Feltham, and I reckon there would have been some overlap with Ryan Sturridge. So I'm thinking, what if Desmond did a bit of talent-spotting while he was there? Suppose Ryan bigged up his operation here – if you can even call it that – and young Connolly thought it sounded fertile ground?"

"What? And they send a hit man up here to wipe out the opposition? And take out an undercover cop while they're at it? It all sounds a bit Hollywood."

"Still."

They were in the briefing room. In his absence, she had added some more lines and notes to the board, including a picture printed off the Internet of a powerfully built man with sandy hair, a moustache to match, and laughter lines around his eyes. His image had clearly been cropped from a larger photograph. He was in evening dress. It made him look more bouncer than tycoon. She had written *Murray Connolly* underneath. Lines spidered off from the photograph to other points on the board.

"Did you find anything to suggest how much he's worth?"

"Nice house in Hampstead, featured in one of the style magazines last year." She shrugged. "I'm no judge, but a few million, certainly. I assume someone's checked out his finances to see if it all adds up. My guess is that anything he can't explain away as legit is slipped into some tax haven or other."

"Have you told Gillingham any of this?"

"Yes, and That was a funny thing."

He looked at her. "What was?"

"He looked almost relieved. Like he was hoping we were on the right track."

"What's wrong with that?"

She looked him in the eye. "You don't understand. It was as if he preferred the idea that some hot-shot gangster might be behind all this than some other alternative."

"What alternative?" He still didn't get it.

"No idea. It was like that sly look he gave me when I said we should do some sniffing behind DCI Sheppard's back."

He went up to the board and looked at it. "I don't know," he said. "I mean, yes, this Connolly could be up to his neck in all this, or maybe someone further down his organisation chain. Or maybe not, and his son being in Feltham at the same time as Ryan was a coincidence."

"And that rumour about the undercover cop who was killed? Who just happened to be reporting to Catherine Sheppard?"

"I'm not saying there's nothing to it, but a rumour's not the same as a hard fact."

"Gillingham said much the same. I think he's gearing himself up to telling us to back off again."

He was surprised once more at how close to the surface his anger was. The veneer was wafer-thin, and he feared it could crack at any moment. "That's not happening, not until I know why Brandon's dead." It took some effort not to raise his voice. "I called his mum on the hands-free on the way back here, you know. Just to see how she's doing."

"And?"

"She's doing badly. But she wanted to talk about Brandon, so I listened. She said he was always changing his mind about what he wanted to do with his life, but there were two he kept coming back to: teacher and copper."

"You said he was interested in the police. Saw you as a role model."

He almost didn't trust himself to answer that without making a fool of himself. He drew in a long breath, then tried to make a joke of it. "God knows why he'd want to do a fool thing like that."

She smiled her crooked smile. "I don't know. He could do worse." She examined the board once more. "You don't suppose he was playing amateur detective? That might explain why he was in the wrong place at the wrong time."

He turned the thought over in his mind. "I can't see it. And surely there would have been something on his computer or phone?"

"True. Although no one's actually looked for evidence of sleuthing."

"I'll get someone to review his recent search history."

She sat down. "We're running out of things to do today. I'm going to press Jason and Joan on that CCTV footage. After that, we need to regroup and think about our next steps."

He plonked himself in the chair next to her. "Frustrating, isn't it? I wanted to get further than this today, before La Sheppard comes waltzing in, telling us to butt out again."

She rubbed tired-looking eyes. "You know, I don't get it. I can't understand why she hasn't already done that. She comes in here yesterday, saying she's in charge and we're off the case. Now we have two more bodies, and she's not even curious?"

A thought formed in his mind. "Your contact at the Met said she might have made a mess with the undercover guy who died, and had to cover it up. And now she could be doing it again?"

"But that just explains why she would want to control everything."

"Unless she knows we'd do our own digging, especially if we're told not to. Maybe it's what she'd do herself."

Archer was out of her seat again and pacing. "You're saying she's giving us some rope so she can come in tomorrow, find out what we know, take it off us and... what?"

"Make it all go away." He frowned. "It would be a dangerous game, but if she's worried enough..." He left the thought hanging.

"Desperate times, desperate measures? Maybe."

He rose himself and went to the board one more time. "You know, for all these questions we can't figure out, for my money it's all coming down to two questions: who and what is the guy we're calling Matthew Butcher? And where the hell is Ben

Loftus?"

16

Claire Taylor's home was on the relatively new Berryfields estate to the north of Aylesbury. Neat, tidy houses in neat, tidy, civilised roads. It was what the sales people liked to call a 'neighbourhood', a 'community'.

Building was still going on and, by the time it was finally complete, the vision was for 3,000 houses supported by a food store, plus other independent shops, cafés and restaurants. There was also talk of sports facilities, a gym, a community centre and a health centre. It already boasted the new Aylesbury Vale Academy and Berryfields Primary School.

It might not be the most affluent part of the town, but Claire was quietly proud of what she had achieved. She had worked hard at school, gone to uni, got a decent job in finance, and scraped together the deposit for her own house while she was still in her twenties.

She'd been able to afford a nice car, too – an Audi. Not a new one, but still, it had made the drive back from Devon a little less arduous.

It had been a disastrous holiday.

She and her three best friends had driven down in two cars, both for more comfort on the long journey and to give them more than one designated driver option once they were there.

Lucy had been the designated driver the night before last. They'd had dinner at a nice pub restaurant they'd heard about. A little too much wine for Claire, Jade and Emma, but strictly J2O for Lucy. No horseplay in the car, though. Lucy wanted to concentrate on the unfamiliar roads in the dark. She'd got a Lady Gaga collection playing on the sound system, and they'd been singing along, just four good mates having a good time.

Then the van had come out of nowhere, barrelling out of a side road right in front of them, going so fast that Lucy hadn't even had a chance to react to the headlamps. She'd hit it broadsides, the sound of the impact immense, the airbags deploying. Claire thought afterwards that Lucy's reactions must actually have been pretty good, or most probably none of them would have survived.

As it was, Lucy and Emma, the front seat passenger, had escaped with a cracked rib or two and, in Lucy's case, a fractured wrist. Claire and Jade had walked away, shaken but otherwise fine. The car was a write-off. The van driver had been breathalysed and arrested.

By the time Lucy and Emma had been released from hospital, everyone was knackered. They'd got some sleep at their rented cottage, then Claire had taken Lucy to the scrapyard where her car had been taken, to get some personal effects and arrange for the vehicle to be held, pending an insurance inspection.

No one's heart was really in continuing with the holiday after that. They'd got some food in from the local supermarket and picnicked for the rest of the day, planning on cutting the trip short and driving home on Sunday.

They'd agreed that none of them would tell their families what had happened until they actually got home. There was too big a risk of mass panic and family dashing over to Devon – something the girls agreed they needed like a hole in the head.

She could console herself with one thought. Her own bed would be much more comfortable than the rather lumpy one she'd slept in at the cottage.

All things considered, it was good to be home.

She turned her car into her small driveway, cut the engine, and stretched. It had been a tedious, tiring drive back, and dropping each of her friends off had taken up a further chunk of time. Now she was just grateful to be home. She saw jammy toast and a couple of cups of tea, and then a nap, in her immediate future.

She toyed with leaving her suitcase in the boot for now, but sooner or later she'd need the things in her wash bag. May as well bite the bullet now, she decided reluctantly. As she lifted the case out, she wondered if she'd ever be able to travel light. She and her mates had each come away with everything but their respective kitchen sinks. At least the case had wheels, so getting it to the front door wasn't too much of a workout.

Her front door key was on the same ring as her car key. As she let herself in, she was debating whether to give her parents a ring, in case word of the accident somehow reached them before they got the news from her. But the thought left her as she closed the door behind her. What was that smell?

Just for a moment, she half wondered if her hunger had manufactured the burned-toast smell that was assailing her nostrils, but she knew that wasn't the case. The smell was real.

Was she getting senile in her twenties? Had she left the oven, or the grill, on the entire time she'd been away? Or had she arrived home just as an electrical fire was starting? She had always mocked her father for switching off every socket in the house before he went out, but maybe he was right.

Shrugging off her light jacket and draping it over the banister, she advanced on the kitchen. Definitely like burned toast, but possibly a bit on the stale side.

Another thought struck her. The kitchen door was open. She always, always closed it before she went out. Another obsession of her dad's, closing all the doors, but a habit that had managed to rub off on her.

Her mouth was suddenly dry. She stopped and listened. A burned-toast smell, a door open that shouldn't be. Was someone in the house?

Suddenly, she wondered if someone had found the spare key. She was forever locking herself out, and had invested in a fake stone in the front garden inside which she hid the emergency key. A few friends and family knew about it, but surely they hadn't been blabbing?

The hairs on the back of her neck prickled. Her cousin Ben knew about the key. She remembered laughing about it with him at her grandad's birthday party. What if he'd shot his mouth off to some of his less savoury mates? Should she get out of there and call the police?

Get a grip, Claire, she told herself. Whoever heard of a psycho killer making himself toast?

As if in answer, she remembered her father telling her about the man known as the Fox, who had carried out a string of armed burglaries, indecent assaults and rapes in Buckinghamshire, Bedfordshire and Hertfordshire in the 1980s. Her dad had been in his teens back then, and had helped his own father put a stronger bolt on the front door and screw the downstairs windows shut.

The Fox had enjoyed quite a reign of terror at the time, and the story had prompted her to look it up online. On at least one occasion he had broken into a house when the victims were out and had calmly made himself a cup of tea and helped himself to some food while awaiting their return.

She was scaring herself, and it was stupid.

"Anyone there?" she called, feeling foolish. She felt her stomach churning as she waited for a response. When none came, she exhaled, called herself an idiot, and walked briskly into her kitchen.

She hadn't been able to see the table from the hall. The figure seated there nearly made her jump out of her shoes.

"For fuck's sake, Ben," she yelped. "You might have said something." That spare key! She ought to get a proper key safe.

Her cousin was clutching his head. Now he emitted a low moan.

"No," he said, "no, no. You're not supposed to be here. This is all messed up, man."

"Actually," she said, "you're the one who's not supposed to be here. So why are you?"

That was when she spotted the gun, lying on the table at his elbow.

"Jesus, Ben," she whispered. "What's going on?"

* * *

The team called it a day and packed up just after 5pm. They still had way too many more questions than answers, and Archer had had to tear herself away, half wanting to stay all night and pick away at dead ends, but knowing she'd feel fresher in the morning after food and a night's sleep.

She'd agreed with Gillingham that it was premature to broadcast that Ben Loftus was a person of interest in four killings. It would stoke up a media feeding frenzy when they were still short of information. All they really knew was that he had supplied a gun to Ryan Sturridge and was now missing.

CCTV footage had been unable to place him in Fairford Leys around the time that 'Raphael' Larkin had been tortured and killed. They had been searching for some of the other vehicles close to the other two murder scenes, but had been staring at screens long enough for them to be goggle-eyed, and at risk of missing something. The viewing would start again in the morning.

Meanwhile, they had circulated Loftus's picture and details to all forces, with minimal information about their interest in him, knowing if that didn't get DCI Sheppard's interest, nothing would.

She sat in her back garden now, watching the sun set, drinking a cold beer before rummaging in the fridge for something to eat, and wondering with one part of her brain whether she should employ a gardener to sort out the untamed jungle that she had done next to nothing with – apart from one weekend's slash-and-burn blitz – since moving in. Most of her mind was still preoccupied with the case, turning things over and over.

As she took another sip of her beer, an overfed tabby cat ambled round the corner and then halted, regarding her with a mixture of insolence and curiosity. She wondered if this was Monty, Dominic next door's cat. As if to confirm her suspicion, it appeared to lose interest in her, sashayed over to the boundary fence and sprang up to the top, where it balanced like a tightrope walker for a moment. Then it launched itself elegantly into Dominic's garden.

She smiled to herself. The cat had looked as if love and care had been lavished on it. She wouldn't mind a little love and care herself.

Realising where such thinking was leading her, she berated herself. In all probability, Dominic Newman wasn't in the least bit attracted to her. She may have upgraded her appearance in the past year, but she'd be kidding herself if she imagined no one would now notice her disfigurement.

And, even if he was a man who saw beyond the physical and, by some miracle, liked what he saw inside her, did she really want another relationship, after her two disasters? It was one thing fantasising about online dating; quite another to see someone and imagine being with them.

Besides, was a next door neighbour really a good idea? She imagined living next to her previous exes: seeing them every day, seeing other women in their lives coming to the house. Awkward and unpleasant.

He'd suggested a drink.

But he was probably just being neighbourly. Suggesting they share a glass of wine wasn't exactly an invitation to move in with him.

She told herself quite sternly to put such thoughts aside. She had her hands full with a murder enquiry and what could prove a messy turf war with the NCA. Now was not the time to start daydreaming about the guy next door. She should concentrate her thoughts on the case.

* * *

Baines and Karen were watching the ten o'clock news when she asked him if he'd had any sightings of Jack that day.

"None," he said. "After last night, I can't say I'm sorry."

"That really got to you, didn't it?"

"Yeah," he admitted. "It did." He paused and then gave voice to a thought that had been in his head all evening. "You know, I think I've worked out why I've been so resistant to trying to find an explanation, especially from a shrink."

"Mmm?" She'd been working hard in the garden for most of the day, and was tired. Baines loved that she'd taken in hand what had once been Louise's pride and joy, which he'd allowed to degenerate into a wilderness since her death. Sometimes, seeing her tending a bed or watering a plant, he was transported back to a time before his world was torn apart. It mixed his emotions beyond his ability to describe it.

"Well," he said, "if you're awake…"

"All ears."

"Here's the thing, then. These dreams and visions, hallucinations, whatever they are… Part of me is terrified by them. Am I losing my marbles? Is Jack trying to contact me in some way?"

She sat up straight and regarded him, her head cocked on one side; one more mannerism she shared with her twin.

"That's what you need to find out."

"Sure. But there's another part of me that doesn't *want* a rational explanation. It *wants* to believe Jack really is trying to get it touch. Wants to keep seeing him. Because maybe that's the closest I'll ever come to having him in my life again. If it's happening because I'm certifiable, maybe part of me would settle for that."

She nodded. "So you're scared that a diagnosis might take all that away?"

He suddenly felt deeply miserable. "It'd feel like losing him all over again."

"You won't lose him," she said, snuggling up to him. "Not really. He'll always be a part of you. You'll probably always dream about him. But seeing things that aren't there when you're wide awake can't be healthy, sweetheart, and what you saw last night…" He saw how troubled she was. "It's getting worse. Your having a breakdown won't help anyone. Not even Jack."

He blinked, his eyes stinging. "I've thought about last night, too. I think maybe Jack wants me to find out who killed those two lads."

She took his hand in hers. Squeezed it. "Then find out," she said simply. "Catch the bastard. But see someone anyway."

He kissed her. "Find me a shrink and I'll go and lie on his couch," he told her. "But I won't talk about my sexual fantasies."

She smiled. "You have sexual fantasies, DS Baines?"

"You'd be surprised."

"Well," she said, her voice suddenly husky, "maybe we should start acting them out. Call it free therapy."

He gave an exaggerated shrug. "If you think it would help... it's got to be worth a try."

* * *

This weekend had turned into a nightmare beyond Claire's darkest imaginings. The car crash, the injury to her mates, and the abrupt end to their holiday had been pretty bad. The drive home had been exhausting.

That was as nothing, though, compared to the mess she found herself in now.

She'd known it was bad, as soon as she'd seen that gun: lying on the table, but still terrifying in its implications. But Ben was her cousin, and they'd always got along well. He occasionally dropped round for a cup of tea and a chat.

He'd started off by telling her he was just in a spot of bother and needed somewhere to crash for a while. It was best she didn't know too much. But the gun said this was pretty serious, more serious than he was letting on, so she'd tried to press him to tell her more.

He'd become agitated, and the last thing she wanted to be around was an agitated young man with a gun.

So she'd tried to make the best of the situation. Then she'd gone and insisted on watching the news.

She'd pretty much ignored the outside world while she'd been away and had just wanted to catch up. Ben had objected, saying he didn't want to watch that crap, and she supposed he'd made more of it than was normal.

"You're welcome here, Ben," she'd told him firmly, "but this is my house. And I'm watching the news."

He'd sat on the sofa, the bloody gun sat next to him like it was his girlfriend, his arms folded and his foot twitching. The item about the shootings in Aylesbury had made the national news,

"Ryan Sturridge?" She'd stared at him. At the gun. Back at him. "Wasn't that your mate?"

He'd just looked at her.

"Ben," she'd said, "whatever you're mixed up in, you're best going to the police."

That was when things changed. He'd decided to tie her up. Just in case she got any ideas, he said. He had actually threatened her with the gun until she had rummaged around and produced some duct tape. He'd made her tape her ankles together and wrap tape around one wrist. Then, with the gun in one hand, he'd ordered her to put her hands together and, with his free hand, wound it around her other wrist.

He still wouldn't tell her what this was all about. He'd just said he was sorry. Said he wouldn't hurt her, even though he was pointing his gun at her when he said it.

Now she couldn't help wondering if he'd actually done the shootings.

She'd had to go to the loo once so far. He'd sliced through her bindings with one of her own kitchen knives and then stood guard outside the toilet while she peed, the door open. His back had been turned, but she had still felt humiliated. Afterwards he had taken her back to the living room at gunpoint and taped her up again. She'd vowed it would be a long time before she went through that indignity again.

He'd made her phone her parents, too. She'd stupidly told him why she'd come home early, and so he'd told her to call them and tell them – and also to say that a work emergency had come up, so she might not be in touch for a few days.

He'd told her to be convincing, and had held the gun to her head for emphasis.

Now he was asleep on the sofa, the weapon by his side. She'd weighed up the chances of getting to it and somehow grabbing it – but, hobbled as she was, she couldn't imagine managing it without waking him, and she had no idea how he might respond.

She felt she didn't know him any more, and that was what scared her the most. He wasn't the sweet, misguided kid she thought she'd known. So, to all intents and purposes, she was trussed up in her own home, with a gun-toting stranger for company, and no one had reason to suppose anything was wrong.

Considering he wasn't the sharpest tool in the box, he'd thought of everything. One of the few things he'd told her was that he'd found her garage key and hidden his car in her garage.

How long did he plan on staying? What would he do to her when he decided to move on?

A tear trickled down her face, and she screwed up her eyes to prevent any more from falling. She was buggered if he was going to see her cry. Not on top of everything else.

17

DCI Sheppard finally put in an appearance at 9am sharp on Monday morning, storming into Archer's briefing after it had been going on for about half an hour.

She bade the team a good morning without introducing herself, then strode up to the board, examining the vast amount of material it contained.

"Can I help you?" Archer demanded when it became obvious that Gillingham wasn't about to challenge her.

"Oh, yes," Sheppard said. "I think you can help me a lot. By telling me what the fuck *that*" – she indicated the board – "is about. Because, to me, it bears an uncanny resemblance to an investigation into a case I told you to keep me up to date on."

Members of the team were staring. Only Gillingham, Archer and Baines were aware of the extent of the jurisdictional row that was brewing. They hadn't wanted to compromise other team members by including them in their defiance of Sheppard and her orders from above.

Archer looked at Gillingham, who found something fascinating about his fingernails to stare at. She could expect no argument or support from that quarter. Yet she found that her patience was in short supply.

"Really?" She heaved sweetness into her tone. "I imagined you'd taken yourself off the case. I mean," she continued, "two more killings here since we last saw you, but you don't call, you don't write…" She affected a shrug. "Still, we've been busy in the meantime, I won't deny that. You'd be surprised what we've found out. I've not had a chance to share it with the team yet, but maybe you'd be happy for me to do that."

She turned to her audience. Baines grinned and winked at her. "This is DCI Catherine Sheppard from the National Crime Agency," she began.

"What sort of things?" Sheppard interrupted.

"Your decision, *ma'am*." She spoke the last word with exaggerated courtesy. "I can brief you and the team at the same time, or we can have a private briefing first."

"Yes, well," Gillingham said hastily, as if roused from a slumber, "I think we'd best adjourn this briefing for a while. Everyone back to their desks. Except DI Archer."

"And DS Baines," Archer said.

Gillingham looked as if he was about to object, then shrugged. "All right."

Sheppard stood, openly seething, whilst the rest of the team filed out, some of them looking curiously at the new arrival. Ashby all but leered at her.

"Right," the NCA officer said when the door had closed on the last of them. She addressed Gillingham. "Let's cut the crap, Paul. What's been going on behind my back?"

He didn't look at her. "Well, I wouldn't say it was behind your back."

It was more than enough pussyfooting for Archer's liking. "Oh, come on," she said. "That's exactly what it is. And you know it, DCI Sheppard. In fact, we did exactly what you hoped we'd do. We used our local knowledge to do some digging, so you could do what you just did – come in here and demand the fruits of our labours all tied up with a neat bow for you to go off and do fuck knows what with. With respect to you both," she threw in, clearly as an afterthought.

Sheppard rolled her eyes. "This is nonsense. I've spent the weekend getting a team and an incident room in place, and getting myself up to speed on the case. I only discovered there'd been more murders when I checked the news on my phone this morning."

"Yeah, right. Well, for your information, we have some intelligence from outside the patch, too."

"Really?" The other woman licked her lips with a pink tongue. "Well, you'd best share that, too."

So Archer did. She laid out her suspicion that a significant crime organisation was looking to expand into the area, and that one Murray Connolly's outfit was top of the list. She added that

Connolly's son, Desmond, had spent time in Feltham in common with Ryan Sturridge, and the possibility that this link had led the family business to turn its eyes towards the Vale.

Sheppard just shrugged. "Interesting theories. We'll be sure to follow them up."

"There's more," Archer said. "I hear a rumour that an undercover cop you were, let's say, associated with infiltrated the Connolly business, got found out, and paid with his life. No one even knows his name. Intriguing when you put that alongside our Mr Butcher, the man with many names."

The NCA woman looked less comfortable now. "Again, interesting. But a bit more of a fairy tale, if I may say so. Where did you hear such rubbish?"

From the corner of her eye, Archer saw Gillingham, suddenly animated, surging out of his seat.

"For fuck's sake," he practically yelled, "can we please cut through all the bollocks?"

Sheppard's mouth fell open. Archer imagined that she'd thought she had the measure of him. Now he'd turned in a way that only his colleagues knew he could.

Not that the woman was fazed for long. She recovered her equilibrium almost immediately.

"Be my guest, Paul." She oozed acid and honey. "Navigate us through the bollocks, if you would."

"Sit down, then," he growled.

She shrugged and slid into the nearest seat.

"Right," he said. "It's about bloody time we all stopped playing games and started batting for the same team. Catherine, you know, and I know, that your interest here is this Butcher character. Whoever and whatever he was, I'm sure you've got your reasons for wanting to keep it 'need to know'."

"Thank you—"

"But here's the thing. The gun that killed him has also accounted for three locals already. Maybe this Connolly family's to do with it all. Maybe there's a link to this cop who was killed a few years ago. Maybe you're on the verge of blowing the lid off something huge. But I don't care."

"Your Chief Constable says you have to care."

"My Chief Constable hasn't been updated yet. But she'll be aware that someone's running around town with a gun that disappeared from police evidence a long time ago, killing people. We've got another kid missing. Killer or victim? We don't know yet."

"What we do know," Archer put in, "is that the Chief won't want to look cagey when the media start asking the awkward questions. And they will. I have it on good authority that the chief reporter from our local rag might already know more than you'd want her to."

Sheppard stared at him. "You've leaked information to her?"

"We wouldn't do that," Archer said. "Besides, maybe at the moment it's just – what did you call it? – an interesting theory. You know – rubbish. A fairy story. Maybe she doesn't have anything yet."

"That sounds like a threat." Sheppard looked at Gillingham, tutting and shaking her head. "Are you condoning this? It could see you back in uniform by Friday, manning speed traps."

Archer held her breath. This was where he would back down. When push came to shove, he wouldn't push his luck. She wasn't sure whether he still harboured the hope of another promotion, but he valued his rank and his salary.

He appeared to weigh Sheppard's words, and then he smiled.

"I can play poker as well as you can, Catherine. Take us into your confidence, and we'll take you into ours. You know about the Connollys."

"Do I?"

He ignored the question. "And we know this patch. We've wasted enough time. We could have been working together properly days ago. It's time for some trust."

Archer doubted she would trust Catherine Sheppard any further than she could throw her. But she knew her boss was right. Found she admired him for taking a stand, too.

She looked at the NCA officer. Sheppard was chewing her lip and looking thoughtful.

"All right, then," she said finally. "It sounds as though your sources are better than I realised. Who *are* your sources, by the way?"

"None of your business," Archer said. "Not relevant."

"You were at the Met, yes?" Sheppard locked eyes with her. "Great potential once upon a time. Now a great career behind you." Her gaze seemed to slide down to the drooping side of Archer's mouth. "Shame what happened to you. And you've gone from city slicker to country bumpkin."

When she'd first arrived in Aylesbury, her career and self-confidence in tatters, that sort of sniping might have either silenced or enraged Archer. She still wasn't the woman she'd been before her injury, but she'd come a long way since then.

"Your point is?"

"Samson Strong. Your protégé, back in the day, right? Now on Serious and Organised. Spoken to him recently?"

Archer felt herself flushing. It was as if she'd betrayed Sam. She tried to play it cool, but she knew the colour in her cheeks would give her away.

"I haven't spoken to Sam for ages. Do you know him? You must give him my regards next time you see him."

Sheppard's smile was knowing. "Fair enough," she said. "This is 'need to know', though. Just the four of us. I don't give a damn how you manage it with your minions, but that's the deal."

"Done," Gillingham said before Archer could protest. She glanced at Baines, could see he didn't like it. But he didn't argue, either.

She felt somehow complicit in a deal with the devil.

Sheppard rose from her chair and went over to the board. She tapped the photograph of Murray Connolly that had been printed off from the Internet and named him.

"I'm going to take it you know quite a lot about him: what he's into, his friends in high places. How he keeps his nose clean."

"Take it as read," Gillingham said. "We'll ask questions if we need to."

"Good. Well, whether he's at the top of the pyramid, or whether he's just somewhere near the top, we're not certain. But I got a man into his setup a few years ago. Deep cover. We set him up with the perfect legend. Sharp cookie, a bit of bad luck, just out of jail. Deals done with a couple of middleweight villains to make sure his CV checked out.

"I won't talk about the things he had to do to convince the organisation he was as ruthless as they are. But it was working. He was climbing the hierarchy, getting closer to the Connollys themselves. I thought another month, maybe less, and we'd have a case. We could smash one of the biggest crime gangs in the south of England, take down Murray Connolly, maybe someone even higher up. Then I got a message from our man. He thought he'd been rumbled. Wanted out."

She didn't look so tough now. The skin seemed stretched over her face like shrunken parchment. Her mouth was set in a stony line.

"I couldn't do it," she said. "Couldn't bring him in without the whole operation collapsing. There were people who had put their lives on the line to get him where he was, who would likely turn up in the Thames. And we'd be back to square one."

She was staring at the floor. "So I asked him to hang on just a little longer. Keep his nerve. I really thought we could end it before they were sure he was one of us. I thought wrong."

It was Baines who asked the obvious. "So what happened?"

"Nothing. Everything. He didn't contact me again. I made discreet enquiries. No one had seen or heard from him. We never did again."

"You think he's dead?"

"I know he is. One thing is known to only a tiny handful of officers." She licked her lips again. "I'll share it in good faith. I got an anonymous tip-off that led me to a lock-up garage in south London. There were traces of blood on the floor – a lot of it. Someone had tried to clean it up, but hadn't succeeded. We had it DNA-tested. I'm sure I don't have to paint you a picture."

Archer felt a chill. "But he must have had a family? Friends?"

Sheppard shook her head. "I chose him carefully. A loner. Only child, both parents dead. No spouse or partner. Not even anyone on the force he was especially close to. No one would miss him, and he'd miss no one. So no one would accidentally blow his cover if they happened to bump into him at the wrong time. No one outside his colleagues to mourn him, either."

"That's pretty cold," Baines said. His stiff posture radiated hostility.

"Yes, well. Walk in my shoes. It was for the greater good. If we could have smashed Connolly's operation…"

"All right," Gillingham said. "What has that to do with what's been happening here over the weekend?"

She let out a bitter laugh. "Would you believe we pulled the same trick again? Another officer with no ties and a carefully constructed legend."

"Butcher," Archer said: a statement, not a question.

"That's one of his names. He had others, as you know – proper IDs in case we had to pull him out fast. We didn't want to repeat what happened before." She shrugged. "I thought it would be a few years before he got near anyone important, and then we got lucky. The firm was expanding, and they were looking to set up right here in Aylesbury. There was a role for our guy. They rented him a house, and suddenly he was on the fringe of meetings with local bad lads they were looking to recruit." She tapped another picture on the board. "I heard the name Ryan Sturridge – he was shot on Saturday night, right?"

Archer nodded.

"I don't think they were that enamoured of him. He had a big mouth and ideas above his station. He imagined he'd be an officer, not the foot soldier they wanted him for. Our guy thought he needed to wind his neck in, or he might be disposed of. Tell you the truth, our guy was scared he might be asked to get rid of him."

"But it didn't pan out that way?"

Sheppard sighed, shaking her head. "I never saw it coming this time. He'd been to a couple of meetings in a pub, and there was talk of someone important coming up to meet people. Maybe one of the Connollys themselves, maybe one of their lieutenants. It could be a breakthrough. Next thing I see is his picture being circulated. So I put a lid on it."

"Why?" rumbled Gillingham. "The man was already dead."

"The operation wasn't, though. They'd invested a bit in this new venture and, if we didn't spook them too much, they might not pull out. If they continued…"

"But now you had no one on the inside."

"True," she said. "But we've still got the Thames Valley Serious and Organised Unit to liaise with. We might get lucky."

"But they're in Oxfordshire!" Baines's frustration was boiling over. "We're right here on the ground. We know who the local villains are, and we're tapped into one or two grapevines too, believe it or not. I mean, what do you think we do all day? Jesus!" He was almost shouting. "How do you think we've managed to piece so much together?"

"Let's all calm down." Archer thought someone had better interrupt his rant before he reopened the rift between Sheppard and the local team. "We're sharing now, Dan, and we're finally all looking at the small picture and the big picture together." She looked at Sheppard. "That's right, isn't it?"

The DCI, who was staring hard at Baines, looked back at her. "So it would appear. All one happy family."

18

The house stood on the outskirts of Hampstead. High walls and electronically operated steel gates made it impossible for anyone to approach the front door unchallenged, and its grounds sat under the watchful eyes of a number of CCTV cameras. The house itself was Georgian in style, with white walls, bay windows, and a swanky porch supported by white-painted columns. Big planters, with flowering plants tastefully organised, stood on either side of the steps up to the porch.

Inside, the property was immaculate, with décor like new and carpet you could imagine sinking to your ankles in if you were heavy enough. The furnishings were a coordinated blend of genuine and reproduction antiques.

One of the rooms leading off the spacious hall served as an office. The man seated behind the desk had an expensive haircut and good clothes. On the walls were photographs of him with stars of the sporting, music and acting worlds. His favourite showed him on Burns Night, in a kilt, next to a prominent Scottish golfer, known for his passion to see the nation independent.

Murray Connolly always smiled when he looked at the photo. It was part of his image: the notion that he, too, was a Scottish nationalist. The truth was, he didn't really give a toss about that, one way or the other. It wasn't as if he had plans to return to Glasgow, or anywhere else in the old country, come to that. He'd found rich pickings down here, made a name for himself, and a fortune, too.

He knew the police would like him to slip up, and that some of the celebrities he mingled with were aware he was a bit dangerous. There were rumours, always rumours, but he was a media darling, and the gutter press knew he'd slap a writ on them faster than they could eat their breakfast if they printed anything they couldn't prove.

And he was simply too clever for anything to ever be provable. Meanwhile, celebs kind of enjoyed rubbing shoulders with a guy who might not be quite as squeaky clean as the gossip columns liked to paint him.

This fuck-up in Buckinghamshire, though. That he didn't like. It was already getting way out of control, and Murray Connolly got nervous on the – very rare – occasions when he couldn't control something. In his experience, control was easy enough to lose, but a damn sight harder to regain.

He stared at the news report on his computer screen. He'd always prided himself on finding the right people to trust, and on letting them use some initiative. He was very rarely wrong in his choices, but he had a nasty feeling he'd made a mistake here.

A tapping on the open door of his office got his attention. His second son, Cameron, leaned against the door frame, tall and rangy with sandy hair and chiselled looks that were a real chip off the old block. Murray smiled to see him. He was his favourite child, although he'd never let on.

The eldest, Fraser, was solid as a rock, would one day take his place, and had the talent to rise to the top in any organisation he chose. But he had no aptitude for getting his hands dirty. When something unpalatable had to be done, it was his father's power, rather than his own, that he wielded.

The youngest, Desmond, was a disappointment. He'd done what no one else in the family had managed to do – get caught drug dealing, of all things. A bit of private enterprise that had brought the police to the family's door. To his credit, he'd done his time and kept his mouth shut, despite offers to make a deal that would have involved selling out his nearest and dearest.

Mind you, that decision had, like as not, been born out of fear as much as loyalty. Blood might be thicker than water, but it could still be spilled.

This whole Buckinghamshire debacle had been Desmond's idea in the first place. The boy had placed his trust in the wrong people, and now look what had happened. Although, to be fair, maybe no one could have predicted how it would play out.

Cameron, though. He had the charisma, the guile and quick wits, and the willingness to do whatever it took. Just as Murray had.

"Got your text, Dad," Cameron said. "Thought I'd better come right away." He had no trace of his father's Glasgow brogue. An expensive education had wiped out any traces there might have once been.

"Appreciate it, son. You've been following the results of young Desmond's efforts?"

Cameron walked into the room and flopped down in the chair across the desk from his father, flinging one long leg across the other. "Can't miss it. Four shootings in one weekend in a town where not much happens. By lunchtime today the TV, the papers and the ghouls will be all over it."

"Do you think Desmond can get the lid back on?"

Cameron snorted. "Des couldn't get the lid back on a jam jar in broad daylight with an extra pair of hands."

"He's young. We all had to learn."

"I know exploiting the potential up there was his idea, Dad, and I understand why you'd want to give him his own thing to make a go of, I really do. And neither of us knows exactly why it's all gone sour."

"I can guess, though."

"So can I. And Des is not the man to sort it out. Des is more likely to join the pile of corpses, and then people will really start asking questions."

"Which is why I want you to get yourself up there. Whatever it takes, nip it in the bud. Take Willie with you."

Cameron raised an eyebrow. "Mad Willie? Are you sure?"

"You know what they say about fighting fire with fire. Just make sure you keep him on a leash."

"Give me the rest of the day. I'll be there by suppertime."

"You'll be there by lunchtime. This thing's like a snowball rolling down a hill. It's not about to slow down."

Cameron rose to leave. "Fair enough. I'll be in touch – using the pay-as-you-go phones."

"Obviously. And Cameron?"

"Yeah?"

"You have my permission to kick your brother's arse while you're about it."

* * *

Claire had awoken feeling stiff from her night in the chair, her bladder telling her she needed to pee again, but her sense of dignity rebelling against a further instance of supervised urination. She knew she was only putting off the inevitable.

When Ben had stirred, groaning and stretching his cramped muscles, she'd envied him and, for the first time since she'd laid eyes on the gun, annoyance with him outweighed her fear.

"I need to get out of this chair, Ben," she'd said. "You're not the only one who's stiff and uncomfortable."

"Tough," he'd retorted sullenly, and she'd bridled.

"Not bloody tough. Who the hell do you think you are? You practically break into my house, threaten me with a gun, tie me up, stand over me when I pee, and you don't even have the decency to let me try and sleep on the sofa – or, God forbid, in my own bed." She drew breath, reaching for calm. "Now, I'm stiff and uncomfortable. I need to stand up for a while. Properly. Which means untying my feet."

He'd made her wait a few minutes, but had cut her bonds so she could eat breakfast. Eating while her cousin sat across the table with a gun in front of him had dulled her appetite, but she had managed a bowl of cereal and a mug of coffee. She didn't know if escape would be possible, but she would need her strength to grab any chance that presented itself.

He still hadn't told her what exactly was going on; whether he'd had anything to do with Ryan's death or the other deaths. She supposed he must have, in some way, but had he actually killed them? Or was he simply scared he'd be next?

Either way, he *was* scared.

After breakfast, he made her return to the chair in the living room.

"How long do you think you can do this?" she asked him as he watched her taping her own ankles together, wondering what he'd do if she refused to cooperate. Would he really shoot her? For all she knew, he'd already shot the four people that the TV news was hinting were connected. That must make a fifth somewhat easier, even someone he liked. Or at least, he had seemed to like her the last time they'd met – under normal circumstances.

He hadn't answered her question.

"You can't stay here forever, you know," she said as she wrapped tape around her left wrist, leaving an end so he could secure her right wrist. At least he didn't bind her hands behind her back, which would have been even more uncomfortable. It was a small mercy. She wondered if, while he was this close to her, concentrating on the tape, the weapon on the carpet at his side, she could take him by surprise – push him over and make a grab for the gun.

The idea had popped into her head. It was risky, and the outcome unpredictable. She might get hurt. There could be a struggle and the gun could go off.

He might be thinking he'd have to kill her anyway, in the end.

"I'm due at work on Wednesday," she pressed him. "Are we still going to be doing this then? They'll wonder where I am."

"You'll call in sick, if you have to."

"We'll run out of food. That milk's long-life, because I wanted some for when I got home, but it'll run out."

"We'll drink water. There's loads of food in the cupboard. In the freezer, too. It's not an issue."

"My parents will expect me to drop round and see them."

"So call them. Say you've got a cold."

She barked a laugh. "You know my mum. She'll be round like a shot, wanting to dose me up with Lemsip Max and the like."

"Shut up!" he snapped. He bowed his head and used his teeth to tear the end of the tape around her wrists off the roll, a brutal, savage gesture. He looked at her like a sullen little boy. "Stop going on."

"All I'm saying is, whatever trouble you're in, you need a plan. So let me help you."

"If you don't shut up, I'll tape your mouth too."

So she shut up, at least for the time being. He slumped down on the sofa. After a few moments he grabbed the TV remote control, turned the set on, and started channel-hopping. He found some dreadful cartoon show and sat staring at it.

"I need the toilet," Claire said after ten minutes or so.

"Christ's sake. Why didn't you say before I tied you up again?"

"You didn't ask."

"Tough, then."

"Stop saying that. What, you want me to piss where I sit? I don't think you'd like the smell any more than I would."

He stared at her for a moment. She could almost hear the wheels spinning as he groped for a retort. Presumably he found none, because he sighed heavily and went into the kitchen, returning with the knife he had used to cut through the tape before. When she was free, he followed her to the toilet, gun in hand.

"I'm shutting the door this time," she said.

"No way."

She was sick of being terrified, she realised. Normally she was scared of nothing. She might be seeing a side of Ben she'd never seen before, but he was still her young cousin, and she thought he was more afraid than she was.

"What are you going to do?" she demanded. "Shoot me for wanting to go to the loo in private? Look at that window in there. You seriously think I can squeeze through it? That's stupid."

The gun barrel rose a fraction. "Don't call me stupid."

"Don't ask for it, then. What would your mum say?"

"Leave my mum out of this."

He was getting worked up. She thought she'd better stop pushing his buttons. But she closed the toilet door on him, and he didn't protest.

As she did what she needed to do, she forced herself to focus on her situation for the first time. Since she had arrived home, she'd been scared of Ben simply because he was the one with the gun. That and the shock of seeing him in this frightening new light. Now she realised that fear wasn't going to get her out of this nightmare. For all she knew, it was only a matter of time before armed police kicked down the door and came in shooting, catching her in the crossfire. She had to try to gain some measure of control.

He'd reacted badly to mention of his mother; plainly hadn't wanted to think about his parents. Maybe she could find a way to reach him. Get him to open up about whatever it was that had led up to this.

"What are you doing in there?" he demanded from the other side of the door.

"You want a running commentary?"

She flushed, washed her hands and face in the small basin, and emerged.

"Right," he said. "Back to the chair."

"Not yet. I want to stretch my legs."

"Who's in charge here?"

She met his eyes, feeling stronger than she had since all this began.

"I really don't know, Ben. You tell me. I don't think it's you, though. I think whoever's in charge is the people you're scared of. I just don't know who that is yet."

"Will you stop fucking talking?"

"No need to swear."

"Back to the chair."

"After I've walked around a bit." She was still looking him in the eye. "Come on, Ben. I don't know if you'd really shoot me at all, under any circumstances. But I don't believe you'd shoot me for a stupid reason, like closing the loo door, or having a leg stretch. You've got the gun. I'm not going to do anything daft. So let's not make this any more unpleasant than it needs to be."

She started pacing the hall, stopping occasionally to work her shoulders or stretch her back muscles. He stood watching her, the gun barrel tracking her every move, as if he feared that she was planning something desperate. But he allowed her to take the exercise, no longer trying to bully her.

She thought maybe the balance of power had shifted, just a fraction. Maybe she could work on that, a little at a time.

Anything was better than being a victim.

19

Archer emerged from the discussion with Catherine Sheppard with mixed feelings. She supposed it was a good thing that the NCA officer had finally deigned to take the local team into her confidence, but she suspected they'd still only been allowed to glimpse the things that suited her.

Even that glimpse had been unsettling. She still wasn't revealing the real name of the undercover officer who had died, but there was no doubt in Archer's mind that she had dispassionately selected expendable officers, who would not be missed, for the most dangerous undercover roles, and was then prepared to burn them rather than jeopardise an operation. She almost certainly wouldn't hesitate to twist the knife in Archer's back, or those of her colleagues, if she deemed it operationally necessary.

She also knew an awful lot about Archer. Well, there the tables could be turned.

Sheppard was still ensconced with Gillingham. Baines went outside to make a call. Archer made a beeline for Joan Collins's desk. She was talking animatedly to Jason Bell.

"Joan, I've got another little job for you," she said. "Use Ibrahim Iqbal if you need to."

"Okay, guv, but we've got some news."

"Is it good? If so, I'm all ears. I'm feeling in need of cheering up."

"It was Jason who spotted it," Collins said. "Tell her, Jason."

Colouring, the Scot gathered up some photographs. As he tidied them up, Archer noted that they all seemed to feature cars – or maybe one car in particular.

"These are all taken from the CCTV footage we've been going over," he said. "Going cross-eyed over, to be honest.

You'll remember, guv, that we haven't been able to place Ben Loftus's car, or any other vehicle of interest, near Raphael Larkin's home around the time he died?"

"Yes."

"Or so we thought." He smiled triumphantly. "Take a good look at these."

She eyed the silver BMW in the photos, then did a double take. "Nice idea, Jason, and I can see it was on the Northfields estate when Brandon Clark was murdered and at Fairford Leys in the early hours of yesterday morning. But that picture from Northfields on Saturday night... it's a different car. Check out the number plates."

"Ah," he said, still smiling, "but then check out the dent in the front offside mudguard."

She examined all three photographs carefully.

"I could really do with a magnifying glass."

Grinning, Collins opened a desk drawer and produced one.

Archer shook her head. "Please tell me you don't have a deerstalker, pipe and violin in there."

She peered through the glass at the area Bell had identified, one photograph at a time. In each case, the car's mudguard had a sizable dent, almost dead centre near the top.

"All right," she said finally. "So unless there's a massive coincidence going on, he used false number plates for the second visit to Northfields."

"False plates in all cases, actually," Collins told her. "Not that subtle, either. They match BMWs owned locally, but not this one."

"How can you be so sure?"

"The number from Friday and Sunday matches a silver Beemer all right. Owner lives in Wiggington in Hertfordshire. Had his plates stolen a week or so ago, but has a high-pressure job and hasn't done anything about it. Seems he made up some cardboard plates and displayed them in his front and rear screens. But on Thursday the car conked out on the way home from a meeting in Southampton. A garage in Winchester will swear they've had it ever since."

"And this one, the one with the odd number?"

"Another local Beemer, guv," Bell said.

Baines had finished his call and came to join them.

"You'll have to play catch-up," she told him.

"Okay," Bell said. "So the second set of number plates were also stolen a while back. Owner – a woman called Jackie Barclay – reported it to the police in Wendover. There's a case number, but they weren't exactly going to put the whole of Thames Valley police on alert for them."

"So you think our killer stole at least two sets of plates to disguise his car?"

"Maybe more," Bell agreed. "We're thinking he was planning ahead for cameras, and wanted plates that appeared to match the vehicle. That way, he thought we wouldn't have evidence of the same car in the region of all three crime scenes."

Baines, catching up fast, stared at the photographs. "The plan might have worked if it wasn't for that dent. I'm guessing that's what gave him away?"

"You should be a detective," Archer said, smiling. "Here," she offered him Collins's magnifying glass, "your first piece of detecting equipment."

Baines ignored the proffered glass. "Shame you can't make out the driver from any of these angles. But suppose we concentrate on the dent. Put out a couple of stills showing that distinguishing mark to all our patrols and ask them to keep an eye out for it."

Collins groaned. "No problem, Dan. Is there a needle we can find in a haystack for you, while we're at it?"

"She's right," Archer agreed. "We can't be sure how many false plates he's got, and the idea of our guys pulling random silver Beemers with dents in..." She shrugged. "Let's do it anyway," she told Collins. "And check if there's been any reports of a silver BMW being stolen. It might not be his car."

Sheppard walked into the office and joined them.

"So we share information, right?" she said to Archer, with no apology for the interruption.

"Apparently. I assume it's a two-way street, though."

"Of course."

"Excuse us," Archer said, taking the other woman's arm and steering her into the corridor.

"So how's this going to work?" Archer wanted to know. "If we really are all going to be playing for the same team, we need a proper mechanism for sharing all – and I mean all – our intel. No more blind man's bluff between us."

Sheppard checked her watch. "Fair enough. But first, I've got to get to Oxford and brief my team there. I'll give you a call later and we can have a proper natter. Maybe over a drink and something to eat. I clocked that there's a pub next door to the station. What's it like?"

"It's fine."

Sheppard stuck out her little and index fingers and held up her hand as if she was making a phone call.

"I'll call you," she said, and was gone.

Archer watched her until she turned the corner at the end of the corridor. She could still hear the woman's high heels, albeit slightly muted by the carpet.

Archer still trusted Catherine Sheppard about as much as she liked her, which was not much. She was still only showing the cards she wanted them to see. Although, Archer had to concede, that worked both ways.

She felt uncomfortable with the whole situation. At the Met it had been the norm to cooperate with other forces and law enforcement agencies. Even here, close to the Hertfordshire and Bedfordshire borders, cross-jurisdiction cases were not uncommon, and nor was working together. There had been dislike and distrust on occasions there too, but nothing like this.

Now, it seemed, they were to have a 'proper natter'. Suddenly they were all girls together. So was the secrecy about to end? She'd believe it when she saw it.

Archer still thought the identity of the man she continued to think of as Matthew Butcher was, if not *the* key, then certainly one of the keys to this case, and so far DCI Sheppard wasn't letting them have so much as a sniff of that.

A man with multiple IDs and no one to mourn him. Who wouldn't be missed.

She returned to the office in thoughtful mode. Baines was back at his desk, Bell was on the phone, Collins was staring at her computer screen. Archer walked up to the latter.

"That job I had for you? It's three now. Jason and Ibrahim will have to run with those plates without you for the time being."

"All right."

"First off, I asked for mock-up pictures of Mr Butcher with blond hair and glasses. Find out where we are with those. I want them handy if I need them. Two, I want you to see what you can find out about our DCI Sheppard."

Collins blinked. "Are you sure?"

"Yeah, if you're not uncomfortable with it. I'm not asking you to hack her personnel records. Well, not unless you're able to do it without leaving a trace."

A crafty smile flitted across the younger woman's face.

"I'm not that clever. I'd bet Ibrahim could do it, though."

"Really?"

"Missed his vocation, that one."

Archer thought about it for a moment. "Ask him, then. If it rebounds, you were acting on my orders, and I didn't say what it was all about."

"With respect, guv, that doesn't usually wash with war criminals. Can I ask why you're interested in her?"

"I'd love to tell you, Joan, but we're doing a lot of that 'need to know' crap. I really just want a decent profile of her. She seems to know plenty about me, and that doesn't seem fair, does it?"

"On it, guv." But she looked disappointed. "What's your next move? If you don't mind me asking."

"Dan and I are going back to the Falcon. I'm thinking there are loose ends there."

20

Baines realised he'd been quiet on the drive to the Falcon. He'd had a text from Karen asking him to ring her, and had called her back at the first opportunity.

"I decided to sound out my HR department," she'd said.

"You decided what?"

"It's not a problem," she'd insisted. "All I said was that I had a friend who needed to see someone." She'd given a nervous laugh. "Most likely they're assuming the friend is me and that I'm the one with the problems. That's the usual thing, isn't it? 'It's not about me, it's about this friend of mine.'"

"Christ. So if they don't conclude I'm nuts, they'll think it's you. That's terrific, Karen."

"The thing is," she'd ploughed on, "you really need to be referred by someone. Either your GP or, if the problem's affecting your work, then your occupational health people can start the ball rolling."

"Look," he'd said through gritted teeth, "absolutely no way am I doing this through work. I had all this occupational health bollocks when Lou died. They wanted me to have grief counselling, and I wasn't having it then. No way do I need it now."

"Maybe you do."

She had said it quietly, but he remembered how his own voice had risen to just short of a shout.

"That was – what? – thirteen-odd years ago! Whatever's going on now, it can't be that. And, I repeat, I'm not involving work in this."

"Your GP, then."

"For fuck's sake!" he'd exploded. "Will you fucking stop it? I thought we'd agreed, I can't do this now. I'm in the middle of a case. I can't commit to any dates for GP appointments right now."

"No," she'd said, anger in her own voice, "we didn't really agree. You said it and that was that. I asked you when you thought you might not be in the middle of a case!"

"I know, I know. But this case…"

"Is different, right. I wish I had a grand for every time I've heard that." She'd paused, then spoken more calmly. "Look, either you want to do this, Dan, or you really don't. It's make your mind up time. I think all these hallucinations, or whatever they are, are messing with your head, but it's *your* head at the end of the day."

"I haven't said I won't go. But you know what the job's like."

"I should by now. But you're allowed the odd medical appointment, surely. You manage to fit the dentist in."

He had no answer to that. "I've got to go. We'll talk about this tonight."

"Bet we don't. And I don't know how long I can stand to watch what's happening to you."

"Later."

He'd hung up then. Now he hated himself, imagining her staring at her dead phone. Annoyed? Upset? Hurt, maybe?

I don't know how long I can stand to watch.

What the hell did that mean?

"Dan?" Archer's voice cut through his thoughts.

"Sorry, I was miles away."

"Slightly worrying, considering you're driving."

She was right. The journey since they'd left the station was a blank to him. "Sorry."

"I said, I don't know what we're going to get out of this visit. I'm a bit surprised they're even opening today."

"I'm not sure the late Raphael will be exactly lamented by his colleagues. Maybe they're banking on a good turnout in his honour today."

"Did you notice Ashby disappeared while we were in talking to Sheppard?"

He nodded. "So we still haven't got his insights into the word on the street about the Connollys, or any other newcomers on the scene."

"Most likely he's about as wise as we are. He's supposed to have this great network of contacts, but now we're calling his bluff, and he finds himself in the spotlight."

"Well, I actually hope there's *something* to all this talk of his. But if there isn't, at least we can enjoy watching him squirm." He sobered. "Always supposing he didn't slip away to leak intelligence to whoever's behind these killings."

"You're really starting to take that seriously, aren't you?"

"Honestly? I can't make my mind up."

A few minutes later, Baines drew up in the pub car park. It was a little ahead of opening time, but there were a couple of other cars around, and they had called ahead to say they were coming and to check that the pub would be open. The door was opened by a tub of lard with a Hawaiian shirt two sizes too small and a goatee beard. He introduced himself as Ricky Martin, than added, "The other one, that is. No good asking me to do the villa loco," before laughing uproariously.

Neither of them bothered to correct his pronunciation, and they managed polite smiles as they entered. He led them to a table in a corner of the bar.

"What can I get you? You can have what you like, as long as it's legal."

"We're fine," Archer said, forestalling any request Baines might have been inclined to make. He would have welcomed a coffee or something.

"We want to talk about Ebenezer Larkin," Baines said. "Your head barman."

"Poor Raphael, yes. Terrible business. Shocking."

"Shocking," Archer agreed. "So how long had he worked here?"

"Couple of years. Came up from London. Good experience and, to be honest, we were desperate."

"And you were all right with him looking the other way while drug dealing went on in your property?"

He scratched his expanse of chest. "You don't let up, do you? You embarrassed me on more than one occasion, officers busting in here, looking for drugs. There weren't any. Poor Raphael's gone, and you still blacken his name."

"What about the dodgy meetings that went on here?" Baines took up the questioning. "Ryan Sturridge, among others."

"Meetings?" Martin shook his head. "Sure, Ryan and his friends used to drink in here. You make it sound sinister. But what do I know? I try to keep myself at arm's length from this place. If I wasn't a member of staff down, I wouldn't be here helping out today. Meetings," he scoffed. "By all accounts, the nearest thing to a meeting that goes on here is you guys."

Baines stared at him, then glanced at Archer.

"Us guys?" she asked.

"One of your detectives comes in maybe once a week, so I hear. Name of…" He scratched his head.

"Butcher?" Baines offered.

"No, nothing like that. Ashford?"

Baines felt every muscle in his body tense.

"Would that be DI Ashby?" Archer asked, with steel in her tone.

"Sounds like the one. Wendy!" he called. The barmaid Baines and Archer had met yesterday appeared from another corner of the bar, a cloth in her hand.

"That copper Raphael reckoned was always in here, meeting with dubious-looking characters? Name of Ashby, right?"

"Yeah, right. Fancies himself a bit of a ladies' man. Really lame chat-up lines."

That sounded like Steve Ashby.

"Mr Martin here—" Archer began.

"Ricky, please."

"Mr Martin says DI Ashby held meetings in here. Is that right?"

"I wouldn't know. Yeah, he comes in once or twice a week, has a drink or a coffee, meets someone. I don't know you'd call it meetings as such. At busy times, you're too run off your feet to notice what the punters are doing."

"Always the same people?"

"Varied. Not many regulars."

Baines's mouth was dry. "He ever meet with Ryan Sturridge? Ben Loftus?"

"Maybe. I'm really not sure."

They showed them both the picture of Matthew Butcher, pressing them on whether Ashby had ever met him. Wendy studied it for a long time.

"I honestly don't know," she said finally. "He looks familiar, but he's got one of those faces, hasn't he?"

"One of those faces?"

"You know. Nice enough looking fella, but lots of people look like him."

There wasn't much more to be gleaned from the pair of them. Baines was feeling decidedly troubled as they got back in the car.

Archer picked up on his mood. "Still think I'm mad wondering if Ashby's involved?"

He shook his head. "It could be that these networks of his are real, and that the Falcon is one of the places he meets his contacts. There was nothing we could really confront him with, though, and we don't want to tip him off that we're suspicious of him, do we? If he really is part of this, he'll talk to people, start destroying evidence…"

"It's worse than that. If he's in on it, then there's a good chance Gillingham is too, or at least knows about it."

He started the car. "Not necessarily. Cutting an old pal too much slack is a long way from being in cahoots with him over a murder."

"Four murders. My point is, are we prepared to take this to Gillingham?"

"Not with what we've got, I'd have thought. For a start, we've no evidence. And, if we had any, I'd be chary about taking it to him unless I knew for sure he was in the clear." He pulled out of the car park, joining the busy Aylesbury traffic. "It's like I said before. The only person above my pay grade I trust right now is you."

"I suppose we could go over Gillingham's head."

"Yeah, right." His laugh was hollow. "Go to them with what? Ashby will provide a perfectly good reason for meeting lowlifes like Ben Loftus in dodgy pubs, and Gillingham will deny all knowledge of it." A new thought struck him. "But say this is a serious line of enquiry. Say Ashby or Gillingham stole that gun back in their Reading days and now they're involved with serious criminals and using the gun to clean up some mess or other. If we start sticking our noses in where they don't want us to…"

"You think we might be next?"

"You don't?" He thought about Karen. It would be a whole new world of pain for her if she got the dreaded knock on the door with the news that he wouldn't be coming home. To say nothing of the risk that he'd be putting *her* in danger as well as himself.

"Maybe. Perhaps we should just turn the case over to Sheppard and walk away."

He changed gear for a roundabout. "Are you serious?"

"I might be. We're both getting more paranoid by the hour, can't entirely trust anyone, and now we're speculating that those suspicions might get us killed."

He glanced at her. "Have you forgotten why we wanted to stay on the case in the first place? Because we thought, at best, Sheppard would be all about Butcher, and not much interested in the local people who've been dying. Like Brandon Clark."

There was a brief silence, before she said, "Are we really convinced that Brandon was as good a kid as we thought? The best we can come up with is that he was in the wrong place at the wrong time."

He felt his hackles rising. "What's your point?"

"We know Ben Loftus was recruiting for this big new operation. What if Brandon was attracted by it? A new challenge? A change from being good? You know he never liked to be bored."

He was utterly dumbfounded. He'd truly thought this case was finally drawing a line under the personal issues and shared misunderstandings that had marred the early days of their work relationship. That the occasional awkwardness and abrasion that had continued to creep in from time to time had finally been put into perspective by the realisation that, for all that, they shared a mutual trust and had each other's backs. Which was more than could be said for DCI Gillingham and many other senior officers around the place.

Now, with just a few short words, she had him on the back foot again.

"Oh, come on, Dan," she said, as if she could read his mind. "Don't tell me the thought hasn't occurred to you as well."

"It hadn't. Since Brandon gave up the gang, I've often thought about him. It's just so rare to see a kid turn away from the wrong path and... I don't know." He wasn't sure he could even explain it to himself. "That family deserved a little bit of luck. Not..." He shook his head, feeling another of those waves of emotion that had pounded at his defences since Friday evening. Simmering rage, threatening to boil over. "Not that."

"But wishing he'd keep his nose clean," she said patiently, "doesn't mean he did."

He felt a surge of hot fury: fury that should have been directed at Brandon's killer, and which finally had a focus on Lizzie Archer. He dropped down a gear, savagely shoving the gearstick into third, his right foot stamping down on the pedal as he flung the car into the right-hand lane, cutting up a guy in a big Skoda. He wanted to get back to the station and get his boss the hell out of his car as quickly as possible, and he didn't give a damn whether he terrified her in the process.

"Dan!" Her right hand shot out, pressing on the dashboard, bracing herself for a collision. "What are you doing?"

He ignored her, concentrating on squeezing every ounce of speed out of the Mondeo that the traffic would permit. There were two cars ahead of him, too slow for his liking, and he closed the gap between himself and the nearest of them, to encourage him to go faster or get out of his way. A tiny gap opened up on his left and he went for it, triggering a fusillade of angry horn blasts.

"For fuck's sake! Dan, stop. Stop the car."

Heedless, he shot up the inside of a line of cars. He'd always been a confident driver, but he knew he was ignoring a voice in his head that was warning him he was barely in control of the vehicle.

Up ahead, a Vauxhall, probably in the wrong lane for the roundabout coming up, started to dither into his path. He jammed the heel of his hand down on the horn. The Vauxhall stopped coming, and Baines was clear for the roundabout. As he approached it, still accelerating, he glanced to his right. A bus was joining the roundabout, lumbering out of its exit.

It would be too tight. He wouldn't make it. He had to stop.

Instead he floored the accelerator, blood pumping hot through his veins.

He thought Archer might actually have screamed, but the howl of the bus's air brakes and the accompanying blare of its horn drowned her out if she did. He missed the bus by a whisker, crossed the roundabout, then barrelled onwards.

Then, abruptly, he slammed on the brakes, violently swinging the wheel to avoid the figure in the road.

There was a flash of blue and white as he narrowly avoided the young man and somehow managed not to mount the pavement. The car stalled. Archer was hunched in her seat beside him, hands over her face, whether to protect herself from flying glass had he hit something and shattered the windscreen, or whether to keep herself from seeing what was happening, he didn't know.

Shaking, he checked his mirror. No dead youngster lay in the road. There was no sign that the figure had ever been there. He wasn't surprised. The anger had left him now, like air from a punctured balloon.

Tentatively, horrified at himself, he touched Archer's shoulder. She pulled away, still covering her face.

"I'm so sorry," he told her. A car had pulled up behind him and was hooting. A little spark of rage flared again and he got out of the Mondeo, walked back and tapped on the driver's window, which slid down.

Baines held his warrant card an inch or so away from the driver's face. "Touch that horn again and you're nicked," he said. "Interfering with police operations."

When he got back to his car, Archer had slid across to the driving seat, trembling. She cracked the side window.

"Get in," she said stonily. "I'm driving. And not a word out of you until we've finished this journey in one piece."

He let her drive, barely registering her cautious handling of an unfamiliar car. His mind was a jumble. Why had Archer's suggestion – that Brandon might not have gone as straight as he imagined – provoked such an extreme reaction? Why had that reaction manifested itself in such reckless driving? And why had the apparition of teenage Jack chosen that instant to appear?

More to the point, what was happening to him? That brief spell of insanity had felt like being outside his own body, watching his self-destructive progress, powerless to intervene.

He felt embarrassed, ashamed and frightened. The person he most needed to talk to was Karen – assuming she was even talking to him after how he had behaved – but for now he knew he owed Archer an explanation. Physical trauma had taken a serious toll on her life already. He could only imagine her feelings at being trapped in a car with a madman at the wheel.

Archer turned into the car park, selected a space, and babied the Mondeo into it. They got out and she locked the vehicle before holding the keys up and then dropping them pointedly into her handbag.

He turned towards the station entrance.

"No," she said. "We're going out for a coffee."

She led the way to a small café and bakery in the high street that he knew she had developed an affection for. It wasn't too busy, and they were able to find a quiet table in a corner, away from flapping ears. Even now, she wouldn't allow him to utter a word until they had drinks in front of them.

"All right," she said finally. "Give me one good reason why I shouldn't report what you just did to the boss. Come to that, tell me why I shouldn't refer you for a psych evaluation."

A number of responses sprang to his mind: *Do what you have to do. I've got a few problems, but they're none of your business. You're making too much of this.*

He knew she deserved a damn sight more than that. Even so, his reply was preceded by a hollow laugh.

"The answer to the second question's easy. I've sort of promised my partner that I'll see a shrink as soon as this case is over. I probably only need one head doctor at a time."

She blinked. "God, Dan. What the fuck's going on with you?"

And there it was. Clam up – or trust her with all the psychological and emotional crap he'd been struggling with for so long.

He wanted this case solved. He knew that – for some reason – it was vital to him that this case be solved. He couldn't solve it by himself, and he and Archer were well aware that too many people around them seemed to be driven by their own agendas. They'd talked about trust. But how could you trust someone if you didn't really know them?

Working with Lizzie Archer wasn't always a picnic. She wasn't one to pull her punches.

When she'd had to, she'd been blunt in her assessment of his performance. He hadn't always liked it, but when he had thought about her words, he had always wound up accepting them.

And that honesty worked two ways. The first week they'd worked together, she'd told him how she got her scar, even though it was plainly something she hated talking about. She hadn't said why whatever treatment she'd had hadn't had more impact on her disfigurement, nor had he pressed the subject. He didn't feel he needed to know. That wasn't the point.

The point was that, if she didn't understand what was going on in his head right now – at least as well as he was able to understand it – then she would never really know him at all.

Was it finally time to open up to her?

Maybe unloading to her would be cathartic. Maybe it would be a disaster. But he sensed that he, and their partnership, had reached some sort of crossroads.

He took a deep breath. And began to speak.

21

Claire studied Ben covertly. He was staring listlessly at some shitty old film on her TV, although she suspected he wasn't really watching it. He'd taken to changing channels when the news came on, ever since his face had filled the screen as a man police were 'anxious to interview'.

Her watch was in the kitchen, removed before he'd taped her wrists for the first time. It didn't stop her keep glancing at where it should be.

"What's the time?"

He looked at her as if she had asked him to explain some aspect of quantum physics.

"What?"

"I asked what the time is."

"I dunno. I don't wear a watch. I use my phone."

"So look at your phone."

"No way!" He became animated. "I'm not turning that on, so they can track me."

"Who's 'them'?"

He licked his lips, not making eye contact. "You know, the feds… or…"

He shrugged.

"Or who?"

"Just shut, up, yeah? Shut up!" He was out of his chair. "Why do you keep asking all these questions? Are you in with them? Trying to trick me?"

The gun had been on the sofa beside him. It was still there. She offered up a prayer of thanks that he didn't have it in his hand, because he was scaring her.

"I just wondered what the time was," she mumbled.

"Fuck the time," he said vehemently. "This is all so messed up. Why'd you have to come home?"

"I told you. We had an accident," she told him. "Two of my mates got hurt, and Lucy's car was written off. We didn't want to stay after that."

"Yeah, yeah. You said." He finally looked at her. "You were okay, though?"

Had he shown concern for her?

"Yeah. Just a bit shaken. I had to drive everyone home, though. To be honest, when I came in I just wanted my bed, but..." She didn't want to sound accusatory, not after he'd enquired after her health. "Well, it wasn't to be. I'm exhausted now."

"Yeah, well, I'm sorry you got mixed up in this."

Maybe he could be reached, the Ben she'd always quite liked.

"I'd really like to know what sort of a mess you've got yourself into, Ben. I know your mate, Ryan, got shot. Is this to do with that?"

His laugh was harsh. "What do you think?"

"I think it must be. But I can't believe you did it. That you shot any of those people."

"You don't know nothing about me."

"I know you're scared now. That doesn't sound like a stone-cold killer."

Just for an instant, his gaze softened, and she thought he might be going to open up to her. Then his eyes narrowed.

"No?" He returned to the sofa and picked up the gun, levelling it at her. "No? Look. No shake in my hand, see?"

"Please," she whimpered, scared all over again. "Don't point that thing at me."

"No? Why not? You think it might go off?"

He strode across to her and pressed the weapon to her temple. "Think it might go off now?"

How had she ever kidded herself that she might wrest some control of this situation from him? That she could reach some decent part of him? The blood in her veins felt like ice and she abruptly feared for her bladder control. She didn't want to die. The thought that her life might end here, like this, made tears flow.

"Please," she sobbed. "Please."

"Please what?"

"Please take the gun away."

There was silence for three beats. Then, "Okay," he said lightly, and the touch of the cold metal was gone.

He turned away and she took a cautious peek at him making his way back to his sofa. There was a swagger to his walk. She'd thought he was little more than a frightened little boy. Suddenly he was a tough guy with a gun, and she realised that she'd provoked that attitude. If he developed a taste for it, she'd be in even worse trouble than she was already.

A big part of her day job was communication and negotiation, and she was good at it. One of the golden rules was to keep the conversation on an adult-to-adult basis and never give the other person reason to feel they were being talked down to. Dealing with her younger cousin, she'd allowed herself to forget that rule.

She knew she'd better not forget again. Her life could depend upon it.

* * *

Archer returned to the office to be immediately accosted by Joan Collins, who had news for her. But she fended Collins off, insisting she had to go to the loo first.

It was just an excuse to think for five minutes.

She'd worked with Baines for a couple of years now, and today she had appreciated how little she really knew about him. He never talked much about his wife's murder, nor his missing son. She'd accepted that he was entitled to his privacy on such a horrific subject, although she supposed she'd always wondered how such a thing could fail to mess you up.

Well, Baines was messed up all right. She was amazed he even functioned, much less did the good job that he did. He'd possibly laid more on her today than she'd necessarily wanted to hear. She'd always privately assumed that Jack Baines must be dead, his remains concealed somewhere, just waiting to be stumbled upon.

She'd also assumed that the rational part of Baines must think that too, deep down, even though she supposed there must be a part of him that would always hope that his son was somehow alive.

But these dreams – and more to the point, these waking visions he described... For the first time, she wondered how close to the edge he really was, and how long he had been teetering there.

He'd told her about his new partner, too. His dead wife's identical twin. She didn't want to judge him, but it didn't sound healthy. From the sound of it, neither Baines's family, nor Karen's, were enamoured of it, either.

He'd already seen a psychic, which Archer found amazing when he'd eschewed any sort of proper counselling. It seemed that the experiment hadn't gone so well. Now, hideously overdue in her view, he was talking about finding some help – except he was still putting it off, claiming that he wanted to see the current case through first.

It wasn't so hard to see now why Brandon Clark's murder had so affected him. A kid he'd come to care for, whose intelligence he admired, and whom he'd seen turn away from a path that would have only led him into darkness. A kid with no father on the scene. It was easy enough to imagine Baines having paternalistic feelings for the boy, his murder being like losing a son all over again.

This analysis she had kept to herself. She knew it was probably amateur psychology of the worst kind. It was better left to the professionals to make that sort of assessment. The real question for her had been what she was supposed to do with the information he'd dumped on her, and how she feared it was affecting his judgement and performance.

He'd said it was only Jack appearing in the road in front of him that had halted his crazy rampage in the car. What was she to make of that? And could she simply let it go?

He'd promised to get help once the current case was over, but she decided she wasn't prepared to let the situation continue.

"I'm sorry, Dan," she'd said in the café, "but that's just not good enough. Not after what I've just seen. I've turned a blind eye to the times you've not seemed all there, but now you're getting downright dangerous."

"It won't happen again."

"Damn right. Because there's only two ways this can go now."

He'd started to protest, but she'd added, "Not for my sake. For yours."

She'd laid it out for him. Either she engaged the force's occupational health team immediately to start seeking whatever support he needed, or she got him signed off on sick leave immediately.

"It's your call," she said. Her voice softened. "Look, I'm here for you, whatever you need. But what you need is help, Dan. You said yourself that you can see that. So go for the first option," she urged. "As your line manager, I can keep this between you, me and the health services. I really don't want to have to involve Gillingham."

"But... Gillingham's one of our possible suspects."

"Exactly. But he's still my boss."

"Karen thinks I probably need a grief counsellor. I think that's ridiculous after all this time."

"I really don't know if it is or it isn't, Dan. I'm not the help you need. What I do know is that you don't seem to have come close to dealing with your losses. That's got to eat away at anyone. I don't think these things get better with the passage of time, not untreated. It's a wonder you're as sane as you are." She knew it was cruel, but it was also no time to pull her punches. "Those are your choices. If you see occupational health as soon as I can get you in, then I'll keep you on the case. And I'll look out for you."

She'd tried to read the look on his face and utterly failed. Surrender? Fury? A sense of betrayal?

He'd finally drawn a ragged sigh. "I suppose I don't really have a choice, do I?"

So now she had one more thing to deal with – all of which was a distraction from an already difficult case. She returned to her desk and, after skimming her email box, beckoned Collins over.

"There you go." The DC laid a photograph in front of her. The original picture of the man they were calling Matthew Butcher had been altered; a face framed by fair hair and nondescript spectacles now stared out at them.

"I'd really like to circulate this," Archer said. "It looks quite a bit different to the other version. But it goes directly against the NCA's wishes. I'll get kicked from here into next year if I ignore that."

"Would you, though?" Baines mused. "This man isn't, strictly speaking, Matthew Butcher. He doesn't look so much like him. So, what if we put it out as someone we're interested in in connection with the killings? We want to hear from someone who recognises him, that sort of thing."

"I don't know." She genuinely didn't. She wanted to stop this killer, but she didn't want to screw up a major investigation, either. "It's above my pay grade."

"Ask the boss?"

He said it gently enough, but she knew pushing when she felt it. It should have irritated her, but somehow it didn't.

"Maybe. Anything else, Joan?"

A slim manila folder was placed in front of her. "That other info you wanted. Before you ask where it came from, though – well, don't ask."

Archer half opened the folder, peeked inside, saw a picture of Catherine Sheppard and closed it again.

"I'll look at this in a mo. Thanks, Joan. Briefing at four, if you'd spread the word."

Baines hovered by her desk after Collins had departed.

"I wanted to thank you," he said. "You know – for listening. For trying to help."

She smiled. "It's what I'm here for. Meanwhile, if you don't pull any more stunts like you did today, we'll say no more about what happened. Fair enough?"

He gave her a weak smile. "Fair enough. Thanks, Lizzie. And I truly am sorry."

"Let's forget it. By the way, I actually have worse driving than that."

"Really?"

"Oh, yeah. Not since my brother was a learner, though, twenty-odd years ago."

22

Archer had taken the material on Catherine Sheppard, gathered by Collins and Ibrahim Iqbal, into the briefing room to examine.

The folder contained Sheppard's CV, but not her personnel file. Although Archer had made it clear to Collins that she didn't expect them to hack into that, she was oddly disappointed that they hadn't. But then she didn't know Ibrahim so well. Maybe he was a stickler for the rules.

The woman was forty-five years old – a little older than Archer had imagined – with an unsurprising career history: the Met, fast-track promotion, the Serious and Organised Crime Agency, morphing into the National Crime Agency. A career that might have taken her higher by now, but there could be a million and one reasons for its apparent stalling.

She'd been married once. Not any more, by the look of it, and Archer was left wondering what had happened. It was hard to imagine Catherine Sheppard in a relationship. Harder still to imagine anyone being in one with her. But maybe she had a softer side. Maybe she'd show it, if that pub meal ever came to pass.

If he'd had qualms about accessing Sheppard's personnel file, Ibrahim still appeared to have dug deep. There was enough material to suggest that an undercover cop had indeed disappeared on her watch. He had even found a name: DS Will Streatham. A photograph, too. He had dark, wavy hair, a high, domelike forehead, a mouth frozen in the act of sneering, and a nose that looked as if it had been broken at least once.

Archer took out her mobile, called Collins at her desk, and asked her and Ibrahim to join her. When they arrived, she thanked them for their efforts so far – and then got to the point.

"I'm just curious," she said. "This Streatham character. How did you come by his name?"

Sheppard had insisted on keeping the dead man's name to herself, so how had these two dug it up so effortlessly?

"It wasn't that difficult," Ibrahim Iqbal said. He was tall and slim with sharp features, a prominent nose, and soulful chocolate-brown eyes behind his glasses. "It's pretty obvious that the guy disappeared on a dark operation that went horribly wrong, and that it's something the NCA would rather stayed buried. But a couple of documents suggesting that an undercover officer was missing found their way onto a shared drive, and the agency were trying to find out what had happened to him. DCI Sheppard's name is mentioned once, in with a load of innocuous stuff."

"Yes, I saw that. You hacked into a shared drive to get it?"

"I wouldn't say *hacked*," the IT man said with a smile. "I'd say I… you know, shared in it."

"So how much information was there about the operation itself? I don't see anything here."

"No, I didn't print that off, but I found a reference to an Operation Stairway."

"Stairway?"

"Don't proactive cases sometimes get names that are supposed to be meaningful, guv?" Collins volunteered.

"Sometimes," Archer agreed. Names of operations were chosen from an approved list decided in advance, a system dating back to the 1980s. "More often, as you know, the names are neutral and unrelated to the case. But we did have an anti-knife crime initiative at the Met called Operation Blunt, and there was an Operation Payback, to do with seizing the assets of organised criminals."

"Stairway," Ibrahim mused. "Maybe something to do with climbing?"

She saw it then. Sheppard had told her that their aim had been to get into the Connolly hierarchy at a relatively low level and find a thread that led all the way to the top.

It wasn't a subject she could share with the team, so she moved on. "So where does this name come from? This Will Streatham?"

"It could be something or nothing," Ibrahim admitted. "I don't even know if it matters. But I managed to get into the staff lists around that period. Of course, a few come and go, and it's clear they've transferred or retired. This guy just vanishes from the list. Now you see him, now you don't. I can dig deeper, but I think my methods might be frowned on."

"No," she said. "I don't want you guys getting into trouble. I'll come back if I think I need any more." She looked again at the picture. "Where did you get this?"

"An internal newsletter a few years before he dropped off the radar. Just newcomers to the then Senior and Organised Crime Agency. Names and pictures."

"And he never resurfaced?"

"No, guv," Collins said. "I mean, we're just putting two and two together, really, but…"

"No, that's helpful. This is great work, thanks. That'll do for now."

After they departed, she pondered for a few minutes, then reluctantly shelved her thinking on these new revelations. She turned on the briefing room computer, looked up a number, and made a call she knew she'd been putting off, then called Baines and asked him to drop in. He arrived a minute or two later, a mug of coffee in his hand.

"I've got you a Wednesday appointment with occupational health," she said. "I had to push for it, and they don't like short-notice cancellations, apparently. So, come what may, you're going."

She brought him up to date on what Collins and Ibrahim had dug up.

"Operation Stairway," he said, as if he was trying the name on for size. "Do you think it's still current?"

"I do," she said, "and I think Butcher was working on it. Somehow he got rumbled by someone who recognised him as a cop and a decision was made to take him out. The only question is this: was it a local decision, or handed down from the top of the food chain? Either way, Ryan Sturridge looks like a loose end to me. One that needed tidying up."

"But..." Baines pulled a face. "These undercover guys are supposed to be good. How did he give himself away?"

"Maybe he didn't. I think 'recognised as a cop' is the point."

"You mean..." He shook his head as if to clear it. "Christ. You really do think it's someone here in the Vale? Someone who'd seen him before?"

"Or someone elsewhere in Thames Valley, I suppose, but closer to home seems more likely. Think about it."

"I am. And I don't like it. I know I've accepted we can't rule out Gillingham or Ashby, but that's a long way from taking them seriously as suspects. Now you're suggesting that one of them might have been taking backhanders from the Connollys or whoever?"

"Put it this way: it would be useful for them to have eyes and ears on the local force, wouldn't it? They'd be a step ahead of our investigations. I'm betting their man saw Butcher going into the meeting and recognised him."

"But he'd have recognised them too."

"Not if he didn't see them," she said. "What if their role was simply to sit in a corner of the bar while the meeting was happening? We know the place had been raided before. This way, they've got someone who can tip them off if there's a problem, but also stall the police. We also know Ashby frequented the Falcon. If it's him, he gives them some crap about meeting a contact and gets under their feet. But if Butcher had seen and recognised them, he'd have reported back long before he was killed."

She felt her mouth twisting into a smile. "The irony with that scenario is that Butcher wouldn't have wanted the local plods poking their noses in either. It could have blown the whole NCA operation."

He was looking grim. "So you're thinking Ashby or Gillingham did the actual shooting?"

Possibilities were unfolding almost as fast as they could articulate them.

"Gillingham couldn't have done the Friday night shootings – we know he was in the station at the time. We don't know where he was on Saturday, though."

"Using a gun that disappeared from the same station where Gillingham and Ashby first met?"

"It could even be the two of them in it together. I know how utterly mad that sounds."

He was pacing. "I wish it did. So are we thinking that Ben Loftus *isn't* the killer?"

"It could still easily be Ben. We still don't have all the puzzle pieces, do we? But hold on." Something else was troubling her. "Say our bent copper recognised Butcher. They thought he knew too much, so they killed him. But why would they see the need to embark on the rest of this killing spree? Why Ryan? And we keep coming back to Brandon. Unlucky bystander, or in it up to his neck? Sorry, Dan, but we have to consider that."

"Fair enough."

She thought he was simply not arguing, rather than taking her suggestion seriously.

"But where does that leave us? Damned if I know."

"Nor me." She was getting a headache again. "This is pretty toxic, isn't it?"

"If we really suspect Gillingham and Ashby, shouldn't we say something?"

"Based on what, Dan? We don't even have circumstantial evidence. Just a feeling and the fact that they worked at Reading. No, we've got to carry on with business as usual for now."

"But keep our eyes and ears open?"

"Yes. Meanwhile, I think I'm going to do three things. One, ask Gillingham about releasing that mock-up and watch his reaction."

He looked at her speculatively. "Why are we still so interested in that? You said Sheppard told you he'd been chosen because he had no one to miss him, nor for him to worry about when he was undercover."

"I don't believe it, Dan. Nobody has *no one*. There must be someone out there wondering why they can't contact him. Someone who can tell us who he really was. Because I really want to know."

"Fair enough. You said there were three things?"

"Two: run the briefing as normal, with him and Ashby present, and keep an eye on them. I told you the boss looked shifty about something before, and Ashby is, well..."

"... is Ashby. Quite. And the third?"

"Sheppard made a throwaway suggestion of a cosy get-to-know-you meal. I'm going to take her up on it, and press her to do it tonight."

"What if she's washing her hair or something?"

"Then I'll make her change her mind."

23

Cameron Connolly glanced at the big man in the driving seat. Willie McMurdo handled the Mercedes well, he couldn't deny that. The calm efficiency with which those plate-sized hands made adjustments to the wheel seemed to give the lie to his 'Mad Willie' nickname. But then, no one had cut him up yet.

Cameron had seen this happen on a couple of occasions. If Willie hadn't already been built like the Incredible Hulk, and if his skin had turned green, it would have been just like the comic book character's transformation when he became angry. As it was, the man's face would turn purple beneath his mop of ginger hair, the veins in his neck would stand out, and those huge paws would grasp the wheel so tightly that his knuckles turned bone-white as he hurled incoherent curses at the offender.

And pursued them.

One fool had actually stopped and got out, looking belligerent and asking what the problem was. Willie had picked him up like a toy and flung him across the bonnet of his own car. He would have gone after him, fists and boots flying, had he not had four passengers, including Cameron, to restrain him. Even then, they had barely managed it, and it had taken all of Cameron's soothing words to calm him down. In the end, Mad Willie had settled for kicking several dents in the guy's car.

It wasn't that Willie McMurdo was out-and-out stupid – far from it. But he was a fry or two short of a Happy Meal, and the volume control on his temper didn't work. Once you turned on the rage, it was at full blast, with no mute button.

And this was the man his father had insisted he bring with him into the volatile situation in Aylesbury. He might as well have given him a jerry can of petrol and a box of matches and sent him to put out a fire.

One thing Willie was good at, if needed, was enforcing. He was good at scaring people, even better at hurting them, and he seemed to enjoy both. If he was multi-tasking, so much the better.

Not for the first time on this journey, Cameron sent up a silent prayer that whatever chaotic genie his brother Desmond had managed to unleash could be coaxed back into the bottle without making matters worse.

Desmond. This whole sorry story was down to their father's sentimental notion that being a Connolly brought with it an entitlement to a senior role in the family business. Giving Des his head in any context was always going to carry a degree of risk. Giving him virtually a free hand in setting up a new venture, in territory none of them knew much about... well, that was just begging for aggravation.

Cameron wished passionately that it could be as simple as writing off the whole sorry episode: withdraw from the Vale and be done with it. But that sort of thing simply wasn't done. If word got out that the Connollys had slunk away from a territory, tails between their legs, some people would seize on it as a sign of weakness. You might as well cut yourself and then go swimming with sharks.

The satnav told Willie to turn right, and Cameron clocked the battered sign for the airfield. Not so long ago, he'd not had the remotest idea that the place even existed, but he'd done his homework.

The old airfield occupied a space between villages, former farmland that had been requisitioned by the government early in World War Two. The actual airfield had been built and occupied by the spring of 1942, with runways, service roads and buildings. The site was originally designated for bomber training, but was subsequently handed over to the United States Air Force, whose squadrons mostly comprised Liberators and Flying Fortresses.

Much of the old airfield was still intact, with its service roads and several of the buildings on one side of the site now supporting industrial units. The opposite side of the site had been returned to farming, with sheep roaming among abandoned buildings.

Desmond had taken on a hangar-like building at the far end of the industrial estate, set apart from the other units. It had been rented by a shell company, registered overseas and with a paper trail that would tie the most talented investigator up in more knots than a Harry Houdini escape trick. Des had wasted no time erecting a tall wire fence around the perimeter, and there was a large, semi-educated primate by the name of Brian Dale stopping people at the gate and enquiring as to their business. At least, that was one way of interpreting the unintelligible sounds coming out of his mouth.

Dale was one of a small team who had come here with Des to get things established. Des had demanded a head of security, and this was what he had got. The head of security's face split into a huge orang-utan grin when he saw Mad Willie behind the wheel, and he all but saluted Cameron. He might have said that Mr Desmond was expecting them but, in all honesty, he might have been asking if they could spare him a banana. Either way, Willie drove through and parked by the building entrance.

"Wait in the car for a bit, Willie," Cameron said.

Willie's father had come down from Glasgow to join Murray Connolly back in the day and had been fiercely loyal, right up until his disappearance during a London turf war – a war that the Connollys had won, but not without casualties. So long as the red mist didn't descend, Willie was equally loyal, and what a Connolly said generally went.

"Right you be, Mr Cameron," Willie said. "Can I put some music on?"

"Sure. Not too loud, though."

Mad Willie was a heavy metal fan and was happiest when the volume was rocking the car and rattling nearby windows. Cameron waited whilst he selected a Megadeth album and then made 'turning down' gestures until he was happy that the noise pollution guys back in Hampstead wouldn't be receiving complaints. Then he walked into the huge building.

It was mostly empty, with just a couple of packing cases, some tables and chairs. Cameron noted with approval that the walls had been soundproofed, which he knew could have multiple benefits in their line of work.

Desmond sat at one of the tables, possibly trying to look like the young Al Pacino in *The Godfather*, but certainly not pulling it off. He was well-built and not bad-looking, although his mouth always looked to be on the verge of whingeing.

"I don't see what Dad had to send you up here for," he began, without rising or offering any sort of greeting. "Everything's under control here."

Cameron raised an eyebrow. "Is that right? What's your definition of out of control, then? An exchange of nuclear missiles?"

"Don't talk stupid."

"Stupid?" Cameron made a show of scratching his head. "Oh, so it's me that's stupid? Let me see now… Dad shows faith in you and – against my and Fraser's better judgement – invests in an operation for you to get up and running here, based on what some tinpot loser told you about the area when you were in jail. That would be after you got caught on some cheap drug deal, right?" He was ticking points off on his fingers. "So naturally you use the same tinpot loser and his chums to recruit a workforce, without running the idea past anyone. Now we've got the first big transaction going down on Wednesday – at no little expense – and all of a sudden the bodies are piling up."

He yanked a chair out from the table and sat down opposite his brother. "Still want to talk about stupid?"

"It's not my fault."

"It never is. Getting sent to prison wasn't your fault. So how come we've now got someone rampaging across your patch, shooting people? Either you sanctioned it, or you've lost control."

Desmond jumped to his feet. "You can't talk to me like that, just because you're Dad's blue-eyed boy."

"He doesn't do favourites, Des, if that's what you mean, That's probably why you're not at the bottom of the Thames wearing a pair of concrete wellies." He waved a dismissive hand. "We can argue about favourites, stupidity and control some other time. We need to sort this bloody mess out, assuming it's not too late. So you need to start by telling me exactly what happened, and how we've come to this."

"I don't need to tell you anything," Desmond pouted.

Cameron sighed. "You do, actually. Dad sent me up here to resolve your little difficulty, and he gave me Mad Willie to help me do it. Don't piss me off, or I'll have to bring Willie in to speed things along. That will give him conflicted loyalties and upset him. And you know how he is when he gets upset."

His brother slumped back down in his chair. "None of this is my fault. Honest, Cam."

Cameron folded his arms. "I'm listening."

Desmond picked at a hangnail. "What you said happened… it's not quite right."

24

Baines came out of the four o'clock briefing, his head spinning. He'd found it hard not to keep looking at Ashby and Gillingham for their reactions to what was being reported. At one point, he'd glanced Ashby's way and found the DI staring at him intensely.

For what it was worth, Gillingham had agreed in a heartbeat to the release of Butcher's doctored photograph, with no obvious concern about hacking off Sheppard or worries about the possible consequences.

The briefing had broken up with Baines no wiser about anything than when he'd gone in. Ashby had followed him out and asked him if he was feeling okay.

"Fine," he'd lied.

Ashby had patted his shoulder. "I know I'm a good-looking guy, and it's none of my business if you're batting for the other side. But you might make it a bit less obvious that you fancy me." And he'd sauntered off, leaving Baines floundering for a suitable riposte.

Plus he now had a visit to some occupational health shrink lined up, something he knew was necessary but was still dreading.

At least Karen would be pleased.

For well over a decade he'd thought he could manage well enough without someone looking inside his head, and it had taken a lot to finally accept that he couldn't do it any more.

But what if his future lay in a cocktail of meds that would reduce him to a zombie-like state?

What if the treatment 'cured' him, so that he never saw Jack again? He still didn't know if that was what he wanted.

Either way, he couldn't carry on like this. He was in danger of damaging every important relationship he had: with Karen at home, and with Lizzie Archer at work in particular.

He knew something about this case was magnifying his problems, and he guessed why. What Karen had implied the other night had been dead right: his dreams, and subsequent sightings, of Jack had roughly coincided with difficult times for him, both personally and professionally, culminating in Brandon Clark's death. It had made a pleasant change to see someone trying to rise above a shitty start in life and fulfil their potential. Now whatever future had awaited Brandon had been erased.

That was why he'd been so incensed at Archer's suggestion that Brandon may have returned to the dark side. It was as if she'd taken a red pen to the script of a feel-good movie, or the lyrics of an upbeat song, and turned it into something black and miserable.

But, since he'd calmed down, he'd found it hard to shake off a sinking feeling that she might have been right after all. Or, at least, he couldn't just close his ears and eyes to the possibility.

Archer was making a call, so he went out to the car park and called Karen. He told her she was right, and he was finally going to see someone.

"Oh, that's great, Dan. At least we'll be doing something. What changed your mind?"

He'd told her then how he'd lost control behind the wheel, how Archer had made him talk to her about what had been going on in his mind, and how he finally had an appointment to see someone.

Her response wasn't quite what he'd expected.

"Very nice," she said in a tone he knew spelled trouble. "You won't do it for me, but one cosy chat with her and you roll over."

"I had no choice. She'd have suspended me, or worse."

"And, of course, your darling job comes first too, right?"

He couldn't believe she was being like this. "I thought this was what you wanted."

"You don't get it, do you? All these years I've been telling you to see someone. When Lou died, you had to play it tough. No compassionate leave for you. Counselling was for wimps."

"I wanted to catch the Invisible Man. You wanted me to."

"But even when that case was well and truly cold, you carried on throwing yourself into your work. Even when you started seeing these fucked-up ghosts. I begged you to get help, but you were too proud – or too fucking stupid. And then, when you finally, *finally* admit you have a problem, you still put off doing anything about it."

He didn't see what she was so angry about. "But I'm doing it now. Well, on Wednesday."

"Yes. Because *she* told you to."

Suddenly, he thought he saw what was going on. "Oh, come on, Karen. I thought you weren't jealous of Lizzie."

"I'm not."

"I've said before. She's not even my type."

"No. Because we know what your type is, don't we? Louise. So much so that you had to have another one exactly like her."

And there it was. The thing they'd both been denying.

"Don't do this," he pleaded. But she had hung up.

Dreading going home, he went in search of Archer.

"Good timing. I've got a date with my new best mate, DCI Sheppard, after work," she said.

He made all the right noises, urging her to pump the NCA officer for every scrap of information she could squeeze out of her.

"Ply her with wine," he proposed. "That might loosen her tongue."

"Oh, I don't know." She waggled her hand. "We'll both be driving, and I'd guess she's a stickler for the rules. I also suspect she could drink a shipload of sailors under the table if the occasion arose."

"Anyhow," he said, cutting the banter short, "I need to pop out for a while."

"Oh?"

"Yeah." He shrugged. "To be honest, it's what you said about Brandon. I'd like to just have another chat with his mum. See if I think there's anything in it."

He saw the quizzical look in her eye. "Do you think that's such a great idea?"

He tried not to bridle. "Why not? I know the family."

She dropped her voice to barely a whisper. "Dan, we've just had a conversation about whether, not to mince words, you might be losing it. Might not be the best time to ask a grieving mother if her son was mixed up in organised crime…"

"Yes, that was precisely how I was going to put it," he said without rancour.

"So how? Maybe I should come with you."

"You're the boss, but I do have a connection with the family. I was going to just ask how they were holding up, and sort of casually ask if anything has occurred to them that they didn't think of before."

She looked undecided. Checked her watch. Then gave a quick nod.

"All right. It probably is a good idea. Just be careful, okay?"

"Discretion is my middle name."

"Oh, bugger off, before I regret it."

He sketched a mock bow, then went back to his desk to sweep up his phone, car keys and his jacket from the back of his chair. In his car, with the engine running, he switched on the sound system and put on *Smile* by Brian Wilson. His dad, who had always been a big Beach Boys fan, had made him listen to the album, maybe ten years ago, and Baines had ordered it online the very next day. It was one of the collections he always had in the car and kept coming back to. And its energy was something he seriously needed today.

Julie Clark was at home, and the smell of baking assailed Baines's nostrils when she opened the door. Brandon's mother wore a flour-coated pink and white striped apron, which she kept wiping her hands on as he followed her into the kitchen. Marcus, sitting at the small kitchen table and playing a noisy game on a tablet, raised a hand and got back to whatever he was killing.

"I decided to bake us a cake," she said. "Thought we needed a treat." She reached for the kettle. "You'll have some tea." It was a statement.

She filled the kettle and switched it on, opened a cupboard to get mugs out, then frowned, stared at the work surface, and picked up a cloth.

The surface looked spotless to Baines. In fact, the whole kitchen, which – like the rest of the house – was always clean and tidy, seemed to have been cleaned to within an inch of its life. That didn't stop her scrubbing away at a blemish only she could see.

Apparently satisfied, she got down the mugs and then took the lid off the teapot.

Baines would have simply shoved a teabag in each mug and poured on hot water, but he knew Julie preferred to make tea the traditional way: the way his mother always had.

To anyone who didn't know her, she would have come across as an ordinary woman who was maybe slightly excessively house-proud. Baines knew differently; that she was barely holding herself together. It took one to know one.

"So," she said a few minutes later, leaning against the worktop and eyeing him over the rim of her mug. "I don't suppose this is a social call."

"Not this time, no."

"So have you come to say you've caught the people who hurt Brandon?"

"Not yet, I'm afraid."

"Have you come to say we can set a date for the funeral?" Her tone was matter-of-fact, yet seemed to contain a thousand reproaches and accusations.

"Sorry," he said.

She blew on her mug and took a cautious sip. "So how can we help you?"

"Well," he began, suddenly feeling awkward, "we haven't talked for a couple of days and I wondered if anything had occurred to you, or to Marcus for that matter, that you didn't think of earlier."

She smiled. "Of course it has. I've just been keeping it to myself, waiting for you to pop round on the off-chance."

He found himself smiling back. "You're taking the mickey, right?"

"Maybe a bit. You think I haven't been thinking about it constantly since Friday?" She shook her head. "I can't think of anyone who'd have done this, apart from Ryan Sturridge. He was the only one who ever threatened Brandon, but now he's dead too, so I'm guessing it wasn't him." Tears rolled down her face and she swiped at them with a sleeve. "I just want my boy back, so we can lay him to rest. And I want the animals who did this punished. It's not asking a lot, is it?"

It seemed a lot right now. Even though he and Archer thought they were close to piecing together what had happened, there was still so much they didn't know or understand.

"You said he was a bit quiet, when we spoke before. He'd said he was just tired. Are you sure he hadn't got himself mixed up in anything?"

"Like what?" He noted an edge of hostility in her tone.

"Had he heard anything from Aaron Briggs lately?"

"Aaron?"

"Or anyone from the old gang?"

"Can you not just spit it out, if you think he was up to something? I know he's not always been a saint, but if he'd got into some sort of trouble, don't you think I'd tell you?" She put her mug down and was trembling. "You know something. What do you know?"

He hesitated. "I can't say too much. But it's possible someone was planning something and getting a crew together. Maybe they contacted Brandon."

"But how would they contact him? I mean, you've got his phone and computer. Surely there would have been a call, an email. Something."

"Maybe they called him on his other mobile."

It was Marcus who had spoken. Baines and Julie both looked at him.

"But," Julie said, "sweetheart, Brandon only had one mobile. You know that. The smartphone the police have got."

"And his pay-as-you-go," the boy said. "The secret one."

"But," she said again, "they searched his room."

"It's not in his room," Marcus said. "But I know where it is."

Exchanging glances, they followed him upstairs and into the bathroom. He pointed to the toilet cistern. "Under the lid. It's too heavy for me."

Baines took out a pair of latex gloves, slipped them on, and lifted the porcelain lid. The phone, a standard Nokia, was in a clear plastic bag, taped to the inside.

"I walked in once when he was putting it in there," Marcus explained.

Julie bent down and took him by the shoulders. "Why didn't you say before?"

He looked puzzled. "You never asked. Besides, Brandon told me not to. Said it was a secret."

She straightened up, her eyes wide. "I don't understand. Why would he have a secret phone? What was he doing?" She closed the distance to Baines, getting in his face. "What was this stuff you think he was approached about?"

"We don't know for sure he was."

"But it was bad, wasn't it?" She wrung her hands. "That stuff with the gun before was bad enough, but this... this is far worse, isn't it?" she whispered. "People are dying."

"We need to see what we can get off this phone," Baines said. "If anything. Until then, it's just speculation. My money's still on him being an innocent bystander. Who knows what this phone is all about?"

"I've got such a bad feeling. This is just a nightmare. Just when I thought it couldn't get worse..."

Marcus reached out and took his mother's hand. "It's okay, Mum. I'll look after you."

* * *

Claire was bored, hungry and tired, and getting fed up with being scared of what Ben might do next. He had dozed off in front of the TV, and some dire American sitcom, complete with braying canned laughter, was now blaring out, doing her head in.

She played back in her mind the call she'd made to her mum while Ben trained his gun on her, reinforcing his warning to say what he'd told her to say – no more and no less. If only she'd had more warning. There must have been something she could have inserted into the conversation that her mum would have picked up on, alerting her that not all was well.

But what, exactly? In books and films, it always seemed so easy. An endearment never used, a reference to a family pet by the wrong name. A subtle emphasis on a syllable. Yet even now, though it was too late, she still couldn't think of anything she might have said.

Even if she had succeeded in alerting her mother that something was wrong, what might that have accomplished? She wasn't sure what was the greater recipe for disaster – her mum turning up on the doorstep, or the police in body armour, waving guns of their own. The first scenario might get her mother killed, whilst what would happen in the second was anyone's guess. The word 'crossfire' sprang to her mind. History was littered with rescue missions ending in dead hostages. It could be a bloodbath.

Meanwhile, when he was awake, Ben was getting jumpier and jumpier. Every so often his right foot would beat a tattoo, as if his leg muscles were spasming. He had a tic in his left eye. And twice, when he'd gone to the toilet, she was sure she'd heard him vomiting.

His responses were entirely unpredictable when she tried to speak to him, too. Sometimes his tone was soft and kindly, and he was all apologies for mixing her up in whatever mess he was in. At other times, his rage was barely held in check, as if this was all somehow her fault. Those were the times he would reach for the gun. Sometimes he'd point it at her.

Overwhelmingly, she had the feeling that time was somehow running out. Things wouldn't stay like this indefinitely. Either Ben would run for it, whatever he was hiding from, or the dangerous side of him would entirely overwhelm his gentler side. If he went off the edge, she didn't think her life would be worth much, however much he might regret pulling the trigger once he'd calmed down. She still didn't know if he'd used the gun before. If he had, that must make each subsequent shooting that little bit easier.

She looked again at the gun on the sofa beside him. Maybe she could get to it, even with her feet and hands bound, without disturbing him. She imagined him, jerked awake by a sudden noise, grabbing the weapon in a panic, training it on the first thing that moved – her – his finger already tightening on the trigger. Too late for him to be sorry, once half her brains were on the ceiling and the rest on the carpet.

Yet she had to do something.

They'd be eating later. He'd untape her feet, take her into the kitchen, tape them again, and then fix up something from the dwindling contents of her fridge and food cupboard. Beans on toast, he'd said.

She allowed her mind's eye to roam the kitchen: to see Ben standing at the cooker hob, stirring the beans. What else could she use? She realised the room was full of weapons. Behind where she always sat was her knife block, a range of quality German knives tantalisingly close. She wasn't necessarily thinking of using one on Ben – she was sure she lacked the courage or the necessary ruthless streak – but what if she could somehow conceal a small one about her person? Cut through her bonds, at least those on her feet, next time he was asleep?

Then what? She had turned the key in the front door when she'd got indoors – which seemed a lifetime ago now – and wasn't aware that he'd removed it. If she could free her feet, if not her hands, could she get to the door, turn the key without waking him, and get outside?

And if so, then what? Run to her next door neighbours? Stand in the street and yell? She needed a solution that wouldn't end with her cousin appearing on the doorstep and shooting her.

She needed to work on the plan.

And, before she could implement it – whatever the plan turned out to be – she needed that knife.

* * *

"My God!" Archer stared in disbelief at the phone in the transparent evidence bag that Baines had brought from the Clark house. "In a toilet cistern? That's such a cliché." She shrugged.

"He probably got the idea off TV. You'd have thought our earlier searches would have turned that up."

"In all fairness," he said, "no one was seeing Brandon as anything more than a victim. There was no reason to take the whole house apart."

"Whatever." She wasn't feeling particularly charitable. She turned to Collins and Bell. "Joan – get hold of Phil Gordon and see whether he wants the phone, or whether he wants it sent elsewhere. Meanwhile, Jason, why don't you see if you can get into it? No need to take it out of the bag. Just push the buttons through the plastic. I don't suppose you'll get far, but you never know."

"Are you sure, Lizzie?" Baines queried. "Maybe we should leave it to the scientists and techies."

"I don't want to wait. I'm seeing Sheppard shortly, and if there's anything I ought to know, I'd like it up my sleeve when I meet her." She looked at Bell. "I don't suppose this is something you can get into with a paper clip?"

He held his hand out. "No, but I'll give it a go."

She handed the phone over and headed for the ladies', where she washed her face, touched up her make-up and made sure her hair was in place, concealing her scar. She wished she could hide the lop-sided sag of her lips, but nerve damage was something cosmetics and a comb couldn't heal.

She remembered Sheppard staring at her. She wouldn't let it intimidate her. She was going to be on top of her game tonight.

She returned to her desk, checked her emails for anything new and significant, then shot a glance at her watch. She had to go.

She was just checking that she had everything she needed when Jason Bell appeared by her desk. His face was pink, but his shining eyes told her that excitement, not self-consciousness, was the cause.

"I broke into Brandon's secret phone," he said. "Piece of cake. He'd used his birthday as his PIN."

"Maybe he thought no one was going to find it anyway. Anything useful? You look pretty pleased with yourself."

His grin would have put the Cheshire Cat to shame.

25

Back in the sixteenth century, the Broad Leys pub and restaurant had been a coaching inn that went by the name of the New Inn. In those days, its site had been part of a toll road in the parish of Walton. Five centuries on, Walton had been swallowed up into Aylesbury and the building had been renovated to provide a more contemporary space without sacrificing too much of its atmosphere. It might be next door to her workplace, but Archer was a virtual stranger to the pub, having only been inside a couple of times since her arrival in the Vale. But she knew the food was good, and it was a handy place to grab a bite to eat.

Despite its being on the doorstep, Archer had still managed to be late. She stepped into a busy restaurant with various groups of diners chatting, studying menus or, as was increasingly the case these days, ignoring their companions in favour of fiddling with their mobile phones. Their activities seemed so futile and trivial after the revelations of the past hour.

What they had found on the phone from the Clark house had changed everything. The implications still chilled her blood like a winter's frost.

Sheppard was already seated at a corner table with what looked like an ice-cold glass of white wine in front of her. She lifted a hand in welcome when Archer entered, and rose for a quick handshake when she joined her. She was an inch or so shorter than Archer, perhaps five feet ten inches tall.

"I'm afraid I've started without you," she said. "I know this is work-related, but I'm technically off duty now. What would you like?"

Archer resolved to do her best to shake off what she was feeling for now. No doubt it would return when she shared her news with Sheppard. She slipped her jacket off and dumped it on a spare chair at their table.

"You know, I think I'll risk joining you. I'll get myself something when we order food. I see you've got some menus." She picked one up.

"It all looks tempting," Sheppard said. "Do you have time to eat?"

"I'll probably drop back in to the office after this, but I don't suppose the world will end for want of an hour or so." She realised she was famished. "Maybe we can squeeze in a main and a pudding?"

Sheppard's smile looked as genuine as it was dazzling. "Let's go for it." She took a sip of wine. "So you transferred here from the Met?"

Archer tried not to bristle. "Maybe I should quiz you on what you *don't* know about me."

"I just like to know who I'm dealing with. But how are you finding it out here? I was surprised to read that you'd traded the Met for somewhere like this, but then I found out about..." – she took another hasty slurp – "...about what happened to you. Has it helped, getting away from the old life?"

At least she was direct. Archer resisted the temptation to touch her scar.

"The honest answer? It's still a work in progress, but I'm trying to make a life here."

"The pace must be different, though."

"It has its moments."

Sheppard sipped her wine again. "Anyhow, I'm uncomfortable drinking alone, so let's pay these menus some attention, shall we?"

They scanned the options and decided to have the same thing: Aylesbury duck breast with vanilla and lime mash, baby corn, bok choi and morello cherry sauce.

"We ought to discuss the case," Sheppard said once their orders had been taken.

"Let's eat first," Archer suggested. "Why don't you tell me about life in the NCA?"

The DCI looked caught off-guard by the question. She stared at the table, as if seeking inspiration, then nodded. "It's good. It's all about making the UK a hostile environment for the serious and organised criminal, so what we do is important. And, as you know, a lot of our work is done in partnership with the police and others."

Archer stifled a splutter of laughter. "Partnership? What, like marching into a station, laying down the law, and telling the local force they're off the case?"

"That's unusual," Sheppard said, unabashed. "Most of the time we're pretty cooperative and softly, softly. But this case…" She stared at her wine glass. "It's high stakes, Lizzie. Is it okay to call you that?"

Archer shrugged.

"All organised crime groups are given a prioritised level of operational response, based on threat and risk to communities. The Connollys are well up the list, because of what they do and the way their empire is spreading. Imagine a spider's web made of pure poison. Every year the spider spins the web a bit wider, but you can never get to the spider itself to stop it doing it.

"I've been working on this for years now, and it's cost me, personally and professionally. Murray Connolly and his boys think they're immune and can go on ruining lives with impunity: the people who get hooked on their drugs, the women they traffic, and anyone who gets in their way."

"Like Will Streatham?" Archer threw in lightly.

Sheppard's eyes widened. Then her features became blank again. "Where did you hear that name?"

"Oh," Archer swirled the contents of her glass, "I like to know who I'm dealing with."

Sheppard stared at her for a long moment, then shrugged. "Where was I? Oh, yes. We do cooperate and collaborate. We use a technique called Organised Crime Group Mapping, and that's shown quite clearly that these people operate in networks – and it takes one network to defeat another. So we work with others to disrupt the organisations and their associates. We try to mess up their business and their way of life. It's all about intelligence and information-sharing and building specialist knowledge."

"I get all that. I just haven't seen much sharing. For instance, I noticed you didn't actually comment on DS Streatham."

"You say you haven't seen much sharing, but I've told you, DCI Gillingham and your DS Baines much more than I wanted to, to help take the Connollys down. As I've said, I've invested a great deal in that. All we need is one breakthrough: something big that we can follow all the way back to Murray Connolly, and that allows him no chance of wriggling off the hook.

"There have been leaks before when we've worked with other law enforcement agencies. It's like we're always ten steps behind. Potential informants disappear, or end up in rivers, or on skips. It depends on what message the Connollys want to send. So you'll forgive me if I'm not as open as you'd like me to be."

To Archer's ears, so much of what Sheppard had said sounded rehearsed, as if they were snippets of presentations or briefings she had made. But she knew now where her weakness lay.

"DS Streatham," she said again. "Come on, Catherine – is it okay if I call you that? I'm pretty confident he was the undercover cop who disappeared and, judging by the way you changed the subject when I mentioned his name, I'm right on the money. You haven't exactly denied all knowledge of him."

The DCI looked about to reply, and then her lip quivered.

"I don't know why you keep throwing that name in my face." Her voice was hoarse. "You know we lost an officer. Why does his name matter? All right, yes. Will was… was…" Her eyes misted. "Damn."

"My God." Archer's instincts kicked in. "When you said he had nobody who'd miss him, that wasn't strictly true, was it?"

"Well, his colleagues would, obviously." She brushed her eyes with her palms.

"Yes, but you said he wasn't close to any of them. That wasn't quite true, was it?"

"You know nothing."

"Have it your way. But I think landing Murray Connolly is at least as personal for you as it's professional."

"Think what you like. I can't stop you."

Sheppard was gaining some sort of control of herself again, but just for a moment there had been a chink in her armour. It was as if her heart had been laid open for anyone to see.

Archer still didn't trust her. But she couldn't help but feel compassion.

"It must have killed you when your superiors wouldn't let you pull him out when it was obvious his cover was blown."

"That was my decision. No one else's. And I haven't said that was Will." She shrugged. "Anyway, I thought we were going to eat first and talk business afterwards."

Right on cue, the food came. The conversation briefly descended into stilted small talk, then they started swapping stories about how they got into law enforcement.

Archer's story was nothing unusual. Her father, Alan Archer, had been on the job himself, retiring as a uniformed sergeant. He'd been proud of his daughter, and had lived to see her make Detective Inspector before succumbing to lung cancer.

He'd been spared seeing her disfigurement, but she chose not to share that with Sheppard.

Catherine Sheppard's grandparents had come over from Jamaica on the *Windrush* in 1948, and her mother was born a year later. She had her first child at seventeen and Catherine, by a different father, two years later. Like Brandon Clark and Ryan Sturridge, she'd never had a father in her life and had grown up on rough streets.

In another family, things might have turned out very differently, but her mother had been determined that both her children should have decent life chances. Supported by her own parents, who were hard-working, dignified and proud to be British, she had worked three jobs and still been there to give the kids a hot meal when they came in from school. She'd nagged them to take their education seriously, and this had paid off.

But Sheppard's brother had been knifed to death on his way home one evening in an unprovoked, random attack. Wrong place, wrong time – just as Archer and Baines had thought might be the case with Brandon. He'd been the same age too: just sixteen.

The police, and one detective in particular, had put tremendous efforts into catching the perpetrators, and Catherine had been in court two years later when the killer and his accomplice were sentenced.

"I knew then that I could do my best at school, get the best job I could, and spend my life doing something mundane. Or I could make a difference, the way those detectives had. That was when I decided what I wanted to do for a living."

"So you made up your mind to become a copper."

"To become a *detective*." She put her cutlery down and dabbed her lips with a napkin. "Someone said something about dessert."

Archer caught their waitress's eye and, after checking out the options, they ordered amaretto poached potted pear for Archer and orange and white chocolate cheesecake for Sheppard. Archer wondered if the other woman normally had such an appetite and, if so, how on earth she kept her figure.

"Lucky with my metabolism, I suppose, although I'm a bit of a jogger too. When the weather's dry."

"I'm thinking of joining a gym."

"You should. Isn't Champneys somewhere near here?"

"Tring, yes. Even nearer to my home."

"Expensive, mind."

Archer nodded. She'd checked out Champneys' website and the fees were not the cheapest. But, frankly, she could easily afford it. The question was whether she would find enough spare time to go and get her money's worth.

"You have to make yourself go," Sheppard said. "No matter how busy work is, you have to ring-fence some 'me' time. What's that old cliché? No one ever wanted: 'I wish I'd spent more time in the office' as their epitaph."

They ordered coffees and the bill when dessert came. Against all her expectations, Archer found that she'd rather enjoyed the DCI's company. It made her almost – but not quite – feel sorry about the bombshell she was about to drop.

They were stirring their cappuccinos when she said, quite casually, "How did you come to recruit Brandon Clark?"

Sheppard had seemingly relaxed, but as soon as the question was out, she froze. She recovered fast, but not fast enough. "I... what?" Her spoon was still in her cup, paused in mid-stir. "*Recruit* him? What are you talking about?"

"Oh, come on, Catherine." Archer put her own spoon back on the saucer. "We found his secret phone. An unregistered pay-as-you-go."

"He had a secret phone?" Sheppard cocked an eyebrow. "So?"

"So Matthew Butcher had an unregistered phone himself, as you know, with lots of unused SIM cards. His killer probably snatched his everyday phone, maybe fearing there was something incriminating on it. Who knows? For the other phone, we reckon he used the SIMs once and then disposed of them. But for some reason, rather than write it down, he had one number stored in the phone's memory on speed dial. Can you guess which number it was?"

Sheppard's attempt at casualness evaporated. Her jaw dropped open.

"Oh, the stupid..." She stopped herself, but it was too late.

Archer stared at her, all the anger she had felt earlier returning.

"I can't believe you did that. You recruited a kid – a child, really – as a snout?"

"I can't talk about all aspects of the operation. And for Christ's sake, keep your voice down."

"Oh, please. You're going no comment? Seriously? I'll see what my superiors think about that. Or your superiors. Or the media, if that's what it takes. Because Matthew Butcher contacted Brandon less than an hour before they were both gunned down." She took a breath. She didn't want to make a scene and have people overhear something they shouldn't. "Brandon Clark wasn't an unlucky bystander. He was meeting your man."

"If you take this story to the press, that'll be your career over."

"And yours."

Sheppard said nothing, but Archer simply let the silence drag out. No way was she dropping this. She'd been seething inside ever since Jason Bell had told her what was on the phone.

"It really wasn't like that," Sheppard finally said, her tone barely a whisper.

"What *was* it like, then? You knew about his background and persuaded him to let Ben Loftus recruit him into the new gang that would be working for the Connollys? Let me guess."

"Lizzie—"

"You checked on local gang activity in the past and noted that Brandon had been a leader but had left it all behind. Maybe you even checked his school records, saw he was getting good grades. You profiled him and thought that he'd make an ideal person to get alongside Ryan Sturridge. The only thing I don't understand is how you persuaded him to do it."

"You're wrong," Sheppard said. "Brandon came to us."

Archer stared at her. "You expect me to believe that?"

"Believe, don't believe. It's the truth." She sighed. "If you'll just calm down, I'll tell you."

"So tell me."

"You already know Brandon was a smart kid. You also know that Ben Loftus was doing the rounds of members of both the old gangs well before Ryan Sturridge came out of prison, telling them there was an exciting opportunity coming and asking them to get on board. Me, I think that was pretty indiscreet, but we do know that Desmond Connolly was in Feltham at the same time as Ryan. We think Ryan bragged about what a big man he was in this part of the world and Desmond – who had probably pissed his father off mightily by getting caught doing some nasty little drug-dealing – saw the chance to get back into his dad's good graces by presenting Murray with a potential new territory.

"Whose idea it was for Ben Loftus to go blabbing all over the place, we still don't know. Probably Ryan's. Maybe Ben himself. But he approached Brandon, who at first wanted nothing to do with it. But then he realised that he might be able to help the police take down some serious organised criminals."

"No." Archer shook her head. "Nice try, but he would have come to us, surely. I mean, Dan Baines is practically a family friend."

Their waitress appeared with a card reader in her hand. "Are you ready to pay?"

"Can you give us five – no, ten – minutes, please?" Sheppard said.

"Sure. Take your time."

The DCI waited until she was out of earshot.

"I told you," she resumed. "He's smart. He understood that this was organised crime and that it was part of something much bigger. He came to us because we're the right people to come to. It was his idea to let them recruit him."

"He probably knew we wouldn't countenance it. I can't believe *you* did. A schoolkid joining a network that kills people, and then informing on them? What were you thinking?"

"It was me he spoke to. I thanked him and said it wasn't happening, for all the reasons you've just mentioned. He said he was doing it anyway. So I thought that making it official was the lesser of two evils. At least he'd have some backup."

"I don't buy it." Another penny dropped in Archer's head. "You didn't really try that hard to dissuade him, did you? Because of Will Streatham. You can go no comment for all you're worth, but we both know he meant something to you. And when they killed him, taking down the Connollys became personal to you, didn't it?"

While Sheppard groped for a response, thoughts of Dan Baines entered Archer's mind. What would he do to get his hands on the Invisible Man, the monster who had destroyed his family and, in so many ways, blighted his life? Seeking justice for loved ones could induce a blind single-mindedness the way nothing else could.

"All right," Sheppard said at last. "You might be right. Maybe Will's death did colour my judgement."

"So you're confirming that Will Streatham was your first undercover man?"

"What's the point of being coy about it? And yes, we were close. We loved each other, in fact. And I'd have done almost anything to bring Murray Connolly and his empire crashing down after he disappeared. But you have to believe me when I say I did try to refuse Brandon's offer. Maybe I should have tried harder."

"And did your superiors know about him?" The other woman's silence and averted gaze spoke volumes. "Jesus," Archer whispered. "But there's one thing I don't get. Matthew Butcher – what is his real name, by the way?"

"That's not important. Trust me."

"Trust you. Yeah, right. But Butcher, or whatever his name is, had already infiltrated the organisation in London. When you agreed to Brandon working for you, how did you know Butcher would be coming out here?"

"I didn't. It was serendipity. But I thought it was a way of getting Brandon off the hook. Only it was too late by then. He told them he'd changed his mind and wanted out."

"But it doesn't work that way, does it? Once you're in, you're in."

"That's right. Maybe he lost their trust at that point. Whatever. I thought, at least now we'll have someone there to look out for him. We even got that phone to him, so Butcher could check in with him, leave him messages, without anything showing up on his regular phone."

Archer glanced at her watch. She was keen to get back to the station and see who was around. She needed to share this sorry story, and the only person she trusted now was Baines. But she just needed a bit more.

"It all went wrong on Friday, didn't it?" she said.

"I knew there was a meeting: my guy. Maybe Desmond Connolly. Certainly Ryan Sturridge."

"Ben Loftus?"

"No. Ryan wanted to keep him in the dark. I don't know who else was present, but I think you might have a dirty cop in your midst, one who recognised Butcher from somewhere."

"We've worked that much out."

"With hindsight, I think they'd already decided Brandon had to go and, once they'd made Butcher for a cop, he was next on the list. I'm guessing whoever pulled the trigger couldn't believe their luck when they found both their targets together."

"And who do you think pulled that trigger? Any ideas?"

"Oh, yes. All this mess had been made by Ben and Ryan deciding to be proactive about recruiting an organisation. Shooting their mouths off. That wasn't what Desmond Connolly wanted at all. So there's a clean-up going on. Brandon Clark and Matthew Butcher. Ryan Sturridge. Raphael Larkin, who hosted the meetings. My money's on Ben Loftus realising he was next on the list and doing a runner. I think Raphael was tortured in case he knew where Ben might have gone, although why they'd imagine he'd protect him…"

"So that leaves Desmond Connolly or one of his henchmen?"

"Or our corrupt copper. Sorry, Lizzie, but someone in Aylesbury nick is probably up to their necks in this. Either they killed four people, or they gave them up to whoever did."

Archer looked Sheppard in the eye. "Does your intelligence tell you who this corrupt copper might be?"

"Unfortunately not. But do you have any ideas?"

Of course she did. Gillingham or Ashby, or possibly both. She and Baines had speculated about it, but all the time Archer had been hoping there would be some other answer. Now those hopes had been dashed. It could be someone else on the team, or maybe even a uniform from the station. But she just kept coming back to Reading and the gun.

She saw again the look that had flitted across Gillingham's face when they'd talked about going behind Sheppard's back to find out what she was really investigating. And a conversation they'd had a year or so back in which he'd implied that he'd made mistakes in the past that might yet come back to bite him on the backside.

"I do," she admitted. "But it's just speculation."

"Care to share?"

Archer thought about it, but came to the same conclusion as before. She'd need pretty good grounds to make serious allegations against two senior officers. Take away the Reading connection, which could be no more than a simple coincidence

– she had no idea who else at the station might have served at Reading at one time or another – and all she had was a weird look on Gillingham's face. Hardly enough to voice her suspicions to this woman. She might be obliged to enter an unholy alliance with Catherine Sheppard, but that didn't mean she trusted her much more than she had when she'd sat down to dine with her.

"No," she said finally. "It wouldn't be right. At best, any suspicions I have are based on instinct."

"A copper's instinct can be as close to evidence as it gets. What about that Scottish lad in your team – Bell? Would his family have had connections with Murray Connolly back in Glasgow?"

Archer had a mental picture of Jason Bell springing open Butcher's metal box with a paper clip.

Learned that in Glasgow.

But she couldn't begin to think Bell was corrupt, much less a killer.

"It's not him," she said. "No way. But I think we need to keep this theory between you, me and Dan Baines for the moment."

"What about telling DCI Gillingham?"

"No." She noted Sheppard's raised eyebrow. "Look, I trust Dan one hundred per cent. Anyone else – including my superiors – I just don't know. But whether it really is one of my colleagues, or someone else behind this, my question is this: have they already got to Ben? Or is he still in hiding? And if he is, where the hell is he?"

26

Cameron Connolly sat on the bed in his hotel room, his phone pressed to his ear. After wringing a full confession out of Desmond, he needed to report back to his father. The whole miserable story had made grim telling, and he was quietly grateful that Dad was at home in Hampstead and hadn't decided to come up and deal with it himself. He might have lost his temper and dispatched Desmond on the spot. For all that the Cameron considered his younger brother a wanker, who could only be a throwback to some arsehole or other who'd managed to pollute the family gene pool back in the mists of time, he was still a Connolly – and the first rule in the family was that blood was thicker than water.

If Dad spilled any of that blood in haste, he'd surely regret it at leisure.

"So let me get this quite straight," Murray said when he'd finished telling the tale. "The guy I trusted as Desmond's wingman turns out to be undercover police?"

"Our own cop was down in the bar and recognised him."

"And meanwhile, the two amateurs that Desmond saw as useful local links turn out to be halfwits who've been bragging all over town that the Connollys are setting up an operation there?"

"I don't think they'd been using our name. Des says not."

"Let's hope not. And so Desmond decides to handle all his problems by himself? And now we've got our cop 'cleaning up' the mess: a kid who wanted out. An undercover cop. A bartender whose only involvement in anything was hosting the odd meeting and taking some cash to keep quiet about it. And one of our young blabbermouths."

Murray Connolly had a way of making you feel you were to blame, even when the trouble was not of your making.

"That's about the size of it, Dad."

His father swore. "And our other young blabbermouth is in the wind?"

"He's not been back home. Ryan Sturridge might have known where he'd hide, but of course he's dead. The cop thought that bartender might know, but if he did, he's amazingly loyal to a punk kid who's nothing to him. Still swore he didn't have a clue after our guy blew both his kneecaps off."

"Jesus. He could be anywhere."

"Except the police are looking for him. His picture's already everywhere. I reckon he's holed up somewhere local."

"And he lives with his parents?"

"Apparently."

"So this is what you do. Get hold of the cop and ask him to ring the parents – as a policeman, not waving his bloody gun around. Can they think of anywhere at all he might be, that sort of thing."

"They'll have been asked all that already."

"So get him to try again. Maybe something's jogged their memories. Who knows? This kid's seen the cop."

"At least he hasn't seen Desmond."

"No. But, much as it grieves me to say this, your brother's right. We need to finish what he started. If we can eliminate this last kid, then we might be in the clear."

"I still think we should forget all about this whole Aylesbury Vale venture."

"Good thing it's me doing the thinking, then. Besides, you know as well as I do that wheels are in motion that we can't stop, at least not without losing an awful lot of cash. And you know how I feel about my cash, never mind my reputation."

"It might be safer writing it off."

"Not going to happen. You just concentrate on finding this Ben Loftus and see that he's dealt with. Afterwards, get rid of the cop, too. Get Willie to do it. He'll enjoy that."

The phone went dead. Cameron stared at it. He thought his father was right, up to a point: tie off the loose ends, oversee

Desmond more closely until the new setup was working smoothly. There was still something that could be salvaged from this fiasco.

So why did he fear that things were about to get worse, rather than better?

* * *

Ben was watching a thriller on a movie channel. Claire marvelled at his stamina. For most of the day – when he'd been awake, that was – he had watched bad TV. She supposed someone had to, or half the TV companies would go bust.

In spite of herself, she'd found herself watching it and wishing real life could be like that. She'd watched the hero, with his hands tied behind his back, palm a piece of broken glass and then saw through his bonds with it. He'd made it look simple.

Getting her hands on a knife actually *had* been relatively simple. Tonight's creation by MasterChef Ben had been cheese on toast. He'd untaped her ankles as usual, so she could walk to the kitchen, and pulled out her usual chair at the table for her, like a waiter.

"Can I stand for a bit, Ben?" she'd asked, trying her best to sound submissive. "I've been mostly sitting down ever since I got home."

He'd shrugged, presumably assuming she didn't pose much threat with her hands taped together, and got on with assembling the ingredients for their feast: sliced bread from the freezer, a block of cheddar and a tub of low-fat spread from the fridge.

"I don't know why you don't have butter," he'd said with his back to her. "Toast isn't the same with this muck."

"Too much fat and cholesterol in butter," she'd replied, edging her way towards her knife block. "The spread is better for you."

"I don't like it."

"You could always pop out and buy some butter."

"Funny."

For a moment, he'd sounded almost like the old Ben.

"If only I'd known you were coming, I'd have got some in."

That was when he'd turned around, a small knife in one hand, block of cheese in the other.

"Or you could have got in a wig and dark glasses so I could go out, what is it, incognito." He frowned. "What you doing over there?"

"I need to stretch my legs. If this goes on too much longer, I'll get a deep vein thrombosis."

He'd actually chuckled. "Your cholesterol spread's not *that* good then."

With that, he'd turned back to what he was doing. If he'd even noticed how close she was to the knife block, it hadn't bothered him. Moments later, she'd removed the smallest knife from the block and managed to slide it into her jeans pocket, sharp side outwards to minimise the risk of accidentally cutting herself.

Rather than go straight back to her chair, she'd continued her perambulations around the kitchen. She'd got more than halfway around – in fact, only a few paces away from Ben – when he'd turned around again.

"I don't like you creeping around behind me," he'd said, the warmth gone from his voice. "Go and sit down."

"What harm am I doing?"

His nostrils had flared. "Why you always fucking arguing with me? You ought to do what I say. That Stockholm thing, yeah? We ought to be bonding, not you being difficult all the time. Now sit down, or no dinner for you."

Before, these mood swings had scared her. This time, it seemed all so preposterous that she had laughed out loud. "Dinner? It's cheese on toast, Ben. You're not Marcus Wareing."

"Who the fuck's he?"

"A top chef."

"Yeah, well, you'd know, with your fancy job and your house and everything. I suppose you eat at his restaurant every other week."

"Oh, sure."

"Top fucking chefs. Go and sit down." He'd picked up the gun.

Even then, a bit of defiance remained. "You're so macho with that gun, aren't you? It gives you permission to swear and everything. Would you really shoot me, Ben?"

He took a pace closer. "Maybe I could start by smashing you across the face with it. See if that shuts your big mouth."

And, just for an instant, she thought he might do it. She'd affected a shrug, trying to cling to a modicum of dignity, and returned to her chair on legs that suddenly felt wobbly. She could hear her mother's voice, worried about her as only her mother could be. *Don't provoke him, love.*

Now she was just waiting for him to fall asleep. He was living on adrenalin, and that had to be tiring. He'd dozed a few times during the day. The next time she heard him snoring, she was going to fumble the knife out of her pocket, cut herself free somehow, and make a bolt for it. What if he woke up, though? What if he panicked, grabbed the gun and pulled the trigger? She might never reach the door, let alone turn the key.

So was she going to make a move for the gun? His sofa was as close as the living room door. If she could get the gun, then it was just a matter of pointing it at him while she called the police. Surely that was a safer bet?

It was risky. But it felt like a plan.

27

Baines was still worrying about his row with Karen when Archer called him and asked him to meet her in the car park in five minutes. He found her pacing and apparently talking on her mobile. As soon as she saw him, she put the phone away, with no pretence of ending a call.

"This is all getting very cloak and dagger," he said. "Should I be worried?"

"I don't know. Maybe."

She recounted what she had learned from her encounter with Sheppard, and he listened without interrupting. When she had finished, he thrust his hands in his pockets and looked back at the building.

"You know, I really didn't want one of our own to be mixed up in this. But it's looking more and more likely. Which one do you think it is?"

She shrugged. "Honestly? Your guess is as good as mine. It could be either Gillingham nor Ashby but, if I had to choose, I'd plump for Ashby. We know he was God knows where when the murders were committed. One of them working with the Connollys seems more plausible than both. But we'll say nothing about our suspicion for the moment, and Sheppard will do likewise."

"It just feels so dishonest, suspecting some colleagues and keeping it from others." He sighed. "Meanwhile, where does all that lead us?"

"If Sheppard's right, then Ben Loftus isn't our killer. But he is a loose end that the killer will want to tie up as soon as possible. He'll be looking for him, and not particularly concerned about who he has to hurt to find him."

"So we have to find him first, right?" He smiled without humour. "That's okay, then. Any ideas?"

"No, but let's think about this. We think he's holed up somewhere. We already know he's not at any of his usual haunts, and not with friends or family, as far as we're aware."

"So...?"

"So God knows."

"Wait a bit, though," he said, his mind racing. "I'm not sure how bright he is – not very, in my experience. But he probably hasn't checked into some hotel where the staff will have recognised him from his picture. I can't see him sleeping rough in his car. He'll know we're looking for it."

"But the car hasn't turned up."

"Exactly. Wherever he is, he's managed to stash it out of sight."

She smiled and nodded. "Very good, Dan. We're looking at a house with a garage, or maybe a lock-up, that he has access to. But who'd know?"

"Maybe his parents. Maybe Laine Shaw."

"Worth a try. Maybe we've been asking the wrong question." She pulled her phone out of her bag. "No time like the present. I really hate doing this, but I'm just going to tell Joan you and I are following up a lead. No details."

He fished his car keys out of his pocket. "No, we don't want to share our thinking with her and then have her be awkward with the boss. If he's involved, then we're in a race to get to Ben first."

"I agree. Damn. I know Joan would keep it to herself if I asked her, but I really don't want to put her in that position."

"It's a bastard, all this, isn't it?" He shook his head in wonder. "Who'd have thought we'd be concealing things from those two and putting our trust in Sheppard?"

"I wouldn't go that far. I still think she might have her own agenda. It takes more than two courses and a glass of white to win me over."

"Did she treat you?"

"What do you think?"

* * *

Archer and Baines had decided to speed things along by splitting up. Archer would take Laine Shaw, whilst Baines spoke to Ben Loftus's parents.

"Tea?" Mrs Loftus asked, almost before he crossed the threshold. "Coffee?"

"I won't, thanks," he said. He recalled that she had served him an unpleasantly weak cup of tea last time he had called, and doubted the coffee would be any better. "I just dropped round on the off-chance you'd heard from Ben."

The boy's father shook his head. "I can promise you we'd be on the phone like a shot if he came home, or got in touch." The corners of his mouth turned down and he wrung his hands. "Like a shot," he repeated. "Sorry. Bad choice of words. Didn't mean to, you know—"

"It's fine." Baines could see both parents were under serious stress. He'd met parents in his time who'd been perfect role models for kids who turned to crime – scumbags themselves, with serious records, who didn't give a stuff about their offspring. He'd even met parents who gloried in their children's criminal exploits. He actually remembered an old lag of a father proudly declaring his son to be 'a chip off the old block' when he was first sentenced to prison. These two were nothing like that, although their earlier laid-back attitude to his absence suggested that a lack of parental control might be one of the reasons their son had gone astray in the first place.

"You must have been racking your brains about where Ben might be," he suggested. "Any ideas you've had, however unlikely, we're prepared to take them seriously."

The boy's father looked a little hurt.

"Again, we'd have told you immediately if we had a clue."

"I know we've exhausted all the obvious possibilities," Baines pressed, "but we're trying to come at it from a new angle."

"What sort of angle?"

He kept his voice light. He didn't want to make too much of this. "It's Ben's car, you see. It hasn't turned up on any cameras so far, and we've had no reports of it being dumped."

"But it could be anywhere," Ben's mother jumped in. "It's like looking for a needle in a haystack, surely."

A bit like a silver BMW, with a distinctive dent, that kept appearing with different number plates.

"You're probably right, but we need to look at every possibility. So we were wondering if there was a lock-up garage, or a friend's house with a garage, that he might have access to. Someone you didn't think was important, or forgot to mention."

Mr Loftus shook his head firmly. "There's no one. Not that he'd go to, anyway, if he was in that sort of trouble. His tearaway mates, maybe, but we gave you all their names, and I'd be amazed if any of them just happened to have a handy garage."

"I still think there's an innocent explanation for him disappearing," said the mother, who had been in denial from the beginning. "I mean, just because Ryan got mixed up with something bad... maybe Ben just met a girl and he's been all loved up instead, unaware you're looking for him."

Baines had thought she was a nice, but pretty stupid, woman on their first meeting, and his opinion hadn't changed. They'd told him then that Ben had never had a proper girlfriend. The notion that he'd gone off on some whirlwind romance at exactly the same time that his so-called best mate had got himself shot through the head was nothing short of laughable.

"I very much doubt that," he said

There was an awkward pause. Baines thought he might as well go. He wasn't going to get any more out of them.

"Well, thank you. I'll be on my way."

"By the way," Mr Loftus added, "you guys might want to work on your communication."

"Yes?"

"One of your colleagues phoned, no more than half an hour ago, asking much the same questions."

Puzzled, Baines asked him who that had been.

He shrugged. "It was a detective sergeant. What was his name? Williams, maybe?"

There was no DS Williams at the Vale, and Baines doubted that Sheppard was likely to have asked her own team to make this sort of enquiry.

"We told him the same we've told you," the man continued. "We're out of ideas."

"You're right," Baines said, alarm bells ringing in his head. "There's obviously been a mix-up somewhere along the line. I ought to speak to the DS. I don't suppose your phone will have stored the number he rang from?"

"Well, yes. It was the last call we had. A mobile, I think. Hang on and I'll write it down for you. I just need to find a pen and paper."

"Here." Baines offered him his pen and notebook. "Write it in here."

"Our family doesn't seem to be having much luck lately," Mrs Loftus said while her husband fiddled with the phone. "What with all this, and Claire."

"Claire?"

"My niece, Ben's cousin. She's had a car accident down in Devon."

"Sorry to hear it," he said, anxious to go and try to trace this number. "I hope she's all right."

"Yes, she's fine, thank God. She was on holiday with friends. Two of her pals had some minor injuries, I think, and their car was written off. Not Claire's."

"Good to know." A suspicion was taking root in his mind. He didn't want to alarm them, but he wanted to check it out as soon as possible.

"Here you are." The husband handed the notebook and pen back to Baines. "I was right. It was a mobile number."

"So, this Claire," Baines said. "Does she live with her parents?"

"Oh, no," Ben's mother said. "She's done really well for herself. Got her own house and everything."

"But she's away at the moment? Would Ben know that?"

"Yes. I'm sure we've talked about it. They get on well. He drops round there for the occasional cup of tea." Mr Loftus's brow creased in thought. "Now I think of it, he does know where she keeps a spare key hidden." Then he slapped his forehead, somewhat theatrically. "Oh, but Claire's home now. They decided to cut their holiday short after the crash. Although she's apparently come down with a cold or something now. Her mum phoned us this afternoon, to see if there was any news on Ben, and she mentioned it to us then. So Ben can't be there, can he?"

"I'm sure you're right," Baines said, trying to keep the concern out of his voice. "And did you mention Claire to this DS Williams? Did you say she'd been away?"

"Yes, I did. I gave him her address."

Now Baines detected a note of doubt in his voice.

"Well, I'm sure, as you say, he won't be there. You may as well give us that address, though."

"No problem," Mrs Loftus said. "I got out the address book for Detective Sergeant Williams."

* * *

One eye fixed on Ben, Claire sawed at the tape that bound her wrists together. She had been watching him for some time, seen how he was fighting sleep. Now he had slid halfway down his seat on the sofa, his head flung back, mouth open and emitting animal-like noises.

The ankles had been a relatively simple job, but the wrists were proving trickier. She'd had to reverse the knife blade and slide it between her wrists without cutting herself. Now she was rocking the handle with her palms, making an awkward sawing motion against the tape.

But it was working. Slowly but surely, the tape was parting, and Ben looked dead to the world. If he could only remain that way, she would be free in a few minutes. The only question then was whether she would have the courage to go for the gun.

* * *

The man who had called himself Williams sat opposite Claire Taylor's home in a silver BMW. A while ago, a BMW would have been a distinctive car. It would have marked you out as someone who had arrived in life. These days, Beemers, Audis and Mercs were more common, and older ones like this drew barely a second glance. And having a selection of number plates to rotate meant he didn't have the inconvenience of having to dump a car after each job and steal another. So long as he continued to be careful and not be seen or noticed, no one was likely to remember one more silver German car knocking around.

It was a shame about the dent, though. It was the one thing that an eagle-eyed copper viewing camera footage might just notice and start joining the dots. But, on balance, he had felt the risk was slim, although his years on the force had taught him that car thieves' luck often ran out. It would be ironic if he was so careful about getting away with murder, only to be observed breaking into a car.

His thoughts turned to the job in hand. He didn't know for sure that Ben was here, of course, although an empty house, his cousin away and an accessible key must surely have been irresistible to a young loser looking for somewhere to hide. What a stroke of luck that his motormouth mother had felt compelled to prattle on about bad luck in the family and the cousin's road traffic accident.

The fact that the cousin had cut short her holiday and returned home raised questions, of course. If Ben was holed up there, what had happened? Had he run for it? Was the cousin shielding him? Had he panicked and killed her?

If Ben was still there, the man knew there was a chance that the doorbell would go unanswered. That wasn't a huge issue. A recce on Google Earth had shown that the rear of the house wouldn't be difficult to access, although he'd probably have to wait until night-time to attempt that. It would involve breaking in, which could be messy. A frontal approach was the tidiest option. If his ID didn't get him inside, his gun would. A few seconds later, it would be over.

The contact from Cameron Connolly had been unexpected, and it was clear that Murray Connolly wasn't exactly ecstatic about what had happened here in the past few days. But it was equally clear that – in Cameron's eyes, at least – the blame was being laid plainly at Desmond's door. Hardly surprising. The boy was an idiot. Although, in fairness, Desmond wasn't to know that the guy calling himself Butcher was an undercover cop, and it wasn't obvious what alternatives there would have been to removing the cop and the kids who couldn't keep their mouths shut – other than closing down the whole Aylesbury Vale operation, which apparently wasn't seen as an option.

It was a shame about the Clark boy, but that was what happened when you got mixed up in something bigger than you.

He looked up and down the street one more time. The coast was clear. He patted his jacket pocket, feeling the reassuring bulk of the gun, then removed the fake, but authentic-looking, police ID from his wallet before getting out of the car.

His earlier fleeting thought about his luck running out had unnerved him a little. So far he had managed to work his evil unseen. Two jobs in the street, nobody about. Quick, efficient killings and away. Now he had to stand on a doorstep and wait for someone to open up. There was always the possibility that, during that time, someone would pull up in their car or come out of their house.

But so what? Who gave someone standing on a doorstep a second thought? Everyone had such busy lives these days, and half the population spent half their time with their eyes glued to their mobile phones. He rather suspected he could be stark bollock naked and no one would even notice.

He was across the road and standing in Claire Taylor's little porch in seconds. In the very unlikely event that anyone spotted him now, no one would be able to see his face.

Holding his ID, he reached for the doorbell.

* * *

Claire stood on slightly shaky legs and looked longingly down the hall at the front door. The keys still hung from the lock. Intellectually, she knew it was only seconds away, even on tiptoe. Yet, all the time she had been cutting herself loose, a terrifying image had been playing itself over in her mind.

She walks down the hall, careful to make no sound, her feet whisper-quiet on the soft carpet. She stops at the front door. As she reaches for the key, she hears a stirring from the living room, then Ben's voice, cursing, then the sound of him scrambling off the sofa.
As she turns to look back, he fills the living room doorway, his gun levelled at her. She starts to beg, but her words are drowned out by the deafening roar of the gun.

No. She had already made up her mind, she realised, that she needed to get that weapon away from him, to neutralise any risk. It sat on the sofa, no more than an inch from his right hand, but his snoring was rhythmical and she knew he was fast asleep. Two or three paces, a reach and a grab, and she would have it. And with it, the upper hand.

She even knew a bit about guns. An ex-boyfriend had been into target shooting with pistols, and he had taken her along one time to see if she liked it. She hadn't. She'd hated it. But she knew about safety catches and the mechanics of shooting a gun. What was more, Ben knew she knew.

She took a wavering step towards him. Stopped. Surely the distance was greater than she'd thought? The sofa still looked three, if not four, paces away, as if the distance was actually expanding as she attempted to close it.

She swallowed. Told herself to get a grip. Took another step.

Froze as something crunched under her feet.

A stray crisp. Holding her breath, she studied Ben's eyelids. They remained closed, his snoring going on, untroubled by the sound. Like someone negotiating a minefield, she scanned the carpet for any other potential sources of noise, and she only took another step when she was completely certain there were none.

She thought that she might be able to reach the gun now, but it would be a stretch and she would risk overbalancing. One more step, to be sure.

Her mouth felt as dry as dust. Three days ago, she'd been enjoying a lovely break with her besties, having a laugh, free of troubles. If anyone had told her then that she would soon be in this situation, hoping to take a gun from her captor and praying he didn't wake up and kill her with it, she would have laughed at them.

Biting her lip, she took that final step. It took her right up to the sofa, her legs only inches from Ben's knees. She was standing right over the gun. All she needed to do was bend down and take it. She exhaled, willing herself to be calm. Slowly, carefully, she began to bend down.

The sound of the doorbell echoed through the house, all but stopping her pounding heart.

Ben's eyes snapped open.

28

Outside the Loftuses' home, Baines called Archer's mobile. She picked up on the third ring.

"Where are you?" he demanded.

"Hi to you, too," she responded coolly. "I'm just heading back, so I'm on the hands-free. Laine was a complete waste of time. Clueless. She seemed far more interested in how much trouble she might be in for possessing Ryan's illegal firearm than in helping us catch a killer. I suggested her life might be in danger, but I really don't think she's hiding anything. How about you?"

"We might have something," he said, glad to get a word in. He told her about the cousin, whose house Ben might have been able to get into.

"So what do we think? She came home, found him there and decided to harbour him? I mean, we don't really think he's the gunman any more."

"It's more likely he's not there, but we ought to check it out."

"Give me the address," she said, "and I'll meet you there."

A couple of minutes later, his phone rang again. He hit the hands-free button.

"Joan just called," Archer said. "Reports are coming in of shots being heard on the Berryfields estate. She thought we might like to know, in view of—"

Baines's heart jumped. "Do I need to ask the address?"

"I'm headed there now."

"Any details?"

"None. Except neighbours on both sides reported hearing what they were sure was a shot, then screaming. They're whistling up all units in the area and putting an armed response team on standby. Oh, and apparently DCI Sheppard's on her way, too."

"*Sheppard?*"

"She was there when Joan took the call. Seems she dropped by for a word with me. About something she should have mentioned before, apparently. Then Joan got the news about the gunshot, and she jotted down the address, said she'd find it on her satnav, and took off."

"Terrific." He thought the NCA officer was all they needed in a potentially explosive situation. His mind raced. "It'll be touch and go who gets there first. She shouldn't approach the house without backup."

"I've told Joan to ask her to wait outside for us." She paused. "Keep an eye out for silver BMWs – you never know."

"Yeah, right." It would be the first break in a long time if the fleeing gunman crossed his path.

"Got to go," Archer said, "I've got another call from Joan."

"Okay, keep me posted."

She had already gone.

Baines itched to put his foot down, but the traffic, whilst not at rush-hour levels, was still busy and slow. Aylesbury had what was described as a ring road, but using it involved numerous roundabouts and it was usually a toss-up as to whether it was any faster than gritting your teeth and driving straight through the middle of the town. It was at times like this that he wished his Mondeo had sirens and blue lights.

As he left the built-up area behind, he called Archer back. "Out of interest, is Gillingham at the station?"

"I asked Joan that. He went out soon after we did. And, of course, Ashby's not there. Long since knocked off for the day."

"So, assuming what the neighbours heard really was a shot – and assuming it's not some crazy coincidence—"

"Which neither of us believes for a moment."

"Which neither of us believes," he agreed, "then either Gillingham or Archer could have called Ben Loftus's parents, posing as this DS Williams."

"They mention the cousin's empty house, and he reaches the same conclusion we have—"

"That it sounds like an ideal hideout for Ben. If it's Gillingham, sounds like he promptly made an excuse before heading over there. And it was just the one shot?"

"Apparently."

Baines processed this.

"That doesn't make sense. Not if Ben and his cousin were both in the house. The killer would have wanted to erase them both."

"I agree. It's gone way too far to start leaving witnesses now. But maybe they weren't both there. Maybe Claire was sheltering Ben and had simply popped out for some shopping when the gunman arrived."

"Maybe. Where are you?"

"Just coming off the roundabout on to... hang on, there's a sign. Paradise Orchard."

"I'm less than a minute behind you, I reckon."

There were two main roads in to the estate: a right turn into the Western Link Road and then Paradise Orchard, off a large roundabout which also accessed Aylesbury Vale Parkway railway station. As he crossed the River Thame, Baines saw a silver BMW hurtling towards him. He got a quick look at the registration number and, as it blasted past him, he had time to clock the bodywork and the driver.

"Jesus!" Baines said. "I think I've just seen that silver Beemer we've been on the lookout for."

"Are you sure? The world's full of silver Beemers, Dan."

"It's got an identical dent, I'd swear, and I'm pretty sure the reg number was one of the ones we're looking for. And if it's just been at Claire Taylor's house..."

"What about the driver?"

He told her what he'd seen. "He's heading back into town. I'm going after him."

The Western Link Road was coming up on his right. The road ahead was clear on both sides, and so was the T-junction, so he used the opening to the road to execute a fast U-turn, his tyres squealing.

"Dan, no heroics. You could be chasing a desperate gunman, and you're not exactly dressed for the occasion."

This was true. Ideally he'd be wearing some body armour, or be armed himself.

"Call the cavalry. I'll just follow. See where he goes."

"Should I turn round too?"

"I think you should see what's happened at that house."

"Okay. Shit, there's another call coming in."

Archer called back moments later.

"There's been a call from the house for police and ambulance," she told him. "A female, seriously distraught. I told Joan you were in pursuit of a silver BMW, headed back into Aylesbury. Any sign of it?"

"Yes, about half a dozen cars ahead of me. For once, the traffic is doing me a favour."

"Try not to let on that you're tailing him."

"Great tip, Lizzie."

"Sorry." It sounded as if she meant it. "I'm outside the house now. Christ, another bloody call. I'll call you back."

* * *

The call was from Sheppard, who was just turning onto the Berryfields estate.

"Where are you?"

Archer gave her location. "There's a squad car here already. I've got Claire Taylor's number and I'm about to call the house."

"You think the killer's still in there?"

"No idea. The woman who rang 999 – presumably Claire – appears to have been pretty incoherent, but she said someone was dying."

She quickly told the DCI about Baines's pursuit.

"Give me his number. I'm going after them."

"Joan's already whistling up armed response, Catherine."

"It could lead us to the Connollys and maybe drop the whole family business in my lap. Give me that number."

Archer obliged, with misgivings, and Sheppard rang off without thanking her. Archer walked back to the two uniformed officers standing by their squad car, awaiting instructions. She could hear other sirens approaching.

"I'm going to phone the house," she said. "See what the situation is before we go approaching the front door."

She had obtained Claire's number from Joan Collins. She dialled it now and a shaky female voice answered. "Hello?"

"Claire?"

"Yes."

"Claire, this is Detective Inspector Lizzie Archer. I'm outside your house. Is everything all right in there?"

"*No!* It's my cousin. He's bleeding. I can't stop it. I think he's dying. I—"

The rest was drowned out by a siren as an ambulance rounded the corner. One of the uniformed police officers flagged it down. The noise stopped.

"Claire, there's an ambulance here. You have to let us in. But neighbours have called saying they thought they heard a shot. Is there a gun in there? Is it safe?"

"There's a gun, but it's safe now."

"Let us in, then."

Moments later the door opened and a dark-haired young woman, her top covered in blood, stood in the doorway. Archer hurried up to her, accompanied by a male paramedic.

Archer showed her warrant card. "Hi Claire, I'm Lizzie Archer. Are you hurt?"

"What? No, no, this is my cousin's blood. You have to help him."

"Where?"

They followed Claire into the living room, where a pale-faced young man sprawled on the sofa, his tee-shirt pulled up. He was holding a blood-soaked towel to his side. The paramedic approached him.

"Hi, Ben," he said. "My name is Rich. I need to see what's happened to you. Can you move the towel for me?"

Wide-eyed, Ben Loftus winced as he removed the towel. There was a fair-sized gash, from which blood still oozed.

"That doesn't look like a gunshot wound," Archer said to Claire, who stood with her arms folded across her breasts.

The younger woman tore her eyes away from her cousin to look at her. "What?"

"His wound. It doesn't look like a gunshot."

"It isn't," Claire said dully. "I stabbed him."

* * *

The silver BMW had left Aylesbury behind and joined the A41 dual carriageway, where it was travelling at, Baines judged, a steady 70 mph in the inside lane.

When his quarry had first joined this road, Baines had been some six cars behind. But, one by one, the cars between them had overtaken the BMW. Now Baines was right behind it. He had subtly reduced his speed to 65 mph, opening up a gap and hoping someone would fill it. So far, no one had. But he had no reason to think the driver had marked him as a tail.

His phone rang. He didn't recognise the number, but he recognised the voice that cut in as soon as he answered.

"DS Baines? This is DCI Sheppard. Do you still have the suspect's car in sight?"

"Yes."

"Where are you?"

He was tempted to be difficult, but decided it was easier to tell her.

"Okay," she said, " I'm going to put my foot down on the dual carriageway and try to catch you up."

"*What?*" This wasn't what he needed. "No, no! I'm just tailing him for now. We've got an armed team on standby. This doesn't need two of us, ma'am. In fact, two people tailing him could raise his suspicions."

"I have done this before, Dan. And this is meant to be a joint investigation. Plus, I hate to pull rank, but I'm pulling rank. Now keep this line open. We need to liaise. Two cars tailing him will be better than one. We can change places and he won't get suspicious. Joining the dual carriageway now. What are you driving?"

Reluctantly, he described his car and gave her the registration number. "You?"

"A black Alfa."

"Very inconspicuous."

"What?"

"Hang on," he said. "He's signalling to come off."

"Damn. What does the sign say?"

"Marsworth and Pitstone."

"Okay, keep giving me information."

As he left the A41, now directly behind the silver car, Baines had the feeling that it was all about to go horribly wrong.

* * *

The man behind the wheel of the BMW had spotted the Mondeo before he left Aylesbury, and had soon suspected that it was following him. Over the years, he'd developed almost a sixth sense about such things, and it had never let him down.

The Mondeo driver was good, but not that good. There'd been something suspicious about the way he'd hurried to join the queue behind him and then studiously kept his distance. He'd even slowed down a little as the cars between them in the inside lane had, one by one, overtaken the BMW.

Police, he assumed – but how were they on to him? Maybe he hadn't been as clever as he'd imagined. He'd thought using the same car for three jobs, even with the fake number plates, with that dent, had been a pretty calculated risk, but this was proving not to be his day.

He was already going to be in trouble with the people he was working for. His plan for erasing the Loftus boy had blown up in his face, although he had no idea what had happened in the house. He'd picked his moment, ghosted up to the front door unseen, and rung the bell.

It should have been simple but effective. Get into the house with his police ID, then produce the gun. Grab a sofa cushion or whatever to muffle the shots. Two to take Ben Loftus down, two more for the cousin, if she was at home.

Bang, bang, bang, bang. Then out again.

But he'd barely reached for the doorbell when all hell had broken loose.

What had unquestionably been a shot had echoed inside the house, closely followed by a girl screaming. He'd got out of there fast, calling his paymasters as he drove away. It was better to let them know what had happened than to have them find out later.

Cameron had been surprisingly good about it. Told him there'd be another opportunity and, even if the police were called, young Loftus probably knew better than to open his mouth.

"Meet us at the airfield," he'd said. "But take the back way."

He'd not been surprised to see the Mondeo still following him when he left the A41 and picked up the B489. He toyed with turning right instead of left at the end of the slip road, but then decided he could easily lose this guy. That, or get rid of him another way.

On a sharp right-hander, he took a nondescript road off to his left, not signalling, leaving it late and then wrenching the wheel round. He heard the Mondeo's tyres scream as the driver braked. He glanced in his mirror and saw him reverse so he could execute the turn. Meanwhile, he took another sharp right, hoping the cop – if that was what he was – wouldn't come round the curve quickly enough to see where he had gone.

The road was devoid of traffic, like an alien abduction scene. He floored the accelerator.

* * *

If Baines had come round the bend any later, he would have been too late to spot the silver car shoot off down another road on the right. One thing was for sure. The guy had spotted him for a tail and was trying to lose him. Pride made him want to give chase, but that wasn't the plan. No heroics, Archer had said.

But he was still sharing an open line with Sheppard, so he kept up his running commentary.

"I don't know that road well," he said. "I don't think it's much used. Bit of a dirt road, to be honest. Middle of nowhere, too."

"So?"

"So maybe I should back off?" he suggested.

"Bollocks to that. If he's running, then let's go after him."

"He could be armed."

"So I'll let armed response know where we are and then get straight back to you."

She broke the connection and he concentrated on his driving, thinking that it was all going to be a fiasco if an armed unit turned out and the guy he was chasing was just late for his tea. It didn't help that he'd never especially liked this road. He wasn't nervous about country lanes like Archer, but this was a tad too winding and narrow for the sort of speeds they were doing.

The BMW hurtled through a series of S-bends. Baines followed suit, but with more caution, and the gap between them widened again as the silver saloon blasted into a straight.

The road was straight and clear for maybe a quarter of a mile, with trees and foliage on either side, blocking out some of the sunlight. Should he try and catch him, maybe even overtake and force him to stop? Or would that be pure folly with a potentially armed killer? So what was his plan? What was Sheppard's?

He had no time to dwell on it because the BMW suddenly swerved dramatically to the left, tyres protesting. It ploughed through some bushes and hit a tree. Its bonnet flew open.

Baines applied his brakes. There was no discernible movement in the BMW, but he could see that the airbags had deployed. He started to get out, and at that moment the BMW's door was flung open and the driver surged out, the gun in his hand levelled at Baines's head.

"Get out of the car," he said. "Now."

29

"Well, there's a lot of blood," the paramedic was telling Ben, "but not a life-threatening amount. Basically, it's just a nasty cut. It needs some stitches, but you'll live, mate."

Claire sagged with relief. Those few moments after the doorbell rang had been playing over and over in her mind. Ben's eyes flying open. Him grabbing for the gun and her going for it too, in a panic. The gun going off, the bullet going God knew where, and then Ben crying out. Her staring at the knife, still in her hand, and the rip across his tee-shirt, the bloodstain spreading.

She'd screamed, first a banshee wail of anguish, and then Ben's name, panicking that she'd killed him or mortally wounded him. He'd let go of the gun, and she'd seized it and dumped it in a kitchen drawer, then run to open the front door, hoping whoever had rung the bell could help them. But there was no one there, so she'd run upstairs and come down with a bath towel to try to staunch the wound. She'd pressed it over the gash, instructed Ben to hold it there, and then dashed to the phone to call the police and an ambulance.

"Are you going to arrest me?" she asked the policewoman after she'd summarised what had happened.

"I don't think so," the woman, who had introduced herself as DI Lizzie Archer, said. "Not if you've told me the truth."

There was something slightly unnatural about the twist of her mouth, Claire thought, as if one side was smiling reassuringly but the other side was less than happy. Maybe she was just tired. She was turning now to Ben.

"You, on the other hand," she said. "Where do I start? Unlawful possession of a firearm. Illegal entry. False imprisonment. How about murder, or conspiracy to murder, while we're about it?"

Ben was still pale, but he didn't look as though he would pass out.

Claire saw the naked terror in his eyes. He was still her cousin. "What?" she said. "No, that's not right. Ben and I just had a little misunderstanding, that's all. I'm not pressing charges. And no way would he kill anyone."

Even though she was saying this, she wasn't sure. Ben still hadn't told her why he had been hiding out in her house in the first place, and there was no escaping the fact that at least one of four recent murder victims – from gunshot wounds – had been well known to him.

She wished now she hadn't been quite so quick to tell Archer what had led to her cousin getting stabbed. She'd dropped him in it – although he had been in it up to his nostrils already.

But he was still her cousin and, right now, she could see in him the little boy she'd once known, although that seemed like a million years ago now.

Archer shrugged. "I'm afraid Ben will have to answer for himself. So how about it, Ben? Claire has already said you were in her house when she came home. You tied her up, but she managed to get free. There was a struggle, the gun went off, you got cut. We're going to be testing that gun of yours to see if it matches a weapon used in four murders, including your mate, Ryan Sturridge. Will we find a match, Ben?"

He shook his head. "No. Absolutely not."

She nodded, evidently accepting his answer for now. "So how did you come by the gun?"

"Bought it, didn't I? Ryan wanted one for when he came out of jail. He told me who could supply it, and what he wanted. I met this dude in a car park. But he said he had a special offer on – buy one, get one half-price. So I got one for myself. I don't even know why I wanted it. It just seemed like a good deal. And Ryan was getting one…"

Even to Claire's ears, this sounded monumentally lame, but also very Ben. She could imagine how the idea of owning a real live gun would appeal to him, as some sort of status symbol, the way some of her male work colleagues coveted Aston Martins and Porsches.

"So come on," Archer was saying to him. "We're pretty sure Ryan met someone in prison and thought he had something tasty lined up here for when he came out. He even asked you to get some people on board. Told you big players would be moving into the area. So who were they? And when did it start going wrong?"

"No comment."

The detective shrugged again. "If that's how you want to play it. We know you're involved in these deaths somewhere and, right now, you're the only person we've got. You've committed enough crimes here for us to hold you, whether Claire cooperates or not. I'd get a lawyer and start talking, if I were you."

"No comment." He looked terrified.

"Please," Claire appealed to Detective Archer. "Give me five minutes with him."

The woman looked about to refuse, then nodded curtly. "All right. Only five minutes, though, and we'll be outside the door if you need us."

She and everyone else filed out. As soon as the door closed, Claire hurried over to her cousin.

"Right," she said, "I don't understand any of this, but you're only making things worse for yourself. What you did to me—"

His face crumpled. "I'm so sorry, Claire. Really, really sorry."

"Yes, well," she sniffed, something of her old pig-headedness returning. "I'm not going to let them make anything of that, if I can help it. But it sounds like you've got an idea who really killed Ryan and those other people. You have to tell the police."

"I'm a dead man walking if I do that."

"Now you're just talking stupid."

He laughed without humour. "You don't get it. The sort of people we're talking about... well, why d'you suppose all those people are dead? If I try to grass them up, I'll wind up dead myself."

"They can protect you."

"You think? These guys can get to you anywhere. They *own* coppers. For all we know, they own that lady with the funny mouth out there." He shook his head, his eyes bleak. "No. My only chance is to say nothing. Let them pin whatever they can on me and take the punishment. Maybe then they'll believe I didn't say anything. Otherwise, they can get to me, even in jail. They might decide to do it anyway, just to be on the safe side."

"You must be exaggerating."

"Trust me, Claire, yeah? I know you're tons cleverer than me, but this is something I know more about than you. Ryan saw what happened to grasses in jail. It wasn't nice."

She continued to try to persuade him, but it was like talking to a wall. After a couple more minutes, Archer re-entered.

"Well, Ben," she said. "Has your cousin managed to talk some sense into you?"

He raised his head, looked her in the eye, and gave her something resembling a smile.

"No comment."

* * *

His hands raised, Baines climbed out of the car. The gunman was bullet-headed, with hair shaven almost to his scalp and carefully groomed stubble. Not Ashby. Not Gillingham. He was vaguely familiar, but Baines couldn't place him. Where had he seen him?

"Not that it makes any odds," the man said, taking a two-handed grip on his weapon, "but who the hell are you, and why were you following me? I mean, I know you're police."

"Detective Sergeant Baines."

"Well, DS Baines, no one's going to miss your ability to tail a suspect when you're gone. I had you straight away."

Baines realised then that this was where it would end for him. This was the man who'd killed, pretty efficiently, at least four people. He wasn't going to hesitate over making it five. Baines wondered why he was still alive. Apart from Raphael, the others had been executed in a heartbeat.

"Just one question," the other man said, as if he was a mind-reader. "And whether I let you live depends on your answer. I asked why you were following me."

If he could have thought of something that would save him, Baines would have trotted it out. He knew, though, that this man was going to kill him whatever he said.

"You had a faulty tail light," he suggested.

"Nice try. I didn't have my lights on. I was wondering how you got on to me. Should I have changed my car?"

"You'll just have to wonder."

"Brave. Fair enough. Well, I'm going to have to change it now. Mine's not going anywhere. So take your keys out of the ignition and throw them to me."

Baines complied with the first order. Was about to obey the second, then hesitated. "Why did you crash like that?"

The gunman looked puzzled. "I don't know. Just for a moment, I thought I saw…" He shook his head as if to clear it. "Never mind that. The keys."

Baines stared at him, taking in what he had said. Then, instead of tossing them to the other man, he flung the keys as far as he could into the adjoining field.

"Very fucking clever."

Baines looked at the man again and something clicked.

"I know you," he said. "The other day, when I was talking to the barmaid at the Falcon. You came and stood next to me, waving a glass and some cash. The barmaid called you Peter, right? Earwigging, were you?"

"Very good. That's one of my talents. The man no one notices, seeing and hearing what's going on."

"You were hoping to hear how our investigation was going. Trying to find out what we knew." He bared his teeth in what he hoped looked like a defiant grin. "Didn't do you much good, did it? And now you're in the middle of nowhere with no car."

It felt like a hollow victory, though. He was still about to die.

"I'll make this quick," the man with the gun said. "On your knees."

* * *

Archer watched the ambulance drive away. There was a uniformed constable with Ben, and a squad car would escort them to the hospital, where his wound would be stitched and dressed. Then he'd be taken to the station to be interviewed under caution.

Claire was standing beside her. "He's scared, you know," she said. "He thinks, if he talks to you, he'll be killed himself. He seems sure they can get to him, wherever he is. What's he got himself into?"

"I wish I could say, but I really can't at the moment, Claire. And I can't help him if he won't help himself."

"He says he might as well top himself as be a grass."

Archer felt sympathy for the girl, who seemed more concerned about her cousin's safety than seeing him punished for what he had put her through.

She felt some pity for Ben, too. There was absolutely no doubt that he was in way, way out of his depth, and his fears were probably well founded. She had encountered enough serious criminals in London who would dissolve their mothers alive in acid for the price of a pint. It was already obvious the lengths this gang would go to, if it meant removing even the smallest risk to themselves, and the most successful criminal gangs had tentacles that reached inside prisons and police forces.

She'd already arrested Ben for unlawful possession of a firearm. Other charges would follow, but she wanted to discuss those with a more senior officer. Which was tricky, given that she didn't yet know how involved her own DCI was in the recent wave of murders.

Yet every time she tried to imagine Gillingham cold-bloodedly pointing a gun at someone's head and pulling the trigger, she failed. Whatever her boss's shortcomings, the image simply didn't tally with the man she thought she knew. Ashby, on the other hand... Was it just because she loathed him so much that she found it so much easier to think the worst of him?

"We'll do whatever we can to keep him safe," she said to Claire. "But I'd be lying to you if I said I could give you any guarantees. He needs to start by telling us what he knows, though." And she suspected that, however little he knew, it would be too much for the Connollys' comfort.

She strongly suspected that, whatever Ben Loftus did or said, and whatever steps the police took to protect him, he was probably right to be afraid. Unless they could get him into some sort of witness protection programme. But she knew that would only happen if he was deemed a valuable enough witness. Somehow, she doubted he was. The kid was trapped in a deadly catch-22.

She left Claire in tears, being comforted by a uniformed policewoman who would later take her to her parents' house. After what she'd been through, she shouldn't be alone.

Back in her car, she tried to phone Baines, but got an engaged signal. She called Collins.

"What happened with that guy Dan was chasing?"

"That's all gone quiet, guv. His phone and DCI Sheppard's are both engaged. I suspect they're talking to each other. I hope everything's all right."

Archer recalled her admonition to Baines not to go in for any heroics.

"So do I, Joan," she murmured. "So do I."

30

"I said," the gunman repeated, "on your knees."

Even now, Baines felt a last spark of defiance. He was damned if he was going to die on his knees, like some sacrificial lamb. The killer had said he'd make it quick for him. Easy.

But Dan Baines didn't do easy.

He'd rather go down standing. Or fighting. He measured the distance between them. If he rushed the man, he'd be a moving target. The gunman might even take an instinctive step back, spoiling his aim. Baines thought he'd probably still get shot, but maybe not fatally. What if he could get within grappling distance of the gunman and still be on his feet? Maybe anything could happen then.

He saw in a moment of absolute clarity that, finally, he had nothing left to lose. He had a slim chance of coming out of this alive.

He bowed his head in apparent surrender, then made as if to drop to his knees. Halfway down, he pushed off with his back foot.

In his school days, he'd been a passable short-distance sprinter. It was a gift that had come in handy in his early days on the force, when having to chase down a villain had been an occupational hazard. Now he was hurling himself across a few yards in the deadliest race of his life, trying to close the gap fast.

His charge took the gunman by surprise. He saw it in his eyes as he stepped backwards. But at the same time, he must have squeezed the trigger, because Baines saw the muzzle flash, and the roar of the gun was like thunder. There was a burning pain in his right side, but he kept going, flinging himself at the killer.

And then he was clubbed across the temple with the gun barrel.

He went down, landing on his wounded side and howling in agony. The world turned grey. He looked up and saw the gunman towering over him, the firearm pointed at his head.

"You've got some guts," the killer said. "I'll give you that. I almost admire you. This is nothing personal."

Even as he spoke, Baines heard a car roaring down the road. It screamed to a stop and he heard the door open. From where he was lying, he couldn't see the newcomer, but the gunman grinned.

"Out," he said to the driver. "Hands where I can see them."

Baines somehow managed to adjust his position enough to see DCI Sheppard emerging from a black Alfa Romeo. When her left hand appeared, it was holding a gun, which she swept up to point at the gunman

"Stalemate, I think," she said. But her voice faltered.

"Catherine," the man said. "I wondered if you'd be joining the party."

These two knew each other? Or maybe Baines had somehow heard wrong. He could feel sticky wetness spreading underneath his shirt and jacket. He was losing a lot of blood.

She looked stunned.

"Will?"

"Will?" Baines's echo was a croak, but understanding was dawning. "This is Will Streatham?"

"His face has changed a bit," she said, "but I'd know that voice anywhere."

The man who was supposed to be dead sounded amused. "When you need to disappear, you don't want to risk a chance meeting with someone who'll recognise you. Maybe I should have got my voice changed too."

"It's a good thing I took the precaution of drawing a firearm before I even came to Aylesbury. Why don't you put yours down, and we can talk?" Her tone seemed light and casual, but Baines could hear the underlying emotion.

The man still had his weapon pointed at Baines. "Oh, I think I'll keep my gun for now. Like you say, stalemate. Not surrender."

"You bastard," she barked, her veneer of control finally cracking. "You utter bastard. You betrayed us all and then faked your own death."

"And now here I am, back from the grave. It's a shock, I know."

Sheppard shifted her grip on her weapon, mirroring Streatham's two-handed stance. "Not a complete shock." Her tone was even once more. "Oh, I was never a hundred per cent sure you were still alive, but I had my doubts about your death right from the start. All that blood on the garage floor looked a little staged."

"Really? I donated two pints of my own blood to that little enterprise."

"Yes, it looked good. Trouble is, that so-called anonymous tip-off didn't ring true. A bit amateurish, to be honest. I'm surprised at you." She tutted. "That was a lot of blood, I grant you, and of course it was yours. But our experts couldn't say categorically that it was enough to be fatal."

Baines's world was swimming. He wasn't sure how much blood loss actually *would* be terminal, but he thought he was well on his way. He was very scared, panic fluttering in his belly, but he didn't want to interrupt this exchange. If he was dying, at least he wanted to know why.

"That wasn't all, though, was it?" Streatham said. "I had a feeling you'd already becomes suspicious of me."

"Maybe it was partly my fault," Sheppard replied. "Maybe you'd been in too deep for too long. I wanted to keep trusting you, but I was your handler. Quite apart from anything else," she added, a little huskily, "I knew the quality of the intelligence we'd been getting from you, and I'd noticed it had started to feel a little soft. And it just seemed that our main suspects were always just a little too far ahead of us for it to just be bad luck."

"I still kept feeding you crumbs."

"Yes. But our successes on Operation Stairway were small beer – nothing to lead us to the top. Someone was tipping them off. Someone on the inside."

"Very clever." His gun hand never wavered, but he was looking at Sheppard. "What can I say? Years of putting my life on the line for a pittance and a modest pension."

"So you came to prefer what the Connollys had to offer. I thought as much, although I had no proof. I kept it to myself, but I half suspected you'd gone bad. I even thought you were responsible for one murder."

"I guessed as much. One more reason to disappear."

"But how did you know I was on to you?"

"You were right, of course. I declared my hand to Murray Connolly about a year before my disappearance. Persuaded him I could be useful to him if I carried on playing the undercover cop. Told him all about Stairway, and how I could keep him one step ahead. But near the end, I heard something new in your tone. It was colder. I could hear the distrust in your voice."

Baines thought her mask of calm was slipping. Her lower lip was trembling, and she blinked rapidly. "I so wanted to be wrong. When you asked me to pull you out, I half wondered if I was."

"But you left me there anyway. Even though I said my life was in danger." He sounded bitter. "So much for our love."

If he'd thought this would work on her emotions, he'd miscalculated. Her eyes blazed with undisguised fury.

"Our love? Don't make me laugh," she sneered. "So it was agreed you should disappear? What? Go abroad, get some plastic surgery to alter your looks, then carry on working on the dark side?"

"Something like that."

"What were you? Some sort of adviser on SOCA procedure, with a bit of enforcement thrown in?"

"We've talked enough."

She ignored him. "So you wound up here. And then one of my people showed up."

Baines was finding it hard to remain conscious. If Sheppard was trying to save his life, it wasn't working.

"Put down the gun, Catherine," Streatham said. "Or shoot me. But I'll blow the DS's head off first."

"You put down the gun," she countered. "There's an armed response unit on its way, and you've nowhere to run."

"Don't bank on that."

"Turn yourself in and give evidence against the Connollys. I can cut you a good deal."

He seemed to hesitate. "What sort of deal?"

Was that hope Baines heard in his voice?

"Helping us nail the Connollys? Big fish like that? We could get you into witness protection. Maybe even make these murders go away."

The killer was silent for a while.

"You can really make that happen?"

"No guarantees, but helping us crack open a big operation has to count for a lot."

Baines didn't believe her, and he doubted the killer would. So Streatham's next words surprised him.

"I tell you what, then. Why don't we both put our guns down, so we can talk?"

"Maybe call me an ambulance while you're talking?" Baines's words sounded slurred, even to his own ears. "Otherwise there'll be one more murder to take into account."

"Maybe," Streatham said. "I'm so tired of all this. How about it, Catherine? On the count of three?"

Alarm bells rang in Baines's head. Maybe the leaking away of his lifeblood had slowed his wits.

"Don't trust him, Catherine," he whispered.

She glanced down at Baines, then fixed her gaze on her one-time lover again. Her face was a jumble of emotions.

"I'm losing patience, Catherine," Streatham said. "Gun down now, or I shoot DS Baines in the head."

"Shoot him," Baines whispered.

Sheppard's finger tightened on the trigger for an instant. Baines could see her hand was trembling.

Then her finger relaxed. "I can't." Her shoulders slumped. "Count of three?"

"Count of three," Streatham confirmed. "One... two..."

As he counted, both bent down. On 'three', Sheppard placed her gun on the ground. Streatham straightened instantly and pointed his weapon at her. He was laughing.

"You expected me to believe all that bollocks? You never really knew me at all, did you?"

Baines knew then that they were both going to die. In the end, whatever Sheppard still felt for Will Streatham had been too strong, and she had given away her only advantage.

The humour went out of Streatham's tone. "On your knees, Catherine."

As the DCI sank to her knees, Baines experienced a surprising sense of calm. He sensed Jack nearby and turned his head to see the boy standing there, plain as day, his expression unreadable.

Baines had never been much for religion, but now he wondered if he was about to see Louise again. What would she say about him sleeping with her sister? He might be about to finally learn the truth about Jack, too.

But then his mind filled with thoughts of Karen. Her last words to him had sounded so hurt and angry. She'd voiced their mutual fear that she was just a poor substitute for her sister, but now he finally saw that his love for the two women was completely different. With Louise it had been the usual boy meets girl thing. But he and Karen had bonded in mutual grief, becoming friends first and lovers much later. He loved Karen for herself, not because she reminded him of his lost wife.

Would she have got over it? Would they have patched things up? He liked to think so. Now they wouldn't have the chance to make it right. Losing Louise had been hard enough for her. He couldn't imagine what this would do to her.

"Just for the record, Catherine," Streatham said, "you were nothing to me but a good fuck."

She looked at Baines, tears glistening in her eyes. "I'm so sorry, Dan," she said.

A single shot rang out.

When he realised he hadn't been hit, Baines glanced at Sheppard, thinking Streatham must have shot her first, but she was alive, her mouth open in shock.

Jack had vanished.

Then Baines looked at Streatham.

The gunman was swaying, his gun hand hanging at his side as if the weapon was suddenly too heavy. His left hand was frozen halfway to his throat. He seemed to have sprouted a scarlet bib, just below his chin.

Sheppard lunged for her weapon. Raised and fired it in a single movement. A second shot rang out simultaneously, somewhere above them. Blood bloomed on Streatham's chest and, in the same instant, matter exploded from the side of his head. He fell to the ground like a puppet with its strings cut.

Baines realised he had been holding his breath. He exhaled and sucked in a fresh lungful. He was shaking. Maybe it was shock, or maybe he really was dying. He was cold, too

Sheppard was already up, gun clasped in both hands, standing in front of Baines and staring into the trees where the shot had come from.

"I can't see anyone," she said. "I thought maybe it was our armed unit, but I don't think so."

"An ambulance would be more use to me now." His voice seemed to come from far away.

She bent down, checked Streatham's pulse, then ran to the car. Came back with a car blanket and stuffed it into the wound. "Hold it there," she said. "I'm calling an ambulance right now. Stay with me, Dan."

She sounded like she was crying. He saw Jack's face floating before him, smiling. Then the world turned black.

* * *

Cameron Connolly walked back down the hill to where his car was waiting. Mad Willie McMurdo trailed behind him, rifle hefted on his shoulder, grumbling that he could have shot all three if only Mr Cameron had let him.

Cameron had to hand it to Willie. The man was as happy as a pig in shit if he was wielding a brick or something sharp to inflict damage on a fellow human being, but he was equally at home with a rifle and a long-range sight if that was called for.

They'd lain in wait for the cop, and Cameron had no doubt that Willie could have taken him out, moving car and all, at the place they'd chosen. But they'd heard the crash, guessed he'd come off the road, and moved quickly to the brow of the hill, where they could see the drama below unfolding.

"The cop was the one we wanted rid of, Willie," he said. "At least one of those others – the woman with the gun – were almost certainly police. And my little brother has made enough of a dog's breakfast of things around here without offing a couple of cops."

He took out his phone and called his father, explaining what had happened. Murray listened to his report, then grunted.

"Not what I'd call ideal. You know, when Streatham came to me admitting he was police, my gut told me to just get rid. I should have listened to it."

"The inside knowledge was useful," Cameron reminded him, "and you can't deny he's been an asset until now. It was just bad luck we turned out to have another undercover guy in our midst. At least our man recognised him."

"Yes, but they'd not have recognised him back, not with his face job. It's not like he was even at the meeting. Desmond should have told us there was a problem, not taken it upon himself to start a massacre." Cameron heard his dad sigh. "I would have just disappeared the guy we knew as Butcher and warned those kids not to shoot their mouths off any more. It's been a fucking disaster."

"And the Aylesbury Vale network's supposed to be going live on Wednesday. We're supposed to be taking our first big delivery. Well, no way can we go ahead with that now. We don't know what Streatham said to those other two before Willie shut him up."

"He won't have said anything."

"We can't be sure of that."

"Even so, I've told you. We've got too much tied up in that damn shipment, and everything's in place. I'm buggered if I'm calling it off now. We go ahead."

Cameron knew finality when he heard it in his father's voice, but he was still far from happy. "It's a massive risk."

"Son, we're in the risk business. Have you not heard? No, we go ahead, but we mitigate the risk."

"How?"

Murray Connolly chuckled. "Just you listen to your old dad…"

31

Archer sat in the corridor at Stoke Mandeville Hospital, nursing a cardboard cup of coffee that was perhaps marginally better than the foul concoction that the vending machine down at the station dispensed.

It was rare for her to be here and not attending a post-mortem, but it hardly made a pleasant change. Baines had been brought in here unconscious and in a bad way after being given a blood transfusion at the scene of his shooting. Apparently he'd lost about five pints of blood and was lucky to be alive. At least the bullet had gone straight through and, by some miracle, missed any vital organs.

She stole a glance at the woman beside her. Karen Smart still looked grey and scared, despite the reassurances she had been given. It had been Archer who'd found her work number in Baines's phone and called her. When she'd announced herself, she thought she'd detected a moment's hostility, but that turned to panic when she explained why she was calling. She'd picked Karen up and driven her to the hospital.

In the car, Karen had confided that she and Baines had rowed on the phone earlier on, and then she dissolved into tears.

"I said some horrible things," she'd said. "I can't help thinking they were nearly the last words I said to him."

Hiding her surprise that all had not been well in paradise, Archer had assured her that all couples fought, and they never expected not to have a chance to make up.

"Trust me." She'd tried to make light of it. "Even coppers survive most days."

A couple in their late sixties appeared at the end of the corridor, the woman holding the man's arm tightly.

"It's Dan's parents," Karen said, rising. She went to meet them, exchanging hugs and kisses with them, and then introduced Archer.

"Well," Archer said finally, "I should leave you all now." She gave Karen a card. "Give me a call, please, after you've seen him."

"Of course I will." Karen surprised her with an impetuous hug. "I'm glad we met. You're not what I imagined."

"Is that a good thing?"

"Yes. I mean… Oh, shit. Look, just thanks for everything. Really."

Leaving the hospital, Archer almost ran into Sheppard, who was carrying a bunch of flowers.

"How is he?"

Archer updated her. "His partner and parents are there, waiting to see him."

"Oh." The NCA DCI shrugged. "Well, I don't want to be a spare part." She held up the flowers. "These are probably not him, anyway."

"Well…"

"I'll bin them. Unless you…"

"I kill everything. It's a nice thought, though. You've spoken to Gillingham?"

"Yes. Let me walk you to your car and I'll debrief you."

"How are you?" Archer asked when they were seated in her car. She was acutely aware that, earlier in the day, Sheppard had seen her former lover return from the dead, only for him to be gunned down.

"I've been better. If you mean am I mourning the bastard – honestly, I don't know. Whoever it was that killed him saved me and Dan, so I'm not about to weep buckets about that. Numb, I suppose, is how I feel."

"So what happens now?" Archer asked. "Are we going to arrest the entire Connolly family?"

"I think you know the answer to that, Lizzie. We've no evidence."

"But you said Streatham named them. To you and Dan."

"And we could make statements to that effect, but it's not the same as proof. It's little more than hearsay. As Paul Gillingham said, the sort of lawyer they can probably afford will drive a coach and horses through it."

"But..." Archer raked her fingers through her hair, disbelieving, groping for straws to grab hold of. "It's a dying man's confession. They can be admitted into evidence in some cases. Can't they?"

"Good luck with that." Sheppard's tone was bitter. "He wasn't confessing as such."

"But his gun. If we get a match to the bullets that killed our four victims—"

"It will prove he killed them, yes. But I very much doubt it will tie him to the Connollys. By the way, we think they do a nice little trade in black market weapons but, like everything else, they cover their tracks too well. I suspect that gun found its way from Reading nick into Will's hand by a very circuitous route. Chances are, we'll never know how. No, our only hope is if we can get Ben Loftus to implicate them. Even then, you'd need a pretty strong story, with evidence to back it up. Otherwise the briefs will say Ben's saying what we told him to say."

"Funny that Ben's in the same hospital as Dan, having his wound stitched and sorted out," said Archer. "I can't wait to get him in an interview room. You might care to join me."

Before Sheppard could respond, Archer's mobile rang. She answered, listened, made a few remarks, then hung up and stared bleakly at the other woman.

"That was Joan Collins," she said. "The hospital has just rung. Ben Loftus is dead."

* * *

Baines was still woozy, but his brain was beginning to function again. He wasn't sure whether that was a good thing or not. Like a loop of film, the moment when he'd believed he was about to die kept replaying in his mind.

He'd tried to make light of it with Karen and his parents, even managing to crack a couple of feeble jokes. He thought he'd scared them more than enough already. It was best, at least for now, if they believed that it had been no big deal. He suspected that Karen had seen right through him, and maybe later he could talk to her about it properly. She'd left, along with his parents, at the end of visiting hours, and for now he was stuck with the emotional fallout from today.

He'd dealt with worse. He could deal with this.

Only he hadn't dealt with it, had he? Not really.

He was aware of a figure standing beside his bed, and looked up.

"Hi," Archer said.

He felt himself frowning. "I thought visiting hours were over."

"You'd be surprised the doors a warrant card can open. But I'll make myself scarce, if you're tired."

"No." He gestured to the chair next to the bed, wincing. He realised he badly wanted her to stay. "Please. Sit."

She eased into the chair. She looked exhausted. Grey-faced.

"Well," he said, "if you've come to cheer me up, you need to work on your technique."

To his dismay, a tear trickled down her face. He'd never seen her cry.

"I was only joking."

"I'm sorry." She swiped at her eyes. "I shouldn't have come. It's been such a bloody awful day. I just wanted to see you. You gave us all such a scare. You..." she gave him a twisted smile. "You gave *me* a scare."

"I scared myself... So, what's happening with the case? Do we know who shot Will Streatham?"

"We think it must have been his own side for some reason. We're not really sure. We're going to regroup in the morning. We found Ben Loftus, by the way."

He felt a surge of excitement. "You got him? Do you think you'll get anything out of him? About the Connollys?"

"No, Dan. He's dead."

"Dead?"

She leaned her head against the chair back. "It was my fault. I should have anticipated it."

She told him then, in flat tones, like an automaton. Having been patched up, at Stoke Mandeville Hospital, Ben had said he needed the toilet before the two uniformed officers with him took him to the station for questioning. He had entered a single WC – the old-fashioned type with an overhead cistern and a chain pull flush – and locked the door behind him. The PC who had accompanied him was calling to him, asking how long he was going to be, when the other constable had come to find them. They got no response and eventually broke the door down, to find Ben hanging by his belt from a cistern pipe. Efforts by hospital staff to revive him had been fruitless.

When Gillingham had heard the circumstances of the boy's death, he had gone ballistic, carpeting both officers and asking what the hell they'd been doing, allowing a vulnerable teenager to lock himself in a cubicle like that with a means of hanging himself. But the truth was that no one could have foreseen that Ben was a suicide risk. But would the media see it that way?

"Gillingham was right," Baines told her. "How could you have anticipated it?"

She barked a laugh. "How? Because his cousin as good as told me. She said he thought his life wouldn't be worth living in prison. I should have taken her more seriously. It seems Ryan had put the wind up him about what happens to snitches on the inside."

"So he took the coward's way out. You can't blame yourself."

"Oh," she said, "I blame myself for a lot more than that. I let you put yourself in danger, and look how that turned out."

It seemed no time ago that she'd been hearing him talk about Jack, and his fear that he might be losing his mind. Now, when he'd never seen her so disconsolate, he was determined to be there for her. Even though he could hardly keep his eyes open.

She must have noticed.

"You need to sleep. I'll drop in again as soon as I can."

"I'll be back at work in no time," he protested.

"I don't think so." She rose, stepped towards him and took his hand. "You get better, you hear? As long as it takes." She bent over and brushed her lips against his forehead. "Get some sleep."

She was halfway to the door when she stopped, slapping her forehead. "Damn it. I meant to bring you something."

He smiled. "Don't worry, Lizzie. You did."

32

It was a dispirited group that convened in the briefing room the following morning. Baines had been banned from work until the doctors judged him fit to return. He'd got out of that occupational health appointment after all, although Archer had already rescheduled it.

It didn't stop Archer from blaming herself. With no one at home to confide in, she'd battled her demons alone, and it had been an unequal struggle.

She'd looked at herself in a mirror in the ladies' just before the briefing and realised how beaten she looked. Applying her make-up had been too much of a bother, and her hair wasn't as immaculately arranged as usual. It was a long time since her scar had been so visible, and it had hurt to realise that people would be able to see it so clearly again. She'd made the effort to do some running repairs to her appearance, but it didn't make her feel any better.

Only Gillingham seemed upbeat. He seemed to have got over yesterday's tantrum and now appeared to regard a death in custody as a comparatively small thing, set against solving four murders.

"I think it'll play quite well in the media," he said, "and the brass seem to agree. Ben Loftus's death was unforeseeable and, at the end of the day, he was a small-time criminal who was involved in murder, and God knows what else, and held his own cousin prisoner at gunpoint. He won't get much sympathy from the public. Compared to the swift, brave action of two of our detectives in helping remove a dangerous gunman from our streets…"

Archer listened to his speech with rising anger.

"You're going to dismiss a confused kid, who got into something he couldn't handle, as a scumbag we're better off without? A kid who didn't actually hurt anyone?" There was a bitter taste in her mouth. "Our officers' 'swift, brave action' nearly got them killed." Something else to blame herself for. She had sanctioned Baines following Streatham. "The only reason they're still alive is that someone – almost certainly the people he was working for – killed Streatham first. They probably decided he was a liability."

Gillingham lowered his eyes. "This really hasn't worked out too bad," he mumbled.

"Not too bad?" Archer's tone was just the right side of shrill. "Just how are you going to explain the fact that an undercover cop who'd been missing, presumed dead, was alive all this time, working for seriously bad guys? Had committed four murders for them and then been killed by them himself? Oh, and the fact that the bad guys are still out there?"

Sheppard cleared her throat. "I know you're unhappy, Lizzie, and I don't blame you. But it's all been agreed. As for the roles of Will Streatham and Matthew Butcher, we're going to play those down as much as possible. There was a reason why we chose them for these dangerous jobs. No one is going to come looking for them."

"You hope," Archer said.

"In fact, we now know Streatham had been using the name Peter Davis here. Your Chief Constable and my director have agreed that we'll stick with that for now."

"In other words, you're going to do your best to bury most of this."

"That's not how I'd describe it." The human being she'd glimpsed at the hospital yesterday, with an inappropriate bunch of flowers, seemed to have retreated back into her hard shell.

"And the Connolly family? Are you just going to give up?"

"Not at all," Sheppard assured her. "I'm even more determined to take them down."

"And how will you do that? Everyone who might have had some useful information on them is dead."

"Actually," Gillingham said, "there might still be one last dice to roll."

"Really?" Sheppard leaned forward. "So tell us."

"It's a bit thin," he admitted, "but while all the excitement was going on yesterday, Steve Ashby came to me saying he'd picked something up from of his contacts about some big thing happening this week."

Archer thought 'a bit thin' might be an understatement when applied to anything to do with Ashby and his contacts, but she resisted the temptation to eye-roll. She still wondered what the deal was with Gillingham and Ashby, but she'd been on the wrong track when she'd thought they might be involved in murder. It could do no harm to at least hear them out.

"What sort of something?"

He shrugged. "All hell was breaking loose, Lizzie, and he said it would keep until today."

"How much does he know about our case?" Sheppard wanted to know.

"I haven't admitted him to the inner circle, if that's what you mean, Catherine," Gillingham said. "But he's not daft. He knows NCA are interested and that it's to do with our murders. It's not so hard to figure that there's an organised crime angle." He looked at them in turn. "Why don't I try to get hold of him?"

"He could be anywhere," Archer murmured.

But Ashby was actually in his office, and he came to join them as soon as the DCI called him. He gave Archer a look that seemed like genuine concern as he sat down.

"How's Dan?"

"He'll be okay," she said. "He just needs to mend now."

"Well, give him my best if you see him."

"I will." This wasn't the piss-taking Ashby she was used to. "The boss says you might have something for us?

"Maybe. I've been chatting up my networks, as you know, to see if anything's going on that might be relevant."

"And...?"

"I spoke to a few villains who'll sell me information sometimes. No one's speaking, no one even wants to talk to me. Which is unusual."

"But unhelpful," remarked Sheppard.

"Yes, except a couple of them had those wall calendars, and I happened to notice that Wednesday's date was circled on more than one."

"Anything written in?"

"No, but—"

"And that's it?" Sheppard sounded exasperated. "Maybe there's some football match on that day."

"Hang on, though," Ashby persisted. "Those people are on the fringes of the drugs scene. So I picked a few more who ought to know if anything important was happening in that area, and said I'd like to meet with them – maybe Wednesday. I said I'd make it worth their while. And you know what the funny thing is?"

"Get on with it, Steve," Gillingham growled.

Ashby blinked. "Sure. Sorry. The thing is, no one's available to meet in the second half of this week. It's as if they're all holding their breath, waiting for something. And knowing that they'll be busy when it happens."

Sheppard drummed her manicured nails on the arm of her chair. "It could be something, or it could be nothing. I don't see that it helps, if no one's talking."

"I don't know," Archer surprised herself by backing up Ashby. "Something significant happening just as everything else is going on? It can't be a coincidence. And we have a day to go on, if Steve's right."

"If," the NCA woman pointed out. She frowned. "But even if he *is* right, we don't have a time, and we don't have a place. If we knew that, we could gatecrash."

"'We', meaning your team, I suppose?" Archer said sourly.

"It's all about the Connollys now. That's my case." She looked Archer in the eye. "But it's on your turf, and your local knowledge is invaluable." Her eyes softened. "If we're going to salvage something from this mess, we need to work together, Lizzie. But first we need a bit more of a lead than we have right now."

Sheppard was right, and the frustration made Archer want to punch a wall. She mentally ran through all that had happened in the last few days. Six deaths altogether. Baines lucky to be alive. And the investigation stalled.

Yet, for some reason, the exercise seemed to clear her mind. Perhaps it was clearer than it had been from the start of this case. She felt a stirring of renewed enthusiasm.

"Maybe we know more than we think we do," she said. "That road where Streatham crashed his car? It's a dirt road. According to my guys, hardly anyone uses it. In terms of the points it connects, it's not even worth a damn as a rat run. But he knew it, and he chose it. That might mean something."

"So where does it lead?" Sheppard seemed interested.

"Well," Archer said, rising from her seat, "let's have a look."

She switched on a laptop and then the projector that was linked to it.

"I'm going to get it up on Google Earth," she said.

A few minutes later she stood by the screen, pointing with her pen. "That's the road. Now, we know they're establishing a new enterprise here in the Vale, and that something's happening tomorrow. Catherine, you have the organised crime experience. You must have some idea as to what it might be."

The other woman pondered. "Most likely some sort of consignment being delivered."

"So they'll need somewhere to take it. Somewhere they can store whatever it is and use it as a base for feeding their supply chain."

"Unless it's women," Sheppard commented. "Although they'd still need somewhere to hold them until they're moved on. And, actually, if they've been imported as sex slaves, they'll be treated almost the same as any other commodity. There could even be an auction."

"Really?" Gillingham shook his head. "I've heard of such things in other countries, but here in the Vale?"

"I'm only aware of it happening at UK airports so far, but that doesn't mean it isn't also happening inside the country."

"So we're looking for something discreet. Hidden," Archer said. "And a decent size, I'd guess."

All four crowded around the screen. Gillingham traced the road with his finger until he came to what looked like a track off to the left.

"Where does this go?"

"What's that?" Sheppard asked almost simultaneously, pointing at an area with a number of industrial-looking buildings dotted around.

"The old airfield," Ashby said. "Some farmland, some industry."

"It's perfect."

"We need to find out if any of the units have changed hands recently," Archer said. "And who has bought them."

Sheppard actually chuckled. "I agree about the first, but as to the second... good luck! It's not going to have 'Murray Connolly' written all over it. If he runs true to form, you'll never trace it to him." She shrugged. "But if it's registered to some obscure overseas company, that's still a bit of a giveaway."

Archer tapped a large building in one corner. "This looks promising."

"Right sort of size," Sheppard agreed.

"We're going too fast," Gillingham complained. "First we need to know if the road Streatham was on is even a viable route to the airfield."

"Paul, how well do you know that area?" Sheppard asked him.

"Not that well." He studied the aerial view. "It looks as if there's a little network of C roads, though, that probably don't see too much traffic. You could try driving it."

"You know," Sheppard said, "we might be able to do better than that. We've got Will's car, and I'm sure he had a satnav. What if he used that to get to the airfield?"

"You might be right," Archer was forced to concede. "If there's a route programmed into the satnav that takes you to the airfield, then he must have been headed there. I'd still like to try that drive, though."

"I'll come with you," Sheppard said. "Let me just get my team checking out the satnav and who holds those units."

"Of course," Gillingham cautioned, "if this turns out to be a red herring…"

"Then we start again," Sheppard said.

* * *

Shortly afterwards, Sheppard was driving back towards the road where she'd had a near-fatal encounter with a killer only the previous day. Archer wasn't sure this would be good for her, had tried to insist on driving, but Sheppard had been even more insistent that she needed to do this.

They'd travelled in silence for about five minutes before the NCA woman spoke.

"I know you're not happy with what's been decided, Lizzie, but think about it. The whole thing with Will Streatham is an embarrassment to the NCA."

"I think that's the least of our worries," Archer said. "Even if we can catch at least one of them red-handed with that consignment, or whatever it is, that's something some hot-shot lawyer for the Connollys will find a way of using against us to undermine our case. I don't give a shit about Streatham," she added. "It was his choice to turn rogue. Butcher, though…"

Archer was still hopeful someone would recognise the mocked-up photo that had been released. Surely, people must have known him before he became Matthew Butcher. But she held her tongue about that. There was no point in antagonising Sheppard.

They drove on, each lost in their thoughts, until they reached the spot where yesterday's standoff had taken place. The area was still cordoned off, with two bored-looking uniforms on guard.

Archer got out, showed them her ID and explained that they needed to get through. She left them moving crime scene tape and got back in the car.

Sheppard was staring ahead, her complexion pale, sweat on her brow, her knuckles white on the wheel.

"Are you okay, Catherine? Catherine? Do you want me to drive?"

"Sorry. Miles away."

"Maybe you should take some time off."

"Me? I'm fine." She put the car in gear and moved forward.

Not for the first time, Archer wondered how yesterday's events would impact on Baines, a man who, by all accounts, had gone back to work pretty well straight after his wife had been murdered and his young son abducted. A man who now kept hallucinating that he saw his son, all grown up, at random times and in random places. She could order him to take some leave, of course, but that could shatter their finely balanced working relationship forever. Whoever occupational health sent him to see, they had better be good. And Baines had better be prepared to open up to them.

"This is where you need to start doing some map reading," Sheppard said.

Minutes later they passed a sign for the airfield, and then they could see the site coming up on their right.

"Don't turn in," Archer said. "You never know who might be about."

"True. Although I fancy a quick gander at that big building we were interested in."

She thought about it. "Sod it, let's go for it. Just drive past, though. Don't make it obvious we're interested."

Archer had seen some big bases for criminal activity before, but this one seemed over the top, especially for a new operation in a rural setting. She knew that organised criminals were increasingly seeking new pastures in which to expand their interests, but she found it hard to believe that whatever the Connollys had planned for Aylesbury Vale justified this much space.

Their working assumption was that Desmond Connolly's interest in the area had been prompted by Ryan Sturridge during their time in prison. Had he been given the Vale as his own turf? And was this great aircraft hangar of a building a testament to his youth, inexperience and, quite likely, stupidity?

As they approached, the wire fencing, high gates, and the casually dressed gorilla by the entrance all spoke of something to hide. The Alfa rolled past at a steady speed, both women avoiding giving any sign that they were at all interested. Archer could feel waves of suspicion emanating from the gorilla of a gate guard – if that was what he was.

"I know him," Sheppard said. "Brian Dale. He's got alleged links to the Connollys. That sort of clinches it."

They returned to the station, where Sheppard dropped Archer, leaving her to update Gillingham while she drove over to Oxford to do the same with her team.

Gillingham looked up at Archer's knock on his door. "How did you get on?"

"I'd say it's promising. Streatham could easily have been headed for that building, and someone DCI Sheppard recognised was controlling access. I just wish we knew a bit more about what's planned for tomorrow, but I suppose that's asking a lot." She hesitated, hating to ask the question that was in her mind, but knowing she had to. "I don't suppose Steve Ashby has any more of his so-called intelligence?"

If Gillingham detected her scepticism, he didn't show it. "Let's ask him. I think he's around." He took out his phone.

Moments later, Ashby put his head round the door and grinned

"Well, this is good timing," he said. "I was looking for you, Lizzie. I might just have a bit more of a lead on what's supposed to be happening tomorrow."

33

Much as Archer hated it, she had to hand it to Ashby. The man was a sleazebag, and his perpetual absences, allegedly cultivating his so-called networks, often seemed a lazy joke, but just occasionally he did produce a rabbit from a hat.

A bloody big rabbit this time, if it led to one of the biggest raids in the Vale's history.

What he had told them yesterday morning had been a mix of hunches and surmise, albeit based on what sounded like hours tirelessly and discreetly asking the right questions in the right places. While Archer and Sheppard had been checking out the old airfield, he'd carried on talking to contacts on the fringes of the local drugs trade as if he already knew what was happening today – and one of the least bright of that cadre had let slip that a delivery was being made somewhere early this morning, with distribution expected during the day.

Much of yesterday afternoon had been spent planning this operation. It should have been an exclusively NCA affair, but Sheppard had been surprisingly keen for there to be a presence from Aylesbury Vale. So Collins sat with Archer in Bell's Ford Focus, just behind one of the factories on the airfield estate. Behind another factory, in Ashby's car, were Ashby himself, Gillingham, Sheppard and Sheppard's deputy, a DI Lee Knowles. Their position gave Sheppard a view of the gates in front of the building they were monitoring. A third car contained other members of Sheppard's team, and an armed team waited in a van a little further off.

All four vehicles were connected by radio, but maintaining silence until Sheppard gave the signal to move.

Archer yawned. It was a couple of minutes before 6am. The Kevlar vest she wore made her feel warmer than was entirely comfortable, and she was acutely aware that, whilst it was bullet-*resistant*, it was not bullet-*proof.* No matter how she tried, she was unable to entirely shake off the feeling that Baines had been lucky on Monday, and she might not be today. But, despite her apprehension, she also felt the anticipation of being part of something potentially momentous. She wondered how long they would have to wait for the delivery – whatever form it would take – to materialise.

If it did materialise, that was. Even if Ashby's source was correct, it always presupposed that the Connollys' plans would go ahead after they had killed Will Streatham. It was obvious that his own side had seen him as a menace and decided to eliminate him. Why his killer had not fired at Baines and Sheppard when they were sitting ducks was less clear, but there had to be a question mark now over whether the delivery would go ahead – despite Sheppard's instance that the family business would have tied up too much cash and kudos in this new operation to pull the plug lightly.

"Heads up," Sheppard's voice crackled in his ear. "Something coming."

Archer's mouth went dry. This could be it. She glanced at her companions and saw her tension reflected in their faces. They were only here as observers, and to provide a local police presence. They weren't armed, and were under instructions not to put themselves in harm's way – which suited her. One close encounter with a firearm was enough for one week for her.

They all watched as a small blue van rolled past. Bell's fingers closed on the ignition key, ready to fire up the Focus.

"As you were," Sheppard crackled again. "It's turned off. Just an early bird on the way to work, I guess."

Adrenalin still coursing through her veins, Archer checked her watch. It was one minute to six.

* * *

"They'd better not be late," Cameron Connolly said.

"They won't be," soothed Desmond. He was praying that his eyes weren't giving away his nervousness.

"Like you'd know," Cameron sneered. "Because you've got

such a great track record up to now, haven't you? If this goes tits-up too..."

Desmond shrugged. "What if it does? I thought Dad had put you in charge. So it's on you now if anything goes wrong, right, bro?"

"I'd keep that flappy tongue of yours under lock and key, if I were you."

"I still say I had everything under control."

"You just keep telling yourself that." Cameron's mobile rang. "Saved by the bell," he said.

Desmond watched him take the phone into a corner of the warehouse, where his brother couldn't hear, as if Desmond was even capable of bollocksing up someone else's phone call, just by being there.

A fresh wave of resentment washed over him. It was all totally unfair. Cameron and Fraser were always his dad's favourites, while he was always treated like the idiot son, the one a few beers short of a six-pack. He'd only done that bit of drug dealing on the side to show that he was as able to run a business as his two sun-shining-out-of-their-arse brothers. No way was it his fault he'd got caught in the act of supplying. Not really.

And hadn't he put his dad on to this promising new territory? Plenty of small-time villains here, but no organisation on the scale his family could bring to the party. Those that were too stupid to see the benefits of coming on board could be coerced by less subtle means. The cop's means, to be precise.

It was Dad who'd sent the enforcer up here as an advance guard, wasn't it? And, when he'd recognised Matt Butcher as police – their paths had crossed a couple of times before – it had been the cop who insisted they should waste him, as well as the kids who couldn't keep their mouths shut.

That Clark kid, though. Desmond knew from Ryan Sturridge that he was getting cold feet and wanted to walk away. That wasn't an option. But when the cop had tailed Butcher, looking for an opportunity to erase him, he hadn't expected him to be meeting the boy on a street corner. The cop had decided to take them both out, and it had all unravelled from there.

Desmond bet that Cameron – or his dad, for that matter – would have done things exactly the same, had they been in charge. But, once it had got messy, it had suddenly become all stupid Desmond's doing.

"Okay," Cameron said, shoving his phone back in his pocket as he returned, "they're less than five minutes away. Best thing you can do is keep out of the way. You say nothing, you touch nothing."

* * *

Archer was beginning to wonder all over again how reliable Ashby's sources actually were. A mean part of her was back to wondering if they really existed. They'd all been here for hours, their flasks of coffee were empty, and Bell had scoffed the last muffin. It was getting on for 6.30am, and her gut told her that an illegal shipment was unlikely to arrive in the middle of the day.

It had started to get light just after five, and now cars were already trickling onto the airfield site. Early starters. Meanwhile, the gates at the front of the suspect building remained resolutely closed. What if they had the wrong building? Maybe the Connollys were using a smaller, less obtrusive, depot elsewhere on the site.

Even so, no vehicles any bigger than an estate car had come on to the airfield so far. Surely a serious consignment of drugs or whatever would rate a larger vehicle?

Collins yawned noisily from the back seat.

"Oh, sorry everyone. I just remembered why I don't do earlies."

Archer laughed. "This from the woman who's usually first in and last out. Assuming you even have a home. I sometimes wonder if you sleep in the office."

"Heads up again," Sheppard said in Archer's earpiece. "This looks a bit more promising."

There was silence for a short while, then, "I think they're going to open the gates," she said. Another, briefer pause. "All right, stand by. I want the goods inside before we go. On my command…"

***

As the roll-up door at the front of the building began to rise, Desmond couldn't help rubbing his hands in gleeful anticipation. Fuck what Cameron said. He knew the truth – that this was all down to him. He'd handled the little teething troubles without any interventions needed, and certainly without a liability like Mad Willie turning up on what Desmond already thought of as his patch.

He tried not to think about the possibility that his commission on this first set of transactions would be reduced, or even withheld. He wouldn't put it past Cam to claim all the credit for himself. But surely that wouldn't happen? After all, Dad had asked him to cut his teeth on this and – what did they call it? Yes, a learning curve, that was what it was.

It would go more smoothly next time.

The door had fully opened, and Desmond heard the throaty purr of the van's engine as the driver applied his foot to the accelerator, allowing the vehicle to roll forward. The guy who had opened the door had his finger poised over the button to close it as soon as the van was inside.

Desmond watched it come, the chink of cash registers jingling in his head, accompanying Jessie J singing about money.

"Come to Papa," he whispered.

***

"Now!" snapped Sheppard. "Go, go, go!"

Archer saw Sheppard's vehicle barrel out onto the approach road to the building, sirens wailing. Bell had turned on his own sirens, the racket all but drowning the sound of his engine gunning. The Focus almost fishtailed as it hurtled into line behind Sheppard's vehicle, her team's car just behind it. Archer glanced back and saw the van carrying the armed unit coming up fast.

Sheppard's vehicle screeched to a halt just outside the gates, the other two cars stopping too. The armed unit sped through the gates, forcing the man on guard duty to leap aside.

"That wasn't the guy we saw yesterday," Archer said, and then everyone was scrambling out of the cars and sprinting over the few yards that would carry them through the gates and into the building. One of Sheppard's team was making sure the gate man didn't do a runner. Sheppard shouted, "Armed police! Nobody move!"

Archer felt her heart pumping like a steam engine, excitement like a drug racing through her veins. Here, right here, was justice, for Brandon Clark in particular – justice that went beyond the death of his actual killer, striking at those who were ultimately responsible. Baines might just sleep a little more peacefully tonight.

Then everyone stopped.

The space inside the building was bare apart from a table holding an electric kettle, jars of coffee and sugar and a grimy mug with a spoon in it. Empty shelves lined the walls. One man stood by the van, whose driver was getting out. Both raised their hands.

"What's going on?" the first man said. He was doing his best to look puzzled, but Archer knew perfectly well that he was laughing inside.

There was a sinking feeling in her stomach. There ought to be more people here than this. And Sheppard had shown them pictures of Connolly family members. These guys were none of them.

"Search them," Sheppard commanded, resignation already in her voice. An armed officer patted down first one, then the other suspect.

"They're clean," he said.

"Are you sure you've come to the right place?" The man who had spoken spoke again. "You look like an army looking for a war. We haven't got one here."

Sheppard looked as if she had bitten into something sour. Gillingham stepped into the breach. "What's in the van?"

"Ah," the man said, "you got us. It's drugs."

He said it with no hint of fear or worry. The DCI looked at

Bell. "Open it up."

The young Scot walked to the back of the van and opened the double doors.

"Empty," he said. "I don't understand, sir."

"Not quite empty." The garrulous suspect was not concealing his enjoyment. "Look again."

Archer joined Bell, her eyes scanning the van floor. Then, without bothering to put latex gloves on, she leaned inside and picked up a small rectangular object.

"It's drugs, all right," she groaned. "One packet of paracetamol."

"Thank God for that," said Mr Chatty. "I've got quite a headache. So I asked Tommy here to drop some tablets round for me."

Sheppard pointed to a door at the back. "Where does that go?"

"Toilet. Why, do you need a slash, love?"

"Call me love again and I'll have your arsehole searched," she said. Then she turned to her team. "Someone check that room out. Two more of you go over this van with a fine-tooth comb."

"You'll find nothing," Chatty Man promised.

"I'm sure." She shook her head, her expression showing a mix of disappointment and the urge to punch someone. "We've been had, haven't we?"

* * *

Meanwhile, packets were being unloaded from a van onto the shelves in the hastily hired building, on the edge of the Buckinghamshire/Oxfordshire border. Desmond watched, arms folded, a warm glow inside. There were enough goodies to start a chain of pharmacies: hard stuff, pills, cannabis. Soon they would hit the distribution network that he had brought together. All right, maybe things hadn't gone so smoothly these past few days, but credit was due to him. He hoped his dad would see that.

On the subject of credit, he supposed some was due to

Fraser. Simply moving the operation had been Dad's idea, but it was his bean-counter brother who had made it work at the drop of a hat, and Desmond knew there was about as much chance of tying it to the family as there was of tying a politician to a dirty deed.

He looked at Cameron, who was presiding over the unloading like the cock of the walk, people looking to him for instructions and approval. Even as children it had been this way: Cameron helping himself to what was Desmond's, Dad telling him not to be such a cry-baby if he made a fuss. Cameron the golden boy.

Back in their childhood, Desmond had told Cameron many times that he hated him. Now Desmond realised with a jolt that it was no longer simply something one child said to another, with no real meaning behind it. He truly hated his brother.

Perhaps Cameron felt his gaze, boring into the back of his neck, because he turned then, locked eyes, and smiled. He ambled over and patted his younger sibling on the shoulder.

"This all seems to be going smoothly," he said. He nodded towards a door to the side which led to a small makeshift office. "Let's pop in there for a word."

They went into the scruffy office, and Cameron closed the door on the hive of activity behind them.

"So," he said, helping himself to the only chair, "it looks like it's all turned out okay in the end. No sign of the police, which is hardly surprising. You know, I almost hope they do raid the other place, now we've gone to all this trouble. Paracetamol," he chuckled. "They'll be spitting blood."

Desmond hadn't liked Cameron's little joke, but voicing that concern hadn't seemed such a good idea at the time. Now his brother seemed more affable, perhaps he could say what he thought.

"Yeah, I'd have loved to see that." He started on a positive note. "But what if the other guys there let something slip? Or they crack under questioning?"

"Oh," Cameron waved a hand airily, "I'd be surprised if they arrested anyone. It'll be embarrassing enough as it is, and they've got absolutely no proof. The building, the van…

nothing traces back to us. The story is that those two guys were thinking of setting up a furniture removal business and changed their minds. They were renting the building from the overseas shell. All cash to a guy in a pub. No name, no pack drill, no paperwork yet."

"So we're up and running?"

"Well, *I* am, Des. Not you. But if you can get your act together – prove you've got some functioning brain cells – maybe you'll get the reins back one day. Although I must admit I like it here. Maybe I'll invest in a property."

Impotent fury bubbled inside Desmond. Losing his temper now would simply prove whatever point was being made. He knew silence was the best policy, however hard he had to bite his tongue. He just held on to his hatred. The time would come when there was only room for one of them – him or Cameron – in this business. And Desmond intended to make damn sure it would be him.

34

Archer arrived home late yet again. Today had been a debacle, and she had been happy to stand aside and let Gillingham and Sheppard decide, behind closed doors, who was going to take what share of the blame. But she knew the reality: Steve Ashby's sources had actually been right, earning him – grudging – respect from her. The stunt with the paracetamol showed that. They'd cancelled, or more likely moved, the delivery, but hadn't been able to resist taking the piss out of the police.

She was embarrassed now to think that she'd allowed her dislike of Ashby, and the apparent freedom Gillingham afforded him, to let her think they'd been a party to murder – perhaps even pulled the trigger. She'd vowed not to be so blinded by prejudice in the future.

When the two DCIs had called her and Ashby in to join them, their waffle pretty much confirmed what she'd thought would happen next. The whole thing was an embarrassing chapter for both forces, and the more that could be swept under the carpet, the better. It left a foul taste in her mouth, and the first thing she did on getting home was to take a beer from the fridge.

Of one thing she was certain: she very much doubted she'd heard the last of the Connolly family, and one day they would surely put a foot wrong. She hoped she'd be there to snap the cuffs on when that day came.

There had been one bright spot in the day. There'd had a couple of calls about the mocked-up photographs of Matthew Butcher, and one of the callers had reckoned Butcher was his second cousin. She'd interview him tomorrow, and another mystery might be solved.

For tonight, though, she planned to treat herself to a takeaway. Live it up a little. But it wasn't a bad evening. Maybe she'd go and sit in the garden and watch the sun go down before she ordered.

As if to thwart her, the doorbell rang. She set her beer bottle down, wondering if it was a late visit by Jehovah's Witnesses. It wasn't as if the bell was exactly overused by visitors.

When she peered through the spyhole and saw Dominic Newman standing there, she felt herself blush. She couldn't deny that he'd intruded into her thoughts more than once since they'd met, and now it was almost as if her thoughts had somehow betrayed themselves, summoning him up in the flesh. He had a look on his face that said apprehension and awkwardness. She remembered his jokey conversation about axe murderers. Perhaps he was one, after all, and had come to confess.

She opened the door. "Dominic." She tried for the right note of warmth, comfortably short of over-enthusiasm.

"Hi Lizzie." He shuffled his feet a little. "I spotted your car on the drive when I called Monty in for his supper and, well, here's the thing." He faltered, then picked up his thread again. "I made myself a curry, and I'm really good at it, though I say so myself and, well, I always make too much, and I bet you haven't eaten, working all day." He stopped for air. "I just wondered if you fancied joining me. We did say we'd have a drink some time." His mouth turned down. "I'm being presumptuous, aren't I? I mean, you don't know me. This was a bad idea."

"No, no," she said. "No, it's very kind." A sensible voice inside her head reminded her that she'd already decided she didn't want to get involved with her next door neighbour. An equally sensible voice pointed out that sharing his leftover curry was hardly getting involved, and he probably wouldn't expect her to drop her knickers in gratitude. A third, more cynical, voice whispered that some men would expect just that for a whole lot less.

"Kind, as in yes please?" he asked. She realised she actually hadn't given him an answer. "Or as in thanks, but no thanks?"

"Sorry." *Sod it, I'm a big girl now.* "No, that would be great. I was planning a takeaway, but home-made curry would be even better. Thank you. Tell you what," she added, "I've got a beer on the go. I could bring it and the rest of the pack, if you like. That is," she added, "if you want me to come now."

"Sure," he said. "I just need to do some rice, so it'll all be ready in ten minutes." He looked pleased.

"See you in five, then?"

"Five it is."

As she brought her beer indoors and locked her patio door, she reminded herself sternly to keep an eye out for an axe, just in case. And she definitely intended to keep her knickers on.

35

Considering that Brandon Clark had become a loner, the church was surprisingly full for his funeral.

It was three weeks since the raid on the airfield had turned into a fiasco. Once the NCA and the top brass at Thames Valley had agreed that the investigation into his murder had gone as far as it could, Brandon's body had been released to his family.

Apart from family members, staff and pupils from Brandon's school were there, along with members of his old gang, a number of community leaders, and a contingent from the local police.

Baines had been touched to be asked if he would like to say a few words in tribute, although this was not the ideal day to be adding to his emotional strain. As it was, he was going to have to skip the wake to make his first appointment with his new therapist. He was still off work – and would be for a few more days, even though he felt fine now – but had been well enough to see someone from occupational health, who had referred him to a counsellor he could talk through his grief, as well as the shooting, with.

It wasn't something he was looking forward to, and his feelings remained confused. Would a mental illness label bring him any relief? Did he actually want to be 'cured', if it meant he wouldn't see Jack again?

Julie Clark's choice of music for her son's funeral had been perfect so far: some hip-hop, or whatever they were calling in this week, mingled with a piece by Elgar that Brandon had been especially fond of. Baines was not in the least surprised to find that his tastes had extended to classical music. Brandon had always had an inquisitive mind and his interests had stretched beyond popular culture.

The hymns had been traditional: 'Abide With Me' and 'All Things Bright and Beautiful'. The vicar said a few words, and then the tributes began: a family friend; Brandon's old bro from his gang days, Aaron. Then it was Baines's turn.

As he took his place in the pulpit, he licked dry lips. He should be used to speaking in public, and this wasn't the first time he had done so at a funeral. Against all advice, he had delivered a eulogy at Louise's. Yet this felt different.

Notes at the ready, he glanced at the sea of faces before him, perhaps seeking some encouragement. Karen sat next to Archer behind Baines's empty front-row seat. To his surprise and relief, they seemed to get on well. Something positive had come out of his shooting after all.

His gaze moved to the back of the church. He wasn't surprised to see Jack standing there, smiling. For an instant, their eyes met, and then his eyes misted. He blinked and the boy disappeared.

He cleared his throat, found that he was calm and confident. Glanced at his notes.

"Brandon wasn't always a good boy," he began. "But he was always a really great kid."

* * *

Archer left the funeral around the same time as Baines and headed back to the office. She really hadn't known the boy as well as Baines had and, although she had liked what she had seen of him, had gone to his funeral more as a courtesy, and to support Baines. She had sensed he was nervous about the tribute he'd been asked to give.

He needn't have been, she thought. He'd spoken from the heart and done Brandon proud.

It had been the first time she'd seen Baines and Karen together. Despite the complexity of their relationship and the baggage that went with it, she'd seen only a devoted, loving couple. She envied them.

She still owed Dominic next door a meal, and she wondered about asking Baines and Karen to join them. Making it more of a dinner party with another couple would ensure that Dominic didn't misconstrue it as some sort of date.

She laughed at herself as she settled behind her desk with a coffee. Dinner party! Like she could cook worth a damn. But maybe if she branded it as an overdue housewarming? She could buy some stuff from M&S, plus a few bottles of fizz... Yes, she should do that.

Assuming Baines was deemed well enough for socialising, she reminded herself. She hoped his first session with the grief counsellor would go okay, and would give him the sort of answers he was looking for.

Meanwhile, all she'd told Gillingham was that Baines needed to be out of the office this afternoon. The shooting helped in that regard. Gillingham clearly assumed it was to do with that, and she did nothing to disabuse him. As far as Baines was concerned, it was a secret she was keeping for him.

She sipped her coffee. He'd been keeping so many secrets at work; so much bottled up, with only Karen to confide in. She was glad to share a little of the burden with him. After all, that was what friends were for.

The thought took her by surprise. *Friends.*

But it did not displease her.

* * *

The waiting room was beige, with a print of red flowers in a vase the sole splash of colour. There was a beige notice board with a selection of dull notices that Baines had tried to take an interest in, but had found his eyes and brain glazing over within seconds.

The selection of magazines on the coffee table in front of him appeared to have been hand-picked to offer him absolutely nothing worth reading. In the end, he'd resorted to fiddling with his phone, but he'd found it hard to concentrate on anything.

So here he was. Seeing a shrink. Officially nuts. At least he was the only person waiting here. In the films, the therapist always announced that time was up after the allotted period, regardless of where the consultation had got to. If that was the case here, then there was no prospect of a GP surgery-style queue building up. That suited him fine. He felt uncomfortable enough as it was without being surrounded by a bunch of other people with Christ knew what going on in their heads.

Karen had offered to come with him and wait while he was in with the therapist, but he'd insisted on doing it himself. She'd declared it to be typical of his pig-headedness, but in a way that implied she'd expected no less.

Karen had urged him to Google his symptoms in advance of the appointment, but he was convinced that that way, quite literally, lay madness. He'd known people who looked up their physical symptoms and came away convinced they'd never see another Christmas, and couldn't imagine what demons could be unleashed by reading up on what sort of mental ailment he might have.

He was fairly certain that Karen had already done more than enough research for both of them, but he'd asked her to keep it to herself for now. He'd find out what was wrong with him soon enough.

If there was anything wrong at all. When he and Karen had had a rare conversation on the subject, they'd agreed that either he had some sort of psychological problem, or the cause of the sightings was supernatural. If he was honest, he preferred the supernatural option. It gave him hope and comfort of sorts.

One thing still preyed on his mind, and he still hadn't decided whether or not to tell the counsellor. He was finding it to shake the feeling that the killer Will Streatham's car had crashed because he swerved to avoid something in the road.

Just for a moment, I thought I saw...

Baines was convinced that Jack had made him swerve. That somehow he had made himself visible to the fleeing gunman. The possibility that someone else was able to see Jack would call into question the whole purpose of this appointment, and was something he'd avoided raising with Karen.

His stomach gave a sudden lurch. What was he doing here? This was a mistake. He could walk out of the door now. This wasn't what he wanted. Not for him. Not for Jack. Panic began to mount inside him. He decided to run for it.

The door into the consulting room opened and a middle-aged woman came out, flashing Baines a smile as she headed for the door to the reception area. She was followed out by another woman, who had short hair, a fringe, and a nice smile.

"You must be Daniel," she said. "Or do you prefer Dan, or Danny?"

"Dan," he said, rising.

She walked over, extending a hand for him to shake. "Tracey Walsh. Pleased to meet you." She had a hint of a Northern accent. Her grip was firm and somehow reassuring. "Come on in."

He wasn't sure what he'd expected, but she wasn't it: no glasses. No white coat. And she was informally dressed in a red top and a pair of dark trousers. A slim gold chain was her only jewellery. She wore flat, comfortable shoes. He thought he might like her.

He followed her into her inner sanctum and closed the door behind him. More beige. There was no desk. In one corner sat a coffee table with two comfortable-looking chairs. There was a sofa in another corner. Some innocuous abstract art on the walls. No personal pictures. Maybe she feared that any picture grounded in reality, however innocuous, might set something off, some association with a deeply buried neurosis or two.

There were a couple of framed certificates, perhaps just to reassure patients that Walsh knew what she was talking about.

There was a box of tissues on the corner of the coffee table, which made him think of the interview rooms at the station, only without the furniture screwed to the floor.

"Shall I lie on the couch?" he asked.

She laughed. "If you want to. I'm not sure how comfortable it would be, given how tall you are. Most clients are okay with the chair."

He sat down, and she eased herself into her own seat.

"This first session will be mostly you talking and me listening," she said. "I've no preconceptions, no idea of what sort of help you might need. Nor, I'm afraid, how long it'll take."

"That sounds ominous."

"It isn't meant to. I do get clients expecting quick fixes, or snap diagnoses. They hope they'll walk out of the first session with a label they can hang on their condition and an explanation for it, and that'll be that."

"And I bet that never happens?"

"Well, it can. But not often."

He nodded. "Well, I came here with no such delusions."

She smiled. "Good. So, first off, I need to know a bit about what's troubling you. How does that sound?"

"Okay. I think."

"Okay then. Now, I understand from your occupational health team that you've suffered a difficult loss. Can you tell me more about that?"

Maybe he'd expected the questioning to lead up to this. Not to have it thrown in straight away, like a hand grenade. The question almost made him panic again.

But then, this was what this meeting was all about, wasn't it? Louise. Jack. The past and the present.

Tracey Walsh was waiting, showing no sign of impatience.

He drew a ragged breath.

"Yes," he said. "I lost my wife. And my son."

THE END

Also by Dave Sivers

Archer and Baines
The Scars Beneath the Soul
Dead in Deep Water

The Lowmar Dashiel Mysteries
A Sorcerer Slain
Inquisitor Royal

Short Stories
Dark and Deep: Ten Coffee Break Crime Stories

DAVE SIVERS

Dave Sivers grew up in West London and left school aged sixteen to embark on a civil service career that took him to exotic places including Rhode Island, USA, Cyprus, Brussels, Northern Norway and Sutton Coldfield.

Along the way, he moonlighted variously as a nightclub bouncer, bookie's clerk and freelance writer, as well as picking up a first-class honours degree from the Open University. Writing has always been his passion and, since giving up his day job, he has launched a second career as a novelist.

The first two books in his popular Archer and Baines crime series set in Buckinghamshire's Aylesbury Vale – *The Scars Beneath the Soul* and *Dead in Deep Water* – reached the top three in the Amazon Kindle Serial Killers chart. His other work includes two hybrid 'crime fantasy' novels featuring personal inquisitor Lowmar Dashiel.

He lives in Buckinghamshire, England, with his wife, Chris.